Welcome to Martin House

C. ANNE BARKER

 FriesenPress

One Printers Way
Altona, MB R0G 0B0
Canada

www.friesenpress.com

Copyright © 2021 by C. Anne Barker
First Edition — 2021

Cover Illustration by Lucinda Howell, @instagram.com/lucillustrations/

ISBN
978-1-03-912253-6 (Hardcover)
978-1-03-912252-9 (Paperback)
978-1-03-912254-3 (eBook)

1. FICTION, SMALL TOWN & RURAL

Distributed to the trade by The Ingram Book Company

Welcome to
Martin House

Acknowledgements

Thanks to my family, *Welcome to Martin House* finally became a reality. My daughter, Cathie Barker Pinsent and my niece, Christina (Barker) Harty, were with me from the start, reading and critiquing each chapter. My niece, Josephine (Barker) Sheppard, proofread and reviewed the entire manuscript, while my neighbour Pat Barker provided helpful input. And through the whole process, my sons, Jerry, Andrew, Kevin, Neil and Colin, as always, offered encouragement and support in so many ways. Andrew was also my go-to computer specialist, skillfully handling my constant laptop problems.

PROLOGUE

Alex Martin's sudden death came as a shock to everyone in Mark's Point. Over the next three days, residents of the small Newfoundland fishing community paid their respects to his widow at the wake and funeral service. Bessie Martin heard the traditional phrase of sympathy, 'Sorry for your troubles, missus' countless times. What she didn't hear was the conversations and speculation regarding her future.

Bessie had lived in the outport community for a quarter of a century. However, she wasn't originally from Mark's Point or even Newfoundland, leading some of her neighbours to believe she would leave the area. Not that anyone wanted to see her go, but with the passing of Alex, many felt Bessie's link to the community was gone.

The Martin home came in for even more discussion and speculation. The house situated on a choice piece of land was the largest home in Mark's Point. It commanded a view of the entire community, with only the local Roman Catholic Church standing higher. Many people would jump at the opportunity to buy the large, well-kept home, which Alex began building in 1946.

Bessie and Alex met in 1940 when he served in the Newfoundland Overseas Forestry Unit in Scotland during World War 11. His logging camp was only a few miles from the town where Bessie lived, and, after meeting her at a dance, Alex was soon making regular visits to her home. Six months later, the couple became engaged just days before Alex boarded a battleship to serve in the Royal Navy for the remainder of the war.

World War 11 finished in 1945, and with peace, Alex's service in the Royal Navy ended. He returned to Scotland, where he and Bessie were married before sailing to Newfoundland later that year. It was November 1945 when the young couple finally arrived in Mark's Point to begin married life.

Their neighbours took it for granted the newlyweds would make a permanent home with Alex's parents. After all, he was an only son, and the house would be his one day. But that winter, Alex was in the woods cutting logs, and word spread that he and Bessie planned to build a home of their own.

When Alex laid the house's foundation the following year, it was noticeably big by 1946 standards. As Alex sketched out his plans and the walls went up, it became evident that the house would be unlike any other in the area.

The new Martin home would have a large sitting or front room. Previously unheard of in Mark's Point homes, a dining room was also planned, causing much discussion, especially since the kitchen was much bigger than in neighbouring houses.

There were five rooms upstairs, which seemed a lot even in a community of large families. When word spread that one of the five would be a bathroom, there was disbelief. In a rural fishing community with no electricity or running water, what was Alex thinking? Their neighbours concluded the grand ideas had to come from Bessie.

When electricity finally came to the community in 1960, indoor plumbing was no longer a luxury. But years before power lines reached Mark's Point, Alex installed a generator. As a result, the Martin home was the first with electric lights, running water, and complete indoor plumbing. Even better, according to the men in the community, when television became available to Newfoundland in 1955, Alex bought a television set.

For years, the Martins' sitting room was the most popular place in the community on Saturday nights. That's when *Hockey Night in Canada* aired on their large black and white television. As the excitement grew over the winter and especially during the hockey playoffs, it was quite possible for more than two dozen males to crowd into their sitting room, from teenage boys to pensioners. Those who gathered in the large room, warmly heated from an oil stove, no longer ridiculed the idea of a sitting room. Now they praised the Martins' foresight in adding the spacious room to their home.

Their house became even larger when Alex's father had a stroke in the late 50s, and it became evident that Mrs. Martin, who had a debilitating form of arthritis, was finding it difficult to care for him. Alex built an extension to accommodate his parents. The additional downstairs bedroom and bathroom made it much easier for the elderly couple to cope and allowed Alex and Bessie to give them a helping hand when necessary. It also made it easier for Bessie to nurse them when her father-in-law suffered another stroke and, as Mrs. Martin's mobility gradually decreased to the point where she became bedridden.

Even earlier, Alex added a covered sun porch that ran the entire length of their home. The new room was the couple's favourite place to relax, offering a spectacular view of the community and harbour, especially when the sun began to set in the evenings, spreading a kaleidoscope of colours over the ocean.

Bessie had settled well into life as a housewife in rural Newfoundland, but there was one difference between the Scottish war bride and most married women. Bessie had no children.

People speculated Bessie might be in the family way when Alex began building their home, but years passed with no sign of children. Women who ventured to raise the topic to Bessie discovered that it was not open for discussion, as did their menfolk when they brought it up to Alex.

Her neighbours never doubted the problem lay with Bessie. After all, one only had to look at the Martin family tree. In this part of the bay, as in several other Newfoundland communities, scores of Martins could trace their roots back to Mark's Point.

Now 25 years later, Alex, a healthy, active man who worked long, hard hours as a fisherman during the season and as a carpenter in the winter, was gone, following a massive heart attack.

Bessie's neighbours felt sure without Alex; not even a large comfortable home was enough to keep her in Mark's Point. There would be no shortage of prospective buyers for the widow's property, and, as they noted, the proceeds from its sale and Alex's boat and fishing gear would be more than enough to keep Bessie in comfort when she settled outside the community.

CHAPTER 1

Bessie's Business

Kavanagh's General Store in Mark's Point was a popular place for residents of the small Newfoundland community. The store, more commonly known as 'the shop,' not only sold groceries and a wide variety of goods, it provided a social atmosphere where news and gossip were equally exchanged and enjoyed. On most weeknights, it was usual to find a dozen or more adults gathered in the shop.

In one corner, men perched on cases of Carnation milk or Campbell's soup. It was their traditional meeting spot. As the owner, Oscar Kavanagh had the highest seat on three tiers of canned goods by the window. The extra height gave him an unobstructed view of the main road. From this vantage spot, he could spot any strange vehicle or RCMP car approaching the shop. Kavanagh's Store was licensed to sell beer, but only for consumption off-premises. Oscar firmly enforced this law whenever strangers, Mounties, or Board of Liquor Control inspectors were in the area.

Tonight, with no outsiders present, beer was flowing freely in the corner. Several women huddled over the counter, studying the new 1971 Eaton's Spring catalogue while discussing flannelette versus nylon nightwear. Behind the counter was Flo Kavanagh, Oscar's unmarried sister, who helped him in the store. Flo, an avid knitter, was clicking away on four needles, forming a pair of traditional grey wool vamps. Flo seldom dropped a stitch regardless of the ongoing conversation and how many times she put her knitting down to serve customers. She was about to start turning the heel of the vamp when the door opened, and long-time resident Lucy Pearce entered the shop.

"What brings you out tonight, Lucy? It's not often you venture abroad after supper. What can I get you?" Flo asked.

"There's no hurry Flo; I'll have a look around. I haven't been out all day, but now the rain's stopped; I thought I'd get some fresh air. There's something I wants, but right now, I can't seem to remember what it is," Lucy replied.

Behind Lucy, Nora Ryan winked at Flo. As Lucy walked around the few shelves in the centre of the shop, Nora whispered.

"Lucy's heard some news; otherwise, she'd never come out at this time of night. She must think it's important. Wait and see how long it takes her to share it."

The words were scarcely out of her mouth when Lucy returned to the counter.

"I wish I could remember what it was I needed. You's not too busy tonight, Flo. Not much happening in a small place like this. How another business could survive here, I don't know."

"Well, I guess Oscar's lucky he don't have that worry, seeing there's no other shop in Mark's Point," Flo replied.

"Yes, my dear, but just think, what if another shop opens? What would he do then?" Lucy questioned.

"What's you talking about, Lucy? Oscar's the only one who needs to be concerned about his business. But then again, if everybody in Mark's Point bought their groceries here, instead of shopping miles away in hopes of getting something a few cents cheaper, he'd have even less need to worry," sniffed Flo, who was well known for her sharp tongue.

Lucy, speaking loudly for the benefit of the men on the far side of the shop, quickly responded.

"Yes, my dear, I knows how hard it is to make a living. That's why I was so surprised when I heard Bessie Martin was starting a business. Like I said to my Jim, 'Why would Bessie start a business?'

"My goodness, poor old Alex's only dead a few months, and she's talking about starting a business of all things. For sure, Alex never left her short of a dollar. Here's people thinking that now she's a widow and has no family, she'll be leaving Mark's Point and all the time she's staying. And not only is she staying, but she's starting a business."

There, she had it out. Famous for discovering news, Lucy had chosen her time and audience for the most impact.

As her words were absorbed and repeated, it seemed everyone had questions. "Where? When? What kind of business?" While comments such as "That's nonsense; Bessie's not staying in Mark's Point." were heard from around the shop.

Lucy was in her element, knowing she had scooped the news. She should be going home to get back on the telephone, but she seldom had such a captive audience. For now, she was the centre of attention as all activities came to a halt. Catalogues, knitting, and beer were forgotten as Oscar clambered for authority by standing on a case of baked beans.

"Now, Lucy, what kind of nonsense is you coming up with now? Bessie Martin starting a business? What next? Not that it makes any difference to me. After all, she's as entitled to start a business as the next person," Oscar spoke loudly in what he hoped sounded like a positive tone.

Inwardly he was apprehensive, wondering about the possibility of competition from a new store. With a population of slightly more than 100, it would be difficult for two general stores to survive in Mark's Point.

"Oh, it's true, all right. I heard Bessie herself say it," Lucy said.

"But what kind of business? Is it another shop Lucy? What exactly did Bessie tell you?" Marge Brown questioned.

"She didn't actually tell me. I just happened to overhear her but didn't catch what sort of business she was talkin' about."

"Oh, that's it. You just thought you heard it," Oscar said, silently breathing a sigh of relief.

"There's no way Bessie Martin's staying 'round here. She's got nothing to keep her."

"She'll have a business," Lucy quickly replied.

"That's what she'll have to keep her in Mark's Point. I was surprised too when I heard her. I got a real shock. But then again, everybody was wondering what would happen to Bessie's big house when she left. Well, with her staying, there's loads of room to put a shop in it."

3

Marge, determined to get to the bottom of the matter, tried to get more information from Lucy.

"When did she say this? If she didn't tell you, who did she tell?"

"The telephone company that's who. I heard Bessie with my own ears. She told them she needed a private line. Her very words were, 'A party line is no longer suitable because I'm starting a business.' Why she'd want a private line, I don't know. After all, since poor old Mrs. Jenny Moss died and Mary Joy moved in with her daughter, the only one she shares the phone line with now is me, and for sure, I don't want to know her business."

"When was this? I never saw any of the telephone crowd out this way, and I've been waiting almost a week to have my phone fixed." Alice Fleming asked.

All eyes turned once again to Lucy.

"Well, eh, let me see. Wasn't they out here yesterday, or maybe it was the day before? Anyway, whenever it was, you can take it for gospel that Bessie is starting a business," Lucy emphatically stated.

Lucy's words were too much for Flo. Although short in stature, compared to her much taller brother Oscar, she was never short of words when it came to quick responses.

"I knows where you think you heard the news. You was listening in on the phone, wasn't you?"

"Well! What next? Trust you, Flo Kavanagh, to think something like that," Lucy sputtered with indignation.

"Now, seeing you've got none of the biscuits I'm looking for, I'm going home. Maybe you should think about getting a bigger selection of groceries Oscar if you wants to keep your customers. Especially now with a new business starting up."

Whether she was disturbed at the possibility of another shop opening or just fed up with Lucy's constant gossiping, Flo had heard enough, and she lashed out verbally at her neighbour.

"That's where you got your news, Lucy Pearce. No wonder Bessie wants a private phone. I just bet she told the telephone company she needed a private line because she don't want you knowing her business anymore. And I don't blame her one bit. Everybody knows you spends half your time on the phone, and mostly you're listening in on somebody, trying to find out all you can."

"Well! If that's the way I'm treated, it's the last bit of news I ever tells you. And me just trying to help your brother. What's more, it's time there was a new shop here. At least, then, customers might get treated with a bit of respect."

With those final words, Lucy flounced across the shop and, grabbing the handle of the door, almost hauled it off in her hurry to exit the premises.

Lucy's news and her abrupt departure had disrupted the normal nightly activities at Kavanagh's Store. The conversation immediately focused on Bessie Martin, just as it had after her husband's death earlier in the year. But now, the issue was not about her leaving Mark's Point or what would happen to her large home. The question on everyone's mind and during the next few weeks revolved once again around the widow's plans. Was Bessie starting a business in Mark's Point? If so, what kind of business did she have in mind?

***

A few weeks later, the much-discussed business was the topic of conversation between Bessie and her sister-in-law, Rose. Since her brother's death, Rose Martin had become a frequent weekend visitor to Mark's Point

"I can't believe we're doing this, Bessie. There will be many surprised people when they discover you're not leaving Mark's Point. They'll be even more surprised when they find out I'm moving back home.

"It's hard to believe that in less than two months, we will open for business. I can hardly wait until the end of the school term. I know this is something we had often discussed since our holiday in Scotland two years ago. But then it was just an idea, something in our future. It seems so much has happened in the last few months."

Bessie Martin glanced over at Rose, who, even while talking, was adding items to the long list of things to be done before the pair began their new venture. Bessie couldn't imagine attempting the enterprise with anyone other than Rose. Smiling, she recalled this wasn't always the case and how before coming to Newfoundland, she had wondered what kind of reception she would receive from Rose's family.

Unlike many servicemen who painted exaggerated pictures of their homes and communities to their war brides, Alex had been brutally honest when describing Mark's Point to Bessie. Although proud of his family and community, he warned her about the lack of electricity, indoor plumbing, and other conveniences, which Bessie, coming from a bustling Scottish town, had taken for granted.

"Why are you smiling? You know some people will have plenty to say about me going into business with you. I can hear them now. 'Rose Martin never did know what she wanted. She don't stick at anything.' Just look at the reaction when I left the convent all those years ago."

"Let them talk. It won't be long before they find out you are staying and what we plan," Bessie replied.

"That's the only drawback about living in a small community; everyone wants to know everybody else's business. It's the one thing Alex didn't warn me about. In fact, that's what I was just remembering; how Alex prepared me for living in Mark's Point.

"He was worried I'd find it too isolated and miss not having electricity and indoor plumbing, and I admit at first, it was hard getting used to it."

Bessie recalled how the welcome she received from Alex and Rose's parents compensated for the lack of amenities. She knew little about rural life and even housekeeping when she arrived in Mark's Point. Growing up in Scotland, she was used to buying fresh bread daily from a bakery and having milk delivered on her doorstep each morning from a milkman driving a horse and cart.

"But no one could have been more patient than your mother, teaching me to mix and bake bread, cook, and sew, and many other things. Thanks to her, I still enjoy doing these things today."

"Mother and Father loved having you here, and look how you cared for them, bringing them here to stay when Father got so ill, then nursing them both through their final illnesses. I know they would be glad to know we are living together in Mark's Point, although I doubt if they would ever have imagined us working together and starting a business."

"They'd be pleased you're making your home here once again, Rose, as would Alex. Mark's Point was his home, and he loved it. And where better to start a business than in the house he built? Although I must confess, if anyone had told me 25 years ago that I would go into business with you, I would have thought them crazy or even run a mile at the idea."

Laughter came from both women as they recalled their first meeting. Bessie had known Alex had only one sibling, but Rose lived at home in 1940 when he joined the Newfoundland Forestry Unit. On his return to Mark's Point, Rose was Sister Mary Bridget, a fully qualified teaching nun living and working in St. John's.

When Rose came home to Mark's Point for a short visit, accompanied by an older nun, Bessie felt uncomfortable in their presence. She had previously met the local parish priest who, once he knew she was not a Catholic and had no plans to convert, openly showed his disapproval of Alex's choice of a wife. Having never encountered nuns before and believing they must share the priest's opinion, Bessie avoided them as much as possible and barely responded to their friendly advances.

"I began to wonder why Alex and my parents thought so much of you. To me, you seemed downright unfriendly. I said that to Sister Theresa, but Sister was wiser than me," Rose recalled.

"I remember her saying, 'The poor girl is probably wondering what to make of us or to say to us. I doubt if she ever met nuns before. We must give her a chance.' Thanks to Sister Theresa, we finally started to speak to each other, and I got to know you. Now just look at us, ready to live and work together. I only wish people around here accepted my decision to leave the convent the same way you did."

The sisters-in-law had become great friends over the years, and now, in their early fifties, they were of one mind when it came to their business plans. Unlike in appearance, Bessie's brown curly hair and rosy cheeks contrasted with Rose's lighter complexion and short, straight, fair hair. At a slim, five foot seven inches tall, the former nun never appeared to gain weight, compared to Bessie, who was two inches shorter and laughingly complained that her body tended to put on inches in the wrong places at times.

A knock on the inside porch door and a loud 'Hello' broke up the women's conversation and announced the arrival of Gabe O'Brien. A long-time friend of the Martins, he was a regular visitor to their home.

Gabe and Bessie's husband Alex had been close friends since childhood, although they differed in many ways. Alex had been well thought of in the community through the local fishermen's committee, church, and school board involvement. A friendly, outgoing man, Alex was known as someone to call on when looking for help.

Gabe, a widower in his late fifties, stopped attending church many years earlier. He was a fisherman and handy with tools, but he rarely got involved in community activities. While some of his neighbours accepted Gabe as a private person who preferred his own company, others considered him dour and somewhat unfriendly.

Even knowing about his close friendship with the Martins, few Mark's Point residents would have guessed Gabe not only knew about the proposed business, but he was helping the women get ready for their first customers.

"I have the board cut out, sanded, and painted white, all ready for your sign. I'm leaving one of you to write the name with black paint. When you gets it done, I'll nail it on a post and stick it up outside your fence. Have you made up your mind what you're calling your boarding house yet?"

"It's not a boarding house; it's a Bed and Breakfast," Rose said.

"'Tis the same thing, isn't it? Just a fancy way people in Scotland have for saying boarding house."

"Indeed, it's not. Trust you, Gabe O'Brien. We are not taking in boarders. We plan to cater to people on holiday. Bed and Breakfast accommodations are popular in Britain. Bessie, Alex, and I discovered that when we holidayed there two years ago. We feel sure they will also prove popular in Newfoundland. Apart from hotels in St. John's or bigger towns, there's nowhere for people to stay, as they travel around rural and small communities. What better place for visitors to stay than here in Bessie and Alex's lovely home? Now, if we could get that idea through your head, we might be able to move on with the work that needs to get done."

"Jumping Joseph, Rose Martin, you never changed much. You're still as bossy as you was as a youngster. Even as one of the youngest students in school, you always had the most prate."

"And you never changed at all, Gabriel Aloysius Ignatius O'Brien. As young as I was then, I still remember Miss Lane calling out your full name in frustration when you sat stunned-like, paying no attention to her or your lessons. Now, if you have finished with the sign, one of the windows in the large back bedroom keeps sticking. Why don't you make yourself useful and go upstairs and fix it?"

Muttering about bossy, interfering women, Gabe turned around and left the house, leaving an indignant Rose staring at his disappearing back.

"What's wrong with that man? He's the most irritating person I've ever met. Doesn't he know there's work to be done?"

"Now, Rose, look at all the jobs he did for us during the past few weeks. Where would we be without his help? I don't know why the two of you can't seem to get on. He's probably out in the shed getting something out of Alex's toolbox so he can fix the bedroom window."

But as Bessie spoke, Gabe, who had enough of bossy women for one day, was at the end of the Martin's long driveway, making his way through the gate leading on to the main road.

"What's wrong with that Rose Martin? She's the most annoying, contrary woman I've ever met. If she thinks I'm doing anything else for her, she can think again. I wouldn't go nowhere near her if it wasn't for Bessie. Why should I put up with her and her bossiness?" Gabe grumbled as he left the Martin property.

As he walked along the main road incensed from his battle of words with Rose, he continued to vent his frustration aloud.

"Who do she think she's talking to? I'm not one of her students to be spoken to like a youngster. I just bet them students of hers were delighted to hear the contrary creature was giving up teaching."

"There's a place for people who talk to themselves, you know," a voice from behind him said.

Turning around, Gabe inwardly swore as he saw Lucy Pearce hurrying to catch up with him.

"What's happening, Gabe? What's that you was saying? I thought it was you I saw leaving Bessie's house. You're spending a lot of time there these days. What's the attraction?" Lucy asked.

"Jumping Joseph, Lucy Pearce. What's wrong with you? Don't you ever stop talking foolishness or asking questions? If I spends time anywhere, it's my business and my business only."

Gabe tried to hurry to put some distance between them, but his stocky body was no match for Lucy's slimmer and more agile figure. Although slightly older than Gabe, her energy was as plentiful as her vocabulary, and she kept in step with him. Not a bit put out by his response, Lucy continued to question him.

"You sure is in a bad mood today. Talkin' about business, did you know Bessie was starting a new business? Maybe you heard her say something about it. Did you? I saw she had some building stuff delivered. Like I said, you've been spending a lot of time there, but you're not building nothing outdoors. Is it inside work you're doing? Is that where she's putting her shop? Her house is surely big enough to put a shop in it, but don't you think that running a shop is a lot of work for a woman alone?"

"What shop? There you go gabbing nonsense again. Bessie's not opening a shop," Gabe growled.

"If she's not opening a shop, what's she doing? There's no other kind of business for a woman to start 'round here, and she's starting a business. I heard her say so myself."

"That's the trouble with you, Lucy; you hear or think you hear something, and you goes running around spreading stories. Just because Bessie's starting a business, it don't mean she's opening a shop."

Lucy instantly pounced on Gabe's last comment.

"I knew it, I just knew she was starting a business, but nobody would believe me. What kind of business? Is it in her house? Is that why you're doing work inside for her? How will she manage to run it by herself? Since Alex died, the poor woman's all alone. Won't it be too much work for her?"

As the questions poured from Lucy, Gabe, furious at himself for blurting out information, tried to set matters straight.

"What's wrong with Bessie having work done or opening a business? What's more, she won't be alone for long, and she won't be running the business by herself."

"What? What kind of business? Who's going to run the business with her?"

Gabe's heart sank once more. He had made things worse by opening his big mouth and to Lucy Pearce of all people. Now he had to go back and tell Bessie what he'd done. What was worse, Rose would find out. It wasn't a good day for him at all.

"I've got to go; I've work to do. I guess it's no good asking you to keep quiet about this," Gabe said.

"Who'd you think I am, Gabe O'Brien? I've better things to do than to talk after you or anybody else. I was on my way to the post office. I'd be there by now if you hadn't stopped me," Lucy replied.

"Is that right? Well then, I saved you a trip. It's Saturday, and the post office is closed. What's more, you're going the wrong way."

"Did I say the post office? I meant the shop. I've got to settle my grocery bill with Oscar and pick up a few more groceries. I'll see you."

With that, Lucy went happily on her way. *I was right all along,* she thought with delight. She couldn't wait to tell Flo and Oscar the news. They'd know better than doubt her words after this. Too bad she didn't know what kind of business it was, but she'd find out; that was for sure.

As she almost ran up the road in her hurry to spread the news, she suddenly realized what Gabe said about Bessie not being alone. *Well, wasn't he the sly one,* she mused? *Just wait until folks hear that bit of news. Not much wonder he didn't want her talking about it and to think Alex had only been dead a few months. Who'd have thought it?"

"Gabe didn't go too far, Bessie. He's coming back up the path. He must have realized how foolish he was, leaving without fixing the window."

"I'm glad he's back, but Rose, don't say anything to him. He's a great help and friend to us, and I don't like seeing him upset."

The words had scarcely left Bessie's mouth before Gabe was coming through the kitchen door. It was evident by his flustered manner that something was bothering him.

"Are you alright, Gabe?" Bessie asked. "I'm sorry if we've been taking you for granted, expecting you to be at our beck and call all the time."

"No, it's nothing you or Rose has done. It's me that's gone and opened my big mouth and to the biggest gossip in Mark's Point. I've gone and told Lucy Pearce you're opening a business, and it's not a shop. That creature! She was gabbing on about you and making no sense at all. She wondered about the shop you was opening and how you was going to manage it alone?

"To shut her up, I told her you was starting a business, but it wasn't a shop. But even worse than that, I went and told her that you wouldn't be alone, that you already had someone to help you, 'though I never said it was you, Rose," a mournful-looking Gabe said.

"The news is out now for sure. If Lucy Pearce knows, the whole world knows," Rose said.

There was silence as they considered the idea of Lucy spreading the news. Then Rose and Gabe looked with astonishment at Bessie, who by now was laughing.

"I'm just thinking about the money we spent getting business cards printed in St. John's when we could have had Lucy providing free publicity. We should have told her from the start we were opening a business," Bessie sputtered through her laughter.

"And you're right, Rose, saying all the world will find out because I'm sure Lucy will get on the phone spreading the news to every soul she knows from St. John's to Port aux Basque. But people had to know, and this may stop their speculation. The more the news spreads, the better for us," Bessie said, still laughing.

"Gabe, you did us a favour because we wondered when and how to break the news to our neighbours. That's one less thing we have to do. I'm also sure you made Lucy Pearce the happiest woman in Mark's Point. She'll have a wonderful time relating this piece of news."

The others joined in the laughter as they each imagined Lucy telling her story in the local shop. Lucy might not know all their business facts, but her flair for dramatics would compensate for any lack of information.

"And she doesn't know everything. She doesn't know I'm giving up teaching and moving home to work with you," Rose remarked.

"And she don't know what kind of business the pair of you is starting. I can just hear the talk in Kavanagh's over the next few days. They'll try to think of every kind of business, but I have my doubts if they'll think of a boarding house, especially one with no name."

"It's not a boarding house. And it does have a name. I'll have you know, Bessie and I put a lot of thought into choosing the right name for our enterprise," Rose snapped.

Bessie looked at Rose and Gabe and sighed.

"What a pair! You are two of the nicest people I know, but somehow you seem to rub each other the wrong way. Yes, Gabe, we have a name for our new business venture. We came up with many ideas and some very fancy names but finally decided we already had the perfect one.

"We are calling it Martin House Bed and Breakfast. After all, Martin is a well-known name in this area, and no one was more hospitable than Mr. and Mrs. Martin. Don't you think Alex would have loved to see the house he built, providing not only a home for Rose and me but also open to visitors? Our Bed and Breakfast will allow people to enjoy his home.

"Rose, you are by far the better printer, so I will leave you to do the sign. We should probably wait until you pick up our business cards in St. John's before the sign goes up. What do you think?"

"You are right. There's still a couple of months before we officially open for business. But when I bring the cards back next week, perhaps the first place we should put them is in the shop. Even better, we can give some to Lucy to pass out. That way, we will spread the news not only in Mark's Point but to all our neighbouring communities as well," Rose said, smiling at the thought.

"That sounds like a good idea, and so is calling your business, Martin House. Mr. and Mrs. Martin was always good to me and lots more. Many a meal they gave away in their time, and nobody could have asked for a better friend than your Alex.

"Now, if someone was to ask me if I wanted a cup of tea when I get that upstairs window unstuck, I wouldn't say no," Gabe said.

By now, he was looking much happier than he had just a few minutes earlier.

"A cup of tea is the most sensible thing I've heard from you all day," Rose replied.

"I'll put the kettle on, and who knows, I may even find a few raisin buns to enjoy with our tea."

CHAPTER 2

First Guests

Humming happily to herself, Rose Martin sat at the kitchen table in Martin House, checking off or placing a question mark by one of the many items on the list she and Bessie had compiled. Looking around the room, she could imagine future guests sitting at the table enjoying a cup of tea with her and Bessie.

'I can see us now on a summer day with the window open and a small warm breeze lightly moving the curtains. I can also picture guests in the fall or winter, enjoying breakfast as the oil stove throws out a cozy and welcoming heat.'

Rose shook her head, laughing at herself. It seemed she spent much of her time lately thinking about the future, but she knew it was because she was happy and anticipating a fresh start.

Time was flying. So much had changed in the past few months. Her only brother died, she had resigned her principal's position, and, in less than a month, she would leave St. John's and return to Mark's Point to open a business with Bessie.

'My life now is much different from what I imagined it would be as a young woman ready to enter the convent.' Rose reflected.

Although she had enjoyed her time as a Presentation Sister, especially when she began teaching, Rose had slowly realized what she had believed was a vocation was, in fact, a love for teaching and not a desire for religious life. But even then, it took 13 years for her to decide to leave the convent. Now, almost 15 years later, her life was changing once again.

"It's strange how things work out, isn't it, Bessie? There's no more talk of you leaving, and people appear to accept the idea that I'm moving home, and we are starting a business together."

"Like most things, it was a seven-day wonder before something else came along to take its place," Bessie replied.

"You are right. The news that a regional elementary school will open this September in Murphy's Cove, and our K-6 school is closing, is now far more interesting. Parents debating the larger school's pros and cons and putting young children on the bus has put our news on the back burner. And that's fine with me. The younger students will love the new school just as the older students did when the high school opened a few years ago."

"I agree, but getting back to our to-do list Rose, your idea of replacing the double bed with two single ones in the biggest bedroom was excellent. That way, if we have a couple who want to share a room but not a bed, we can accommodate them. We still have double beds in the other bedroom and both our rooms. If there is a demand for single beds, we can do the same in the second spare bedroom. Then too, there is your parents' bedroom downstairs with two single beds and the adjoining bathroom. We can use it ourselves if we have a crowd or give it to older guests or someone who might find it difficult using the stairs."

Rose said Bessie's bed plan made good sense, then suggested using quilts made by her mother and Bessie as bedcovers.

"They would make the rooms a colourful and welcoming sight to our guests. But, thinking about the twin beds, we need to get them soon. What if I buy them when I'm back in St. John's and arrange with Murphy's Trucking to pick them up? Dave Murphy takes his truck to the city several times a week."

"Great! And with our joint business bank account now open, you can write a check for the beds and anything else we might need. Having a partner who not only shares in the running of Martin House but handles the financial side of the business is great," Bessie replied.

"Speaking of business and finances, Bessie, there are people who will wonder why we are doing this. I can hear them now.'Those two women aren't short of a dollar; why are they starting a business?'

"Others will see us as greedy and not satisfied with what we have. I don't know if it's worth explaining that this is not all about money, that we started talking about this long ago as something we knew we wanted to try."

"Don't worry about it, Rose. It's just something else for people to discuss. The Martin name has been well talked about ever since Alex died. The best way to deal with talk is to ignore it, and people will soon get tired of the subject. Anyway, I'm sure our business will prove a success because there isn't anywhere else for visitors to stay in this area."

"Now, where are we with our to-do list? When we first began the list, I thought we'd never get through it. There was always something else to add. Apart from running up some new curtains for the kitchen and dining room, only a few odds and ends are left. You did a fine job picking out the material, Rose. By the time you come back next weekend, I'll hopefully have the curtains made and hung."

Rose said making curtains was a job she would never want, recalling how her mother gave up on her ever learning to sew a basic stitch, let alone use the sewing machine.

"Did I ever tell you when I entered the convent, some of the older sisters thought embroidery would be a good pastime for me. It didn't take them long to realize their mistake. I'm hopeless at any kind of sewing or craft," Rose said with a sigh.

"Yet, you are such an accomplished musician. You play the piano, organ, accordion, and recently you've taken up the guitar. That's a talent I wouldn't mind having. I imagine when Father Kiely hears you're home to stay; he'll come looking for you to play the organ in church and to get a choir started once again."

The telephone rang before Rose could respond, and Bessie went to the living room to answer its summons. Now and then, Rose would hear the murmur of her sister-in-law's voice but whoever was on the other end appeared to have plenty to say. Several minutes later, an excited-looking Bessie reappeared.

"You'll never guess," she said, her Scottish accent strongly emphasized as it was apt to do when she was excited.

"We have our first guests, and they are arriving in less than two weeks."

"What? We won't be open then. Who are they, and how did they find out about us?"

Bessie began laughing.

"I'll give you one guess who spread the news of our Bed and Breakfast, but even then, you would never guess the news had reached the United States. That was a Patsy Hollinger on the phone from New York. She was a Kennedy from Muddy Brook Cove before she married an American service-man stationed in St. John's during the war."

Rose remembered Patsy and her younger sister Molly, saying they were slightly older than her. As young adults, they had often gone to the same garden parties and dances.

She recalled both Kennedy girls leaving Muddy Brook Pond to work in St. John's when she entered the convent. Like many Newfoundlanders, the Kennedys found employment when American bases in Newfoundland opened. Although not at war in 1940, the United States signed an agreement with Great Britain to provide battleships and war supplies. In return, the United States was allowed to build three bases in Newfoundland, which, at the time, was a British colony.

The agreement created much-needed work for Newfoundlanders who flocked to the Fort Pepperrell Military base in St. John's, the Naval Base in Argentia, and the Air Force Base in Stephenville. Jobs in construction proj-ects, on-base employment with the Americans and spin-off work in nearby communities became plentiful for males and females.

It was in St. John's that Patsy and Molly met their American future hus-bands-to-be, recalled Rose.

"So they were war brides, just like me. The only difference is I came to Newfoundland while they left for the United States," Bessie said.

"Patsy told me this is only her second trip to Newfoundland since she left. When her father died in the 50s, her mother moved to New York to live with her. Mrs. Kennedy will celebrate her 75th birthday soon, and this trip back home to celebrate the event was arranged by Patsy and Molly. Mrs. Kennedy has a sister and a nephew living in Muddy Brook Cove, and she can't wait to see them and her old home. And by the way, the nephew's wife happens to be Lucy's cousin," Bessie said.

"So, I guess it was Lucy who passed on the news of our business. You did say she would spread the word better than any advertisement. But there's still three more weeks of school, and we didn't plan on opening until I finished teaching. I can't believe this is happening so soon. But why aren't they staying in Muddy Brook Cove?" Rose queried.

Mrs. Kennedy sold her family home when she moved to the States, Bessie explained. In addition to the mother and her two daughters, Patsy's husband would join them on the trip. They originally planned to stay in St. John's and make a couple of day trips to Muddy Brook Cove, knowing Mrs. Kennedy's sister, who shared her home with her son, his wife, and their family didn't have room for them.

"Patsy phoned her aunt and spoke about their plans, not thinking there was anywhere in this area offering accommodations. Hearing about our business from Lucy's cousin, the family was excited and want to come here for at least four days. They are so happy to know they can stay in this area."

"And that's how news spreads, with a helping hand from Lucy. She must be upset that you managed to get a private telephone line. Look at all the conversations she's missing. I'm sure she would love being on a party-line with you now, especially when guests begin using the phone. You made a wise move Bessie when you requested a private line."

"I know. Now at least we have the privacy to make calls. Alex was usually a patient man, but he would get annoyed if he used the phone and knew Lucy listened to his conversation. Once, he was so mad I had a hard time convincing him not to go over to her house and have it out with her.

"But that's enough about Lucy; let's talk about our first guests and see what else we have to prepare before their arrival. Isn't it exciting, Rose? We are actually doing this. Our business is about to become a reality."

The following two weeks flew by as Bessie, with Rose's help on weekends, ensured everything was in perfect order and ready for them to begin their new venture. The house was shining, extra bread, muffins, and cookies were baked, and as the women worked indoors, Gabe was equally busy, mowing grass and finishing outside jobs.

"Just imagine, Bessie, any time now, our first guests will arrive. I wonder what they'll be like and how we'll get on with them. I know they will love the house and we have beautiful weather today, which is all good, but what will they expect from us? I'm excited but also nervous."

Rose said she was initially happy their guests were arriving on a Friday evening, and she could get off school early to be there. Now she wasn't so sure because she was worried she would let Bessie down.

"Nonsense Rose. You are the most capable person I know. I'm sure all they'll be looking for when they arrive is a friendly face, a cup of tea and comfortable beds. You provide the friendly face, I'll get them a cup of tea, and the beds will do the rest," a laughing Bessie said.

"But seriously, Rose, this isn't like you at all. You've met them before, and you say Mrs. Kennedy and her daughters were always a friendly family. There is nothing to worry about."

"Don't forget, Bessie, it's almost 30 years since I saw them, and they haven't lived in Newfoundland since then. Goodness knows what they are like now or what they will expect, especially with them coming from the States."

"Now I know you are stressed, Rose. That comment is not like you at all. People are people regardless if they live in the United States or anywhere else. All we need to do is treat them as we'd like to be treated, and I'm sure things will work out. But it's too late now to worry because I believe that's them turning into the driveway. Don't go running away. Everything's ready, so let's go outside and meet them together."

"Wow! Isn't this grand, Patsy?" said a tall, smiling man as he opened the front door on the driver's side of a station wagon and looked around appreciatively at his surroundings.

"Hi, ladies, I'm guessing you are our hostesses. We sure are delighted to meet you: what a beautiful view and home you have.

"I'm sorry, I'm so happy to be here that I've forgotten my manners. I am Max Hollinger. Let me introduce you to my wife Patsy, and Molly Thomson, my sister-in-law. Last but certainly not least, here is my mother-in-law Gertie, or as we all call her, Nan Kennedy, who has longed for this day to come," he said as he helped an elderly woman out of the vehicle.

"Hello, I'm Bessie Martin, and this is my sister-in-law, Rose. Welcome to Mark's Point. You are our first guests to Martin House Bed and Breakfast, and we are every bit as excited about your visit as you seem to be. Come on in, the kettle just boiled, and I'm sure you're ready for a cup of tea."

"It's lovely to meet you, Mrs. Martin, and to see you again, Rose, although it's many years since we last met. I'd love some tea, and I am sure the others would too, especially Mother. Right now, she's too busy breathing in that wonderful smell of the ocean to talk, but we don't want you going to a lot of trouble for us," answered Patsy.

It was easy to see the relationship between the female visitors, Bessie thought. All three were small, slender women, but Mrs. Kennedy's hair was now silvery white where the sisters had dark hair.

"It's no trouble at all, and call me Bessie. Come in and make yourselves at home," she quickly responded.

Meanwhile, Rose was greeting the other guests as Max Hollinger continued to admire his surroundings.

"Just look at that view. What a lovely little village, and look at those green hills rising from the brilliant blue ocean. The breathtaking scenery makes a perfect backdrop to your village. To think we'll be enjoying these views for the next few days. It's easy to see why you longed to come back home, Nan."

An hour later, it was as if they had always known each other. After seeing the bedrooms and expressing their satisfaction, the American guests had enjoyed their choice of tea or coffee with a selection of sandwiches and some of Bessie's homemade sweet bread and tea buns. As they relaxed in the large sun porch facing the community and harbour, the five women reminisced about past events and people they knew, while Max was content to sit back, listen to their stories from the past and enjoy the view.

"Isn't this gorgeous, Patsy? We are actually looking at the ocean. I never imagined it like this, with twinkling silvery ripples and magnificent hills way off in the background. It's powerful and yet so peaceful," said Max.

The words were no sooner out of his mouth when the peaceful moment was interrupted by a shrill 'Hello, anyone home,' coming from the kitchen. The relaxed setting changed as both Rose and Bessie jumped to their feet.

"You stay with our guests Bessie and leave this to me. I'm fairly sure I know who it is. I will see what she wants."

Before Bessie could object, Rose was on her way to the kitchen, where she discovered Lucy with an empty cup in her hand.

"Oh, it's you, Rose. I'm wondering if Bessie can do me a big favour. I started baking 'cause I never knows when company will arrive. Then I found out I didn't have enough sugar. I thought maybe Bessie could loan me some. I don't need a lot; that's why I brought a cup. Where's Bessie? Is she busy? I don't like bothering her if she's got company. She do have company, don't she?" Lucy asked, the words tumbling out of her mouth in her usual rushed conversation style.

"You won't be bothering Bessie. I can give you what you need. We have plenty of sugar. Just give me your cup, and I will look after it," Rose said, taking the cup from Lucy.

The sound of laughter coming from the front of the house brought a quick reaction from Lucy.

"You do have company. Don't tell me you've got your first customers. Oh my! It wouldn't be Patsy and Molly Kennedy, would it? They was friends of mine when we was growing up. I'd love to see them again. It's alright if I just pop through, isn't it?"

"I'm afraid not. Our guests have just arrived, and no doubt are tired after all their travelling. Bessie and I decided that unless guests ask to meet people, we won't bother them with visitors," replied Rose.

"But I'm not what you'd call a visitor; I'm your closest neighbour. They wouldn't be staying here if I hadn't told my cousin about your business. And I've known them for many years. I'm sure they'd want to see a familiar face."

"What about your baking? Shouldn't you be getting back to your cake or whatever it is you intend to make? I'll tell them you called and would love to see them. Perhaps they may want to drop over and see you sometime during their stay and sample your baking. I'll be sure to pass on your message. Here's the sugar you need. I'm sorry I don't have the time to stop and chat, but I have to get back to our guests," said Rose, as she gradually ushered a reluctant Lucy out the door.

Smiling faces and almost expectant looks greeted Rose on her return to the sun porch. Bessie was the first to speak.

"Wasn't that Lucy? Did she want something?"

"What does Lucy always want? She was looking for news, that's what, but I soon got rid of her."

After blurting this out, Rose's face turned all colours as she suddenly remembered their guests.

"I'm sorry. Lucy is your friend. I had no right to say what I did, especially since she came to see you, although she said she needed sugar. She wanted to come through here, but I stopped her. However, I did tell her I would pass on her message. I must apologize. You are our first guests, and I turned away your friend," said an unhappy-looking Rose.

Her expression quickly changed to bewilderment when she saw everyone laughing.

"Poor Rose, we are not laughing at you," Molly said.

"Patsy and I grew up with Lucy, who, of course, originally belonged to Muddy Brook Cove. We'd be surprised if she changed from the very nosy child and teenager that we knew. Even my mother remembers her reputation, and I'm sure Max has heard some of our Lucy stories over the years. When Bessie said it was probably Lucy, Patsy and I were betting on whether you would manage to get rid of her. I thought she would push her way through here, but Patsy was sure you could handle her. I guess Patsy was right.

"Unless Lucy has changed over the years. I have to admire you for being able to get rid of her so quickly. The Lucy I remember was like a dog with a bone. Once she had an idea in her head, she'd never let it go."

"I guess Lucy faced Rose wearing her principal's hat. She is well used to dealing with all kinds of students, so she knows how to handle Lucy," Bessie said, laughing at the thought.

"I don't know how I helped. I only knew we were having a pleasant evening, and I wasn't having Lucy spoil it by coming in and asking questions all night."

"Well done, Rose. I can see life is never dull around here. I know we are going to enjoy our stay in Newfoundland. I would like to meet nosy Lucy before leaving to see if she lives up to her reputation. Patsy has often said that the New York Police Force would solve far more crimes if they employed someone like Lucy to question the witnesses." Max said.

A far more relaxed Rose joined in the laughter brought on by Max's comments. As Bessie looked around the room, she reflected on the evening's events. The dream she shared with Rose of starting their own business and welcoming visitors to their home had begun. She knew all their guests wouldn't be like their first visitors, and no doubt, there would be bumps along the way, but they had set their dream in motion. From now on, life as they knew it was going to be different.

Later, when the guests had gone to their rooms for the night, Bessie and Rose happily reviewed the day's events, delighted with the response they had received from their guests.

"If we had picked them ourselves, I am sure we couldn't have nicer people as our first guests. I know you were nervous, Rose, wondering how we would get on with them and what they would expect. To be truthful, so was I, although I tried not to let you know."

"And there I was, admiring you for being so calm and acting so profession-ally as if expecting paying guests was something you did every day. I'm glad you didn't tell me how you felt because that would have probably finished me. But aren't we lucky to have such lovely people as our first guests? It's almost as if we had been friends for years. I believe it is a good omen for the future. Just think, Bessie, our Bed and Breakfast is officially open. There is no turning back now. We have a new business, and I know it's going to work out."

"I feel the very same way. Ever since Alex died, I've felt rootless, as if my life had no real purpose. The rumours I was leaving Mark's Point might well have come true if not for you. If you hadn't decided to take early retirement and return home to stay, the idea of opening a Bed and Breakfast would have remained a pipedream."

"Nonsense Bessie. You are more than capable of running the business by yourself. However, this was a dream we shared, and I had no intention of letting you have all the enjoyment. That's why I'm here, ready to start a new phase in both our lives. I know all our guests won't be as easy to get along with as the Kennedys, but between us, we'll make sure that while they are here, they have a good experience."

"That's what I was thinking earlier. Our Bed and Breakfast business is going to work out. What's more, I know we will enjoy entertaining visitors and hope our guests share that enjoyment. Now I don't know about you, but I'm calling it a night. Max said he would be ready for breakfast at about eight, but I can look after him, Rose, if you feel like relaxing in the morning."

"Our first breakfast in our new business? Not on your life! We will make this the best breakfast Max has ever had. I'll be downstairs bright and early."

CHAPTER 3

A Toast

Bessie and Rose were up early the following morning, prepared to make breakfast for their first Martin House guests. After finishing their breakfast and with things well in hand, they sat at the kitchen table, enjoying a second cup of tea when Max walked into the room.

"Good morning, ladies. Isn't this a beautiful morning? It was wonderful waking up to the fresh air smell of the ocean coming through our bedroom window. I hope you don't mind me getting up at this hour. I thought about going for a walk earlier, but I wouldn't want your alarm to go off and startle everyone. Patsy would probably murder me if I woke her."

Bessie and Rose looked at their American guest with puzzlement. Why was Max talking about an alarm? There were only alarm clocks in the house, and they were rarely used, Bessie told him.

"What am I thinking? Of course, you don't have a house alarm. No one would break into a home in this peaceful place. But in New York, burglar alarms are becoming more common. It's different here in this quiet, safe village."

"Peaceful and quiet? I guess you didn't hear the boat engines when the fishermen went out early or the loud 'cock a doodle doos' when the roosters belonging to Ben Ryan and Pat Martin began competing with each other.

Then there's the seagulls and crows; they start their loud conversations at daylight. Things are anything but quiet most mornings in Mark's Point." Rose said with a smile.

But Max said those were sounds of nature and village life. To him, they were beautiful sounds and not at all disturbing.

"I guess everyone looks at things differently," Bessie said.

"But don't worry about waking us while you're here because we're early risers. Now, are you ready for your breakfast, and what would you like to eat this morning?"

"Could I just have a cup of coffee for now and wait until the women get up to have breakfast? I'll drink my coffee, and then if it's okay. I'll take a walk around the village."

"That's no problem at all. The coffee is ready, and remember, if you come into the kitchen and see anything you want, help yourself. We want you to make yourself at home."

"You're spoiling us, giving us much more than we ever expected," Patsy said, coming into the kitchen.

"You're up early, Honey. Did I wake you?" her husband asked.

"No, not really, although I heard you moving around. I think it's because I'm so happy to be back home in Newfoundland that I couldn't stay in bed any longer. I looked in on Mother and Molly, and they're awake, but it will take Mother a bit longer to get washed and dressed. There's no way she'll come downstairs until every hair on her head is in place.

"I guess you want to go walking, Max. But knowing you and how you talk to everyone, what about putting a time limit on your stroll? Bessie, when do you plan to have breakfast?"

When Bessie and Rose discussed breakfast times earlier, they decided to be flexible and work around their guests' preferences. She explained this to Patsy, who then asked if a half-hour would be alright, giving her mother and sister time to get downstairs and allow Max to walk.

"That suits us, but Max, before you leave, what would you like for breakfast? And Patsy, if you can ask your mother and sister what they want to eat, we'll start preparing the food," Bessie responded.

It wasn't too long after Max left when Molly and her mother came into the kitchen with bright 'good mornings' to everyone.

"What a great night's sleep I had. It must be the fresh Newfoundland air, and of course, the bed was wonderfully comfortable," Mrs. Kennedy said.

"Where's Max? Although knowing him, he's probably up and on the go long before us."

"You're right. Max couldn't wait to get outdoors and go exploring. However, he did promise to be back soon because he didn't have breakfast, and we can't have Bessie and Rose waiting all hours for him. It's not that he would deliberately inconvenience you, but after almost 30 years of marriage, I've learned that Max forgets all about the time when something or somebody interests him."

But true to his word, Max was back in less than 30 minutes, sniffing appreciatively at the smell of frying bacon and toasted bread. Somewhere along his travels, he had picked up a small beef bucket. Considering the way he carried it and kept looking inside, it wasn't empty.

"What have you there, Max?" his mother-in-law asked.

"You look as if you found a fortune. Were you down on the beach picking up rocks and shells?"

"No, although I did go walking along the beach road. That's when I saw fishermen working at small tables on the pier where all the boats are tied up. I didn't plan to intrude because I saw they were busy, but then a man called out to me, telling me to come over. When I went there, he said the fish in this bucket was mine. I told him he must be making a mistake, but he was insistent. I offered to pay for them, but he wouldn't take my money.

"And guess what? He knew I was staying here, saying if my wife or mother-in-law had forgotten how to cook codfish, he was sure Rose or Bessie would fry them up," a bemused-looking Max said.

"That sounds like Gabe O'Brien. It's just like him to take things for granted. Not that Bessie or I would mind cooking the fish for you, Max, but Gabe can be a know-it-all at times."

"Oh no, he wasn't like that at all, Rose. He was real nice, and guess what, Patsy? He invited me to go out in his boat with him on Monday."

When Patsy asked her husband if it was to go fishing, Max sounded and looked confused. Confessing, he wasn't exactly sure what he would be doing because the fisherman not only talked fast, but it also sounded like he mentioned a dance. Max didn't like to ask him to explain but did understand when the fisherman said he would see him later to arrange a time in the boat.

"You're going dancing in a boat? If I didn't know you better, Max, I'd say you were drinking. You must have heard him wrong," Mrs. Kennedy chuckled heartily.

"I didn't say it was a dance, Nan. I said it sounded like a dance, almost like an Irish or Scottish reel or jig. That's it; I think he said jig. In fact, I'm sure that's what he said. Why are you laughing? I'm not making it up."

"I think Gabe must have invited you to go jigging," Bessie said, trying to keep her face straight.

"Don't be offended by us laughing. I know exactly how you feel because I found it difficult to understand much of what people meant when I first came to Mark's Point. I had never heard some words before, and others, such as jigging, had a completely different meaning. To a Newfoundlander, jigging is a way of fishing for cod. Gabe must like you if he invited you to go fishing."

"I should have known I had it wrong. When I was in the Army and stationed in St. John's during the war, I couldn't understand many words or sayings. Even now, Patsy and Nan Kennedy can surprise me with a strange word or meaning."

"You'll enjoy going out in Gabe's boat. In the meantime, I'll put the fish in the fridge while you sit down and have breakfast. Now, ladies, you can start because your breakfast is ready. If you tell me how you want your eggs, Max, I'll start cooking them," Bessie said.

"But what about the fish? What will we do with it? Can we eat it?"

"Max! Don't bother Bessie or Rose. We can bring it over to Aunt Meg's when we visit her later this morning. Perhaps we can cook it there for lunch. Unless you want the fish for your lunch, Bessie?"

"Not at all, Patsy. We can have fish anytime, but you don't have to take the fish away. We will cook it for you later. What time do you think you might be back this evening because we can have it then?"

"But we can't bother you. Martin House is a Bed and Breakfast, and you don't serve other meals. We are happy to stay in such a lovely home and certainly don't expect you to cook at night," Molly said.

Rose interrupted, saying she would love to have them come for supper because it was probably her last opportunity to see them. She was returning to St. John's the following day to begin her final week of teaching. She and Bessie had already discussed the idea of inviting the family to a meal. It would be a celebration to mark the opening of their new business, Rose said.

"Well, that's settled," Max said.

"I'd love to have the fish tonight, and Patsy, Molly, and Nan, you are all acting polite, but I have the feeling Rose and Bessie speak their minds. If they didn't want us for dinner tonight, I'm sure they wouldn't invite us. Am I right, ladies?"

When laughter from all the women greeted his announcement, Max continued enthusiastically.

"Thanks, Bessie and Rose, you sure are wonderful hostesses. Now I'm hungry and ready for some of the lovely breakfast I could smell as I was coming up the garden."

"Poor Bessie and Rose, I should have warned you about my husband. He is anything but shy and always says what he thinks. But I don't want him steam-rolling you into doing things that you're not supposed to do for guests."

"Don't you worry. Max is correct when he said we wouldn't invite you for supper if we didn't want to do so. Now, what about returning for six o'clock, and we will have our meal then?" Bessie asked

"Six it is. I'm driving the car, and I will make sure my women folk are back in lots of time for supper. You can count on me because I'm sure looking forward to a home-cooked Newfoundland meal."

Max's much-anticipated meal was over many hours later, and five happy and well-fed guests were relaxing in the sun porch. Gabe, the fifth guest, was invited to the celebration as a thank-you for his work before the business opened.

"This is terrible sitting back, waiting for Bessie and Rose to bring tea and coffee after them providing such a wonderful dinner," Molly said.

"And what a meal! It was as good as any I ever had in a Boston restaurant. I thought we might have fried fish, but that starter of cod au gratin, followed by poached salmon, potatoes, and vegetables, was delicious."

"I know. I had forgotten just how good fresh fish could be. And those desserts were out of this world," her sister added.

"I have to get the recipe for the trifle. Rose says it's a recipe Bessie brought from Scotland, just like those tea buns she gave us last night."

"The trifle was tasty, but my favourite was the boiled pudding. Which reminds me, Nan Kennedy, it's far too long since you made a boiled pudding. Why did you stop making them?"

Max's wife and mother-in-law started laughing at the question.

"Perhaps if you looked at your stomach, you might be able to guess. I had to ask Mom to stop making so many puddings because we were both putting on too much weight."

"Who's putting on too much weight?" Rose asked as she entered the room, carrying a tray of cups and saucers. Behind her was Bessie with a milk jug and sugar bowl.

"My women folk are ganging up on me, telling me to look at my stomach. I never saw any of them thinking about their weight by turning down any of that delicious meal."

"I have to agree with you, Max," Mrs. Kennedy said.

"We all ate as if we had never seen food before. I know we already thanked you, Rose and Bessie, but seriously, it was a wonderful meal and one we won't forget in a hurry. We also need to thank you, Gabe, for the fresh fish. One thing I miss in the States is being able to get fish right from the water. Max, I must admit I've also missed boiled puddings. When we go home, I'll start making them again. Now Patsy, a question for you. Did you talk to Rose and Bessie? Did you ask them?"

"No, mother, give me a chance. What mother wants to know, really what we all want to know is whether we can stay longer than our original booking? It is beautiful here, and you've made us so welcome that we would love to extend our stay at Martin House," said Patsy

"We know you have to return to town to finish out the school year, Rose, which means you will be working alone, Bessie, but we wouldn't expect you to serve us. We could easily get breakfast for ourselves. What we would love to do is spend our entire vacation in Mark's Point instead of several days in a St. John's hotel," Molly added.

"Please tell us you have room for us," Mrs. Kennedy said.

"We have no other bookings, and it certainly isn't too much work to have you stay longer. We'd love to have you, wouldn't we, Rose?"

"I would be delighted. This way, you will still be here when I return on Thursday."

"Thank you; I'm so glad we can stay longer. There are many places I want to go to and people to visit. You have such a lovely home here, and if you were our flesh and blood, we couldn't feel more welcome," Mrs. Kennedy said.

"Speaking of places to go, Patsy, did you tell Bessie and Rose about our invitation from her neighbour?"

"No, Max, I was trying to forget it. Well, not really, but visiting Lucy Pearce is not high on my list of things to do."

"When did you see Lucy?" Rose asked.

"We didn't see her, but I swear she must have timed our journey to Aunt Meg's house because we'd barely landed when the phone rang. Shirley, my cousin's wife, answered it, and when she said the call was for me, I got a shock for a second, thinking there might be a problem with our boys at home. But it was Lucy, greeting me like a long-lost friend, inviting us for dinner, and of course, asking all kinds of questions. To get off the phone, I said I would talk it over with the others and get back to her."

"Lucy didn't intend to wait for an answer, however. She called back about half an hour later, and this time, she asked for me," Molly said.

"She wondered if we had decided when we were coming for dinner. To end the conversation, I told her we would come on Monday. You might not believe this, but before we left Aunt Meg's, she called again and told Shirley to make sure we knew she was expecting us for dinner at noon on Monday. Why is she so eager for us to visit? It's not like we were best buddies growing up, so why is she acting as if we were?"

"If you ladies don't want to visit Lucy, then we won't go," Max said.

"Why go somewhere you won't enjoy, especially when there are so many lovely people and places to see around here? It's not worth having any of you upset. Do you have Lucy's phone number, Bessie? I'll give her a call and say we are making other arrangements."

Quickly breaking into the conversation, Mrs. Kennedy told Max to hold on a minute.

"I remember Lucy growing up, and yes, she was nosy, but she came by it honestly because her mother, Agatha, was also nosy. However, I also remember Agatha as a good neighbour, and although she was nosy, she was never malicious. I haven't seen Lucy for years, but I will accept her invitation for the sake of her mother. And girls, would it kill you to go to Lucy's house for a meal?"

Rose and Bessie were smiling at each other during Mrs. Kennedy's stern talk to her daughters.

"Rose, does Mrs. Kennedy remind you of anyone?"

Before Rose could reply, Gabe answered the question.

"It's like hearing Mrs. Martin speak again. She never had a bad word to say about anyone, and although she was usually a quiet woman, she'd never let you talk ill of people."

Laughing, Rose said, "I don't often agree with Gabe, but this time he's right. It could have been Mother talking. As annoying as Lucy could be at times, Mother always defended her and would relate her good points."

"That's true, but then Mrs. Martin was a saint and never saw anything wrong with anyone. On the other hand, I've had my ups and downs with Lucy. However, she's not a bad person, and on the plus side, you'll enjoy your meal because she is an excellent cook," Bessie admitted.

"Thank you. Now, girls, I hope the two of you were listening. Can we consider this matter settled and that we will be accepting Lucy's invitation?"

"Yes, Mother. We know better than disagree with you when you get that certain look and address us as girls. Anyway, although this is a holiday for us all, it's your birthday treat, and it's all about what you want to see and do. Right, Molly and Max?"

With both her younger daughter and son-in-law echoing their agreement, Mrs. Kennedy nodded approvingly.

"Good! Before we know it, the time will rush past so let's enjoy every minute of it while we can."

"Speaking of time, I had better get off," Gabe said.

"I guess you good people will be going to church in the morning and wanting your beauty sleep. Don't forget, Max, you are coming out fishing with me on Monday. I have extra oilskins and jiggers, and Bessie says you wear the same size of rubber boots as Alex, so that's looked after.

"Bessie, is it okay if I come over tomorrow and look through Alex's fishing gear for some jiggers and a splitting knife? I'll be hauling my nets, but I think Max would enjoy cod jigging. We are sure to jig a few cod, and when we get back to the wharf, and I unload my catch from the boat to the buyer, I'll show you how to fillet any fish we jig, Max. But I have only one good knife as I lost my other when it fell off the cutting table and into the harbour water a couple of weeks ago."

When Bessie told Gabe to take anything he needed from Alex's gear shed, he thanked her before telling Max it would be an early rise on Monday.

"You might need to set an alarm clock as we will be leaving from the wharf around five o'clock. Okay?"

Gabe was surprised when laughter greeted his mention of an alarm clock.

"No need to worry, Gabe, I'll be there on time. The ladies tell me alarms are unnecessary in Mark's Point. Therefore, I will count on one of them to make sure I'm awake and ready to go. Gosh, I just can't wait for Monday to come. What a holiday this is turning out to be. Too bad, Nan Kennedy, we didn't think of celebrating your birthdays in Newfoundland years ago."

"Don't forget Max, Bessie and Rose have just opened their Bed and Breakfast, and we are their first customers. We wouldn't have been able to stay in Mark's Point before now," his wife said.

"You're right, and I think we should mark the occasion. Hold on just a minute, Gabe, there's something we need to do, but first, I must run upstairs. Patsy, as Bessie and Rose said, 'Make yourself at home' Why don't you get out some glasses?"

With that, Max left the room, leaving a puzzled-looking group of people. Patsy, picking up the tray and empty teacups, was right behind him. Within a few minutes, the couple came back. Max had a bottle of rum in one hand and a bottle of wine, while Patsy had exchanged the cups for glasses.

"I knew we had these bottles with us for a good reason. Now ladies and Gabe, take your choice of wine or rum. We need to toast Bessie and Rose's new business. It's our pleasure to be your first guests, so fill your glasses. Nan Kennedy, would you like to make the toast?"

"Thank you, Max. The toast is a wonderful idea. I would be proud to make it. Does everyone have a drink?

"To Martin House and to Bessie and Rose, whose idea it was to open this much-needed business, allowing people like us the opportunity to return home to Newfoundland. May you have many successful years ahead of you. I hope your guests will always be as appreciative and thankful as we are for the wonderful hospitality shown to us by two amazing women. Congratulations,

Bessie and Rose! And thank you for giving my family the honour of being your first guests in Martin House."

"Thank you, Mrs. Kennedy. I'm sure Rose is thinking the very same thing as I am, that we couldn't have asked for better guests, and that goes for each member of the Kennedy family; sorry, Max, but that's how we entered your names in our reservation book.

"We're delighted you are staying longer and not only because we are enjoying having you stay with us. When Rose returns from St. John's later this week, she will pick up our first Martin House guest book, with a photograph of our home on the cover. We originally thought you would be gone and miss signing the book. Now you will be the first people to sign, and that's the way it should be."

"I agree," Rose said.

"And before we retire for the night. I want to propose a toast to our guests. Bessie and Gabe, let's raise our glasses and toast the extended Kennedy family. You are a pleasure to host, and you have given us the confidence to continue with our new business. Thank you all."

CHAPTER 4

Gabe's Problem

Bessie was upstairs in Martin House, making up a bed with clean linen in a guest bedroom. Her thoughts were on the Kennedy family members who were now on their journey home as she did so.

There's a different feeling in the house this morning since they left. Even the weather seems to sense the change. After a week of warm sunny days, it's a dark and overcast morning. I wouldn't doubt we will have rain later this morning.

"It seems so quiet in the house since the Kennedys left yesterday. I know they arrived here less than two weeks ago, but it's almost as if we always knew them," she said to Rose when she returned downstairs.

"I was just thinking the same way, Bessie. They only left yesterday, and I already miss them, but we're not going to be very professional business owners if we get too attached to our guests. And speaking of guests, I had hoped by now we might have some bookings."

But Bessie pointed out that it was still only the end of June, and there were two full months of summer ahead. They had known it would be slow going at the start, but she said they had to remain optimistic that business would pick up.

"Anyway, Rose, I thought if we don't have anyone booked for next week, I might go to St. John's and help you pack up."

"I'd enjoy your company, although I haven't much packing to do with just my clothes and some personal stuff to bring back. Renting my house furnished to a pair of Memorial University professors from England will work out quite well. They want it for a year, which gives me time to decide whether to sell or rent it. If I sell, I have to decide what I am going to do with my furniture, and it's not as if we need any more furniture here."

"There is something I thought we could use, and that's a freezer. Bakeapples and blueberries will be ripe in just over another month. Then partridgeberry season starts in September. I usually jam the berries, but it would be a good idea to freeze some to use in muffins and pancakes for our guests' breakfast. We could also freeze bread as well as fish and meat for our use."

Rose suggested they buy a freezer in St. John's and have Murphy's Trucking pick it up and deliver it to Martin House. At the same time, she could ask Dave Murphy to pick up some boxes and a trunk from her home.

"I'm glad you're not making a hasty decision about selling your house, Rose. I sometimes feel I pushed your retirement ahead by deciding to open the Bed and Breakfast two years earlier than we originally planned."

"That's nonsense, and you know it, Bessie. I was the one who first brought up the subject. I am more than ready for retirement. I can always return to teaching later since the school board gave me the option of a year's leave of absence if I change my mind.

"And speaking of teaching, I have mail to send to the Department of Education that I must get to the post office today. I'll buy some extra stamps and pick up our mail while I'm there." Rose said, slipping on a jacket.

She had no sooner gone through the door when she popped back, asking Bessie if she was expecting Gabe because he was on his way up to the house. Bessie thought he might have arrived to look at the store door lock, which at times stuck. He had said it might only need some oil, and now Bessie remembered she was supposed to pick up a tin of oil at the shop.

"That's okay. After I get the mail, I'll drop by the shop and buy some. If I take my car instead of walking, it won't take long."

Meeting up with Gabe in the driveway, she told him she'd be back soon with the oil.

"Why's Rose telling me about oil? I'm not looking for oil," Gabe said to Bessie as he entered the kitchen.

When Bessie explained that she thought he had come to look at the store door, Gabe admitted he had forgotten about it because he had something else on his mind.

"I came to talk to you about Angela and Maggie. I'm hoping you and Rose might be able to help me with a problem."

"I'll put on the kettle, and we'll have a cup of tea. While I'm doing that, tell me how Maggie is doing and what Angela is up to now."

Bessie could see that Gabe looked out of sorts, but she knew that wasn't unusual when he spoke about his only child. Even as a young girl, Angela tended to butt heads with her father, and when Gabe's wife Meg died suddenly, the trouble escalated. Gabe and his teenage daughter were continually at loggerheads without Meg's calming influence, especially over Angela's determination to leave school and Mark's Point. Gabe's refusal to let the 16-year-old leave school finally resulted in her running away. Despite the efforts of Gabe and the RCMP, the missing teenager had disappeared. Two years later, without any notice or explanation, Angela returned home. She was noticeably pregnant, and within a month of her arrival, she gave birth to a baby girl and named her Maggie.

From the time she was born, Maggie was the joy of Gabe's life. A loveable, friendly child, Maggie began following her grandfather everywhere as soon as she learned to walk. Over the next few years, life could be no better for Gabe and Maggie. But it was evident Angela was unhappy, and she made no effort to hide her longing to leave the community. At the time, Bessie, like many others, wondered how much longer Angela would be satisfied to stay in Mark's Point. One month before Maggie was due to register at the local school, the question was answered. Angela took her five-year-old daughter and left the community.

Although Angela kept in contact with her father and had made several trips home with Maggie on holiday, she never seemed to settle in one place or one job. It was also evident that living in Mark's Point would never be an option for Angela.

Bessie could see Gabe was upset, and she wondered how a mother could drag her child around the country, knowing how much it worried her father.

"Here's a strong cup of tea, just how you like it. Help yourself to some biscuits. Have you heard from Angela, and is she bringing Maggie home this year?"

"I had a letter yesterday from Maggie, and I've been wondering ever since how to deal with it. Maggie wants to come home for the summer holidays. Inside the letter was a note from Angela telling me if I sent the airfare, Maggie would come home by herself for the summer."

"That's great news, Gabe. Just imagine Maggie with you for two months. I would love to see her again. But you said there was a problem. What kind of problem? Is it something that will stop Maggie coming home?"

But Gabe said that maybe they should wait until Rose came back before he explained everything. He added he was determined that Maggie would get home this year, that it was two years since he saw her. From reading her letters, Gabe often felt she was lonely. His granddaughter was almost 13, but she was still a child, and he believed she spent too much time on her own.

"Angela needs a good shaking. There is no stability in the child's life at all. How can Maggie have a normal childhood or make friends when they move around so much, and she's attended different schools?" Bessie interrupted.

"I know, and I worry about Maggie. You knows I'm not a church-going man, but I always pray that no harm comes to Maggie."

Gabe must be upset. It's unlike him to talk about personal matters, especially those relating to Angela.

The ringing phone broke into Bessie's thoughts, and excusing herself, she left the room to answer it.

The caller asked for Miss Martin and sounded disappointed to hear she was not available. Asking whether she could help him, he said he had hoped for information from Rose.

"My name is David Nolan. I'm a teacher, and it's through the school system that I know Miss Martin. Would she be available to talk later this afternoon if I call back?"

When Rose returned a few minutes later, Bessie relayed the message. Although Rose knew David Nolan was the vice principal of an elementary school in St. John's, she had no idea why he would be calling her.

"I barely know him or how he would know I was here. I wonder where he got our phone number. I guess I'll find out this afternoon. But enough about him, what's wrong with Gabe? He says he's been waiting to talk to us. Do you know what he wants?"

"He needs our advice with a problem, and it concerns Angela. He's hoping to get Maggie home this summer. Let's go through and see what we can do."

Gabe looked relieved when the women came into the room, almost as if he counted on them to sort out his dilemma.

"Rose, I told Bessie how Maggie wrote asking could she come home for the summer and that Angela agreed she could if I sent the airfare. What I never told you, Bessie, was the same thing happened last year."

"You sent the money for the fare? But if you did, why didn't Maggie come home?" Rose asked.

"Because I don't think Angela wanted her to come. I did send money, more than enough to buy Maggie's ticket and new clothes. Then Angela said Maggie was too young to travel alone. I offered to go up there and bring her home, but Angela told me Maggie had changed her mind and was going to a summer camp in Ontario."

Bessie said she found that hard to believe, adding Maggie would never turn down a chance to come home to Mark's Point.

Gabe had also found it difficult to believe and had tried phoning Maggie. Angela would say she was in camp and having a wonderful time.

"I come to accept that, thinking Maggie was growing up and changing; that's why she went to the camp. I found out after that it was a day camp in the city."

"Which probably cost little or nothing at all. I remember going to a principal's national conference in Ontario, and one of the workshops I attended was about the benefits of summer camps regarding education. We had speakers from the YMCA and the Salvation Army, and both groups ran summer day camp programs for children in Toronto," Rose recalled

"It was something like that where Maggie went, and although she liked it fine, it was only for a few hours each morning. It meant she was all alone the rest of the time her mother worked. That's why I wanted to talk to both of you. Maggie wants to come home, but I want to be sure the same thing don't happen again."

Rose suggested buying the ticket in Newfoundland and mailing it to Maggie.

"That might sound okay, Rose, but it means we have to depend on Angela to get Maggie to the airport," Bessie interrupted.

"Considering what happened last year, I wonder if Angela would let Gabe buy the ticket then stop Maggie from using it. I don't understand why you never told us about this, Gabe. If you felt you couldn't speak to me, why didn't you tell Alex? You know how much he cared for Maggie. We were both disappointed when she never made it home last year."

But Gabe said he couldn't tell anyone he sent Angela the money, and she never bought Maggie's ticket. It made him ashamed that she was his daughter.

"Never be ashamed to talk to Bessie or me, Gabe. Now while Bessie was talking, I've been thinking. Can we leave this until tomorrow? I have a good friend, Sister Bernadette Moran, who lives and works in Toronto. She's a teacher, but her students are adults who need to learn English. I remember her telling me that the nuns living in her Toronto convent had different professions suited to their work with immigrant families and people in need. I believe one of the sisters is a social worker, and another is a lawyer. Let me call Sister Bernadette tonight and see if I can get her involved in this."

"Do you think she'll help us, Rose?" Gabe asked, looking hopeful for the first time since he arrived.

"I'm almost positive she will, and I can guarantee Sister Bernadette can handle Angela. She'll get to the bottom of this and definitely won't tolerate any excuses or lies."

Gabe said he should have told Alex and Bessie the year before, but it was too late for regrets. If they could get Maggie home this summer, he would be a happy man.

"We're glad to see you looking better. You had me worried when you came in earlier. All kinds of things were going through my mind because I felt it wasn't good news as soon as you mentioned Angela. But now that Rose is looking into this; I'll change the subject.

"What about you fixing the lock on the store door, Gabe, and then stay and have lunch with us? We're feeling a bit lonely today now the Kennedys have left to go back to the States, and we'll enjoy your company."

"I'll get to it right away, and thanks. I'm starting to get hopeful that Maggie will come home this year," Gabe said as he went outside.

As the two women relaxed that night, Bessie said it had turned out to be a good day, even though they had no guests.

"And it's all thanks to you, Rose. You helped that young principal, you made Gabe a much happier man, and again thanks to you, we have more guests arriving this week."

"Nonsense Bessie, we both helped Gabe. Without your involvement, I'm sure he would never have looked for any help from me. As for David Nolan, we won't know if I helped until later this week. I hope he does accept the principal's position at the elementary school in Murphy's Cove. A new school needs fresh ideas. From the sound of him, he has lots of ideas and energy."

Rose thought back to the phone call from the young teacher who knew nothing about the school area. A fellow teacher advised him to contact Rose and provided the phone number of Martin House.

"He certainly had lots of questions for me. Did I tell you his wife is also a teacher? She was offered a French teaching position at the high school. They want to come and see the schools and this area and hopefully meet some of the staff. Being young and from St. John's, moving here would be quite a significant change for them.

"It was good of your friend Jean telling him about our Bed and Breakfast. We have them booked into a double room for Wednesday and Thursday nights. Two days should give them lots of time to discover whether they want to move to this area. Hopefully, they will decide to take the positions. It would be a nice change to have people move here instead of having our young folks leaving for St. John's or the mainland. And Rose, they might not be on holiday, but we have booked our second lot of guests."

Bessie spoke of the declining population in the area. Because fishing was the only industry in the area, many young people left for other parts of the province or the mainland, often quitting school early. Murphy's Cove, the largest and busiest of the 14 communities on this side of the bay, had a fish plant that employed almost 200 people from the area, including students. Unfortunately, she added, it only opened seasonally during the spring and summer fishery. The only full-time employment appeared to be in small shops or post offices.

"How often did Alex wish that another industry would open to encourage young people to stay in the area? Martin House is not an industry, but we will stay open all year, that's if we keep getting guests."

The school board could be another good source for their business, Rose said. School board specialists travelled to schools in the district and often needed accommodation.

"I remember talking to a reading specialist who got caught out this way in a snowstorm and was stranded. He said a local teacher put him up, but he felt terrible because he knew he took her son's bedroom while the teenager slept on a couch. I'll give our business cards to the school board office and tell them we have accommodations available."

"You are full of good ideas today Rose. Although I have to say your idea of phoning Sister Bernadette was the best idea yet."

"Yes, I'm pretty happy about that myself. Sister Bernadette is the right person to deal with Angela. There should be no good reason to stop Maggie from coming home this summer. I can just imagine Angela's face when Sister Bernadette and Sister Patricia, who is a social worker, turn up at her door."

"I remember Gabe's face, Rose, when you told him Sister is making sure Maggie not only gets her ticket but she, or one of the Sisters, will take her to the airport to catch the plane. It was like a cloud lifted and for the first time today. he stopped looking like a defeated man."

"Yes, I noticed that too, especially when Sister asked to speak to him, and he could hear for himself how she planned to help Maggie. Gabe is going to send money to Sister tomorrow to buy the ticket. When you said he could have your car to pick up Maggie at the airport, instead of driving his old truck, it was like his last worry was gone, and he actually smiled," Rose said, laughing.

"Now, Rose, Gabe smiles quite often. It's just that you don't see that side of him because the pair of you are usually sniping at each other. From what I heard from Alex, your feud with Gabe started in school, and neither of you ever seem to forget it. However, Gabe was definite today that he wanted your help, which is a sign he thinks of you as his friend."

"I think a friend is too strong a word to describe the relationship Gabe and I have. Not that I regard him as an enemy, far from it, but Gabe O'Brien can be a difficult person to get along with and to know," answered Rose.

When the telephone rang, and Bessie rose to answer it, Rose began laughing.

"Saved by the bell! I know for sure you were ready to defend Gabe, but now you'd better answer the phone before the caller hangs up."

As Rose listened to one side of the telephone conversation, it was evident from Bessie's reaction that it was good news and concerned their business. When Bessie asked the caller when they would arrive and for how many nights, Rose knew for sure they had more guests on the way. Her sister-in-law's big smile when she concluded the call was all the confirmation Rose needed.

"By your expression, I would say we have more guests. Who are they, and when do they arrive?"

"They are arriving tomorrow night, and their names are Sue and Bob Newman. It's not a coincidence that they, like the Kennedys, come from New York.

"Max told them about us. He met them today at a hotel parking lot in Port aux Basques. He noticed their New York license plates, and of course, had to talk to them. They arrived off the Sydney ferry this afternoon while the Kennedys sail tomorrow."

"And Max being Max, I'm sure he told them all about his holiday in Mark's Point. He is going to make a great ambassador for our business," Rose said.

"It wasn't only Max who gave us a great review, that was Mrs. Newman on the phone, and she's been talking to the Kennedy women. She says she heard wonderful things about Martin House, the hosts (that's us), and Mark's Point. Her husband also heard all about Gabe from Max, and now he wants to go fishing. Mrs. Newman wondered if we could book Gabe, saying they didn't expect Gabe to take her husband fishing without paying for his time."

"I didn't think we would be taking bookings for Gabe when we booked our guests. However, I suppose with buying Maggie's air ticket and with fish prices starting lower this year, Gabe can use all the extra money he can get."

"That's the right attitude, Rose. I'm glad you feel that way."

"Alright, but on the topic of Gabe, I have one last thing to say. Gabe O'Brien is not a saint. I grew up hearing that kind of talk from Alex and my parents, but I never did see any wings or halo on him."

"And I agree, but then again, I never met any saints in my lifetime. My last word on Gabe is, he's a good man, and even you must admit he's always been a friend to the Martin family. And now that the topic of Gabe is closed,

I just remembered Mrs. Newman's last words. She said hearing about Martin House and Mark's Point from the Kennedys; she knew this was the kind of home and community she and her husband had dreamed of discovering when they decided to come to Newfoundland."

"What a lovely thing to say," Rose said with a huge smile.

"It's the kind of recommendation any business or community would love to have. After hearing that, I am even more sure that we did the right thing in starting our business."

"I know how you feel. I hope our next two lots of guests will also enjoy their time with us. The Newmans are staying until Saturday, which means they will be here when the young teachers arrive. Getting two bedrooms ready for our guests will be our first job tomorrow morning, Rose. Things are starting to get busy around here, and that's a good sign for Martin House Bed and Breakfast's future.

"And now we have that settled; I'm going to put the kettle on. There's nothing better than a cup of tea to put the finishing touch to a good day."

CHAPTER 5

Traditional Pursuits

I t was a calm day on the water, or what Gabe O'Brien would describe as a perfect morning for fishing when he left Mark's Point harbour with his latest 'fishing mate.' It was American Bob Newman's second day of fishing, and Gabe had been pleasantly surprised by his reaction to the boat and the hours spent on the water.

Not a big talker by nature, especially with strangers or when out in his boat, Gabe had worried the American would either talk incessantly or get bored at the lack of activity when not jigging fish or hauling nets. But Bob proved to be an ideal fishing companion, interested in everything and asking what Gabe considered sensible questions.

Today, Gabe planned to extend the trip and check his lobster pots, much to Bob's pleasure. As Gabe started up the boat motor again, Bob asked him how he knew where to place his nets or jig for codfish.

"I've got markers. The church is one, and another could be a hill or maybe a small bay, and I knows when I'm facing north, south or any direction."

"But how can the church or a hill help you?" a puzzled Bob asked.

"If you looks now, even this far out, you can see the church tower. Do you see it? Fishing folks from Ireland or England were the first settlers in most of Newfoundland, and they usually built their churches on the highest piece

44

of land, where they came together as a community. That's so the fishermen could see the church towers far out in their boats to guide them home. The church is my first marker, and if you looks right, you can see that point of land sticking out, and that's another marker. A mile further along, there's a small bay I often use as a marker for my herring nets, 'cause I knows if I go a mile straight out, that's the best place to find herring," Gabe explained.

Gabe told Bob that people always said Mark's Point got its name from an early fisherman called Mark who chose the bay's point, with its sheltered harbour as a marker when he fished.

"That was well over 150 years ago. I suppose it's right, 'cause it's also said that Mark's Landing got its name from the same fellow who landed and made his home down there," Gabe told Bob.

Meanwhile, back in Martin House, Bessie was in the kitchen when Bob's wife Sue tapped at the open door.

"Mrs. Martin, is it okay if I hang around the house until Bob returns from fishing. I thought he'd have returned by now because he left several hours ago. They were back by this time yesterday."

"You don't have to ask whether you can wait here, Mrs. Newman. We want you to feel this is your home when you are in Mark's Point. If you'd like to go through to the sun porch, you can watch for Gabe's boat coming into the wharf. Gabe did tell your husband that they would be out longer today because he had to check his lobster pots. One other thing, Rose says she feels she is back in the classroom when you call her Miss Martin, so please call us by our first names," Bessie said.

"I will if you agree to call me Sue. Do you mind if I just stay here and talk to you?" she asked.

"Not at all, but I'm just about done here. What if I make us a cup of tea, and we both go into the sun porch and relax?"

"I'd like that, but only if you're sure I am not taking you from your work. I've been admiring your lovely home. I'd love to have a sun porch like yours, with windows not only along the front of the house but one on each side, so you have a complete view. Of course, I don't have this spectacular view of the ocean that you enjoy every day. You are so fortunate to live in this home and community."

Sue told Bessie that her husband planned to retire next year, and they were seriously thinking of leaving New York for a quieter lifestyle. It was one reason they were travelling across the States and Canada, looking at communities where they might spend their retirement years.

"Ever since we arrived in Newfoundland, Bob keeps saying it would be a lovely place to live, and Mark's Point has to be one of the most beautiful communities we've seen."

"It's a big decision to leave one's home and especially one's country. I know because I left Scotland to move here. I had Alex, of course, but I can honestly say I never regretted my decision," Bessie said.

"And I can't imagine living in Mark's Point without Bessie," Rose said as she came into the kitchen through the back door.

"Although this is where I grew up, I would never have made a permanent move home if Bessie hadn't decided to stay when my brother Alex died."

"You are just in time for a cuppa, Rose. Sue and I decided to take our tea into the sun porch and watch for Gabe and Bob coming into the harbour. Are you going to join us?"

"I'll be with you in a few minutes. I need to make a phone call, and then I'll be through."

Once the tea was ready, the women took theirs and settled down in the sun porch, where Bessie placed her cup on a side table before picking up a bag containing wool and knitting needles.

"Do you ever just sit still, Bessie? You never seem to stop, and now, when you have an opportunity to relax, it looks as if you are going to knit."

"This is my way of relaxation, that and reading. I enjoy both, and knitting is something my grandmother taught me when I was a small girl. She didn't believe in idle hands, and she always kept busy."

Sue admired the beautiful colour of wool and asked Bessie what she was knitting?

"It's going to be a sweater for Gabe's granddaughter. Her 13th birthday will soon be here, and I thought a sweater in this deep rose wool would suit her blonde colouring. We're looking forward to seeing Maggie soon. She lives in Toronto but is coming to Mark's Point for the summer,"

"And maybe sooner than we thought," Rose said as she entered the room.

"Were you talking to Sister Bernadette? Did she speak to Angela, and did she see Maggie?"

"To answer all your questions, yes. It looks as if everything is going to work out. However, Gabe needs to phone Sister Bernadette, who is not teaching today, so she can explain what travel arrangements she hopes to make for Maggie."

"Gabe is going to be so excited. Maggie is his only grandchild, and there's a special bond between them," Bessie told her guest.

"I'm glad for Gabe, and now you'll be able to give his granddaughter the sweater instead of mailing it. I was just admiring the lovely sweater Bessie is knitting. Do you knit, Rose?" Sue asked.

Laughing, Rose replied she had no talent or interest in knitting or any other kind of craft. Saying Bessie was the knitter and quilter in the house, she asked their guest if she liked the quilt on her bed? It was one of Bessie's creations, she told Sue.

"Yes, but I learned quilting from Rose's mother and many of the quilts in the house we made together. Don't listen to Rose talking about other people's talents; she is a gifted musician."

Sue said being a musician was a great gift to have, adding she must tell her husband Bob, who loved music and played the guitar. He mostly played and enjoyed country and western music. Sue admitted to having no talents in either music or crafts but did enjoy cooking when she was at home.

"Rose, you asked if I liked the quilt on our bed. I think it's gorgeous. Is there a craft shop nearby where I can buy a couple of quilts? My good friend is looking after our house while we are away. A handmade quilt would make a wonderful thank you gift for her. It would also be nice to have one as a spread on my guest room bed where I can show it off to my friends."

Bessie said there were no craft shops in the area, but she knew two local women who made and sold quilts and would contact them to see if they had any available.

"Would you do that for me, Bessie? Do they live near here?" Sue asked.

They were sisters, Alice Brown, living in Mark's Point and Mary Fleming, in Mark's Landing, and Bessie said she would phone Alice.

"We have mostly patchwork or scrap quilts on our beds because they are so colourful. The sisters make their quilts from patterns, and some of them are beautiful. Finding patterns and even material wasn't easy at one time. I must show you the quilt I have on top of my bed. Mrs. Martin made it and gave it to me when I first arrived here as a bride from Scotland. It is the Double Wedding Ring quilt pattern."

Bessie recalled her mother-in-law saying her generation never wasted a scrap of clothing that came from dresses, shirts, pants and coats. What wasn't handed down to younger family members or turned inside out to reuse would be set aside for quilts or rag rugs.

Flour bags were always in great demand for many sewing projects, especially for quilt backing and sometimes lining. There were few quilt patterns to choose from then, but the Double Wedding Ring was one most women knew. Mrs. Martin sometimes ordered quilt squares from Eaton's or Simpson's catalogues or advertisers in *The Family Herald*.

"Now, if my eyes don't deceive me, I believe that's your husband and Gabe, just coming around the point in boat. It will be a half-hour or more before they finish for the morning. Gabe has to get his fish out of the boat and into pans to be weighed by the buyer who trucks it to Murphy's Cove fish plant. And if he has lobsters, he will have to move them into the holding box he keeps in the harbour. "

Almost an hour later, Bob and Gabe sat down to a late breakfast at the kitchen table. Rose and Sue had driven to the wharf, asking Gabe to return to Martin House to phone Sister Bernadette. On the way back, Bob, a tall but wiry man in contrast to the more robust Gabe, enthusiastically described his early morning fishing activities.

As soon they entered Martin House, Gabe wanted to phone Sister Bernadette, but Bessie insisted he first sit down with Bob and eat breakfast, saying the men must be hungry after spending five hours in a boat.

When he finally made the call and returned to the kitchen, it was evident Gabe had good news.

"Maggie is flying home on July 9, that's next Friday. Sister Bernadette knows of a family flying to Newfoundland then, and Maggie can travel with them. Isn't that wonderful! Sister Bernadette wanted to know if this was okay before she went back to Angela's apartment and told Maggie the good news. I said to go ahead, that it can't be soon enough for me."

As Gabe was speaking, Bob jumped to his feet. Thanking Bessie for the tasty breakfast, he said he and Sue were in the way and would leave Gabe and the women to discuss their business.

"No, Bob, you are not in the way. I want you to share the good news. My granddaughter Maggie, who I haven't seen for two years, is coming home. It's the best news ever. Thank you, Rose, and how can I thank Sister Bernadette? Although the money order I sent her hasn't arrived yet, she's buying Maggie's ticket today.

"Wait until Maggie finds out she's coming to Newfoundland. Bob, I told you that this was a good day when we got all those lobsters, but it don't hold a candle to my Maggie coming home. It's too bad you and the missus will be gone when she arrives, and you won't meet her."

Bob walked over to Gabe and shook his hand.

"Congratulations, Gabe, this is great news. Sue and I are happy for you and who knows, perhaps we will meet Maggie. We are going to St. John's for three days, but we were hoping the ladies would allow us to stay here on our way back. What do you say? Do you think you could put up with us again because I'm hoping for more fishing time with Gabe?"

"That's not a problem. Just give us the dates, and we will book you in. I've heard about golf widows, Sue, but it appears you're going to be a fishing widow, considering the time your husband is spending in a boat," Rose said with a smile.

"I'm only too glad to see him happy. Bob runs his own construction business, and he works far too hard. I've been after him for years to take a break and get away from it all. These past two days, he has been more relaxed than I ever thought possible. But he's not the only one. I think this holiday in Newfoundland is turning out to be the best medicine in the world for both of us."

Bob's fishing activities for that day weren't over yet, Gabe said, reminding him they would return to the boat to get their bucket of jigged cod.

"Then you will get your first lesson in filleting fish. Perhaps the women might want to cook some cod fillets for supper. There's at least a dozen codfish, and whatever the women don't want, we will salt. At one time, we had to salt all our fish if we wanted to sell it. Salting fish is a long process, and making quality salt fish needs good weather to dry it properly, so our fishing income was always at the mercy of the weather. Thankfully, we have a modern fish plant now in Murphy's Cove that takes our catch straight from the water, making life much easier for fishermen in these communities."

Gabe spoke about his lobster catch, saying he told Bob that he and Sue must have at least one lobster meal before returning to the States. After all, he said Bob brought him good luck that day with an above-average catch. The lobster buyer made his weekly collection in Mark's Point on Saturday morning. If and when the women were willing to cook the lobsters, Gabe said to let him know, and he would deliver a half dozen of the large shellfish to Martin House.

Bessie told Sue that she had phoned Alice Brown and asked her about the quilts when Sue and Rose went to the wharf. Unfortunately, she and her sister sold the quilts they had to a salesman Alice met in Kavanagh's Store.

"They sold them for $40 each, which in my eyes was sheer robbery considering the material and time they put into making them," Bessie said.

"Gosh, I would have gladly paid twice that amount and even more if the quilts were as good as the one on our bed. It's terrible to think someone would take advantage of them. Bessie, I don't suppose you know anyone else who might sell quilts?"

Alice suggested another woman living in Murphy's Cove South, and Bessie said she would give her a call.

Gabe had gone home, and the Newman's were upstairs in their room when Bessie returned from making her phone call. On seeing the look on her face, Rose had a feeling that the conversation had not gone well.

"You don't seem happy. Who was the quilter you phoned, and what happened? Didn't she have quilts for sale, or are they too expensive?"

"She has quilts for sale, and they're not expensive. It was Mina Lynch I called, but something didn't feel right. It was almost as if she couldn't wait to get me off the phone. I may have imagined it, but if I didn't, I wonder what was wrong?"

"Mina Lynch; wasn't she also a war bride?" Rose asked.

"I thought the two of you might have been friends. I never met her, but I remember Mother mentioning her a couple of times in letters. She wrote, saying she was glad there was another young bride from Scotland in this area and hoped the pair of you would become friends because she didn't want you to be lonely."

"Yes, she was a war bride, but we never got a chance to be close friends. For one thing, I never liked her husband Herbert, and neither did Alex. He once said Herbert Lynch was a troublemaker and a bully, and he would prefer not to have anything to do with him. Those were strong words coming from your brother because he rarely spoke ill of anyone."

Bessie said she had liked Mina. But because she didn't drive at the time, she had no transportation to visit her. Alex was always fishing or working at something, and when he was free, Bessie didn't feel like asking him to drive her to the home of a man he didn't like. She did manage to visit a couple of times, but Mina lived with her in-laws at the time. Bessie said she never felt welcome, and there was always a strange atmosphere in the house. Then too, Mina never returned her visits.

"But what happened now, Bessie? Did she say she had quilts for sale?"

"She has quilts for sale, but it was her hesitation about having visitors to her home that bothered me. When I said I might bring Sue over sometime today to see the quilts, Mina immediately had an excuse for us not to come. However, she seems eager to sell her quilts and told me she would call me tonight to arrange a time to get together."

"It all appears a bit strange, and what I am going to say may sound stranger, but do you think she could be afraid of something or someone? The reason I ask is that I have dealt with students and mothers who acted that same way, and there was usually a reason behind their behaviour."

As Bessie thought back and remembered Mina's husband, she told Rose she could be right. Mina was probably ashamed or even scared of him.

"From what you say about Mina, it sounds as if she is a private person and probably too proud to tell anyone if there is a problem. Does she have children?" Rose asked.

Bessie said Mina had three daughters, recalling she was married for years before the first girl was born. She remembered the occasion because she knit an infant's sweater set when she heard Mina had a baby girl. Alex drove her to Murphy's Cove South to see Mina and the baby, and by then, the family had a home of their own.

"I remember there was quite a bit of talk about their house because it originally belonged to Herbert's grandmother. She left it to Mina when she died, not her grandson or her son, which was most unusual.

"That was the day I realized what sort of man Herbert Lynch was. He ridiculed Mina in front of me, saying she took years to produce a child, and after that long wait, all she managed to have was a girl. I thought it was the most terrible thing I had heard.

"But he hadn't finished talking. He turned to me and said, 'I suppose I should be grateful she isn't barren like you.' He began laughing then, saying he was only joking, but I knew he wasn't making a joke. I remember thinking, thank God Alex made an excuse not to come into the Lynch's home. I don't know what he would have said or done if he heard what Herbert had to say."

Alex wasn't wrong when he described Mina's husband as a bully, Rose said. Considering his actions, she wondered if he was also a wife abuser. She asked how old were Mina's daughters.

Bessie said the oldest girl, Christine, would be twenty because she was born in 1951, but she didn't know the other two girls' ages or names. Christine no longer lived at home, Bessie said, recalling talk when she abruptly left school.

On hearing this, Rose exclaimed, "Chrissie Lynch, she was called Chrissie!"

"I had a feeling there was something familiar about this. Chrissie left school before she finished Grade X1. I know this because I met her principal at a meeting in St. John's a few years ago."

Rose recalled how the principal, hearing her family home was in the Murphy's Cove school area, asked if she knew Chrissie or her family, saying she was a brilliant student who suddenly quit school. He felt she should have gone on to university or at least completed Grade X1. He even went to her home to convince her parents to get her back in school but was unsuccessful. Chrissie had already gone away. However, his comment, wondering how a smart young girl could have such an ignorant man as a father, was one Rose always remembered.

"He thought I might know why she left school, but of course, I had no idea, and, at the time, I didn't connect Chrissie with Mina Lynch."

"I never heard why she left school or her home. There was speculation that she might be having a baby, but I also heard Alice Brown's daughter

Laura, Christine's best friend, said there was absolutely no truth to the story. The last I heard, Christine was living in Nova Scotia," Bessie said.

"Well, one thing for sure. If Mina calls and says to come over to see her quilts, I'm going with you and Sue. Something doesn't seem right, and you know me, I won't rest until I discover what it is."

"If she does ask us over, I hope it will be in the morning or early afternoon because we have the young teachers arriving tomorrow night. One of us has to be here, Rose, to welcome them and show them around."

The following afternoon, Bessie and Rose accompanied Sue to Murphy's Cove South. Their American guest was excited at the thought of getting one or more quilts.

"You ladies are so good, driving me in your time off to see quilts. Is this lady a friend of yours, Bessie?" Sue asked.

"You did say she was Scottish and a war bride, and I'm guessing your husband was probably a friend of her husband. Did they go to Scotland together when World War 11 began?"

"I knew Mina quite well at one time, but we had different lives, and she was busy looking after her growing family. And although the men sailed on the same ship to Scotland after joining the Newfoundland Forestry Unit, they didn't spend much time together because Alex later enlisted in the Royal Navy."

Alex was her only brother, Rose added, and although they had their share of arguments, he had always looked out for her.

"Alex was also a good son to our parents, but as my father always said, the best thing Alex ever did was to go to Scotland and bring back Bessie as his wife."

"Your Father was tormenting Alex when he said that. You both knew whatever you did was always perfect in his eyes. You had wonderful parents, but they had one flaw, they only saw the best in people. As a result, I often felt some people took advantage of them."

"Gosh, Bessie, and Rose, it sounds as if you had a wonderful family life. Do you mind me asking you, Rose, did you ever want to get married?"

There was silence for a minute before Rose began laughing.

Instantly Sue began to apologize.

"There I go again, me and my big mouth. Bob keeps telling me to think before I speak, and I always mean to do so. I am so sorry, Rose. I had no right asking such a personal question. Please forget, I ever asked. You've been so nice to me, and I would hate to become bad friends with you or Bessie."

"Not at all, Sue, there is nothing to apologize for," Rose said through her laughter.

"If you were here a bit longer or got talking to Lucy Pearce, you would soon know why I never married. I joined the convent when I was 19."

Before Rose could continue to explain, Sue gave a small gasp.

"Oh! I never realized you are a nun. You do know that Bob and I are not Catholics."

At this, Bessie joined in Rose's laughter.

"Rose hasn't been a nun for many years, and neither one of us cares what religion you are," she said through her laughter.

"I don't belong to any religious denomination. I believe in God, but I have never found it necessary to belong to a certain religion to do so."

Rose said she entered the convent in 1942 and trained as a teaching sister.

"I left the Order in 1955, and it wasn't because I lost my religion. I just realized I didn't have a vocation. I returned home that spring, thinking my parents would be upset at my decision, but instead, they, Bessie, and my brother Alex, could not have been more supportive. However, there are still people in Mark's Point who feel I let the community down by leaving the convent."

"As Alex would say, who cares what people think. He believed it was the start of a new life for you, Rose and decided to give us driving lessons. Although you said you didn't know what you would do, Alex was sure you would return to teaching, and he was right. He said we should both learn to drive, that having a license would give us independence. It would give me the freedom to travel and that wherever you taught, you could drive to school. I think he was also making sure you would return home for weekends and holidays."

"And do you remember how surprised we were when we passed our driving tests, Bessie? We got even bigger surprises the following week. That's when Father had two new cars delivered, one for each of us."

"Those cars were the talk of Mark's Point for ages. Some people were convinced Alex was starting a taxi service, probably because it was rare to see one new car, let alone two because most men drove trucks, not cars. Your father joked he only bought the cars to have two personal drivers at his command, but it was just another example of your parents' kindness. I drove that car almost ten years before I traded it, and Rose used hers to drive to school each day," Bessie recalled.

"Wow, you tell lovely stories. What great lives you have. I thought life would be slow in a small community, but you make it sound exciting," Sue said.

"Speaking about small communities, we're coming to Murphy's Cove South, where hopefully you will find quilts you like. We just go through the main road, and Mina's house should be the first one in the second lane."

Ten minutes later, the women were in Mina's home. The outside could use a coat of paint, but the interior, although shabby, was shining. When Mina brought them into her living room, Sue gasped with delight at the sight of four colourful quilts spread over a couch and chair.

"These are absolutely beautiful. Are the quilts all for sale, and how much do they cost?"

Mina replied they were all for sale and the going rate was $45. However, hearing Sue wanted two quilts, she would sell them for $40 each. At this, Sue gave a disbelieving snort.

"Ridiculous, look at the work and time that has gone into these quilts. They are worth at least twice that much to me, and I would love to have all four of them. However, I only brought enough money to buy two quilts. I will pay for them now, and could you put the others away for me? Now that I know where you live, I will return and buy the others."

Later, when the women were driving home, there was silence in the car. Bessie was thinking back to the visit. Everything had appeared well when they met Mina and her daughters, Katy, who would start her final year in high school, and Isabelle, about to enter grade eight.

But Bessie kept remembering Katy's face when Sue spoke about returning the following day. Katy looked worried until her mother quickly said she or the girls would not be home the next day. When Sue asked about dropping by another time, Bessie saw the same look of apprehension on the younger girl's face.

Mina said if Sue was sure she wanted to buy all four quilts, she could take them that day. Her next suggestion was even more surprising. Rather than have the women return with the additional money, she suggested Rose give it to Father Kiely after Sunday mass, and she would get it from him.

All this was running through Bessie's mind when Sue suddenly spoke up.

"I know I read too much into things. Mina and the girls were nice people, and I couldn't help admiring their beautiful reddish-blonde hair and colouring. And the quilts are gorgeous, but I had a weird feeling in that house. I don't think it's a happy place. Bob would say I was crazy, and I'm sorry if I'm offending you, but I can't stop thinking something wasn't quite right."

"I don't think you are crazy, Sue," Rose replied.

"There definitely was an atmosphere in that house. I can't put my finger on it. Mina and the girls were delighted you bought the quilts, and Mina's look when you said you wanted all four and would pay double, was priceless. If someone gave her a million dollars, I don't think she could have looked happier, but even so, there was something wrong. What did you think, Bessie?"

"You're both right. The girls looked apprehensive when you spoke of returning to pay for the other two quilts. I also remember how Mina was definite about the time we should come to see the quilts. I don't think she wanted us there when her husband was home. I know he wasn't a nice person when he was younger. Perhaps he never improved. It could be that Mina and the girls are embarrassed by his behaviour and didn't want us to witness it."

"I think you may be right, Bessie. That's why I said I wouldn't mind passing along the money to Father Kiely," Rose said

"But there's a bright side to this experience. Mina is a good contact for us if a guest is looking to buy a quilt, and I think she can use the extra money. Look, we are almost home, and the first thing I plan on doing is filling the kettle. Let's put our visit behind us and look forward to a good hot cup of tea."

CHAPTER 6

Dinner Guests

B essie and Rose stood on the steps of Martin House, bidding their latest guests goodbye. Bob and Sue Newman had booked into accommodations in St. John's but planned to return to the Bed and Breakfast for a few more days. The women had enjoyed hosting their latest guests and were looking forward to their return.

"I think they will enjoy their stay in St. John's, especially now they know David and Sharon. I wondered if young people like the Nolans would find anything in common with Sue and Bob or us, but they fit in well. It's nice that the two couples arranged to get together for a night out in the city."

"I think everyone enjoyed themselves on Friday night, Rose. What a talented group of musicians we had gathered here. It was like having a band with Bob on guitar, David playing your accordion, you on piano, and Sharon singing so beautifully. And who would ever think that Bob could do such a great Elvis Presley impersonation? Even Gabe enjoyed himself. I haven't seen him so relaxed for ages."

Rose agreed with her sister-in-law, saying she believed it was the news about Maggie rather than the music that relaxed Gabe.

"He's a different man since knowing Maggie is coming home and that her travel plans are in place. The other good news is David accepted the principal's position in the elementary school, and Sharon will teach at the high school. I'm sure the students will like them. Now all they need to do is find somewhere to stay. Hopefully, they'll find a decent house to rent when they come back in two weeks. We must be doing something right, Bessie. We've had three lots of guests, and two couples are returning. Wouldn't you say that's a good recommendation?"

"Yes, I've been feeling good about our business, but since visiting Mina, I can't get her and the girls out of my mind. There was an atmosphere in that house, and it wasn't good. There's something about those girls' faces that haunts me.

"Which reminds me, Rose, it's tomorrow you see Father Kiely and give him the money for Mina. I've been feeling guilty since Mina mentioned his name because he was a regular visitor here. He and Alex enjoyed each other's company, and he sometimes dropped in for a cup of coffee and a chat. Alex would bring him back for dinner whenever there was 11 o'clock Sunday mass, but I've never invited Father Kiely since Alex died. When you see him tomorrow, why you don't ask him to come to dinner?"

But Rose felt the invitation should come from Bessie and suggested she call him, adding the priest had often inquired about Bessie when she spoke to him at weekend masses. With the mass schedule for Mark's Point changing the following day to 11 o'clock each Sunday during July, Rose said he could come to Martin House after mass."

"I'll phone him right away, and I'll also ask Gabe. There's no need for him cooking for one when we are preparing dinner," Bessie said.

"You are asking Gabe to dinner when Father Kiely is here? Is that a good idea? The last time Gabe was in church was probably at Alex's funeral."

"Yes, and that was the last time I was in church, too," Bessie sharply replied.

"Gabe is a good man, whether he goes to church every week or not. And another thing, Gabe was Alex's closest friend and often came here for Sunday dinner. Father Kiely and Gabe always got along well."

"Now, Bessie, don't get me wrong. I was just thinking of Gabe. It's less than two years since Father Kiely came to this parish, and I don't know much about him. It didn't occur to me that he and Gabe might know each other. I just didn't want Father Kiely, or any priest, putting Gabe on the spot, asking him why he didn't attend church."

"I'm sorry I jumped on you like that, Rose, but religion can be a very touchy subject with me. As you know, religion wasn't a part of my life until I met your brother. That's why I never thought it would matter to my family where we were married. However, some of my relatives refused to attend our wedding because it took place in a Catholic church, and that really hurt me. I thought I was finished with bigotry when I came to live in Newfoundland, but I discovered I couldn't have been more wrong."

"What do you mean?" Rose asked.

"Father Heaney was the parish priest when I came to Mark's Point. I wasn't here a month when he started pressuring me to convert. When that got no results, he went to Alex and your parents, telling them they needed to convince me to change my mind. He was furious when they told him it was my decision and refused to discuss it further."

"I never knew this, but remembering Father Heaney, it doesn't surprise me. He was one of those priests who thought it was his way or no way. Most of his parishioners feared him, but he should have known it wouldn't work with our family," Rose said.

Bessie said if the priest stopped then, it would have been alright, but when he realized he wouldn't get help from the Martin family, he changed his tactics.

He decided to preach about hell and damnation at Sunday mass and told his parishioners not everyone would go to heaven. The priest said a heathen lived among them who had no religion and would spend the hereafter in hell. It didn't take the Martin family long to realize who he meant.

"What! Why didn't I hear about this? And what did Alex and my parents do after that sermon? Priest or no priest, I can't see my family letting him get away with that."

"Alex and your mother left mass while he was still preaching. Your father stayed, but only because he was determined to have it out with Father Heaney.

"After mass, he told the priest he could take a lesson in Christianity from me. The following day your father sent a letter to the Archbishop, and within a couple of months, Father Heaney had left the parish for good. Although Alex and your father were furious, I will always remember how upsetting it was for your mother. I can still see her crying, saying she couldn't believe a priest could be so cruel. That's when Alex said not to tell you. It was over, and there was no need to have you upset."

"That was terrible, Bessie, but attitudes and opinions on religion have changed a lot since then, and no one knows that more than me. Remember the summer I came home just after you arrived? When you didn't go to mass, I asked Mother if you were sick. When she said you weren't a Catholic, I took it for granted that because you married Alex, you planned on joining his faith," Rose recalled.

"It came as a shock when Mother said she doubted if you had any intention of becoming a Catholic and that whatever you decided was your business. The main thing, she added, was that you were a good person. She also said Alex could have made no better choice when he asked you to be his wife. My mother was one of the wisest people I ever knew, and I've always remembered that conversation. It certainly made me think twice about some opinions I held."

"That's enough talk about religion. I don't know why it is always such a controversial subject. It's one topic I always try to avoid. However, I will say this; Father Heaney was an exception. Since then, I have known several parish priests, and, as your mother would say, they were 'good men' and always welcome in our home. Now with that spiel over, I will call Father Kiely and invite him to share our meal. Then I'll call Gabe."

The following day, after a hearty meal, Father Kiely pushed back his chair from the table with a satisfied sigh.

"Bessie, as usual, that was a wonderful meal. I have to admit that I've missed Sunday dinners at the Martins."

"We can remedy that, Father. Whenever you have 11 o'clock mass in Mark's Point, you are welcome to come here for dinner, and Gabe, that invitation is also open to you."

"That's a date. However, there is a problem. I know I'll have no trouble remembering to come for dinner because of my Sunday schedule, but Gabe, how will you remember when you don't attend mass?" the priest said.

Rose gave Bessie one horrified look and was about to say something when Gabe spoke.

"Well now, Father, as I've told you before, unlike some people I could name, my stomach don't need no ringing of a church bell to remind my brain when it's time to eat."

Bessie joined in the men's laughter while Rose looked on in bewilderment.

"Oh, Rose, your face is a picture," said Bessie.

"I told you that these two were friends; what I forgot to mention was the insults they enjoy trading. But I'm warning both of you that we will have Maggie with us for dinner next Sunday, and I don't want her thinking you are fighting."

"Is this your granddaughter? Is she coming for a holiday?" Father Kiely asked Gabe.

"Yes, she's flying home next Friday," Gabe replied with a huge smile.

"We are all excited about her arrival. She's a lovely youngster who will soon be a teenager. Alex was her godfather, and she meant a lot to us," Bessie said.

"Yes, and you should have been her godmother. That's another foolish rule the church has, Father. Bessie couldn't be Maggie's godmother because she wasn't a Catholic," Gabe said with a snort of disgust.

But Bessie said she didn't need a title to care for Maggie. However, she did have a title in one way because Maggie, like her mother, always called her Aunt Bessie.

"And although I haven't seen Maggie since she was a small child, I'm hoping I'll also become her honorary aunt. I'm looking forward to having a child around," Rose added.

"She'll be here in just five more days. I wonder if she has changed. Do you think she'll be happy enough to spend the whole summer here? I sometimes wonder if this was a good idea. Maggie is getting older, and it might not be much fun for someone her age to stay with an old fella like me."

"I always knew you were foolish, Gabe O'Brien. Do you think Maggie would have asked to come if she didn't want to be here?"

"I have to agree with Rose, Gabe. I think your granddaughter is a lucky girl to have a grandfather who cares so much. I only wish all the young people in my parish were so lucky," Father Kiely said, looking quite solemn.

When the priest spoke, Rose and Beth looked at each other, their thoughts returning to the Lynch girls. Rose wondered if Mina's girls were in

Father Kiely's mind when she suddenly thought of the money Sue had left to pay for the quilts.

"Father, I just remembered about an envelope I have belonging to Mina Lynch. She asked if I could give it to you, saying she would pick it up at Benediction this evening. I'll get it for you."

Father Kiely looked startled for a second but quickly recovered and asked Rose if she knew Mina well.

"I only met her the other day, but Bessie has known her for years."

"We know each other mainly because we both came to Newfoundland as war brides, and although we were quite friendly at one time, I'm sorry to say we grew apart. However, Rose and I visited her this week with one of our guests who wanted to buy quilts from Mina," Bessie said.

"I'm glad you saw Mina. She's a nice woman and a caring mother. She doesn't go out much, and I'm sure she could use a friend. Do you think you might see her again?"

"Mina makes beautiful quilts for sale. Rose and I think she will be a good contact for any of our guests who may be interested in buying a quilt, so hopefully, we will see her again."

"Wonderful, and did you meet her girls?"

"Yes, we met two of the girls who seemed proud of their mother's skill as a quilt maker. Mina has another daughter Christine, I remember seeing her when she was a baby, but I believe she lives on the mainland somewhere."

"I haven't met Chrissie, that's what Mina and the girls call her, but I know her mother is immensely proud of her. She lives in Nova Scotia and is not only attending university classes; she also works part-time. I heard she always did well in school, and I know both her sisters are excellent students."

"They would have gotten their brains from their mother, then, because Herbert Lynch is an ignorant brute of a man. Sorry, Father, I don't usually like speaking ill of people, but that man is spiteful and mean. I've had many a disagreement with him during Fishermens' Committee meetings. I don't like him, and to tell the truth, I don't know anyone who can stand the man."

Seeing the concerned look on Father Kelly's face, Rose decided to lighten the mood.

"And that's the sermon of the day, according to Gabe O'Brien. Now Gabe, while we have you here, I have a question. Why don't you and Maggie stay at my house on Friday night? I'm going into St. John's, probably on Wednesday, to remove the rest of my things before the professors begin renting my house on July 15. I'm coming back on Saturday, but before I leave St. John's, I want to take Maggie shopping."

"I can't because I'll have Bessie's car, and she'll need it, but I did wonder if Maggie needed any new clothes. I usually send her money at the end of the school year to buy summer clothes, and I haven't so far. If she do need clothes, is she big enough to go into a shop and buy them herself? I'll pay, but I can't go shopping for girls' stuff," Gabe said with a worried look.

"Rose and I have already discussed this, and I won't need my car, which means you can stay overnight, so that's settled, but there is one other thing. Rose and I want to buy clothes for Maggie. I see your face Gabe, and I know you're getting ready to object, but just listen to what I have to say. We would have never got our business up and running without your help, and you refused to take a penny for your work. It's our turn to repay you. Rose is looking forward to taking Maggie shopping, and you wouldn't want to deprive your granddaughter the pleasure of a shopping trip, would you?"

"I believe the women have the better of you, Gabe," laughed Father Kiely.

"One thing my father always said was, 'Never argue with a woman,' and I always listened to my father. He would also tell his children that we should always use the talents God gave us. And Rose, I understand you have a musical talent our parish could use."

"She sure put her talents to good use the other night, didn't she, Bessie? We had a real good time. Rose was on piano, Bob on guitar, and the other fellow, a schoolteacher, was a real good accordion player. The teacher's wife and Bob were singing too. You should have heard them, Father," Gabe said.

"I would have enjoyed hearing them. What about inviting me when next you plan a 'time'? I don't play the piano, but I strum the guitar on occasion. But getting back to you, Rose, we really could use an organist and a choir in church. Will you consider taking over the job?"

"I am surprised you waited this long before asking her, Father. I told her ages ago that you would ask once you knew she was home for good. Go on; Rose put him out of his misery. You know you will do it."

"Yes, but let's not jump into this right away, Father. What about putting a notice in the church bulletin asking adults and students who would like to sing in a choir to come to a meeting? That way, we'll see what interest there is. Even if we only get a few people, we could start practicing. If we began singing as a choir during mass, it might encourage more members."

"Wonderful Rose. I would have asked you weeks ago if I thought it would be this easy. A choir is going to make such a difference during mass, and having someone to play the organ will be great."

"If I thought the choir might cut down on the length of your sermon, I might even consider attending mass now and then. Don't look so hopeful, Father; I said I might, not that I would," Gabe said, laughing at the priest's expression.

Rising from the table, Father Kiely looked over at Gabe and, slowly shaking his head, said, "I would stay and argue with you, Gabe, but I have a meeting this afternoon and have to get on the road. I'll have to live with the hope you might show up at mass.

"But Gabe, if you do, give me plenty of warning, please. I wouldn't want to scare my parishioners by falling out of the pulpit in shock."

Father Kiely's parting shot left Bessie and Rose in a fit of laughter and Gabe shaking his fist in mock anger.

"One of these days, I'll get the last word and the last laugh with that man."

As the priest, still laughing, walked outside, he almost bumped into an older woman.

"Excuse me; am I at the right place? When I went to Murphy's Cove, I heard there was a house that provided accommodations in Mark's Point, and by the sign at the end of the driveway, I'm hoping this is it," the woman said.

"Yes, this is Martin House. Come inside, and I will introduce you to Bessie and Rose, who are sisters-in-law and partners in their newly opened Bed and Breakfast."

With this, the priest opened the door and called out to the women.

"Did you forget something, Father? Or did you come back for another bout with Gabe?" Rose asked, then looked confused when she saw a stranger accompanied him.

"Rose, this lady wants to ask you about accommodations."

Turning to the newcomer, he said, "I'm sorry for my lack of manners, this is Rose Martin, and I am Father James Kiely, the parish priest in this area."

"I'm Margaret Wilson, and I am delighted to meet you. My husband and I left St. John's early this morning on what I call a scouting expedition. We're not looking for accommodations today, but for two nights at the beginning of August. We've been invited to a wedding in Murphy's Cove and need a place to stay that weekend. The groom is the son of our friends, and we are looking forward to the wedding," Mrs. Wilson said.

"Now that you have met Rose, I will leave you in her capable hands. It was nice meeting you, and hopefully, I will see you in August," said Father Kiely.

"Why don't you get your husband, and we can talk about accommodations," Rose told their visitor.

"In the meantime, I'm sure you could both use a cup of tea. I'll put on the kettle, and when you return, don't bother knocking; just come right in."

The following Saturday, on her return from St. John's, Rose gazed in amazement at the names in the Martin House reservation book, which had significantly grown thanks to Mrs. Wilson.

"My goodness, I was only gone four days, and look at our reservations. I often wondered if the time would ever come when our reservation book had guests' names. Now, look at the August 6-7 weekend bookings. Who would have guessed Mrs. Wilson's visit would result in our first full house? We must remember and thank her when she comes next month."

"Yes, Rose, it's hard to imagine having the four upstairs rooms full with eight adults and our first child guest. They are all attending the wedding in Murphy's Cove. What a good week it has been. Sue and Bob came back on Wednesday, just after I booked in two sisters from Ontario, who were making their first visit down east. The sisters stayed for two nights and thoroughly enjoyed travelling around this area. We also have another reservation for later this month, and that's in addition to David and Sharon," Bessie boasted.

"I would have liked to meet the sisters. I'm sorry you had to look after them as well as Bob and Sue by yourself, but hopefully, that was my last visit to St. John's this summer."

"You needed to be in St. John's. Now tell me about Maggie, and how did you enjoy shopping for a cot. I can't get over us not thinking of children's furniture when we opened, especially since we advertised our Bed and Breakfast as suitable for all ages."

"Maggie helped me pick out the furniture. What a lovely young girl she is, Bessie. When it came to the right size of beds, she was a great help. With her flight arriving at two o'clock, we had most of the afternoon to go shopping. We bought a cot and ordered a highchair and what is called a junior bed. It was Maggie who thought about the highchair. She also very seriously informed me that although a child might be too big for a cot, an adult bed wasn't suitable, so that's why I bought a junior bed."

"What about clothes for Maggie? She has grown so much in two years," Bessie said

"I think she was a bit overwhelmed at first when Gabe and I told her she was going shopping for clothes. Maggie's certainly not a greedy youngster. She picked out a top and shorts, insisting they were enough. I finally got her to start choosing clothes by saying it looked like Gabe and I would have to pick her clothes, and neither of us had any fashion sense. We had a good laugh at that, and she did choose a few more tops, pants, and a dress. Then early this morning, we went shopping for sandals and sneakers, and she picked out a jacket she liked."

"How did you manage to get Gabe into a shop?" Bessie inquired.

"He didn't have to go inside a shop. We went to the Avalon Mall, where he could sit on a bench while we shopped. Although the Mall opened four years ago, it was his first visit. I believe he was fascinated by all the shops and how many people were shopping in one place. He met a couple he knew from up the shore, and when the woman went into some of the stores, her husband and Gabe were only too glad to sit down on one of the many available benches and talk."

Bessie was glad everything went well, saying she didn't need to ask Gabe how it went for him.

"He is a different man whenever Maggie is here. I still get furious when I remember what Angela did last year. I'd like to see her and give her a piece of my mind."

"Never mind, Bessie, I believe people like Angela get what they deserve. Now, changing the subject, I bought the freezer we wanted and arranged with Murphy's Trucking to bring it and the children's beds when they return from the trip to town on Wednesday. I wonder if Lucy will be around to see the delivery. If she sees we have a cot and highchair arriving, we may have a visit from her. I can hear her now, announcing our purchases in Kavanagh's.

'What do them two women want with baby furniture when one's a widow and the other's an old maid? There's not much hope of either of them making use of it,' Rose said, in an almost perfect imitation of Lucy's voice and actions.

"Rose Martin, what are you like at all?" Bessie asked, trying to control her laughter.

"Alex once told me how he found it hard to believe you had chosen to enter a convent. When I asked him why he grinned, saying you were better suited to go on stage as a comedian or a ventriloquist. It stuck in my mind as a strange thing to say because, at the time, I couldn't see that side of you, but I've learned what he meant since then.

"When you go to mass tomorrow morning, perhaps you should think of going to confession. I would tell Father Kiely what you said about one of his parishioners when he comes to dinner tomorrow, but knowing him and Gabe, they would probably have a good laugh."

"There will be five of us for dinner tomorrow now that Maggie is home," Rose said.

"I meant to tell you that there will be seven of us. Sue and Bob are leaving for home on Monday, and I thought it would be nice to invite them to dinner. They are delighted to know they will meet Maggie, but I think Sue is a bit apprehensive about meeting Father Kiely."

"Sue will be alright. After all, she got over the shock of me being an ex-nun," Rose said, laughing again.

"If I didn't know you better, Rose Martin, I'd say you'd been drinking and not the tea you just finished. I think it's time we went to bed. It's been a long day, and it looks as if tomorrow is going to be a busy one."

"I won't be long getting to bed. I find driving always makes me tired. I forgot to tell you that I'm picking up Maggie in the morning. It was Gabe who asked if she could go to mass with me. Of course, I agreed, and when I did, Maggie was pleased, saying she would wear her new jacket and sandals to church."

CHAPTER 7

Parting Gifts

On the final morning of Sue and Bob's visit to Martin House, the American couple appeared in the kitchen, asking if the women would do something for them. Bob held an envelope that he said was for Gabe to thank him for making his holiday enjoyable.

"I've tried paying him for all our fishing trips, but he refuses to accept money and won't even talk about it. You are his good friends, and I'm hoping you might talk some business sense into him. He needs to charge a set fee for taking people out in his boat. I don't think he realizes what a wonderful thing it is for people like me.

"When I say this has been the most amazing holiday Sue and I have had, I mean it. Not only did you ladies make us feel like we were at home, but Gabe also provided the most relaxing pastime for any man. I know people who spend a fortune on holidays and will never have this kind of experience. Others pay hundreds of dollars to psychiatrists, hoping to find the peace and tranquillity experienced in Gabe's boat."

Bob said he knew Gabe well enough by now to realize if he tried to give him money, he would refuse it again. However, determined Gabe would get paid, Bob thought by having Bessie or Rose give it to him once they left Mark's Point, Gabe would have no option but to accept it.

"And, if we had been here on Maggie's birthday, we would have given her a gift. She is such a good kid, and I hope she has a wonderful birthday," Sue said, handing Bessie another envelope for Maggie.

"Now, Bessie and Rose, the hardest part of all this is saying goodbye. What Bob said about staying with you and our visit to Mark's Point goes double for me. If Bob didn't have to get back to look after his business, we would stay longer. But you haven't seen the last of us. We will definitely be back."

A few minutes later, the American couple pulled out of the driveway to shouts of goodbyes and with promises to tell all their friends about Newfoundland and Martin House.

"It's going to be quiet around here without Sue and Bob. What a great pair they are. Knock on wood; we have been lucky so far with our guests."

"You are right, Bessie. We haven't had anyone who has been demanding or difficult to please. I am going upstairs to strip the bed and get the bedding into the washing machine. It's a lovely day to put it on the clothesline.

"By the way, I forgot to mention that Maggie is coming here for a music lesson. When we walked home from mass the other day, I told her about starting the choir and how I would play the organ in church. She wanted to know if it was difficult learning to play the organ. It turns out she would love to play a musical instrument, so I suggested she try the piano and I'd give her lessons while she was in Mark's Point. I saw her yesterday, and she wanted to know how much a piano lesson cost. When I said there would be no charge for her, she shook her head, saying she couldn't take free lessons. Don't you think she sounds just like someone we know well?" Rose asked.

"She's Gabe's granddaughter for sure. But if she doesn't want free lessons, how is she going to pay for them?" Bessie asked.

"I think that's settled. I said when the blueberries ripen in a few weeks, we'll need several gallons to make muffins and pancakes for our guests. I suggested we would buy them from her, and perhaps other people might like to buy some. That's when she asked why we would want any because she always went berry picking with her Aunt Bessie, who picked three or four times the amount she ever could.

"Trying to come up with a reason why we'd want to buy them, I sort of implied that you had bad knees. After that, Maggie was only too willing to pick blueberries for her poor Aunt Bessie. Needless to say, paying for music lessons wasn't mentioned again," Rose said with a grin.

"Rose Martin, what a nerve you have. I might be a wee bit overweight, but there's certainly nothing wrong with my knees. And another thing, I enjoy berry picking, especially berry picking trips with Maggie. We've had some great times, leaving in the morning with a picnic lunch and not coming back until late afternoon. What am I supposed to do now?"

"Don't worry, Bessie, I'll think of some way to allow you and Maggie to go berry picking. Who knows, I might find a new miracle cure for your knees," Rose said, laughing as she left to go upstairs.

She was no sooner gone when she was back in the kitchen. Instead of bed sheets, she had an envelope in her hand.

"I found this on top of the Newman's bed, addressed to both of us," Rose said.

Withdrawing an American $50 bill and a note from the envelope, she began to read.

Dear Bessie and Rose,

What wonderful friends Bob and I discovered when we came to Martin House. Although the Kennedys were full of praise for your hospitality and the community's beauty, we had to experience it ourselves to appreciate just what it is you have in Mark's Point.

We have travelled extensively (mainly for Bob's business) and stayed in many hotels. Nowhere could we get the service, laughter, entertainment, and particularly the friendship we found in your home.

You say your business is a Bed and Breakfast. It is that, but it is so much more. You both went out of your way to make our holiday memorable. What you offer to your guests is unique. I wish we could bottle it and bring it back to the States.

As you know, Bob is a businessman. He owns a large construction company with over 100 employees. Making money has been a way of life with him for too long. Bob believes your rates are much too low for the service you provide. I think he would also like to give Gabe a good shaking for his lack of business sense. But seriously, I think this holiday taught him that there is far more to life than making money.

Thank you, Bessie and Rose, for everything. Please accept this gift as a small token of our appreciation. See you next year for sure!

Your friend always,

Sue

"What a lovely letter, but there was no need for money when they paid for accommodation. I certainly never expected it, but it is so like something Sue would do," Bessie said.

"Yes, and knowing both her and Bob, I wouldn't doubt there is also money in Gabe's envelope, and speaking of Gabe, he and Maggie just passed the window," replied Rose.

"Aunt Bessie, how are your knees?" Maggie asked as she came in and crossed the kitchen to hug Bessie.

"Yes, Rose, just how are Bessie's knees?" asked Gabe.

"And don't you go laughing! Ever since you told Maggie that Bessie had bad knees, she's been worrying about her. I thought when you was in the convent; you might have outgrown your foolishness."

"You were in the convent, Aunt Rose? Are you a nun? Is that why you were a teacher?"

As the questions poured out of Maggie, Bessie and Gabe laughed at the expression on Rose's face.

"Yes, Maggie, your Aunt Rose, was in the convent. You sit down with her and get her to tell you all about it. And don't worry about my knees; it seems they suddenly got much better."

"And when she finishes telling you about her life in the convent, ask me about her life as a student at Mark's Point school. I can tell you some good stories about your Aunt Rose," Gabe added.

"Yes, Maggie, I was a teaching sister. I lived in the convent, and it was a good life, but I decided I could also have a good life outside the convent. Now, don't you mind your grandfather's nonsense, because if there are school stories to tell, I'll be the one doing the telling. We are starting our music lesson in a couple of minutes, just as soon as I strip the clothes off the

Newmans' bed. But speaking about Sue and Bob, what about those envelopes, Bessie?"

"I know Rose is trying to change the subject, but Sue and Bob did ask us to pass on these envelopes. Here is yours, Maggie, and give this one to your grandfather."

When Maggie opened her envelope, she gasped with delight and held up an American $20 bill.

"Look Pop, look, Aunt Bessie and Aunt Rose, just see what Mr. and Mrs. Newman gave me. It's $20. Look what this note says, *A birthday gift for a beautiful girl who will soon become a teenager, love from Sue and Bob.* But it's not my birthday yet, and how did they know I will be turning 13?" she asked.

Gabe was silent at first when he opened his envelope to find his money. As he removed the enclosed letter and began to read, it was evident from his expression that he was far from pleased with the contents.

"Nonsense, all nonsense! If I wants to take somebody fishing, I'm not looking for money. Bob put $100 in this, telling me to put gas in my engine and buy more jiggers because he plans to return next year. Leaving me money when I already said no is bad enough, but then he says I need a business plan because once your guests know I'll take them out in my boat, I'll need what he calls a proper rate of payment," said an indignant Gabe.

"Why are you so stubborn about this. Bob is just trying to help you, and it certainly makes good sense to give customers a set price. What kind of business would Martin House be if Bessie and I didn't set rates to let our guests know in advance what their accommodation cost?" Rose asked him.

"Jumping Joseph! Rose Martin. You've got to be the most annoying, know-it-all woman I ever knew. I'm not running a business when I asks people to come fishing in my boat. You don't invite someone and expect payment. I don't want to hear another word about the subject," Gabe said belligerently.

Bessie glanced at Maggie, who by now was looking apprehensive as the discussion began heating up.

"What's the matter with the pair of you. Can't you see you are upsetting Maggie? You both need to keep your opinions to yourself," she said, giving Rose and Gabe stern looks.

"Maggie, you are a lucky girl getting $20. Have you any ideas about what you are going to spend it on?"

"I don't need any new clothes because you and Aunt Rose bought so much for me already. It is the most money I ever had, and it would buy lots of things."

"I'm glad for you, Maggie. If you want to give it to me for now, I'll bring it home while you go and have your music lesson," her grandfather said.

"That's what I can spend it on. I can pay for my music lessons. We are still starting today, aren't we, Aunt Rose?"

"Yes, we are, but before we start, I need to tell you there will be no charge for your lessons. As your grandfather said, you don't ask for payment when you give someone an invitation. You didn't ask me to give you music lessons, I volunteered, so there is no charge. Isn't that right, Gabe?" Rose said, giving him a look that defied him to debate the issue.

"I guess your Aunt Rose is right," Gabe muttered.

Bessie broke in, saying people should never charge each other when doing things for a family member."

"And Maggie, as far as we are concerned, you are part of our family. You took your Aunt Rose by surprise earlier by saying you had to pay for lessons. Not wanting to insist the lessons were free, she used the excuse my knees were bad to come up with the idea of you picking berries and getting repaid in piano lessons."

"Does that mean you can still go berry picking, Aunt Bessie?"

When Bessie said yes, Maggie's face lit up.

"Good because I love berry picking. When I was in grade six, my teacher told us about farmers and growing vegetables and fruit. She asked us to write an essay on harvesting. I wrote about how we went blueberry picking. My teacher asked me to read it in front of everyone and gave me an A on my essay. She said I was the only one of her students to take part in a harvest.

"I wrote that I was a good berry picker, but that you Aunt Bessie was a champion picker, and you used the berries in jam, pies, and puddings. When I finished reading, some of the kids in my class said I was lucky, and they wished they could come to Newfoundland."

"And we are lucky you came to Newfoundland this summer because we missed you last year. It won't be long before the blueberries are ripe, and as soon as they are, we will pack a lunch and take off berry picking," Bessie answered.

"What about you, Aunt Rose? Will you come berry picking with us?"

"I don't think so, Maggie. Unlike your Aunt Bessie, I have never enjoyed crawling through bushes, getting sunburned or being bitten by hordes of black flies. No, my dear, my talents don't extend outdoors at all."

"She is absolutely right. I once convinced her to come berry picking with me, but never again. She constantly complained from the time we left the house until we got back. She was so busy complaining I don't think she picked any berries. However, her talents do extend to the piano, and if you want to learn music, you will have a good teacher in your Aunt Rose."

"Well, thank you, Bessie, for those kind words," Rose said, laughing.

"I guess I'm forgiven for telling Maggie you had bad knees. So, with that, Maggie and I will adjourn to the sitting room and begin her music lesson."

As they left the kitchen, Gabe shook his head.

"I sometimes wonder about that sister-in-law of yours. Fancy her telling Maggie you had bad knees. You knows how that youngster worries about things. Now I'm off. Maggie says she wants to walk home, and I'm going back to do some weeding in my cabbage garden."

"Before you go, and while Rose has Maggie occupied, can we talk about her birthday? In just over two weeks, she turns 13, which is a milestone for her. She's looking forward to becoming a teenager. Do you have any plans made because Rose and I would like to have a party for her? What do you think?"

"To be truthful, I know nothing about throwing a birthday party. If you plan it, I'll pay for whatever is needed."

"There's no need for that. It will be our treat and something we will enjoy doing for Maggie."

"I was thinking of getting her a bicycle. She hasn't had a new one since she was small. You don't think she is getting too old for bike riding, do you, Bessie?"

But Bessie thought it was a great idea. Maggie probably missed not having one, she assured Gabe, because all the youngsters in Mark's Point seemed to have bicycles.

"Maggie will have lots of company while cycling, and she's old enough now to ride to some of the nearby communities. As for the party, you can tell Maggie about it. Then Rose or I will talk to her and see who she wants to invite and what food and decorations she wants. But the first thing I need to do is get the bedclothes from upstairs. Rose made two attempts to strip the Newmans' bed but got sidetracked. If I don't get the bedding washed and out on the line soon, the best of the day will be gone."

Bessie had the laundry done and was pegging the sheets on the clothesline when Maggie came out of the house.

"Is your music lesson over for today? How did you like it?"

"I loved it, but Aunt Rose says half an hour is enough for my first few lessons, but later if I still like it, she will keep me longer. I'm going home to help Pop in the garden. He says he will show me the difference between a young plant and a weed."

"That will be a good lesson to learn. Who knows, maybe next term, your English teacher will ask you to write an essay on growing crops, and you will have firsthand experience."

Pleased at the idea, Maggie took off running down the garden path while Bessie went indoors to discover Rose writing in the reservation book.

"Another booking?" Bessie asked.

"One old, one new. That was Sharon's mother, Mrs. Dawson, who called. She plans on coming here with Sharon and David next week. She wants to see where her daughter will be working and living."

Listening to Rose, Bessie sensed something was bothering her sister-in-law and asked was there anything wrong.

It appeared Mrs. Dawson had heard so much from Sharon about the beautiful quilts Sue bought she wondered if Rose could get one for her. Sharon had a birthday soon, and knowing how much she admired the quilts, her mother wanted to surprise her with one. Mrs. Dawson asked if she mailed a cheque to cover the cost, would it be possible for Rose to buy a quilt and hold it until she arrived.

"I don't mind buying a quilt, and I told Mrs. Dawson there was no need to pay for it until she arrives. However, it means getting hold of Mina again, and I have mixed feelings about that."

"I see why you are bothered, but I'll call Mina. Since we took Sue there, I can't get her and the girls out of my mind, and I feel I should do something. Asking about a quilt is a good excuse for me to get in touch with her. I'll do it right away before I change my mind."

A few minutes late, Bessie was back in the kitchen, looking much happier than when she left to make the call.

"I wonder if we read too much into our trip to Mina's house. She seemed delighted to hear from me, almost as if it was a common occurrence. I spoke about the quilt, and she has one on hand. However, it has predominately blue colours, and she suggested I ask Mrs. Dawson if her daughter would want a blue quilt. I also asked about the price because I know $40 or $45 is too low, but I don't think everyone is like Sue Newman and will pay double the amount. Mina says she would make enough to cover the cost of her material and work if she got $45, but I think $60 seems a reasonable price to pay for the work she puts in each one."

But Rose had already asked Sharon's mother if she had a colour preference, and luckily Sharon was partial to greens and blues. When Rose asked Mrs. Dawson what she was willing to pay, she said handmade quilts sold between $70 and $100 in a St. John's craft shop.

"I think $60 is quite a bargain considering all the work Mina puts into each one. I will call her back and arrange a time to pick it up."

Later that afternoon, Bessie, accompanied by an excited Maggie, set off for Murphy's Cove South. Bessie had invited Maggie to go with her, hoping to discuss her upcoming birthday party. They had less than a mile of the journey left when they came upon two teenage girls at the side of the road who appeared to be trying to attract their attention.

As she slowed down the car, Bessie was surprised to see the girls were Mina's daughters, and the eldest was carrying what appeared to be a bulky jacket or coat. When she brought her car to a complete stop, the girls approached as she wound down her window.

"Hello, Aren't you Katy and Isabelle? Do you remember me?" Bessie asked.

"I came to your home with an American lady to buy quilts from your mother. I'm on my way there now. Why don't you jump in the back, and I'll drive you home?"

"But you can't go to our house today," the younger girl said.

"What Isabelle means is that our Mom is not there. But we have the quilt you wanted," Katy quickly interrupted and produced what appeared to be a stuffed pillow from inside the coat she was carrying.

"Mom said she's sorry. She didn't want you making a wasted trip, and that's why we brought the quilt. She put it in this big pillowcase to keep it clean. You don't have to pay us. Mom says to give the money to Father Kiely."

Completely taken aback and at a loss for words, Bessie stared at the girls until Maggie asked if they were still going to Murphy's Cove South.

"Maggie, this is Katy and Isabelle, who are Mrs. Lynch's daughters. And girls, this is Maggie O'Brien from Toronto, who is spending the summer with her grandfather in Mark's Point. Girls, I understand that your mother can't see me today; however, I think you've done enough walking for now, and Maggie would like to see your community. We were thinking of treating ourselves to an ice cream from the shop. Why don't you get into the car, and I will treat all of us."

The two girls stood looking at each other as if they were uncertain whether they should accept the ride when Bessie settled the issue. Getting out of the car, she took the quilt from Katy and opening the trunk, took it from the pillowcase, and placed it inside a large flat cardboard box.

"I didn't know if your mother would have anything to wrap a quilt in, so I brought this cardboard box. The last time we were here, Mrs. Newman was so delighted with her quilts, she held them all the way back to Mark's Point.

"Now, girls, get into the car. I'm not having you walk any further. Why don't I drop the three of you off at the brook just outside your community, and you can show Maggie the swimming hole. I saw some youngsters swimming there the last time I passed by. I'll go on to the shop, get the ice cream and bring it back there for us all to enjoy. How does that sound?"

With Maggie agreeing wholeheartedly and the sisters now looking much happier about getting into the vehicle, Bessie returned to the driver's seat and starting the car headed toward Murphy's Cove South.

Several hours later, she related the day's events to Rose, who appeared to get angrier by the second.

"I knew it. There's something terribly wrong in that house. Why would Mina ask you to come and then not be at home? Why didn't she phone you and arrange another time to pick up the quilt? And those poor girls, walking all the way carrying a quilt in a coat. It almost sounds as if they were hiding it."

"I thought of that, and I asked myself the same questions as you are asking now. Remember how I mentioned the looks on the girl's faces when we went to Mina's home? I saw those looks again today. It was almost as if they were worried about something, and I am sure they didn't want me going to their house. That's why I suggested stopping by the brook.

"I was so glad Maggie was with me because she chattered away to them as if nothing was wrong, and they responded to her. When I returned with the ice cream, they seemed more at ease with me. Maggie certainly likes the girls and has invited them to her birthday party. I offered to drive them home as we left, but they said they weren't ready to return.

"The question is, what do we do now, or are we reading too much into this? After all, Mina might have the best reason in the world for not being home," Bessie said.

"If that's true, why didn't she phone you and explain? I don't think we should ignore this. You said Maggie invited the girls to her birthday party. Isn't that a good reason to phone Mina?"

"Let's not make any hasty decision. After all, there could be a good explanation for what happened today. That reminds me; I forgot to take Mrs. Dawson's quilt from the trunk of the car. Why don't you put the kettle on Rose while I fetch the quilt? I could use a good cup of tea about now."

CHAPTER 8

House Hunting

It was late afternoon, and Bessie was in the garden watering some newly planted flowers given to her by Nora Ryan when she saw David's car turning into the driveway.

Leaving the flower bed, she greeted the young couple and Sharon's mother, Agnes Dawson. It was Mrs. Dawson's first visit to Mark's Point, and she spoke enthusiastically about its natural beauty and how much she had looked forward to meeting Rose and Bessie.

While David and Sharon decided to walk around the community to stretch their legs after the long car ride, Bessie brought Mrs. Dawson upstairs to the bedroom she would have during her stay. She also had the quilt made by Mina to show her guest.

"What a lovely quilt, Mrs. Martin. I'm so glad you managed to get it. Sharon will be delighted when I give it to her on her birthday. She asked me why I was taking a suitcase when we only planned a two-night stay. Little did she know I would be putting her birthday gift inside it," Mrs. Dawson said.

Listening to Martin House's most recent guest who, with her rosy cheeks and dark hair, was an older edition of her daughter, Bessie's thoughts returned to her recent visit to Murphy's Cove South when she picked up the quilt Sharon's mother was now admiring. A week later, she still wondered why Mina gave her daughters the quilt and had them walk so far to deliver it.

Leaving Mrs. Dawson in her bedroom and returning downstairs to the kitchen, Bessie wished she felt better about the whole situation. After a great deal of discussion, she and Rose had decided to let the matter drop, with the hope that Mina might call with an explanation. Now she wondered if they made the right decision.

"I see David and Sharon have arrived. Are they going to start looking for a place to rent this evening?" Rose asked on her return from the local store.

"They are, but they have gone for a walk now because, in David's words, 'They are dunched' and needed to get the kinks out of their bodies after the long drive. Sharon's mother, Mrs. Dawson, is upstairs admiring the quilt. All three are driving to Murphy's Cove and Murphy's Cove South in about an hour. I offered to get them something to eat, but they stopped for a late dinner on the way and are not hungry. However, I have the kettle on because Mrs. Dawson agreed to have a cup of tea."

The words were scarcely out of Bessie's mouth when Mrs. Dawson tapped on the open kitchen door, asking was it alright for her to come in. After being introduced to Rose, the three women were soon seated at the kitchen table, enjoying a cup of tea and chatting away as if they were long-time acquaintances.

"I told David this is where we would find you," Sharon said, returning from her walk.

"Bessie and Rose, you want to watch this woman. If she doesn't drink all your tea, she'll have your ears bent double because she dearly loves talking."

"Be careful of how you talk to me, young lady," her mother said, laughing.

"Who knows how many of your students I might meet during our search. I'm sure they'd love to hear stories about their future French teacher."

As Sharon and David joined the women around the kitchen table, the conversation centred on possible homes in the area. Students from 14 communities attended the two schools, and with Murphy's Cove almost in the centre of the district, the farthest any bus travelled was about 22 miles each way. The young couple didn't want to live too far from the schools but were willing to rent anywhere in the area to get a decent home.

"There is one home in Murphy's Cove available, but apparently, it's been empty for a few years, and there's another in Murphy's Cove South. We thought if we looked at those two first and travel as far as Freeman's Beach East this evening, we could visit the other communities tomorrow."

Any other plans David had, were put on hold when a knock on the outside door and footsteps in the porch announced a visitor.

"Hello Rose, hello, Bessie, and you must be the new teachers looking for a place to live. And is this another one of your guests, Bessie?"

Despite walking in on the conversation, Lucy Pearce appeared entirely at ease in the Martin kitchen.

After making introductions, Bessie asked Lucy if she could help her, was there something she needed?

"No, my dear. I'm here to give these lovely young people some help. I knows you're looking for a place to stay, and I've been asking around. I've made a list of all the empty houses from Mark's Point to Upper Penny's Cove and all the way to Freeman's Beach.

"I knows how busy you and Rose is, Bessie, that you don't have the time to do all this work. Like I said to my Jim, 'What's neighbours for, if not to help their friends who's trying to make a living by renting their rooms to strangers?' Here's the list, and I want no thanks for it."

As Lucy paused for a breath, her eyes were taking in everything in the kitchen

"Is that new curtains, Bessie? I guess you needed them to freshen up the kitchen if you wasn't going to paint it. Where did you get the material? If you just had some more to make chair cushions to match, it would make all the difference to your kitchen."

The young couple and Mrs. Dawson looked on with amazement at the non-stop bombardment of words that came from Lucy, but she wasn't quite finished.

"Now, my dears, would you like me to come with you and show you where all these houses is? I knows the story behind every one of them, what house is good and what's wrong with another. You really needs to get settled in a nice place. Like I said to my Jim, 'If we don't get those young teachers a comfy home, they might not stay. If that happens, what would we do then for a principal in our brand-new school and for a high school French teacher?' No, my dears, we needs to get you a nice house to stay."

Mrs. Dawson was first to recover and interrupt the verbal onslaught.

"That is so kind of you. I can't get over how good everyone has been to David and Sharon. They've had so many offers of help, and although they already know of some houses, I am sure your list will be useful. We are meeting up with different people in the communities who have volunteered to show us the houses, isn't that right, David?"

With a look of gratitude to his mother-in-law, David agreed before thanking Lucy for her thoughtfulness.

"When we first came to see the schools, we weren't sure if we wanted to teach in this area, but the longer we stayed, and the more people we met, made us realize that this was the place for us."

"And that's the reason I came along on this trip. Sharon and David had so many positive things to say about the area and about the welcome they received from Bessie and Rose; I had to see it for myself," his mother-in-law added.

"Martin House is a beautiful home, and you women are doing a wonderful job. I had never heard of a Bed and Breakfast before now, but I wish more communities would offer what you provide here. I'll be telling all my friends about it. You must be proud of your neighbours, Mrs. Pearce. They are certainly putting Mark's Point on the map."

"Oh, I knows that for sure. Wasn't I the one that got them their first customers? Isn't that right, Bessie? That's why I come now, because I'm only too happy to help any of Bessie and Rose's customers.

"But there's another reason I'm here. I heard you're starting a choir in church, Rose. Now, I'm not much for holding a tune, but my Jim's a wonderful singer. The problem is my Jim is a shy and quiet man. Like it says in the good book, he hides his light under a bushel. I tells him he needs to show people what he can do. Will you ask him, Rose, or should I get Father Kiely to talk to him? I knows he would make a wonderful addition to your choir."

"Why don't you leave it with me, Lucy? I'll watch for Jim and talk to him about it when we meet. The choir could certainly use men. I wasn't in school with Jim because he was older, but I remember Alex saying he had a fine voice."

Delighted with the praise for her husband, Lucy left, but not before inviting Mrs. Dawson and the young couple to drop into her house at any time.

"Wow!" Sharon exclaimed.

"Does anyone else have the feeling that a whirlwind just passed through?
I thought you were a great hand to talk, Mother, but I have to say that hands
down, Mrs. Pearce has you beat."

Bessie interrupted the laughter that followed by advising her guests they
should get on their way before Lucy decided to return. Within ten minutes,
they were gone, and Bessie and Rose found themselves alone once more.

"I suppose in her way, Lucy is trying to be helpful, but she is so nosy, and
she doesn't know when to stop talking. And intentional or not, she always
manages to get a little dig in here or there," Rose said.

Trying hard not to laugh, Bessie had a question for her sister-in-law.

"I'm guessing you didn't appreciate her hint about making cushions to
freshen up the kitchen or her offer of help to her friends who are trying to
make a living by renting their rooms to strangers?

"But seriously, since Mrs. Kennedy spoke up defending Lucy, I've been
trying to think more positively about her. I know she's naturally nosy, but
because Lucy talks so fast, I wonder if she doesn't realize what she's saying
at times? However, it was nice to hear her praise Jim and his singing. I seem
to remember hearing that he used to sing at concerts when he was a young
man. I wonder why he stopped?"

"Bessie! Do you need to ask? I'd say he couldn't get a word in after he
married Lucy, let alone a song. She starts most of her sentences with the
words, 'Like I said to my Jim,' or 'Like I told my Jim,' Not much wonder
he's so quiet. But I wasn't putting Lucy off. I will try to convince Jim to join
the choir. It would be good to have a few men come to our first practice
next week.

"Now, while we have some time to ourselves, what about Maggie's birthday party? It's only a week away, and we need to make some plans. We don't
even know how many guests she wants to invite. What if we call her and see
if she can come over after supper, and we make up a list of things to be done."
Rose suggested.

Later that evening, the sisters-in-law and Maggie were happily going over
the party's final list of requirements. In addition to the Lynch sisters, Maggie

had invited four other girls. They included 14-year-old twins Lily and Pansy Brown from Mark's Point, and Maggie's cousins on her grandmother's side, 12-year-old Jenny Long and 15-year-old Martina Ryan.

"Jenny and Martina live in Murphy's Cove, but Aunt Teen is driving them over for the party. I told Aunt Teen about asking Katy and Isabelle, and she says she will bring them when she comes. Martina and Katy are best friends in the same class, and 'though Katy lives in Murphy's Cove South, Aunt Teen usually picks her up when the girls have things going on after school hours."

"That's settled, but are you sure you only want six girls? We've plenty of room to have more, and once your Aunt Rose and I get baking, there will be lots of food," said Bessie

But Maggie was happy with the girls she had invited. Apart from the twins, the only other girls about her age living in Mark's Point were Theresa and Nell Martin, and they were on holiday in St. John's.

"I talked to Mom last night and told her about my birthday party here. She said when she was a young girl; you always helped my Nan with her birthday parties. She also said they were the best parties in Mark's Point. Mom says she doesn't feel so bad about missing my birthday because she knows I'll have a wonderful birthday party with both of you here."

"I used to enjoy your mother's parties and helping your grandmother. Did you know, Kate, that your Nan was my best friend, just like your grandfather was your Uncle Alex's friend? She was a lovely woman, and I certainly miss her. I wish you had known her. Now, are you sure there's no one else you want to invite to your party?"

"I almost invited Michael Ryan and the twins' brother Bobby to my party, but I was glad I never. The twins asked me if I invited Bobby, and when I said no, they said good, they wouldn't come if he was there. Michael heard them and said he'd never go to a party with a bunch of foolish, giggling girls anyway. Then Bobby said birthday parties were only for babies," related Maggie.

"Sounds like typical teenager behaviour," Rose said.

"Give them time, and they'll enjoy each other's company. But few growing boys can resist birthday cake and cookies. What if you put some aside for them after the party?"

Maggie had just agreed this was a good idea when the teachers and Mrs. Dawson returned from their house search. After being introduced to Maggie and discovering she was entering grade 8, Sharon asked what extracurricular activities were available in the local high school and how Maggie participated.

"I don't live in Newfoundland, but I wish I did," Maggie said.

"I'd love to go to school in Murphy's Cove with my friends. Isabelle Lynch would be in my class, and I'd go on the bus with the twins, Lily and Daisy. I start a new high school when I return, and I don't want to go there. The school is too big, and I won't know anyone. I wish we lived with Pop all the time and never had to go back to Toronto."

Bessie was taken aback by Maggie's outburst. Although she rarely mentioned Toronto, Bessie hadn't realized Maggie might not want to return to Ontario or was unhappy in school. Making a mental note to talk to Maggie in private later, she changed the subject by asking her if she would like to help prepare a snack for their guests, who could probably use a cup of tea after their search.

Later, when Maggie had gone home, and Sharon was in the kitchen with Bessie helping wash up the dishes, she apologized for assuming the young girl would be attending the local high school.

"I knew she was Gabe's granddaughter, but I never realized she didn't live full time in Mark's Point or that her parents weren't here. She'll probably be okay when she goes to high school. The thought of change and having to make new friends is often upsetting for students entering a new school."

"I'm afraid that's not the problem with Maggie. If you stay in this area, you'll soon discover she's had too much change in her short lifetime. What she wants is the kind of life she has in Mark's Point with Gabe. Not that Maggie doesn't love her mother, but Angela is a single parent with little education or training who keeps changing her low-paying jobs and addresses. She can't give her child the stability she has with her grandfather.

"Maggie adores Gabe, and she has friends and far more freedom in Mark's Point than she could ever have in Toronto. However, staying here is not an option for Maggie because Angela will never return here to live. But I'll talk to Maggie and try to find a way to make her think more positively about her new school."

Bessie and Sharon went on to talk about the teachers' search for a place to rent since their first attempts, which saw them visit four communities, had proven fruitless.

"I'm sure you would prefer to live in Murphy's Cove, close to both schools, but you might find a more suitable house somewhere else," Bessie told Sharon.

"We still have about eight or nine houses to see. Five of them are on Mrs. Pearce's list, and hopefully, something will work out. Tomorrow we are going to start with the communities closest to the school and work our way outward. David wants to leave about nine, which gives us several hours to search before returning to St. John's."

"You shouldn't commit to renting any house until you see them all. Why don't you start your search at the farthest point in Mossy Brook, then return through the communities this way? That should bring you back here just in time for lunch.

"Before you object, Rose and I have already discussed this and are prepared. I know a couple of take-outs are on your way, but I don't think they open until later in the afternoon. That's because they are more like hang-outs for teenagers than restaurants, with pool tables and other games. Let's go and see what David and your mother have to say."

With her plan of action laid out, Bessie soon had the others agreeing it was a good idea. It would leave them three more communities to visit in the afternoon on their way back to St. John's.

The following morning after the guests left to go house hunting again, Gabe dropped in. He had ordered a bicycle for Maggie and planned to pick it up in Murphy's Cove on Thursday. Because it was a surprise birthday gift, he wondered if there was some way the women could occupy Maggie to allow him to go to Murphy's Cove, return with the bike, then hide it in his shed.

"That's not a problem. I'll change the time of Maggie's music lesson, and afterward, we can keep her busy with plans for her party on Monday. She enjoys her music lessons and would come every day if I let her, but I only give her lessons twice a week because I don't want her getting bored."

"I know Maggie is enjoying playing the piano, and she also likes to sing. She and the twins are planning to go to the choir practice next week. Who knows, I might have to go to church one of these days to hear them sing," laughed Gabe.

"You could do worse things, Gabe O'Brien," Rose sharply replied.

Before Rose and Gabe could begin another war of words, Bessie changed the subject by asking Gabe if everything was ready. Rose wondered what Bessie meant and was surprised when Bessie said she asked Gabe to come so they could discuss Rose's parents' home.

"What about my parents' house, and why are you both looking so serious? I know we must soon decide about the house, Bessie. It has been empty since Mother and Father came to live with you and probably needs interior work. Alex always kept the clapboard painted and the garden in order, but I should have taken more interest in our home, not left it all for him to maintain."

"Thanks to your brother, the inside of your parents' home is also in top condition. Alex did a lot of work in the house. I know because I helped him put in new kitchen cupboards last year," Gabe said.

"You did? I never knew that. Why didn't Alex ever speak about it? I would have paid my share of the cost."

"He didn't want you to know, at least not until he finished working on it. You always said the house belonged to both of you, but Alex insisted it was your house, a place of your own for when you retired, even if you decided to sell it. It was his special project to work on it in his spare time. He took his time doing the renovations, and apart from some painting, he almost had it finished."

Rose looked with astonishment at Bessie and Gabe and, for once, was lost for words, but Bessie had more to add.

"I didn't tell you before because Alex planned to finish it and give you the house keys on your birthday this year. Your birthday is not until October, and with Gabe's help, I wanted to carry out Alex's wishes and surprise you then.

"However, you probably heard me tell David and Sharon not to make any decision about renting a house until they saw all the available homes. I said that because Gabe has worked overtime this last week, finishing the painting in your house on the chance you might consider renting it to them. They are a fine young couple, and I am sure they would appreciate and look after it. What do you think?"

By now, Rose, who was not known for showing her feelings, was looking tearful. It was evident it was a huge surprise.

Overcome, she sat down and tried to take in Bessie's news. She had many happy memories of growing up in the house, but because it had remained vacant for so many years, she had thought it would require a great deal of work before it was habitable again. Finally, she spoke.

"To think Alex did that and never once mentioned it. I want to see the house. Why don't the three of us go there now?"

Ten minutes later, Gabe was pointing out the many improvements made in recent years. Although the sturdy two-storey, three-bedroom house was over 60 years old, the inside was now as modern as any newly built home.

"Alex put a lot of good work into this home. Besides the new kitchen cupboards, he built closets in the two big bedrooms. The year before Mr. and Mrs. Martin moved in with you, Bessie, they had the bathroom installed, but it was pretty basic. Alex updated it, added a new vanity, and installed a bigger water pump just last year. Didn't he do a great job through all the house?"

"With your help, Gabe. Well, Rose, what do you think?" Bessie asked.

"I never imagined this. It's ready for someone to move in and deserves to be lived in again. I can see Sharon and David making a home here. What a wonderful job Alex did, and you too, Gabe. Let's go back to the house and talk about this."

Sitting in the kitchen and drinking tea, Rose was still trying to get over the surprise of visiting her childhood home and seeing the time and care Alex had put into it.

"It has been somewhat of a shock. I keep thinking of Alex doing all that work and me not knowing. It's all ready to move into, but Bessie, you know I consider Martin House my home now."

"And this will always be your home, but Alex wanted you to have an option. As far as he was concerned, the house was yours, whether you chose to live there, sell it or rent it."

"It deserves to be lived in now, and I can't think of a nicer couple than Sharon and David to occupy it. But I don't want them to feel obligated to rent it because it is mine. What if you show them around the house, Gabe, and say it belongs to a friend who has just decided to put it up for rent? If they want it, we can then tell them the story behind it. How does that sound?"

After agreeing with Rose's idea, Gabe left for home while the women prepared lunch. When their guests arrived around noon, they didn't look as if they had a successful search.

"We still have three communities to visit, and who knows, we might yet find a good house. If not, we'll have to settle for one of the others that are available, even though they are not ideal," Sharon told the women.

"We might be able to help you. Gabe was here earlier and is coming back after lunch to see if you are interested in looking at a home that has just become available for rent in Mark's Point. He has the keys and would show you around the house," Rose said.

"What kind of house? Is it in good condition? We would love to live in Mark's Point. Who owns it?" Questions came tumbling out of David and Sharon.

"Gabe will answer all your questions later, but for now, come and enjoy your lunch. Bessie has made a lovely pot of soup, and you have the choice of different sandwiches. You want to eat up as you still have a long afternoon ahead of you," Rose urged the young couple.

About half an hour later, Rose and Bessie had cleared up from lunch and sat waiting for Gabe and the Nolans to return from viewing the house.

"I hope I am not pushing you into this, Rose. You just learned about the house this morning, and now Gabe is showing Sharon and David around it. You haven't said much, and I wonder if I did the right thing telling you now; if I influenced you in deciding to rent your home?"

"Not at all, and if you think I am quiet since I heard, it's because I've been doing a lot of thinking. I hope David and Sharon like the house and want to live there. But there's something else I want to talk about, and that's the rent. Martin House is your home, but you've insisted we are equal partners and share in any profits since we opened for business. Now it's my turn. I want to put my parents' home as my investment in the business. I have no idea what the going rate for rent is, but I want it included in our business income. That is only fair, and I don't want any argument."

"Alex always said you were too independent by far, but if you're sure, then I will agree. You never know when we might want to make improvements down the road to Martin House or your home, and with a guaranteed rental income, we have that option for the future. Now let's stop talking about money because they will soon be back. I am sure the three of them will be ready for a cup of tea when they return, so I'll just put some water in the kettle and put it on to boil."

CHAPTER 9

Musical Times

With no guests staying at Martin House, Bessie and Rose were taking things easy, enjoying time to themselves, as they relaxed and chatted over a mid-morning cup of tea.

Rose was still getting over her surprise on learning her family home was ready for occupancy. Knowing her deceased brother, Alex, was responsible made the surprise even more special.

"I can see your face now when Gabe and I told you about the house. Then when you saw the house and how Gabe had finished Alex's work, I didn't know if you were going to laugh or cry," Bessie said.

"There have been so many good things happening in Martin House this past week. What with Sharon and David finding out they could rent your parent's house, and Maggie and her friends having so much fun at her birthday party, there's been no shortage of happy faces around here."

"You're right, Bessie," Rose said.

"Knowing our family home was ready to be lived in was a big surprise and the perfect solution for Sharon and David. I keep remembering their reaction when they realized the house was available. They began to worry they might have to settle for something they didn't like or even one without water and sewerage.

"And didn't the girls have a great time and lots of surprises at Maggie's birthday party?" Rose added.

Getting Maureen Mackey to come to the party was a fantastic idea, she said. When the girls discovered the young hairdresser came to give each girl a manicure, they were delighted. Hearing they could choose from a variety of nail polish colours was another surprise. But, when Maureen said she would demonstrate how to apply make-up, Rose said she never saw a more excited group of girls.

"If we brought the girls to a top salon in St. John's, they couldn't have been any happier."

Laughing, Bessie replied they had Lucy to thank for the idea. She was always first off the mark with news and couldn't wait to relate how Maureen, who was getting married in August to Jerome Maloney of Mossy Brook, had moved home from St. John's. She also knew Maureen, a trained beautician, planned to open a hairdressing salon in Mossy Brook after her marriage.

When she heard this, Bessie contacted the hairdresser, who not only agreed to attend the party; but refused payment for her services, saying it was good publicity for her business. She insisted it didn't cost her anything because she would use makeup and nail polish samples.

"Maureen is hoping the girls and their mothers will become customers when she opens for business. Her boyfriend renovated the house his grandfather left him, which will be their home, and he has an addition almost completed that will be Maureen's beauty salon. Things are certainly looking up with another business opening in this area," Bessie said.

"Remember how Oscar was worried that Martin House would be competition for his shop? But between us buying extra groceries and our guests dropping in for odds and ends, it gave him additional business. Now with Maureen opening, he's sure to start worrying again," Rose said, laughing at the idea.

Bessie wanted to know what difference a hairdressing salon in Mossy Brook could make to Oscar's shop?

"With your naturally curly hair, you might not think of home perms, but Oscar will. He stocks Toni's and other brands of home permanents. Who do you think will bother with a home perm once Maureen opens for business?

I'm sure women will want to have their hair done professionally. Watch out then; it won't be long before Oscar starts putting on a poor mouth again."

"Perhaps you're right, but getting back to the party, I was glad we didn't have anyone booked in here Monday night. It meant the girls could stay for as long as they wanted with no worry about disturbing guests. The sun porch was ideal for them listening to their music and for Maureen doing the girls' beauty treatments."

"It's probably a good job. Maggie didn't invite any boys. Can you imagine their faces if they saw nail polish and make-up produced at the party? Although no doubt they would have enjoyed themselves when it came time to eat.

"And now the party's over; it's a good time for me to think about going to St John's. The professors seem to have settled into my house, and Joe Marsh has papers for me to sign about the tenancy. Joe's a good lawyer, and he's also going to straighten out my parents' house."

Anything else Rose planned to say came to a halt when they heard a knock. Bessie, who was closest to the back door, rose to answer it and discovered teenagers Michael Ryan and Bobby Brown on the doorstep.

Surprised by the boys knocking and waiting outdoors, when it was rare for Mark's Point residents to do so, she asked was anything wrong. Shuffling their feet and looking far from comfortable, the boys appeared lost for words until Michael finally plucked up enough courage to speak.

"Thanks for the cake and stuff from Maggie's birthday, Mrs. Bessie. It was some good, wasn't it, Bobby?"

When Bobby didn't answer immediately, Michael poked his friend, making him jump.

"Eh, yeh, it was all good."

"I'm glad you enjoyed it, but there was no need to thank us. It was really Maggie's idea. Are you coming inside?"

The two boys looked at each other, and then Bobby said, "You ask."

"Ask what? Is there something I can do for you, or are you looking for something?"

"We was wondering if the other missus, Maggie's Aunt Rose, was here. We wants to talk to her," a resolute-looking Michael finally got his request out.

Bessie stepped back, telling the boys to come in. When they entered the kitchen, she told Rose that the boys came to speak to her. However, she said, perhaps they would like some milk and cookies before she left them to discuss their business.

The boys appeared to be struck dumb at the sight of Rose. Giving Bessie grateful looks, they accepted the seats she offered at the kitchen table.

"The boys enjoyed Maggie's cake, Rose. Isn't that right, Bobby?"

A swift nod came from Bobby, who seemed mesmerized by Rose.

"It's too bad we haven't any left, but what about snowballs. Do you like them or date squares?" a smiling Rose asked.

"We likes them all, don't we, Bobby?" Michael quickly said, but the only response he received from his usually talkative friend was another nod.

The women smiled at each other over the seated boys while putting out milk and cookies.

"Isn't this lovely having Bobby and Michael visiting us, Bessie? We are more used to seeing girls. We enjoy their company, but what I like about young men is their hearty appetites.

"When Mrs. Bessie and I make cookies, we usually make a big batch, but we find the girls only eat one or maybe two at the most. I hope we don't have that problem with you," Rose said as she placed a large plate of mixed cookies on the table.

"Oh, no, missus. We eats a lot, don't we, Bobby?"

Bobby finally appeared to have found his tongue when he answered, "Yeh."

Seeing the boys eat and gradually relax, Bessie thought it was a good time to leave them to talk to Rose.

"Now, you have something to eat; I'll leave you three to talk."

A look almost of panic came across Michael's face as he looked from Bessie to Rose and back again at Bessie. On seeing this, Rose said she was sure Bessie didn't need to leave; perhaps she could also help the boys with what they wanted. There was silence for a minute, and then Michael spoke.

"Do you play music?" Mrs. Bessie.

"Only on the radio or the record player, I'm afraid," Bessie replied.

"However, my sister-in-law does. She will be playing the organ in church. Are you thinking of joining the church choir? The first practice is tonight."

Two very emphatic 'Nos' from the boys quickly answered that question.

"How can we help you then?" Rose asked.

"The twins says you plays the guitar. They heard you at Maggie's birthday party, and we knows you gives Maggie piano lessons. We wants to know if you'll learn us how to play the guitar. Bobby and me wants to learn the guitar so we can have our own band one day. Don't we, Bobby?" said the spokesman of the duo, speaking in a rush.

"Yeh! We've got guitars. You forgot to tell her that Michael," Bobby, who now seemed to have found his voice, finally spoke up.

"That's right, and we can pay. We've been cutting out cod tongues on the wharf and selling them. We often goes out in boat with our fathers, and our fathers say we can catch our own fish this summer and dry and sell them. That's how we got our guitars last year. So don't worry, missus, we've got money."

Rose looked with astonishment at the two boys and seemed at a loss for words. Although she played the guitar, she had had never considered passing on the skill.

"Is there anyone else around here who plays the guitar? I never took guitar lessons. It's just something I started trying on my own, and I don't know if I would make a good teacher."

"But Mom says you're a principal, that's even smarter than a teacher, and she says you was a nun and that all nuns knows about music."

"Yeh, your mother did say that, and my mother said we wasn't to bother Mrs. Bessie and Maggie's Aunt Rose," Bobby said.

Looking earnestly at the women as if trying to convince them, Bobby continued speaking.

"She said the pair of ye might be busy with visitors. But Mrs. Bessie, we looked to make sure there were no strange cars in your driveway before we come to your door, so we're not really bothering ye, are we?"

Bobby's logic amused Bessie, who assured him they weren't bothering them at all. However, Rose appeared lost in her thoughts, and the boys watched her anxiously, waiting for her to speak. Finally, she seemed to have reached some sort of decision.

"I'm glad to know you are interested in music, but let me think about this. That doesn't mean I'm saying no. I have some things to do in the next couple of weeks, including a trip to St. John's, but when I come back from town, I'll give you an answer. Will that do for now?"

"Okay, missus, we'll wait, but is you really thinking about it, not just putting us off?" Bobby asked Rose.

When Rose said she would seriously consider the guitar lessons, he let out a big sigh of relief.

"Thanks, missus. Is it okay to call you Mrs. Rose instead of Maggie's aunt, even though people say you're not a missus?"

"They are correct. I never married."

By now, Rose was finding it difficult to refrain from laughing.

"And Miss Martin sounds like I was still a teacher, so what about Miss Rose?"

"Okay, Miss Rose, but if those sisters of mine ask you for guitar lessons, remember we asked you first. Anyhow, they don't have guitars, and they're not getting a loan of ours, right, Michael?"

"Right. They only wants to play the guitar because we said we did. They're always trying to copy us or spoil our fun. Girls! What are they like at all?" a disgusted-looking Michael asked.

"Come on, Bobby, let's go and let the womenfolk get on with their work. Thanks, Miss Rose, and thanks, Mrs. Bessie, we'll see you around."

"Yeh, thanks a lot, and if ye needs any help around here, we're good workers, aren't we, Michael? Bye!"

Bessie and Rose tried to control their laughter when the boys took off outdoors. It became increasingly difficult for them to do so when Michael and Bobby, unaware the kitchen window was open, continued their conversation outside.

"That wasn't too bad, was it, Michael? I knows Mrs. Bessie, and she's always okay, and Miss Rose is not nearly as scary as I thought she'd be."

"I wasn't scared, not one bit," Michael announced bravely.

"My Nan Morris always says, get to the point. That's what I did; I up and told Miss Rose we wanted to learn the guitar."

"I didn't say I was scared. I just said Miss Rose wasn't scary. That was some good cookies she and Mrs. Bessie made. Think we'll get a lunch when she learns us the guitar?"

The women didn't hear Michael's answer to Bobby as the boys passed out of earshot, finally allowing them to laugh freely.

"What a pair of characters they are. Michael tries hard to act grown up, and I thought Bobby, who is usually a chatterbox, had lost his tongue. But they appear so serious about learning to play the guitar. What are you going to do, Rose, about giving them lessons?"

"I thought I might talk to David when I'm in town. He mentioned getting a youth club started when he discovered no organizations for the young ones in this area. With our school closed now in Mark's Point, the building belongs to the parish and would be perfect for guitar lessons or crafts. David plays the guitar, and he would be a much better teacher than me. I'll tell him about the boys' interest in guitar lessons, and hopefully, he'll agree to give them lessons."

"You'll have two exceedingly happy boys if he agrees, although if the lessons took place in the school, Bobby would miss out on any lunches he hoped to enjoy. Weren't the boys hilarious? I don't know how I kept my face straight. When Michael said, 'Come on Bobby and let the womenfolk get on with their work,' he looked and sounded just like his grandfather Joe," Bessie recalled with amusement.

"Poor Bobby, I bet his sisters give him a hard time. It's bad enough having one older sister, but I doubt if he gets a word in edgewise with twin sisters like Pansy and Lily. I think Maggie might have liked to invite him and Michael to her party, but the twins were adamant that they wouldn't attend if their brother did," Rose said.

"Which reminds me, Rose; when you are in St. John's, why don't you look for a gift for Maureen. She refused to take any money for her work at Maggie's party, but she won't be able to refuse a wedding gift."

"That's a great idea, and we should make a list of anything else we might need. Now it's time I looked for hymn music for tonight's practice. I wonder how many will turn up at the church for practice."

Arriving at the church later that evening, Rose was pleasantly surprised to see at least a dozen people waiting inside with Father Kiely.

"I hope you don't mind me attending your first choir practice Rose. I spoke to Jim Pearce, who was apprehensive he might be the only male in the choir, so I assured him I would be here. However, I see his niece Kelly has managed to convince her boyfriend, Sean Ryan, to come, so you have at least two men, and it's early yet. I know two or three women from Muddy Brook Cove are coming, and hopefully, some parishioners from Mark's Landing will also make it."

"I'm glad, Father, that you spoke about the practice after mass on Sunday, encouraging parishioners from all three communities to take part in the choir. By the way, do you have any hymn preferences? I was thinking of asking those who turn up if they had favourite hymns."

"Be careful what you ask for," laughed the priest.

"I happen to know Meg Joy and her sister Mary Clare Brown from Mark's Landing are proud of their Latin skills. They informed me they knew all the mass responses in Latin and, knowing you were a former nun, they were sure you would be delighted to have experienced Latin singers."

"I hope you told them we stopped using Latin in church years ago."

Still laughing, Father Kiely told Rose it wasn't his place to interfere in the choir.

"I believe you are enjoying this, but I'm not worried. I'll just make sure I ask for your advice if the women mention Latin during our practice. They probably think the priest is always right and will accept your decision when you tell them Latin is no longer used in church."

"Hi, Aunt Rose and Father Kiely. The twins came with me, and there's a couple of their friends from Muddy Brook Cove. Bobby and Michael are outside the church. I wonder if they are coming into practice. Are you staying, Father?"

"I wouldn't miss it, Maggie. Your Aunt Rose wants to know what hymns people enjoy, and I can't wait to hear my parishioners' favourites. Did you have any you particularly liked when you were in Toronto?"

"I like the Salvation Army ones. I often went to their youth group on Friday nights with some friends from our apartment building. We always had a good time playing games and doing all kinds of things, and that's where I learned the hymns."

Rose, who already knew about Maggie's attendance at the youth club, was pleasantly surprised by Father Kiely's reaction to this information.

"I like their music too. I always enjoyed the Salvation Army band playing at parades and special events. I'm glad, Maggie, you had a youth club to attend. The Army has many excellent programs for all ages. I'd like to see some sort of youth club in this area."

"Remind me to talk to you about that when you come to dinner on Sunday, Father. I know someone else interested in seeing a club put in place for young people. But now our prospective choir members are here; it's time to get this show on the road."

Two hours later, Rose was telling Bessie all about the practice. Between teenagers and adults, 16 parishioners turned up at the church.

"I was pleased with the turnout, and there are some good singers among them. I thought of asking them for their favourite hymns, but Father Kiely told me the last time the older women sang in church, it was Latin. Instead, I told the choir we would try some of the old familiar favourites and newer hymns. I couldn't believe how well everyone accepted this and how enthusiastic they were about singing."

Rose laughed, remembering her worry that different ages and sexes might not work in a choir. However, the enthusiasm of the group made working with them a pleasure. She had thought several practices might be necessary before singing as a choir in church, but her singers were anxious to begin, even asking to get together again to allow them to do so."

"I agreed to have another practice on Saturday night, and from what I hear, they all plan to attend. Then Maggie told me on the way back from church that our two young friends, Michael and Bobby, might consider joining us. It appears they got talking to Father Kiely, who told them that instead of always using the organ to accompany the hymns, a guitar might be used at times, especially when David becomes a full-time member. That was all it took for them to change their minds about becoming choir members. It didn't hurt either that Sean Ryan, one of Michael's older brothers, was there with his girlfriend, Kelly Pearce."

"Sean is in the middle of Nora and Jack's five sons, while Michael is the youngest. There are no girls in the family, but I'm sure Michael doesn't miss having sisters knowing how he feels about girls. Meanwhile, Bobby not only has the twins to order him about, but he also has two smaller sisters," Bessie said.

"Poor Bobby, it's a wonder he gets a word in at all. But I also have some more news."

"The Anglican Church in Murphy's Cove is celebrating its 50th anniversary next month. Father Kiely says their bishop and several former clergy members plan to attend. Parishioners will host the visiting clergymen, but they haven't found a place to stay for the bishop and his wife. Not only is the rectory quite small, but Reverend and Mrs. Paul have three pre-school children. The bishop and his wife are childless and quite a bit older than the Pauls, which means the rectory is probably not the most suitable place for them to stay."

Rose related how Father Kiely, a good friend of the Anglican minister, had offered to accommodate the bishop and his wife overnight in the Catholic parish house. The only problem was when the parish housekeeper retired months earlier, Father Kiely, who didn't mind looking after himself, replaced her position with a part-time secretary to relieve him from many office responsibilities.

"The bishop wants to spend two or three nights in the area to allow him to visit other communities in his diocese. Both Reverend Paul and Father Kiely agreed that staying in the Catholic parish house for that length of time is probably not a good option, especially since there is no housekeeper. That's why the minister is going to be contacting us. He knows we operate a Bed and Breakfast and he says paying for accommodation for these special guests is the least his parish can do."

"It's good to see a Catholic priest and an Anglican minister so friendly. Attitudes have certainly changed in recent years. Can you imagine Father Heaney becoming friends with someone he would call a 'Protestant,' let alone thinking about having an Anglican Bishop to stay in his home?"

Rose agreed with Bessie, saying it appeared as if younger clergy like Father Kiely and Reverend Paul led by example.

"They certainly have a different attitude now when it comes to other religions. When Father asked Maggie if she had any favourite hymns, she said she liked those played by the Salvation Army. He agreed with her choice, telling her he always enjoyed hearing their band during parades and other special events."

"I always enjoyed listening to the Salvation Army band when I lived in Scotland. On Saturday nights, uniformed members of the 'Sally Annes,' as most people affectionately called them, would go around the pubs to pass out copies of *The War Cry* newspaper and accept donations from customers drinking in the bar. Meanwhile, the band would be outside playing rousing hymns. We'd be coming from the pictures, or movies, as they say here, and we'd always stop and listen to them. Gosh, that wasn't yesterday. I wonder if they still do that today?"

Bessie had barely finished speaking when the telephone sounded. Rose, who had risen to put the kettle on, went into the hall and answered it. Several minutes later, the kettle was whistling, and Rose was still talking on the phone. Bessie had the tea steeped and cups on the table before her sister-in-law returned to the kitchen.

"That was Maureen on the phone. Guess what? She wants me to play the organ at her wedding on August 28. Father Kiely is marrying them in the church in Mossy Brook, and the reception is taking place in Turner's Club in Freeman's Beach."

"That's where the reception is happening next week, the one that our group of guests staying attend. I remember how some people reacted when George Turner announced his plan to build a club in Freeman's Beach. They said he was crazy, that it would be a waste of money. That was almost four years ago, and it has proven popular for dances and wedding receptions. It's the only club in the whole area, and it draws people from the 14 communities. But getting back to Maureen, did you agree to play at her wedding?"

"Yes, I did. Jerome's cousin in St. John's would play, but she is expecting a baby in October. Her doctor wants her to rest and not to travel, especially over rough roads."

"Music has certainly been a popular topic of conversation today. It started with you playing guitar at Maggie's birthday party, which led to Michael and Bobby's request for lessons," Bessie said.

"Then you had choir practice, and now you'll be playing the organ for a wedding in Mossy Brook. It's a good job you moved back home, Rose because it looks as if your musical talents are in great demand. Now, let's pour up the tea before it gets cold; it should be well and truly steeped by now."

CHAPTER 10

Mina's Story

Bessie was cleaning windows in the sunroom when she saw Maggie coming up the garden path. Turning to Rose, who was dusting furniture, she asked if Maggie had a music lesson that morning.

"She's on the path on her way up here, and she usually has the twins in tow unless she is coming to practice."

By the time Bessie reached the kitchen, Maggie was already there. She held an envelope, which she passed to Bessie.

"Aunt Bessie, this is for you. It was inside a letter to me from Isabelle and Katy thanking me for inviting them to the party and for the great time they had. They asked me to give you this letter. When I showed it to Pop, he said I had to cycle here with it right away."

Bessie had a funny feeling as she took the envelope from Maggie. Realizing it must be from Mina, Rose suggested to Maggie that she might like to practice some of her piano pieces unless she was in a hurry. With Maggie happily occupied, Bessie opened the letter, which was as she had guessed from Mina.

Dear Bessie,

Thank you for letting my girls attend Maggie's birthday party at your home. They are still talking about the wonderful time they had.

My main reason for writing is to ask if I can visit you on Thursday night when your sister-in-law Rose has choir practice. Father Kiely will be there, and he asked my girls and Martina Ryan to attend. He suggested that he drop me off to visit you while they are in church, but I didn't want to show up without asking you first.

I will understand if you don't want to see me. After all, we have not been in close contact over the years, and the way I treated you recently was far from friendly. But if you don't mind me visiting, would you telephone me on Wednesday afternoon.

Thank you

Mina.

When she finished reading, she handed the letter to Rose, who had returned from seeing Maggie settled at the piano. Rose read it and said, "I think you should see her."

"And I will for sure, but it makes me wonder if there is something wrong, especially when Father Kiely is involved in this. Whenever Mina or the girls' names come up in conversation, I can tell he worries about them. Did you notice how pleased he was to know Mina's girls were attending Maggie's party?"

"It's almost lunchtime now. I'll call Mina this afternoon. The worst thing about this is I'll have Mina on my mind until I see her tomorrow night, and you know what kind of imagination I have."

"I may not be as imaginative as you, Bessie, but since I met her, Mina often comes into my mind, and although I've never met her husband, I still feel he is at the root of her problems."

The following night when Bessie opened the door of Martin House to invite Mina inside, she was slightly apprehensive as she imagined her guest to be but offered a time-proven cure for all occasions.

"Come on in; I've got the kettle on for a cup of tea."

Giving a small nervous laugh, Mina replied that her grandmother always said a hot cup of tea was the best remedy for all that ails a body.

"I'm not sure if it's a cure used by all grandmothers or is it a Scottish one because my Granny always said the same thing," Bessie answered, smiling.

She had a good feeling that the cup of tea was helping to break the ice. Watching Bessie putting out cups, Mina spoke up again.

"My girls are so pleased I'm visiting you. I've heard all about your lovely home and the food you and Maggie's Aunt Rose, as the girls call her, made for the party. The party was the highlight of their summer, and they wrote my oldest daughter Chrissie with all the details. It's not often they have something exciting to tell her. They said they felt like film stars getting their nails and make-up done."

"They are nice girls, and it's good to see how well they and Maggie get on together. Now drink up, and if you like, I'll show you around our home or, as Rose and I now call it, Martin House Bed and Breakfast. I don't think you were ever here, which I hope we can remedy in the future. You know, it was my mother-in-law's hope that you and I, both coming from Scotland, could see more of each other, but ten miles was a long distance back in the '40s."

"Did you have nice in-laws?" Mina asked, almost wistfully.

"The best anyone could have asked for, and I miss them almost as much as I miss Alex, who was everything a wife could ask of a husband."

On hearing these words, Mina's face crumpled, and her eyes glistened with unshed tears. Despite her attempts not to cry, her emotions won out, and she gave way to muffled sobs.

"That's it, cry away. I have the feeling you've held those tears in for far too long. My granny also used to say that everyone needed 'a guid greet,' or as our neighbours here would say, 'a good cry,' once in a while".

Rising, Bessie went along to the downstairs bathroom and got a warm damp face cloth and towel, which she handed to Mina, but not until she was sure Mina had finished crying.

"That's better; you needed a guid greet. I'm going to top up your tea, and for all you heard about our baking, you haven't touched a bite. Before we chat, enjoy one of Rose's delicious pineapple squares."

Although evidence of Mina's tears showed on her face, she now looked more relaxed and even helped herself to one of Rose's squares.

"I don't deserve this. You are far too good, especially since it's my fault we didn't remain friends. You made an effort, but I never did," Mina said.

"I have a feeling that wasn't your fault. Am I wrong, Mina?"

"No, you're not wrong."

Later that night, when Bessie told Rose about Mina's visit, she compared the way Mina's words started pouring out to a person mute from birth who suddenly discovered they could speak. Mina began her story by recalling meeting Herbert in Scotland.

She married him, thinking he was everything she had dreamed of in a husband but began to have doubts when her brother begged her not to leave Scotland. He saw a side of Herbert that Mina didn't want to believe.

"After I arrived in Newfoundland. I saw the truth of my brother Andy's words when Herbert became a different person. He mocked me and often spoke with contempt about my home and, even worse, my family who had always made him so welcome."

Mina continued with her tale of disillusionment, how the couple lived with her in-laws, who made no bones about their dislike for the 'foreigner' who stole their son and brother. Mina's mother died when she was young, and she had looked forward to a relationship with her mother-in-law. But there was nothing motherly about Mrs. Lynch. She ridiculed Mina's housekeeping efforts, her inability to make bread and to cook traditional Newfoundland meals.

"Nothing I did was good enough for her. I couldn't split or salt fish. I didn't know how to work in the garden, make hay or tend the animals. Everyone who came into that house heard how stupid I was. 'She can't even talk proper.' How often did I hear that phrase from his family? Mr. Lynch was nice enough when we were alone, but he was afraid of his bullying wife."

Mina said the one person in the family who went out of her way to make her feel welcome was Herbert's grandmother. She lived just a few doors away, and Mina described her home as an oasis, where she felt safe.

"I think Nan Lynch realized how unhappy and homesick I was and knew it would get no better unless something changed. She came up with the idea that she needed help in her house, asking me to come each morning to do some housework," Mina recalled.

Mina may have helped the older woman, but Nan Lynch taught the young Scottish war bride everything she needed to know about running a rural Newfoundland home. The two women became close friends, and for the next few months, Mina started to believe her life was getting better.

When she discovered she was pregnant, she and Nan Lynch were delighted, making plans to sew and knit for the baby. Even Herbert seemed happy, but his mother and two sisters made it clear pregnancy was no excuse for laziness. Mina's share of outdoor work still had to be done. An early frost that Fall, resulting in a coating of ice on the planks of the family's fishing stage, ended her baby's chance of life. At eight months pregnant, Mina was cleaning fish in readiness for salting when she slipped and fell. She went into labour later that afternoon, and with the local midwife not called until it was too late, Mina suffered through 16 hours of labour before delivering a still-born baby boy.

It was Bessie whose eyes then filled with tears as she imagined the heart-break and wished she could have been there for her fellow war bride. She realized how lucky she was in comparison to Mina.

But out of that tragedy came a change for the better for Mina. Nan Lynch, who knew nothing about the birth until the following day, was so outraged she demanded Herbert bring Mina to her home to rest. Determined to help Mina, she insisted the young couple make a permanent home with her. Herbert was pleased with the arrangement, but his mother and sisters were furious. They accused Mina of telling lies to Nan Lynch and plotting to make them look bad.

Although not a perfect husband, Herbert was much better away from his family's influence. Two years later, when Mina became pregnant again, she, Herbert, and Nan Lynch were happy. The two women made baby clothes and plans for the expected arrival until Nan Lynch died suddenly from a massive heart attack before the baby was born.

"I was facing the birth of our baby without the one person on whose support I could always depend. Then on the day Nan died, my mother-in-law gleefully informed Herbert and me we had to find another place to stay, that as Nan's only son, it was now her husband's house, and she intended moving in."

But Mina's mother-in-law's plans were thwarted from the grave when, after Nan Lynch's funeral, the parish priest asked the family to gather for the reading of the will. Nan Lynch left her son a piece of land while Mina received her house and everything else. Furious at this, Herbert's mother threatened to go to court, but although the priest had written out the will, signed by Nan

Lynch and witnessed by him and her friend, it had had also gone to a lawyer to ensure the document was in order and could not be changed.

"As far as I was concerned, the house belonged to Herbert as much as it belonged to me, but he began to resent me owning Nan's home. Soon, he followed his mother and sisters' example, saying there was something underhand about how I got the house. Even the birth of Chrissie or knowing his mother had wanted to evict us from Nan's house failed to change his opinion that I had cheated him and his family out of their rightful property."

"What kind of man treats his wife in that way?" Bessie asked angrily.

"I guess he, like his father, is afraid of his mother. Growing up in Scotland, I met all kinds of people, but I never met anyone like her. She's a spiteful, mean person who has no feelings for anyone, even her own family. It's a terrible thing to admit, but my girls are afraid of their grandmother and never want to visit her. I feel sad about this, as my granny was always a positive influence in my life."

"Why do you stay with Herbert or even in Murphy's Cove South. If the house is yours, you could sell it and leave. Your oldest daughter left; why don't you take the younger girls and join her?"

There was dead silence for a minute before Mina replied.

"Yes, the house is mine, and at one time, things were so bad that I threatened to sell it and take the three girls away. That was the year Chrissie started grade 11. She was a good student and was looking forward to going to university the following year. That summer, she worked in the fish plant in Murphy's Cove, making good wages. Herbert demanded her pay packet, saying it was for house expenses. I wanted at least half of it put away to help Chrissie go to university the following year," recalled Mina

But Herbert had no intention of that happening. Mina related how he went to the plant manager, telling him he would be collecting Chrissie's pay each week. When the manager said he wouldn't do it, Herbert threatened to sell his fish to an outside buyer who was always looking for new business. The manager wasn't intimidated and refused to pass over the pay envelope until Chrissie, afraid of what her father might do, begged him to give it to Herbert.

When it came time to issue her first cheque, the manager asked Chrissie to report to his office. She had worked 50 hours that week at $1.25 an hour, which was above average at the time, but the plant workers, even women and students, always got top wages. Her earnings were $62.50, but her wages were in two envelopes. One, which the manager told Chrissie to put away, held a cheque for $25. In the envelope, to be picked up by her father, was $37.50, the balance of her wages. On questioning the amount he received, Herbert heard it was students' wages.

"This went on all summer until Chrissie returned to school. Then somehow, Herbert discovered other students had earned more than Chrissie. That's when all hell broke loose," Mina said, shuddering as she recalled what happened next.

Failing to intimidate the plant manager after storming into his office, he took his rage home, demanding the remainder of Chrissie's wages. During the summer, she saved $200, but it wasn't in the house.

"Chrissie gave her cheque each week to Millicent Murphy, owner of the store in Murphy's Cove, who banked it for her. Millicent is a good woman who's been a friend to me and the girls over the years. I wouldn't have been able to start making and selling quilts if she hadn't encouraged me and given me credit to buy the supplies I needed."

As Mina recalled the events which followed her husband's discovery, Bessie could see she was close to tears again.

Mina had never before seen Herbert so overcome with rage. He cursed and yelled and then started throwing dishes and even chairs around, terrifying the three girls. They began crying, and as his temper grew worse, Chrissie blurted out she didn't have the money that Mrs. Murphy was looking after it for her. With that, he walked over to Chrissie and, grabbing her shoulder, he pushed her outdoors, saying they were going to Murphy's Cove to get it.

But like the plant manager, Millicent Murphy was a match for Mina's husband. When he went to her shop, cursing and demanding Chrissie's money, she refused to give it to him, telling him she would call the RCMP if he made any more threats. Things might have escalated if it wasn't for Dave Murphy. Hearing the yelling as he parked his truck for the day, he rushed in and witnessed Herbert's fury. Taking a firm hold of him, Dave dragged him outdoors, telling him he would thrash him within an inch of his life if he saw Herbert's face again in his wife's shop.

Herbert took off, leaving Chrissie behind. When Dave and Millicent brought her home later, they had a long talk with Mina. Knowing of Herbert's temper from previous incidents, they couldn't understand why Mina stayed with him. They begged her to make a new life for herself and the girls by leaving. It was Mina's house, and Herbert couldn't stop her from selling it.

Herbert never appeared until the following evening, just after Mina and the girls finished supper. He refused the food Mina offered him, and it was apparent he had been drinking. It was evident there was only one thing on his mind when walking over to Chrissie. Herbert asked if she had his money now. When the terrified teenager said no, he slapped her across the face. The force and shock of the blow sent Chrissie flying into the table and on the floor.

"I think I could have murdered that man then. I grabbed an iron skillet and ran across the kitchen in front of Chrissie, telling him if he laid one more hand on her, I'd kill him. In my frame of mind, I could easily have done it. Poor Chrissie was lying on the floor with this awful mark on her face, with the two younger girls screaming in fear yet standing over their sister, trying to protect her from their father. That's when I told him it was my house and I could sell it, take the girls, and leave him. That stopped him in his tracks. He gave me such a look, then turned and left."

Mina's husband didn't return home that night but came back accompanied by his mother the following day. The younger girls were in school but Chrissie, not wanting anyone to see the large bruise on her face, was home. Herbert came straight to the point, saying Chrissie would be sorry for stealing from him; he intended to get his money by taking her out of school and putting her to work.

Before a shocked Mina could respond, her mother-in-law gleefully announced there were people in St. John's looking for serving girls, and she was going to help her son find a job for Chrissie. Mina, she said, had always thought herself better than anyone else because she came from Scotland. Her mother-in-law said Mina had passed on her high and mighty airs to her daughters, talking about going to university as though they were too good for Murphy's Cove South and their family. As for selling the house, she said, Herbert would set it on fire rather than seeing it sold, a home that rightfully belonged to his father.

"That's when I exploded. For 20 years, I had been a quiet, mousy creature, saying and doing nothing to upset Herbert or his family. I had put up with their insults, threats, every kind of indignity that could be imagined, just to keep the peace and to protect my daughters. But that day, the mouse turned and, as my father would say, the tinker came out in me. I was so furious that these two monsters would dare speak that way to me about my daughter that the rage, built up over all those years, came pouring out. I could endure any threat or insult they wanted to throw at me, but they crossed the line when they threatened Chrissie and her future."

To Mina's amazement, she saw apprehension in the faces of her husband and his mother. For too long, they had ruled by bullying, and now they were on the receiving end of Mina's fury. Herbert started to bluster that he was leaving, he wasn't listening to such foolishness, but Mina wasn't ready to let either of them go.

Saying they would only leave when she had done with them, and it was up to Herbert if he returned or not, she turned on her mother-in-law. After giving her opinion on her mother-in-law's character, Mina finished by saying Mrs. Lynch didn't know the meaning of the word mother or grandmother, and she was never to enter the house again.

"I told them Chrissie would not be going to work and that my mother-in-law would never have a say in what any of my daughters did. The $200 was never Herbert's money; it was Chrissie's hard-earned wages, and if I had allowed her, she would have given it to me because Herbert barely contributed enough to feed us. I remember saying the only way Chrissie could have a better life was to get away from them. She needed a good education to do so, and her money, and any she earned in the future, would be saved for that purpose."

As Mina recalled her words and actions from that day four years earlier, Bessie wondered how she would have coped if Alex and the Martins had been like the Lynch family. She also had many more questions. Herbert had returned to his home, but what kind of life did Mina and her girls have now? And what happened to Chrissie? Why did she leave school and Murphy's Cove South?

Bessie was about to ask these questions when the porch door opened, and voices came from the kitchen.

"I guess choir practice is over for tonight. I'd better put the kettle on again. Rose and Father Kiely are sure to want a cup of tea. What about the girls?

Let's go through and see what they would like to drink. I also promised to give you a tour of the house. We can do that while the kettle boils."

Later, when the visitors had left, and she and Rose were clearing up, Bessie told her they had been right in their suspicions.

"I wish we had been wrong, but Mina's husband is a brute. Even worse is a person we never considered, her mother-in-law. The woman is a bitch!"

At Rose's shocked look, Bessie said, "Yes, I know, I did say bitch, and truthfully, it's not a strong enough word to describe that woman when I think of the hell she's put Mina through. While Mina was talking, I kept thinking, what if Alex or your parents had been like the Lynch's? Could I have survived? Mina is an amazing, strong woman who has endured a terrible life. I don't know how lucky I was to marry into your family."

She related Mina's story to an unusually quiet Rose who waited until Bessie had finished the whole sorry tale before asking questions.

"What about now, and what happened to Chrissie to leave school and home? Why did Mina put your letter inside Maggie's? Does the mother-in-law still cause trouble, and what about that husband of hers? Did he ever strike Mina or the other girls?

"I haven't got all the answers because Mina was still talking when we heard you come in. As for putting my letter inside Maggie's, that's because her sister-in-law runs the post office in Murphy's Cove South. Mina usually posts her mail at the office in Murphy's Cove and has any private mail sent to Millicent Murphy. She told me when we were upstairs that she doesn't want any of the Lynch family knowing her business."

"Is that why there was so much secrecy over the quilts? And it's probably the reason Mina doesn't seem to want visitors," Rose said.

"We never spoke about that, but I think it must be. Anyway, Mina asked could she come back another time, and of course, I said yes. If I can do anything to help her or the girls, I will. I just can't believe the kind of life she has led with that family."

"Father Kiely spoke about bringing the girls back again to choir practice, and he hopes to convince some women to attend," Rose told Bessie.

"There's no organist in Murphy's Cove, but he thinks if he even gets a small group of adults and teenagers to practice the hymns with us, they can sing without music during mass, and it might encourage others to sing."

"So perhaps Mina might get back when you have your next practice. That would be good. I have a feeling she needs to get a lot more off her chest. We were just about to talk about Chrissie and why she left school when you returned. I wouldn't doubt that old witch of a mother-in-law had something to do with it."

"Good, I see you're starting to calm down, using witch to describe that awful woman instead of the 'B' word, which is not like you at all."

Bessie laughed, saying, "Rose, you've got that nun's look on your face again. I could use far stronger words to describe Mina's relatives, and I've used them on occasion. I grew up listening to my father, who had a very colourful vocabulary, although my mother would tell him off in style if he ever swore in the house. I often think of my parents when I hear old Jimmy Jack Joy cursing and then see his wife, Mrs. Molly, prayer beads in hand, quickly making the sign of the cross and starting to pray. I wonder how many sets of rosaries she's worn out praying for him."

"Maybe she should try Mrs. Lizzie Duggan's remedy," Rose said

"What remedy is that?"

"You mean to say Alex never told you about Mrs. Lizzie from Muddy Brook Cove? I find that hard to believe because he always enjoyed telling that story.

"A good many years ago, long before he went overseas, Alex and I were at the back of the church talking to our priest Father Malloy when we saw Mrs. Lizzie filling up a big bottle with holy water from the font. Father Malloy asked us if Mrs. Lizzie had anyone sick because he saw her filling up bottles with holy water before then. When we said we didn't think so, he decided to question her.

"Yes, Father," said Mrs. Lizzie.

"It's my Timothy that's sick. He's got a sick tongue he has. For sure, the divil's in it. He curses he does, and every time he does, I splashes holy water over him. That stops him. It's an awful affliction Father, but with the help of the holy water, I'll cure him.

"I remember Alex thought it was one of the funniest stories he'd heard. Then about a year later, he came home from fishing and told us Timothy had stopped swearing. The poor man died the night before from pneumonia.

Alex always said a chill from all the holy water Mrs. Lizzie threw on him probably caused Timothy to get pneumonia."

"Alex had lots of stories, but I never heard that one before," Bessie said.

"Still, it's nice to be able to smile after listening to Mina's story. There are some terrible people in this world, and her in-laws fall into that category."

"Now I've got you smiling. I'm going to change the subject. I tried all the girls singing without adults for one hymn, and I must say they did a wonderful job," Rose said.

"There were nine of them because the Martin girls are back from holiday. We also had Mina's girls and Martina Ryan and her cousin, with Maggie and the twins. I wish Bobby and Michael were there to sing with the girls, but they stayed outside the church again, saying they're waiting until the principal, Mr.Nolan, comes until they join. Of course, they also asked when I'm going to St. John's. When I said next week, and I didn't forget about the guitar lessons, their faces lit up."

"It seems they are pretty serious about learning to play. I can picture the boys playing guitars and singing hymns in church."

Laughing, she said it would be one church service she would gladly attend.

"You never know what might happen. Now I don't know about you, but I'm having one last cup of tea, and then I'm having an early night."

CHAPTER 11

Rose's Unexpected Guest

M aggie had been coming to Martin House regularly for piano lessons from Rose since returning to Mark's Point. Noting her enjoyment and how well she was progressing, Rose had increased her classes. But she was running out of suitable music as Maggie went quickly through the available music books.

Finishing a lesson one Monday afternoon, Rose spoke of her pleasure with Maggie's progress and how she planned to look for more music when she went to St. John's the following day.

"Am I really doing okay, Aunt Rose? Do you think I'm good enough to play something for Pop the next time we are here together? He hasn't heard me play yet, and I want to give him a surprise."

"I'm sure he'll be pleasantly surprised. Hold on a minute, Maggie, that sounds like a knock on the back door, and with your Aunt Bessie gone to Murphy's Cove, there's no one else to answer. Whoever it is, they are certainly impatient; there's another knock."

As Rose walked into the kitchen, she was annoyed to hear yet another loud knock.

Shouting, "I'm coming," she narrowly avoided a raised fist poised to knock again as she opened the back door.

Her first impulse to berate the impatient caller halted when she saw a small, elderly man with pure white hair standing on the doorstep holding on to a battered suitcase.

"What took you so long? Is you the missus that runs this boarding house because I needs a place to stay? Well, is you letting me in or not?"

Speechless, Rose took a step back, allowing the old man dressed in what appeared to be his Sunday best of a black suit, white shirt, and tie to push past her and enter the kitchen. On seeing Maggie, who by now was in the kitchen, he addressed Rose again.

"Good, I sees you've got a serving girl. Well maid, what's you waiting for? It's a while before supper so stick on the kettle. I'll have a mug of tea. Now missus, which one are you, the foreign one or the nun, and how much do you charge your boarders?

His questions finally got a response from Rose.

"There are no nuns or foreigners here. Who exactly are you, and where did you come from? Haven't I seen you before? And this is not a boarding house; we do not provide meals."

Ignoring Rose's answer, her visitor continued to speak.

"I'm only looking for a place to stay until I finds a woman. Now, while your maid gets me a mug of tea, I've something I wants you to do. Phone the priest and tell him I needs him to come here right now."

Rose looked with astonishment at the man who wanted to be the latest guest in Martin House. For once, she was at a complete loss for words.

"Aunt Rose, are you alright? Will I put on the kettle?" a bewildered-looking Maggie asked.

Assuring Maggie everything was fine and she would take care of the kettle, Rose said it was time the young girl returned home. She then accompanied Maggie to the back door, telling her to go home quickly on her bicycle and ask Gabe to come to Martin House.

"Are you going to phone the priest or not, and what about my tea?" her impatient visitor asked when Rose returned to the kitchen.

"First of all, I am not your servant, and secondly, you still haven't told me your name and where you live," Rose replied, trying to keep her annoyance under control.

"I'm Philly Moss, and I did live in Mossy Brook, but no more. That's why I wants the priest. He'll straighten things out for me."

Hoping Father Kiely would solve her unwanted guest's problem, Rose put in a call to the parish house in Murphy's Cove. Inwardly praying the priest was home, she was relieved when he answered. As she began to explain the problem, she was surprised by his response.

"That's where he is! Thank goodness. Please keep him there, Rose, and look after him. I'll be with you as soon as I can."

"Keep him here? I don't think he has any intention of leaving," an indignant Rose replied.

With another assurance he was on his way, Father Kiely hung up, leaving Rose to wonder what was going on and why her unwanted visitor was looking for a priest.

"Look after him," she muttered, remembering the priest's words.

"Oh, my God! I suppose he's not sick, that he won't die on me," she spoke aloud.

Rushing back into the kitchen, she was relieved to find her visitor sitting where she left him. However, her relief turned to irritation when Philly, who Rose now believed had to be her worst nightmare, began questioning her.

"Well, did you get him? When will he be here?"

"Yes, I got him, and he'll be here as soon as he can. In the meantime, I'll make a cup of tea, but only because I need one myself."

"Is you the owner of this here boarding house then? I'm glad that the foreign heathen and the nun is gone. I don't know who the worst of them was."

"Is that right? And did you ever meet this terrible pair of women?"

"No, thank God, but I heard about them. They're trouble like most wimen. That's what's got Newfoundland as bad as it is, wimen who don't know their places. Well, I'm not putting up with one of them no more."

Ignoring Philly's rant, Rose filled the kettle and put it on to boil before laying out cups and saucers on the table. But her visitor soon showed his dissatisfaction with this arrangement.

"You're not thinking of putting my tea in that little thing! It's a decent-sized mug of tea I want. My missus don't know much, but she do know how to make a mug of tea."

Rose, who was finding it increasingly difficult to keep her temper, was quick to respond.

"Is that right? Then I suggest you go back to your wife and ask her to make you some. I'm not running a restaurant, and I certainly didn't invite a cantankerous old so and so like you here."

"You talks some fancy. Did you take lessons from that old nun that used to be here, or was it the foreigner you learned from?"

Philly was saved from what would have been a blistering response when Rose, looking out the kitchen window, saw Gabe running up the garden path much faster than she could ever have imagined.

Gasping for breath, he burst into the kitchen, shouting, "What's wrong?"

When Gabe saw Rose's visitor, a look of confusion spread across his face.

"Philly Moss! What in the name of God are you doing here? Is it you that's got my granddaughter worried to death? And, anyway, how did you get here?"

"That's a nice greeting coming from you, Gabe O'Brien, and what's you talking about, worrying people? I'm only looking for a place to board for a while until I get things sorted out. And that all depends on Father Kiely. I'm waiting for him to come."

"Anyways, I didn't know that maid was your grandchild. What's she doing in this house? Oh, I get it; now I sees the rights of it. This is your missus. I didn't know you had another missus. Is this where you lives? That's even better; I'll have someone to play a game of cards with now."

A vehement NO from Rose and an equally emphatic one from Gabe appeared to confuse Philly.

"What do you mean, no?" Does you have a grandchild or not and, does you all live here?"

"You ask too many questions. And although it is absolutely none of your business, I'll set you straight. But only because I don't want any rumours or lies spreading in these communities. I am nobody's missus. Maggie is Gabe's granddaughter, and both are my friends," an indignant Rose sputtered in frustration.

"And another thing, you asked earlier about a nun and a foreigner. I'm the nun, at least I used to be, and my sister-in-law who owns this house, and the one you described as a foreigner, is from Scotland if you want to consider

Scotland a foreign country. We operate this as a bed and breakfast business, not a boarding house. So now, with us being the two worst kinds of women in your mind, what possible reason would you have to stay here?"

Rose, fully expecting a saucy answer, was shocked when her visitor began laughing.

"You've got a good one here, Gabe. I likes a woman with spirit, and this one's got spirit all right. And you says she's not your missus?"

Whatever Rose or Gabe might have had in their minds to say was interrupted when the back door abruptly opened, and shouts of "Bessie, Rose, are you okay?" revealed a flustered Lucy. As she rushed into the kitchen, her husband Jim, now entirely out of breath, followed her in.

"I spied an old man come up your garden path, and the next thing I sees is young Maggie taking off like a bat out of hell, and I says to my Jim, 'Mark my words, Jim, there's something wrong over at Bessie's and Rose's place.' I thought of phoning you, but the next thing I see was Gabe, driving like crazy in that old truck of his, coming over the road. When he started running up your path, I knew for sure something bad was going on. Like I said to my Jim, 'We've got to get over there; for all we knows. somebody might be dead, didn't I, Jim?"

Without waiting for an answer and barely drawing a breath, it became evident Lucy's power of observation wasn't affected by the happenings when looking around; she suddenly recognized Rose's visitor.

"Is that you, Philly Moss? What's you doing here all dressed up like a dog's dinner? Is it you that's causing this uproar?"

"Questions, questions, questions! My Lord, Jim Pearce, how does you put up with this one at all? I bet you never gets a word in. Yes, nosy Lucy, it's me, but what I'm doing here is none of your business, so why don't you get on your way. You're not wanted here."

"Mind your manners. This is my home, and Lucy is my neighbour, and she's here out of concern, not like some people I could mention," said Rose, who found herself in the unusual position of defending Lucy.

Completely ignoring Rose's withering looks and sharp voice, Philly turned to Jim.

"You lives right close to here, don't you, Jim? By George, that's grand. Gabe, who else can we get to make up a foursome for a game of cards tonight?"

"What makes you think you will be here tonight, let alone playing cards?" Rose snapped at him.

Turning to Lucy, Rose thanked her for her concern and apologized for her bad-mannered visitor.

"I don't need no thanking, Rose. Like I says to my Jim all the time, what are neighbours for if not to help one another? I hope you and Bessie knows that me and Jim are always there for you. And don't you go apologizing for that old reprobate. Everybody knows he's a contrary old goat. I don't know how his wife Jean puts up with him. If he were my man, I wouldn't put up with his nonsense."

"And if I was your man, I'd shoot myself. You're nothing but a..."

Before Philly could say any more, Gabe let out a roar.

"Enough! That's more than enough from you. Jumping Joseph! Don't you realize you are in somebody else's home? You can't carry on like that. Rose, I'll drive Philly home. His family is probably looking for him, wondering where he's got to."

"That's all right; someone's coming to get him. I'm sorry I worried you all, but everything is under control now. Thanks for coming, especially when I know how busy you are," Rose replied.

"Are you sure, Rose, that you'll be okay with that old nuisance? Me and Jim wouldn't want to leave if we thought you needed help."

When Rose assured her that she would be fine, Lucy turned to her husband, saying they should go home.

"I just remembered there's a few things I'm running short of, and I needs to get to the shop."

As Lucy and Jim left, Rose saw Gabe shaking his head. They both knew why Lucy had a sudden need to get to Kavanagh's. Without a doubt, Philly Moss and his appearance at Martin House would be the main topic of conversation that day in the local shop. Rushing there to relate this news must be why Lucy overlooked Rose's words that someone would be coming to pick up Philly Moss.

Leaving Philly in the kitchen, Gabe and Rose went through to the back porch, where Gabe said he had no intention of leaving yet.

"I'm staying until I knows what's going on with that old so and so. How did Philly manage to get here?"

"I don't have a clue. His family must have known he was gone but not where he went. I spoke to Father Kiely, who was relieved to know he was safe. Philly wants to talk to him. That's why I phoned the parish house and why Father Kiely is on his way here. Lucy will be sorry to have missed him. Although I shouldn't speak ill of her; after all, she did come ready to help."

"Was it help, or nosiness brought her here?" Gabe dryly asked.

"Where's you gone, missus, and where's that priest?" Philly yelled from the kitchen.

"I'll go talk to him and keep him occupied until Father Kiely gets here. Then I'll leave, but until then, I'm not leaving you alone with him."

"I'm not helpless, you know," Rose was quick to respond. "Apart from his tongue, what harm can he do?"

"He's a contrary old goat who thinks women are nothing but servants. You're not as tough as you think. Anyways, Bessie would be mad if I left you here alone with him."

Their conversation came to a halt when a knock, followed by the door opening, announced Father Kiely's arrival.

"Where is he? Is he alright?"

"Yes, Father! Apart from worrying Maggie half to death and being his usual contrary and ignorant self to Rose, Philly is perfectly fine," Gabe answered in a sarcastic tone, entirely unlike him.

"Anyway, what's the old bugger doing here bothering people? I hope you can sort this out, Father."

"I believe it will take more than me to sort old Philly out. I get some unusual requests from time to time, but from what I'm hearing, I don't know if even the Pope can do what Philly wants," the priest said, shaking his head.

"Well, it's about time you got here," Philly grumbled when Father Kiely, accompanied by Rose and Gabe, entered the kitchen.

"And if you thinks you are getting me to go back to that woman, you can think again. I'm after telling you what I'm looking for. I wants a 'nulment from her. She's useless and won't carry out her wifely duties. So, I'm entitled to a 'nulment, isn't I."

Rose and Gabe looked at each other in astonishment, and both opened their mouths to speak at once. As Gabe said he would get going, Rose told the priest she would go to the sun porch, leaving him and Philly to talk in private.

"Yes, you get on Gabe, but missus, you can stay. With you being a nun, maybe you can help. What's you looking so stern like for? It's not like I'm looking for a divorce. All I wants is a 'nulment. That way, I can get married again."

Looking at him with astonishment, Rose finally found her tongue and asked how old he was.

A gleam of what might be hope, spread over Philly's face as he answered he was 87.

"You're 87 and talking about leaving your wife. For sure, there's no fool like an old fool. You've got to be mad," Rose said with a disgusted look at Philly.

"Gabe, I need some fresh air after listening to that foolishness. I'll walk outside with you."

With another muttered "Old fool" directed at Philly, Rose exited the kitchen and the house.

"What's wrong with her at all," Philly asked Father Kiely.

Shaking his head, the priest wondered how best to proceed and how he could convince Philly to return home.

"You do know Philly that your wife Jean is worried to death. You walked out of the house and wouldn't tell her where you were going. The last she saw was you walking down the road carrying a suitcase. What's going on, and what do you think you are going to accomplish by leaving home? You've upset Jean, who says you've been acting strangely for weeks. I don't know how you got here, but your son Bob is on his way to bring you home."

"And he can just turn right 'round and go back again. As for you, you're my priest; you're supposed to help me, so I'll tell you one more time what I wants. I wants a 'nulment. I knows the church don't give divorces, but it do give 'nulments. I knows 'cause I've heard about movie stars that got 'nulments from the Church. If they can get one, so can I, and what's more, I'm staying here 'til I gets one. I knows you're only a young fellow and can't do it yourself, but go talk to the bishop or the pope; I knows they can fix that kind of thing."

"But you've been married for over 60 years, and you and Jean have a large family. Think about them. You're upset right now, but I'm sure when you get over what's bothering you, you'll realize an annulment is not what you want. And look at your age; where do you think you're going if you leave your wife?"

"Wife! You call her a wife? She refuses to do her wifely duties. She says she's too old for that sort of thing, and not only does she want me out of my own bed. She says I needs to sleep in another room, so I don't bother her. Now, what do you think of that, Father? If I wasn't a Catholic, I could get a divorce, but a 'nulment will have to do. Then I can get another missus. Tell me one thing, Father, wimen that used to be nuns, is they 'lowed to get married?"

Almost choking inside, Father Kiely thought it was good for Philly that Rose had left the house. He could just imagine her reaction. Meanwhile, he had a problem and had no idea how to handle it. But Philly had some more words of wisdom to impart.

"And as for family, me and the missus had 14 young ones and a lot of good they are. They all takes the side of their mother. Bob is making a wasted trip; there's no way I'm going back home.

"Now, Father, you looks puzzled. That's because you is only a young fellow, and you don't know the troubles wimen causes in married life. But that one Rose, the one that was a nun, she's some sharp, and I bet she knows. Get her in here; I'm sure she'll sort this out, and I knows she won't mind me staying here. Tell me, Father, is there something going on 'tween her and Gabe O'Brien. I don't think she's interested, but why's he hanging about acting as if he owns the place?"

Oh Lord, send me strength, Father Kiely prayed inwardly, wondering how he could sort out this problem, which was unlike anything he had encountered during his nine years in the priesthood. He was sure Rose didn't want Philly staying at Martin House, and he wished Bob Moss would come soon. Bob, recently retired as a postmaster, was a sensible fellow who might be able to talk his father out of his crazy ideas.

While asking Philly to stay where he was until he spoke to Rose, Father Kiely went outdoors and found Gabe with Rose.

"Jumping, Joseph! Father. That man's crazy and don't blame it on his age. Philly Moss has always been a bit off, and for some reason, he's always fancied himself as a lady's man. How a sensible woman like Jean Moss ever married him, let alone stayed with him for all those years, God knows. That poor woman will go straight to Heaven, she's had her Purgatory on earth, and it's called Philly Moss. Now he's here tormenting Rose."

"Gabe, why don't you go inside and sit with him until I talk to Father. We won't be long, but I don't want Philly alone; someone needs to watch him. Oh my, here's Bessie arriving. I was hoping to have this problem fixed so she wouldn't have the bother of it. Drat, that man, why did he have to come here of all places?" Rose complained.

Gabe went inside, leaving Rose and the priest waiting for Bessie, who was surprised to see them outdoors.

"Wasn't that Gabe I saw as I was parking my car, and why, pray tell me, am I getting a welcoming committee to greet me today?" a smiling Bessie asked.

As she looked from Rose to Father Kiely, Bessie realized there were no returning smiles.

"What's wrong? There is something wrong, isn't there?" she asked.

With that, Rose gave a half-laugh, saying, "Yes, and no."

"There's nothing wrong, but there is one big problem sitting in the kitchen. We have an 87-year-old fool who wants an annulment from his wife after more than 60 years of marriage and is planning to stay here until he gets it. All I can say after listening to his foolishness is that the woman must be a saint to have put up with him for 60 minutes, let alone 60 years."

"Rose is correct about Philly wanting an annulment Bessie. I know I can depend on you two and Gabe to keep this to yourselves, although goodness knows he may have broadcast his intentions to the world for all I know. To be truthful, I am completely at a loss. However, Philly seems to think that you, Rose, being a former nun and a sensible woman, probably knows how to fix an annulment for him far better than a young, innocent fellow like me."

Trying hard to suppress a grin, the priest continued, "I should also tell you that Philly fully believes he will get an annulment and may be looking at you, Rose, as a replacement for his wife. He was trying to find out from me what Gabe's intentions are towards you and why he was hanging around Martin House."

A red-faced Rose sputtered in frustration and rage.

"The nerve of that creature; who does he think he is? I'm going inside now to straighten him out for once and for all."

"Hold on, Rose," Bessie interrupted.

"Would this be Philly Moss you are talking about, and how did he end up in our house? I only left a couple of hours ago. What on earth has been happening since I went to Murphy's Cove? And by the look of you, I don't think you should talk to anyone until you calm down."

Bessie heard the story of Philly and the priest's dilemma in trying to solve the problem. Asking Rose to stay put, Bessie and Father Kiely went indoors, where it was evident Gabe was only too happy to see them arrive so he could leave.

"And who's this fine-looking woman you brought to meet me, Father?" said Philly, instantly moving his slight body from a slouch to full attention.

"I am Rose's partner in this business. I understand you have given Rose and my friends a hard time. You need to understand that you cannot stay here. We have a full house of guests arriving this weekend, with every bedroom occupied."

"You's the foreign one then. You do talk different, not that I mind, so long as I can understand you. Now, don't you worry about a bedroom for me. I'm sure you've got more than one settle or daybed in a house this size. And is it you that owns the house? It must be worth a good penny," Philly said, giving Bessie a speculative look.

"Which is none of your business? Your business will see you going home or moving on somewhere else because you won't be staying here," Bessie emphatically stated.

"Will you listen to this hard woman. Where's the other one? Father, what do you think of this one trying to throw me outdoors and me nowhere to go," Philly said mournfully.

"And that's a lie!" said a voice from the kitchen door.

"You've got a perfectly good home. You chose to walk out of it and to leave Mother, and it's sorry you'll be for that foolish act."

"Excuse me, Mrs. Martin, but Miss Martin told me to come in. I'm Bob Moss, the son of this ungrateful scoundrel. The problem is my mother has always been far too good for him. In fact, she has herself worn out tending to him. 'Get me this, do that, fetch me this.' I don't know who you think you are the way you bark orders to Mother, but it's stopping right now. I've spent the last half hour talking with some of the family by phone, and we all agree that

Mother needs a break from you. She'll be leaving Mossy Brook tomorrow to do so. You can have the house all to yourself."

"What do you mean she's leaving? She can't leave me. Who will look after me? I'm an old man. I needs your mother to look after me," Philly cried plaintively.

"Is that right? Maybe you should have thought of that before you announced you were leaving Mother and wanted out of the marriage. Because of your age, your family won't abandon you the way you wanted to leave Mother. But, mark my words, there will be changes. By now, Mother should be at my house, and tomorrow I'm driving her to St. John's, where she will stay with Betty for a few days. Madonna has been begging Mother for years to visit her in Halifax, and it's finally going to happen. She's having a holiday and a well-earned rest."

Bob Moss didn't give his father any chance to argue. Instead, he continued to unveil the plans he and several of his siblings had made. Jean Moss would fly to Nova Scotia within a week, and, with three other members of her family now living on the mainland, Bob hoped she would extend her holiday and visit them. Meanwhile, Philly would return to his own home, and although he would be alone, his family would see to his main meal at noon each day. However, breakfast and supper would be his responsibility.

"Didn't I tell you, Father, that my crowd was all agin me? What's a poor old man to do? I can't live by myself. Tell him, Father, they can't make Jean leave me," cried Philly, who by now had lost his arrogant manner.

"And that's another thing, you pulled Father Kiely into this mess, not only embarrassing yourself but our whole family. Asking Father to get an annulment; what next? Don't you think he has enough on his hands without your foolishness? You'll be the butt of jokes for years to come because a story like this will get out. Mark my words."

"But he's a priest. He's not allowed to say anything." Philly smugly replied.

"Not when you're the one telling everybody. You got Jimmy Jack to drive you here and told him about your plans to get a new woman. You also saw Aunt Mary Jones when you were waiting for your ride and told her. How far do you think that news has flown? Now come on, get your case, and let's go. I'm sorry, Father and Mrs. Martin, for all this bother. My father is coming with me, and there will be no more talk of annulments," Bob said.

As a much-subdued Philly walked out accompanied by Bessie, Bob stayed behind to speak to Father Kiely. When Rose and Gabe saw Philly coming with his suitcase, their relief was evident.

"It looks as if you have come to your senses at last. I don't know what you was thinking about," Gabe said.

"I'll thank you to keep your nose out of my business Gabe O'Brien. I knows it was you that turned the missus here agin me. We was getting on fine until you turned up. I never took you for the jealous kind."

Turning to Rose, Philly continued, "It was real good meeting you. If you comes to Mossy Brook, why don't you drop in? I'll be all alone and glad of a bit of female company."

Rose was saved from replying when Bob Moss came outdoors. Taking his father's suitcase, he told him it was time to be on the road.

Watching them walking down the garden path, Father Kiely turned to the others, asking was there any chance of a cup of tea? After the Philly affair, he was sure they could all use one.

"Not until I am sure Philly Moss is in the car pointing out of Mark's Point, and Father, I hope you don't think I'm uncharitable, but I never want to see that man at our door again," Rose said.

"I don't think you have any worries. Bob believes this was just a plan of his father's to get more attention from Jean and his family, which backfired. He says Jean will be gone for at least a month, and by that time, Philly will be so glad to have her back, he will forget he ever mentioned annulment. So, what about that cup of tea? Are we having one or not?"

CHAPTER 12

A Call For Help

It was the morning after Philly Moss's unexpected visit, and Rose and Bessie were sitting at the kitchen table enjoying their second cup of tea after breakfast. Rose, who was leaving later that morning for St. John's, completed a list of items she needed to get in the city. She planned to return on Thursday but wondered if she could accomplish all she needed to do in two days.

Adding music to her list made her think of Maggie, and she asked Bessie if the teenager mentioned getting a birthday card or a phone call from her mother.

"No, and I was going to ask Gabe. But the only time I saw him alone was yesterday, and with all the racket over Philly Moss, it went completely out of my mind. I'm starting to think Angela hasn't been in contact because, knowing Maggie. she would be only too happy to share the news." Bessie said.

"I just added music for Maggie to my list, and I want some different hymn music too. I think the best idea is to check with a couple of organists I know and see what they are playing in their churches these days."

As Rose continued writing, Bessie recalled how they were both frantically adding items to the same small book just a few weeks earlier. Then they were trying to remember everything they needed before opening Martin House to guests. Rose was still making notes, but now it was mostly to remind her of things she needed as a piano teacher, church organist, and choir leader.

"Most people retire and move from the city for a more relaxed and less busy life but not you, Rose. And news of your musical talent is spreading, at least it has to Murphy's Cove."

Rose asked Bessie what she meant.

"When I was in Millicent Murphy's shop yesterday, she was saying a couple of her customers came to Mark's Point for mass on Sunday. They said the choir did a great job and how nice it was to hear the organ being played in church, especially since they have no organist or singing in their church now."

"I'm glad they enjoyed it, and if Father Kiely has his way, there will be singing in their church. That's why he brought the girls over last week to practice and hopes to convince some adults to make up a choir.

"Now, Bessie, are you sure it's alright for me to leave this morning. It seems I'm always taking off, but I need to get things straightened out legally with my house in St. John's and the family home here. Hopefully, this will be my last trip to the lawyer. What about you? When are you going to take a few days off and have a break in town?"

"Maybe in September, but for now, I've plenty to keep me busy here. And that reminds me, Maggie and I are going berry picking tomorrow morning. I'm looking forward to it. I also promised Maggie we'd make a boiled blueberry pudding the following day because it's Gabe's favourite dessert. She wants to learn how to make it so she can surprise him by making one."

"I would have thought partridgeberries were more to Gabe's taste than blueberries, considering how sour they are," Rose said with a laugh.

"And maybe that's why you like partridgeberries because they're also sharp, just like your tongue when it comes to Gabe," Bessie quickly responded.

"I hope you don't come out with comments like that in front of Maggie. She'd be hurt to hear you speak that way. And whether his taste is sweet or sour, I notice Gabe was the first one you called on for help when Philly Moss appeared on the scene."

"That's because Maggie was here at the time. She was going home, and it only made sense to get him."

"Nonsense! Lucy and Jim live much closer, and you could have asked Maggie to get them, but no, Gabe was the one who rushed to your rescue."

"I might have sent for him, but that was a mistake. He acted as if I was helpless, and I don't need him or any man to protect me. I only asked him because I thought Philly might listen to him more than he would to me. Anyway, that's enough about Gabe O'Brien. Have we got everything we need for the weekend? With the crowd coming for the wedding on Friday night, can you think of anything we may have forgotten? I'll be back on Thursday, but you can always get me by phone at Jean's house," Rose reminded her.

Bessie's thoughts turned to the upcoming weekend and the houseful of guests they had booked. After Mrs. Wilson's visit, they heard from her several times. During her most recent phone call, she asked how far from Martin House was the nearest restaurant. The guests' wedding was taking place in the afternoon, with the reception starting at 6 pm. The group would need to eat between breakfast and the wedding and asked about local restaurants.

There was no restaurant nearby, but Rose, who answered the phone, was sure a meal could be arranged at noon in Martin House and promised to get back to Mrs. Wilson once she discussed it with Bessie.

"I think your idea of the guests having a light breakfast and then brunch at noon will work well, Rose. If we serve it buffet style, everyone can help themselves. We can make a big pan of scrambled eggs, and our guests can choose from bacon, ham, and baloney with toast, tea, or coffee. By serving a light breakfast and brunch later, there's no need to charge them extra. Attending a wedding is expensive enough, and we want to make their weekend an enjoyable experience."

Mrs. Wilson was delighted when she heard what the women planned.

"I keep telling my friends that I found a jewel in Mark's Point when I came upon Martin House. No other hotel or accommodation owners would do so much for their guests as you two ladies. My friends are all looking forward to this weekend, not only for the wedding but also to stay here and to meet such a pair of enterprising women," Mrs. Wilson said when Rose returned her phone call.

Everything seemed in place for the wedding guests. Even the mass schedule was working to their advantage. A couple of years earlier, Saturday night masses, introduced to the parish, resulted in Holy Family Church having a monthly rotation mass schedule. During August, Mark's Point's weekend services would take place on Saturday nights. That meant Rose would be available on Sunday morning to help Bessie prepare breakfast before the guests left for home. Bessie thought it was unlikely the guests would want to leave early on Sunday after celebrating the night before, which meant it could be noon or later before the house emptied. With Father Kiely celebrating mass in Murphy's Cove and Mossy Brook, he wouldn't be having dinner at Martin House, and she and Rose would have a light meal later in the day.

"It seems Saturday night mass is catching on with parishioners. When first introduced, many older people thought it was sacrilegious. Some parishioners even travelled to neighbouring communities to attend Sunday mass instead of their church on Saturday night. The younger people were quick to accept it but not the older folk," recalled Bessie.

"And we still have parishioners who feel that way. You were saying Millicent Murphy mentioned people from Murphy's Cove attending mass here on Sunday morning. There were at least a dozen older people who had a mass the night before in their community but chose instead to travel miles to attend Sunday mass," Rose replied.

"And talking about travelling, it's time I got ready. It's a good day for driving, and the forecast calls for nice weather all week. The quicker I leave, the more I'll get done in town today. I was wondering, with all the upstairs rooms filled for the weekend and us using Mother and Father's room with the twin beds, have we enough single-sized sheets, or should I buy some more?"

"It wouldn't hurt to have some extra sheets in both sizes. We bought additional towels and facecloths before we opened, but at the time, we decided we had enough bedding between my sheets and those you had in St. John's. It makes sense to have spare sheets on hand."

"All right, I'll buy a couple of pairs in both sizes. I had planned to go to Bowring Brothers, and if I don't get them there or in one of the other shops on Water Street, I'll try the Avalon Mall."

A few hours later, Bessie was alone in the house, enjoying a sandwich for lunch, when the telephone rang. *Why is it that the phone always rings when I sit down to eat,* she thought?

On answering the phone, the female caller identified herself as Sister Bernadette from Toronto and asked if this was Rose's sister-in-law Bessie.

"Hello, Sister. Yes, this is Bessie. I'm sorry you missed Rose, but if it is important, you may reach her later today in St. John's."

When the nun said she wasn't looking for Rose but had called to speak to Bessie about Angela O'Brien, Bessie was immediately apprehensive, wondering what she was about to hear about Gabe's daughter.

"What's wrong, Sister? What has Angela done now?"

"She has done nothing wrong. I understand you had issues with Angela in the past, but that's not why I am calling. I'm calling because Angela needs help."

"What kind of help and what sort of scrape has she got herself in?" Bessie asked, finding it hard to imagine strong-willed Angela asking anyone for help.

"As you know, Bessie, I only met Angela when Rose asked me to arrange Maggie's transportation to Newfoundland. What I saw was an unhappy young woman struggling to raise her daughter on a low income. Since then, I have kept in contact with her. You were upset hearing about Maggie's cancelled trip. However, what you don't know is the money her father sent for Maggie's fare last year saved his daughter and granddaughter from being evicted from their apartment at the time."

"What!" a horrified Bessie exclaimed.

As the nun continued to speak, Bessie became even more horrified hearing Angela and Maggie had been struggling financially for a long time. Angela's minimum wage job left barely enough to pay for essentials, let alone for extras. Sister Bernadette, noticing how difficult things were for the young mother, reached out to her. But Angela was adamant she was not a charity case and didn't need help.

"I knew she was finding it difficult to make ends meet, but I didn't realize just how bad things were until last week. Angela's landlord evicted her from her apartment and kept her furniture in lieu of payment. She either had to lose her furniture or go to court for failure to pay almost three month's rent. She was left homeless, with only a few personal belongings of Maggie's and her own. She stayed with a friend for a few nights but knew it wasn't a long-term solution. Yesterday, she was desperate enough to ask for my help. That's why I am calling you."

As Sister continued to talk, Bessie went through a range of emotions as she realized she had never considered Angela's feelings or how she might be managing. Bessie remembered how she condemned the young mother's actions, not thinking how difficult it might be for her. Instead, she had focused only on Gabe and Maggie and how they were affected.

"I arranged for Angela to stay at a hostel for women right now. But she and I have talked at length about what has happened and what she should do. Her biggest worry is Maggie and where they will stay when she returns to Toronto, but I believe she needs to look much farther ahead. I work with immigrant families, and Angela is in a similar position to many of them. The only difference is that most immigrants have a good education and little English, while Angela speaks well but has little education."

Angela may have confided in Sister Bernadette but had no intention of asking her father for help. Bessie's mind was in turmoil as the nun continued speaking, trying to take in all she was hearing. She was quickly brought back to reality when she heard her name mentioned.

"What was that, Sister? I thought I heard you say Angela wanted to talk to me."

Bessie was sure she had misheard. There was no way Gabe's daughter would ask to speak to her. In the past, they had exchanged harsh words about how Angela treated her father and the lifestyle she had inflicted on her young daughter. Bessie explained this to the nun, who said that could be why Angela wished to speak to her now.

"When I asked Angela if she had an aunt or female relative she trusted to give her sound advice, she immediately mentioned you. She told me after her mother died, you were always there for her, but at the time, she never appreciated it. She remembers you were upset when she left school, telling her she would regret her decision.

"Will you talk to her? I think she has bottled up her problems for too long and was too proud and perhaps stubborn to ask for help. Talking to me, a stranger, was a start, but now she is ready to talk to someone she trusts, who will be understanding but firm when necessary. We cannot sugar-coat Angela's problems, but with help, she can work on resolving them. I'm willing to help Angela, and I have some ideas, but she also needs someone like you in her life right now."

Bessie found herself agreeing to talk to Angela later that night.

"I will talk to her, but Sister, I do have a condition. Once I talk to Angela and can help her, it has to be with Gabe's knowledge. I won't go behind his back. Will you tell Angela that and, if she agrees, she can make a collect call to me tonight. I'll be home and, if someone does happen to be here, I will ask Angela for a phone number and call back later," said Bessie.

Before saying goodbye to the Sister, she promised to get in touch with her the following day.

Over the next two hours, Bessie couldn't get Gabe's daughter out of her mind. She thought about and dismissed several ideas and always returned to the same one. But before speaking to Angela, Bessie wanted Rose's input. Waiting until she knew Rose would have arrived in St. John's, she called her sister-in-law. Following a lengthy conversation, Rose was in complete agreement with the plan. Sister Bernadette was next to hear how Bessie wanted to help Angela. Not only did she approve of the idea, but she also expressed her pleasure for Bessie's quick and positive response. Now, all Bessie could do was wait for Angela's phone call that night and hope she was receptive to the proposal.

She found herself restive, unable to settle down to the chores she had intended to do.

Why am I so uptight about the upcoming conversation. It's not as if Angela is a stranger. After all, I've known her since she was a child. I must relax, or else I'll be stressed out and no use to Angela.

Just then, Bessie remembered the monthly reading material package that arrived from her brother Duncan in Scotland. He continued a tradition her mother began when Bessie first came to Newfoundland by sending her *People's Friend* magazines and *Sunday Post* newspapers. Reading them would take her mind off the upcoming phone call, and settling down in her easy chair with a cup of tea, she prepared to enjoy a peaceful interlude. Beginning a short story in the magazine, she finally found herself relaxing.

"Hello! Is you here, Bessie?"

Oh, my Lord, thought Bessie, jerking upright. *Of all the people I don't want to deal with this afternoon, Lucy tops the list.*

Rising reluctantly, she went through to the kitchen, where Lucy stood holding a covered plate in her hand.

"How is you, my dear? I saw Rose leaving this morning. Off to town, is she? When I finished baking this afternoon, I said to my Jim; I'm taking some cookies over to Bessie and having a nice visit. She's going to be lonesome in that big house all by herself.

"I guess Rose has business in St. John's. Has she? Is she got over that old Philly Moss landing on your doorstep yet? The nerve of him, thinking he could move in here. Like I said to my Jim, 'I knows Bessie and Rose don't have much customers, but who'd want the likes of that old thing as a boarder?' I tells my Jim that it's a blessing that you two's not short of a dollar; that you don't be depending on customers."

Bessie was about to give Lucy a sharp reply when she remembered Angela and how she had quickly judged her. Instead, she tried to think of something positive to say to her neighbour and focused on the cookies Lucy had uncovered and placed on the table.

"You have been busy, Lucy. Those cookies look delicious. Mrs. Martin always said you had the lightest touch with pastry in Mark's Point, and she always enjoyed your cookies. I was sitting in the sun porch, having a cup of tea. Would you like a cup?"

"Well, if you are sure you have the time, I'd love a cup of tea. What's neighbours for if not to share a cup of tea and a yarn," a delighted Lucy said.

I've done it now, thought Bessie, hoping Lucy wouldn't stay too long.

"I don't usually relax in the sun porch in the afternoon, but I'm having a lazy day because I have the next few days planned out. We are getting ready for a full household of guests this weekend."

"This is a lovely room, Bessie. I mind when your Alex built it. People wondered what next he was adding on to the biggest house in Mark's Point. When you moved in and put in a generator, you were the first to have power in Mark's Point. Then when Alex bought a television, no one around here had ever seen one before. Mind how all the men would come to your house every Saturday night to watch 'Hockey Night in Canada?' My Jim dearly loved those games."

Without waiting for a response, Lucy continued to address Bessie.

"I sees you had a couple of customers last week, but they only stayed the one night. I'm some glad you've got more customers coming, and my Jim will be happy to hear it as well. He don't say much, my Jim, but he's a caring man, and he wants to see you make a go of your business. Any time you needs help from him or me, don't you be shy asking."

As Bessie assured Lucy that everyone knew Jim was a kind man, she also thought he was a saint to put up with a wife who talked continuously. Lucy, beaming with delight at the compliment paid to her husband, proceeded to live up to her reputation by relating the latest comings and goings in Mark's Point and its neighbouring communities. Trying to appear alert, Bessie was only half listening to her neighbour, who jumped from topic to topic.

Lucy continued to gossip with news of Kate Brown's pregnancy and what the twins were saying about having another brother or sister. She spoke about Maureen Mackey's upcoming wedding before wondering why the Mounties were making so many visits lately to Muddy Brook Cove.

Bessie focused on Lucy's rambling when she heard Rose and Gabe's names mentioned in the same sentence.

"What was that you were saying about Rose and Gabe?"

"I was saying it's nice they is such wonderful good friends, 'though I always thought they was too much like one another to really like each other."

"Of course, they are good friends. Why wouldn't they be? Gabe is and has always been a friend to all the Martin family. He was Alex's closest friend, and since Alex's death, he's been a tremendous help to both Rose and me, especially when we were getting the Bed and Breakfast ready for business."

"And some close-mouthed he was about it too," Lucy said.

"Fancy him knowing all the time about your business and not saying a word about it. And I see he's been working on Mr. and Mrs. Martin's house. Is Rose thinking about selling it?"

"Oh, no. Didn't you hear? Rose is renting it. I thought you would have known. David and Sharon, the young teachers you met, are going to be living there. Won't it be nice to see new residents in Mark's Point?" Bessie asked, inwardly delighted with Lucy's look of astonishment.

Within minutes Lucy departed, no doubt anxious to share the latest news about David and Sharon moving into Rose's house. Looking out the window, Bessie saw her headed in the direction of Kavanagh's shop.

That solved the problem of getting Lucy to leave. Now, if only Angela's issues could be so quickly resolved.

She was still thinking about Angela's situation when the telephone rang that night. It was only seven-thirty, six o'clock Ontario time, when

Bessie answered an operator, asking if she would accept a collect call from Angela O'Brien.

When she agreed, a tremulous voice said, "Aunt Bessie? This is Angela.

"I hope you're not mad at me getting Sister Bernadette to phone you, but I didn't know who else would be willing to listen. How are Maggie and Dad? I missed Maggie's birthday. Did she have a good birthday?"

Angela began crying as she spoke about Maggie, making it difficult for Bessie to control her emotions.

"Angela, I'm glad you thought of me, and of course, I'll listen. You know you are important to me, and you should also know I'll do anything I can to help you. Don't worry about Maggie; she is great as usual, and I believe she enjoyed her birthday. Rose and I did, although I'm sure she missed not having you here."

A weeping Angela said she had been thinking of Maggie, wishing she could have been there to celebrate her birthday.

"It was the first time I ever missed her birthday. You and Aunt Rose are so good to her, while I never even sent her a card or phoned her. Maggie's a good kid, but she must think I forgot her birthday or didn't care, and I know Dad must be furious. I don't blame him or you if you hate me after the way I let Maggie down."

"No one hates you, Angela. Maggie not only adores you; she is proud of you. As for your father, he could never hate you. He loves you, but he also worries about you and the kind of life you share with Maggie. Your Uncle Alex often said that you and your father disagreed so much because you were so alike. You are both too independent and stubborn for your own good. Neither one of you will ever back down and admit you're wrong, and you've both been wrong many times."

Regardless of what happened in the past, Bessie assured Angela that Gabe would always be there for her and Maggie whatever problems she had.

"Now, Angela, I haven't spoken to your father about this, but he will have to know. However, before that happens, let's see what we can do now. I know you are missing Maggie, so why don't you come home for a holiday and spend time with her and your father. We can work out your problems while you are here, giving you the time you need to make plans.

"Before you say no, let me say it won't cost you a penny if you want to come home. I spoke to Sister Bernadette about you flying to Newfoundland on Thursday. Rose, who is in St. John's right now, would meet you and drive you home. We all care and want to help you. What do you think?"

For a few seconds, there was absolute silence before Bessie heard a fresh burst of sobbing.

"I can't come. I won't be able to pay the fare back, and I need to find a new and better job for Maggie's sake."

"There will be no paying back. It's a gift, and not only to you. It's also for Maggie and Gabe, who will be delighted to have you home. And there is time enough to think about a job and your future when you get home. What I want you to do now is hang up and think about this, even it takes all night. You may want to talk it over with Sister Bernadette, but I want you to call me back by tomorrow morning with your answer. When you agree, and I sincerely hope you will, we will start making arrangements."

As Bessie continued to assure Angela that coming home for a visit was the best solution, the young woman gradually seemed more open to the idea. Before hanging up, she agreed to call early the next day with her decision. Angela also promised to talk to Sister Bernadette.

Bessie imagined Maggie's reaction if her mother decided to come home. Just then, she remembered the berry-picking trip she and Maggie had planned. They hoped to leave at ten the following morning from Martin House, bringing a packed lunch and making a day of it. Now with Angela calling in the morning and having to contact Rose and Sister Bernadette to make travel arrangements, there was no way she would manage to leave at that time. She decided to call Maggie.

"Maggie, would it be alright if we leave to go berry picking a bit later tomorrow? I have several phone calls to make, and I'm also expecting people to call me. We might still be able to go before lunch, but for now, I'm not sure how long my business will take."

When Maggie said she didn't mind waiting, Bessie smiled to herself, imagining the young girl's excitement if her mother decided to come home. Hanging up the telephone, she knew there was little else she could do that night and decided to finish reading the magazine story Lucy had interrupted that afternoon.

A few minutes later, Bessie was relaxed in her comfortable chair, magazine in hand, and a cup of tea on the side table, when the telephone rang.

One thing for sure, there's no rest for the wicked. When the operator said she had a collect call, she knew Angela had made up her mind.

"Aunt Bessie, it's Angela. Were you serious about me coming home?"

When Bessie assured her she was, Angela began to cry, saying, "If you're sure you want to do this, I want to come home."

"Of course, I'm serious and want you to come home. It's the answer I wanted, and I know Maggie and your father will be so happy. First thing in the morning, we, that's Rose, Sister Bernadette, and I, will start making all the arrangements and, as soon as I can, I will call you, so stay close to the phone. Now go and relax and have a good night's sleep. I know I'll rest well now we have this settled."

"Thank you, Aunt Bessie, thank you so much. I'm so happy and looking forward to coming home. I will get up early and wait to hear from you. Thank you, and good night."

When the phone call ended, Bessie felt a deep sense of relief.

I think this is the best solution for everyone. Now I need to call Rose and Sister Bernadette. Once that's done, I'll relax the best way I know how by enjoying a good cup of tea and reading my Scottish magazines.

CHAPTER 13

A Surprise For Maggie

B essie's late husband Alex often said his wife had a built-in alarm clock. Summer or winter, Bessie woke up at 7.30 each morning. So, when she found herself wide awake just after six o'clock on Wednesday morning, she knew there had to be a reason.

Her thoughts went to guests, wondering if she had an early breakfast to prepare, but with Martin House empty, that wasn't the cause of her unrest.

What is on my mind? Do I have somewhere to go or something to do?

It wasn't until Bessie remembered the blueberry picking trip she and Maggie had planned for that day that the reason for her unrest came to mind.

Angela's phone call the previous night, resulting in her decision to accept Bessie's offer to provide a plane ticket home, was emotional for both women. Instead of waiting until the next day, Bessie had immediately set the wheels in motion, calling Rose in St. John's and Sister Bernadette in Toronto. If everything went as planned, Sister Bernadette would bring Angela to catch her flight the following day, and Rose would meet her at St. John's Airport before driving her home to Mark's Point.

Bessie knew the decision was the right one. Angela's visit would be a wonderful surprise for Maggie. Although Gabe's first reaction would be like her own, wondering what kind of trouble his daughter was in, he would want to help her. But with neither Maggie nor Gabe aware Angela was even thinking of coming home for a visit, it was up to Bessie to break the news.

Knowing there was little chance of getting more sleep, Bessie decided to get up, have her breakfast, then get her bedroom ready for the weekend guests. She would change and launder the bedding, and once she had it hung outdoors, she would make up the single beds in the downstairs bedroom.

It was the first time guests would use Rose and Bessie's bedrooms, which meant emptying their closets to provide space for guests' clothes. It was the only negative about having a houseful of guests, and it was something they would have to consider for the future.

By eight o'clock, Bessie was outside pegging bedding on two clotheslines. She had also changed Rose's bed, knowing her sister-in-law would have enough to do when she returned from St. John's. As she felt the warm, soft breeze on her face, she could imagine guests in bed enjoying the fresh air smell from the sheets. Pinning the last pillowcases on the line and looking across the harbour to the wharf activity, Bessie wondered whether Gabe was one of the fishermen gathered around the splitting tables.

She considered driving over that way and asking him to stop in later. Still, knowing how everyone's actions were observed and discussed in the small community, she decided against doing so. Recalling Lucy's insinuation the night before about Rose and Gabe, she laughed inwardly, wondering what her neighbour might say if she saw Bessie on the wharf looking for Gabe.

Still chuckling at the thought, she was about to enter the house when she heard a horn blowing and turning around; she saw Gabe's truck at the bottom of her driveway. He had the window down and shouted out to her, but unable to understand what he was saying, Bessie began to walk down the garden path towards him.

"I saw by the lines of laundry you were up bright and early this morning, and I thought you might like some fish. I knows you and Maggie plan on going berry picking later, but I filleted cod if you fancy some."

"I'd love a fillet for my supper, but would you have a few minutes to spare as there's something I need to talk over with you?

"If you get me a bowl to put the fish in, you can tell me what it is when I bring your fish back," Gabe replied.

It would take more than a few minutes to explain what was happening with Angela, and knowing Gabe was probably hungry after fishing for hours, Bessie decided to make breakfast for him.

"I'm keeping you from going home to eat, so I've put some bacon on to fry, then I'll cook you a couple of eggs," she told Gabe as he came into the kitchen.

"I won't say no. I'm feeling peckish, and bacon and egg sounds good. I'll just put these couple of skinned cod fillets in your fridge. You said you wanted to talk to me; is there something you needed doing?"

Bessie looked at him, wondering where to start, then deciding to get right to the point; she said, "I've been talking to Angela. and she's flying home tomorrow."

"My Angela? She's coming home? What on earth made her decide to come now? Not that I don't want to see her. I knows for sure Maggie will be some glad. But with her phoning you, not me or Maggie, is there something wrong? There's got to be some reason for her suddenly wanting to come home. She's not come to take Maggie back already, is she?"

Assuring Gabe this wasn't the reason Angela was returning, Bessie told him everything she knew. He never moved or spoke as she told him about Angela's recent eviction and how she came close to losing her apartment a year earlier. While talking, Bessie continued to cook, and when Gabe's breakfast was ready, she placed it in front of him. Returning to the table with tea and toast, she saw Gabe had yet to touch his food.

"Eat up, Gabe, while it's hot. I know Angela's news is a shock, but don't you think she is doing the right thing coming home? That way, we can work out things together and see what's best for her and Maggie."

"Of course, I knows it's the best thing. Angela should be home, but why wouldn't she tell me about her problems? Am I that bad a father that she couldn't come to me for help?"

"You are not a bad father, and I'll tell you the same thing I told Angela last night. The problem is you are both too much alike. I'm sure Alex told you that more than once. Proud, stubborn, and too independent by far describe the pair of you. Neither one of you would ever ask for help for yourselves. I'd say the only reason Angela went to Sister Bernadette and agreed to talk to me is that she was concerned for Maggie. Now, I'm going to pour myself up a cup of tea. Any more talking can wait until you eat your breakfast."

Gabe ate in complete silence, except when a sound came from him, almost like a soft sigh. Bessie stole an occasional glance at him, knowing he probably had mixed feelings about the news he was trying to absorb. When she saw he had finished eating, she asked him what he was thinking.

"I'm still trying to get my head around this news. I wish Angela knew she could ask me for help. It's a terrible thing to know your daughter feels she must ask others instead of coming to her father. It's like she don't trust me."

"That's nonsense. Do you think Angela would leave Maggie with anyone but you? She didn't call you because she feels she's let you down again. Now let's think about Maggie. Will you tell her Angela's coming home, or should we ask Angela to call Maggie?" asked Bessie, who would prefer to see Angela calling Maggie but felt it should be Gabe's decision.

"I think Maggie would like to hear from her mother. She never once complained about not hearing from Angela on her birthday, but she must have wondered why. I'd see her every time the phone rang, rushing to answer it as if expecting a call," Gabe said.

"Then I'll phone Angela and get her to call Maggie this morning as soon as everything is settled. I think you should tell Maggie that because Angela couldn't be here for her birthday, and if anything changed, she wanted her flight booked before letting her know.

With Gabe in agreement, he left for home, leaving Bessie to clear away the kitchen. It wasn't yet nine o'clock, and with Ontario 90 minutes behind in time difference, it was too early to call Angela.

When I make up the single beds in the downstairs room and vacuum upstairs, it will be time to call Toronto. I wonder when we will settle everything, and Angela can call Maggie.

But before she had the clean breakfast dishes back in the cupboard, the phone rang. On answering, she discovered she wasn't the only early riser that morning when an exuberant Rose spoke.

"It's all settled. I went to the airport and have Angela's ticket paid for and ready to be picked up at the airline counter in Toronto."

"As early as this? I thought it would be much later before I heard from you. Gabe was here on his way back from fishing, so I told him about Angela coming home. Now the ticket is bought, I should call Angela. Maybe I should wait for a while as it's only about 7.30 in Toronto."

"I'd say she is well awake by now. She'll be too excited about coming home to sleep late. Even I was up bright and early this morning. The travel agency didn't open until ten, so Jean suggested I go to the airport, and it proved to be a quicker way to arrange things. Angela has the first flight down from Toronto tomorrow and will arrive at one o'clock, which means I'll have her home before supper time."

"What if we all have supper here? Maggie wants to make a blueberry pudding for Gabe, and we could have it for dessert," Bessie said.

"That sounds good. I should be home in Mark's Point around 4.30, and I'll bring Angela to Gabe's. If we eat an hour later, it will give them some time together before coming for supper. In the meantime, I'll call Sister Bernadette and let her know what's happening."

When the call ended, Bessie went into the downstairs room to make up the beds she and Rose would be using. While spreading the bottom sheet on the first bed, she remembered she hadn't asked Gabe to put the junior bed together for the young guest they expected that weekend.

Once she made up the beds, Bessie decided she couldn't wait any longer to phone Toronto. Hoping Angela was up, she rang the number only to have the phone answered immediately.

"Angela, everything is arranged. You'll be flying home tomorrow, and your ticket will be waiting at the airline counter. Rose has already talked to Sister Bernadette, who will contact you to arrange your transportation to the airport. Rose is meeting you in St. John's and will drive you home."

Tears muffled Angela's answer as she thanked Bessie, telling her that one day she would pay her back.

"You'll pay me back today by phoning Maggie and telling her you're coming home. I already spoke to your father this morning, and although he got a shock, he's only too happy to know you are coming home. We both feel you're the one to call Maggie and think you could say this visit is a late birthday surprise for her."

"I'll call her right away. I can't wait to speak to her or to see her tomorrow. Thank you again, Aunt Bessie; thanks for everything."

Within five minutes, Bessie's phone rang again, and an excited Maggie was telling her about the phone call from Angela.

"It's a wonderful surprise for you, Maggie. I know your mother wanted to be here for your birthday, but this is the next best thing. Did she tell you Aunt Rose is picking her up at the airport and driving her home? When I talked to Aunt Rose, we decided to ask you all for supper once they arrive. Remember, you are coming here to make a blueberry pudding tomorrow. It will be your mother and grandfather's turn to be surprised when they see what a good job you make on the dessert."

Maggie squealed with delight before asking Bessie if she knew when she would be ready to go berry picking.

Now, with all her phone calls over, Bessie suggested Maggie come to Martin House in half an hour, and from there, they would make their way to the berry hills. When Gabe came to the phone at her request, she told him about the supper plans and then mentioned the junior bed. He accepted the supper invitation and promised to put the small bed together the following day.

Several hours later, Bessie and Maggie sat enjoying their lunch on a grassy spot high above Mark's Point.

What a great day this is, and what better way to spend time with Maggie, Bessie thought, glancing at her one-gallon bucket filled with large juicy blueberries, while Maggie's had almost as many.

"I would say by the time you add another half dipper of berries; your bucket will be full, Maggie. I'll need to look to my reputation as the top berry picker considering how fast you are picking," Bessie said, smiling at her young companion.

"You're joking, I know, Aunt Bessie. Nobody can pick berries as fast as you. I'm getting a lot because it's a good year for berries, and they are some big. If you look from a distance, you'd think the bushes were blue instead of green because they're loaded down with berries. Can we come back again another day?"

"I'm hoping to come a few more times because your Aunt Rose was right when she said we're going to need lots more berries this year. That's one of the reasons we bought a freezer. We want to freeze berries to have on hand for muffins and pancakes, and we plan to keep some for desserts."

"Good, maybe Mum will come with us when she's here. She's like Pop; she loves blueberry pudding. They're going to get some surprise when they know I helped make the pudding tomorrow."

Maggie was quiet for a minute as she looked over the bay and at Mark's Point, which lay below them.

"Aunt Bessie, isn't Mark's Point the most beautiful place in the world? Do you think maybe Mom is coming home to stay? When I blew out my birthday cake candles, that was my wish."

Oh no! Have I done wrong in asking Angela to come home? Now Maggie has her hopes built up that somehow her mother will stay. How do I answer her questions?

Trying to keep her tone light, Bessie laughed.

"You are looking at Mark's Point on a beautiful summer day. You haven't lived here in winter since you were a small girl, and believe me, it can be far from beautiful then. In fact, it's bleak and even scary at times, especially when we have a storm and the wind blows across the bay. Then the house starts shaking, and you wonder if it will blow down."

"But we have winter in Toronto, where the snow never stays white but turns grey and dirty with all the traffic. I remember how white the snow is here and sliding down Church Hill or your garden. I used to love doing that and, if we stayed here, I could go to school in Murphy's Cove with my friends," Maggie replied.

"What about your mother? There's no work here for her, and to be happy, she needs to have something to do. You have to think of her."

Maggie's face clouded over, and she admitted she hadn't thought about work for her mother.

"But Aunt Bessie, Mom works hard, and she's tired a lot. She's smart, and I wish she could get a good job in Newfoundland, but she likes Toronto better than Mark's Point, so I guess we will be going back there. Anyway, I still have another month of my holidays before I have to leave."

Then a sudden thought seemed to cross the teenager's mind.

"Aunt Bessie, you don't suppose that's why Mom is coming, that she wants to take me back early?" she asked almost fearfully.

"I know that's not the reason. Your mother told me she has missed you a lot and felt bad about not being here for your birthday, so get that thought out of your mind. Now let's fill your dipper, and then we will go home. We can come back next week when we have more time and make a day of it and, as you said, maybe your mother will join us. She was a fast berry picker when she was young. Think of all the berries the two of you can pick together. Perhaps you can bring some back to Toronto."

Maggie appeared considerably happier when Bessie spoke about Angela. Picking up her dipper, she moved to a blueberry bush and started picking berries again.

Later that afternoon, as Bessie cleaned her berries before putting some in the fridge for the following day's pudding and the remainder in the freezer, she wondered what plans Angela might make? Whatever Angela decided, Bessie hoped the results would improve both her and Maggie's lives.

Since first speaking to Sister Bernadette and hearing about her work in adult education, Bessie kept thinking about the possibility of Angela completing her high school education, which would allow her to attend a college and train for a good job. She knew it was what Angela needed, but would the young mother now see the importance of education? She wondered what would be the best way to approach the topic. There was also the question of finances. What would Angela and Maggie live on if she did go back to school?

I think I need to talk to Sister Bernadette tonight and see what possibilities there may be in that direction. If there are programs to help immigrants better their English, surely there's one to help adults improve their education.

"It's called upgrading," Sister Bernadette told Bessie later that night.

"And it's what Angela needs if she is ever going to improve her job prospects. I did mention the possibility of more education to her, and she seemed receptive to the idea. I don't know what's available in rural Newfoundland, but we have excellent upgrading courses in Toronto. An allowance is paid to participants, but it wouldn't be nearly enough to live on for both Angela and her daughter. She would have to attend day classes and work nights and weekends to pay their rent and food. Or she could work during the day and go to night school.

"Being a single mother is going to make it that much harder for Angela to make a decision, but in the end, I see education is the only course open to her if she is to improve her future and Maggie's. She could go on barely making ends meet, but don't forget, when Maggie returns, Angela not only needs to find another apartment, which means a month's rent and a security deposit, she must furnish it. How is she going to manage this in a few weeks when she is not even working?" asked Sister Bernadette.

Lying in bed that night, Bessie kept thinking about Angela's circumstances, knowing she would face challenges whatever she decided to do. It would take far longer to graduate from night school, but regardless if Angela chose day or night classes, she would also have to work. It meant Maggie would often be left alone. Renting an apartment was another necessity, and as Sister Bernadette pointed out, that was a significant expense.

Bessie's thoughts kept returning to a remark made by Sister Bernadette that inexpensive accommodation was available at hostels for single women.

What if Maggie stayed in Mark's Point until Angela furthered her education? It would allow Angela to live in a hostel and attend day classes while working evenings and weekends to cover her board and expenses.

She mulled over the idea, but even knowing Maggie would love to stay and attend the local school, she believed it unlikely the mother and daughter would agree to live apart. It was Bessie's last thought as she dropped off to sleep.

After nine the following morning, Gabe arrived to assemble the child's bed, which would be needed when Martin House filled up with guests that weekend.

"Not out fishing this lovely morning, Gabe?" Bessie asked.

"No, not that I wasn't up early enough because Maggie has been on the go since the crack of dawn getting things ready for her mother. Not only has she got Angela's bedroom turned inside out, but she also ordered me outdoors so she could wash the floors. Then she tells me she's coming here to practice this afternoon, and while she was gone, I had to promise to keep the house tidy," said Gabe

"Rose encourages Maggie to come here and practice the piano whenever she can. She'll be wanting to show her mother how well she is doing with her lessons. It's good to see how interested she is in music, and I'm also glad she wants to help you around the house," said Bessie.

"I don't mind her helping out now and then, but she's on holiday, and anyway, I wouldn't want her getting too particular and house proud," Gabe said.

That night following supper, Bessie was reminded of Gabe's words when he bragged about her housekeeping skills, much to Maggie's embarrassment.

"And not only is she as good as any woman around the house, look at all she's learned in just a few weeks. Angela, did you ever think Maggie would be able to play a song on the piano or to make a blueberry pudding like the one we just had for supper?"

"You are right, Dad. I'm getting plenty of surprises tonight. You've certainly learned a lot between piano lessons from Aunt Rose and Aunt Bessie's cooking lessons since you came home, Maggie. You're a lucky girl having them and your grandfather in your life. I hope you appreciate all they do for you."

Later that night, when the O'Brien's had gone home, Angela was the main topic of Rose and Bessie's conversation.

"I didn't know her well, and it must be seven or eight years since I last saw her, but Angela is not what I imagined her to be," Rose admitted.

"She was full of questions about Maggie and Gabe, and although I know she and her father don't agree on a lot, it's evident she cares for him. I enjoyed her company and found it easy to have a conversation with her."

Bessie agreed Angela had matured a lot, saying the old Angela never seemed appreciative of what people did for her.

"At one time, she seemed to have a permanent chip on her shoulder, as if the world was against her. I often wondered where she got that attitude because her mother was one of the happiest and most appreciative people I ever met, and while Gabe might not always show his feelings, he is a good man. Tell me, Rose, did you get a chance to bring up the topic of her finishing her education."

"I never came right out and asked her if she had thought of returning to school, but I did speak about the importance of a good education and how it opens doors when applying for employment. Angela said that leaving school without graduating had prevented her from getting a good job. She worked in a factory when she first went to Toronto and was well paid. It was enough to cover all her household expenses and a babysitter after school and during holidays for Maggie. However, the factory, like many others, closed, and the only work she's been able to get in recent years was in fast food places or stores that paid minimum wages."

"Not much wonder she couldn't pay her rent. That might just be the push she needs," Bessie said.

"We may not have to do as much persuading as I imagined to get her back to school. As she was leaving, she said she knew we had a busy weekend with a full houseful of guests, but hopefully, we might be able to sit down and talk on Monday. I guess we'll have to wait until then, but one thing for sure, she and Maggie can't go on living the way they have these past two years."

Two days later, Angela was far from the women's minds as they prepared a buffet brunch for their guests. While Bessie put the finishing touches to the meal, Rose was busy in the dining room, accompanied by their youngest guest, four-year-old Melinda White.

"This will be your seat, Melinda. You have a special corner seat because you are a flower girl." Rose said.

"Did you see my dress? Daddy says I look like a princess when I put it on, and Nanny and Poppy say I'll be the prettiest flower girl ever."

"And what does your Mommy say?" Rose asked the little girl.

"She says fancy finding her pencil from school here. She says she thought you would always be a pencil, and she says…"

"Melinda! You talk far too much, and Miss Martin was my principal, not my pencil. Come away and stop being a nuisance," a laughing voice interrupted from behind them.

"That's alright, Josie. Melinda is helping me set the table and telling me all about her flower girl dress. She is a chatterbox, but then so were you when you were much older than Melinda, or have you forgotten?"

When Rose began to laugh, Josie White grinned.

"I guess I was, or so my teachers and especially my principal kept telling me. You know I still can't get over the surprise of seeing you when we arrived last night. I didn't know you had retired as principal and living here. I hadn't even heard of Mark's Point before now. What a lovely community it is."

"That is what I kept telling you and your parents all along," Mrs. Wilson said, coming into the dining room as Rose and Josie were talking.

"I knew this was an ideal place to stay. Anyway, Bessie says she is ready to start bringing through the food, and we need to call everyone and tell them we are about to eat."

As the guests served themselves buffet food, Bessie looked around with satisfaction. It was the largest group of guests she and Rose had hosted, and everyone seemed appreciative and getting on well together. She smiled, remembering the surprise Rose and Josie White got when they saw each other the night before. The former principal and student were laughing as Josie promised to spread the news of the Bed and Breakfast to all her school friends who, she said, would jump at the opportunity of having their former principal serve them breakfast.

This is what I imagined when I first envisioned Martin House as a Bed and Breakfast. Guests around the table, enjoying a meal and each other's company in the home Alex built. He would have loved this.

Just then, Rose came over and quietly spoke.

"You know what I was thinking. Alex would be so happy, seeing his home filled with people enjoying good food and good company. He would absolutely love it. What do you think, Bessie, when you see this happy crowd? Doesn't it make you glad you decided to share your home with others?"

"Were you reading my mind, Rose, because that's exactly what I was thinking? It's wonderful to see everyone so pleased with things here. Now, seeing our guests have everything they need right now, what about rereading my mind and tell me what else I'm thinking?" Bessie said with a smile.

"I don't need to be able to read your mind because I see you eyeing up the teapot. I know for sure you are ready for a cup of tea. I'll go and get our cups."

CHAPTER 14

Angela's Plans

O n Monday, after catering to the largest group of guests ever hosted in Martin House, Rose and Bessie began changing beds and cleaning bedrooms. With several loads of bedding and towels to be laundered, they were grateful for the fine weather to dry the washing outdoors.

Yesterday was also a good day, Bessie remarked, wishing they could have started the laundry then, but nobody in Mark's Point would ever hang clothes outdoors on a Sunday.

"Just imagine the talk if we hung out the washing yesterday. I don't know what harm it does, but your mother never did, and I've always respected her beliefs," Bessie said.

"I know what you mean. I often did my laundry on a Sunday when I was in St. John's, and although I had neighbours who hung their washing outdoors, I'd put mine in the dryer. Even then, I felt guilty thinking Mother wouldn't approve."

"We should get at least four lots of bedding washed today. We'll strip the beds upstairs, and that way, we can get back in our rooms tonight. It's going to be a busy day because Angela's coming to talk about her plans," Bessie reminded her sister-in-law.

"I'll get out of the way when Angela arrives to give her privacy."

"Nonsense Rose. You're probably the best one to talk to Angela, and you did say she seems to realize she needs more education to get a better job. I don't know what time she is coming, but I hope she waits until this afternoon, which will give us time to get the washing and bedrooms finished."

But the first visitors of the day weren't waiting until the afternoon. It was just after nine o'clock when Rose, hanging out the first load of laundry, spotted two little figures coming up the path. As they came near, she recognized them as the postmistress's youngest daughters.

"Good morning, girls. What are you doing up so early on this lovely morning? Can I help you with something?"

"No, it's Mrs. Bessie, we wants," said the biggest one, who looked about six years old.

"That's right; it's Mrs. Bessie we wants," her sister parroted.

"You girls look enough alike to be twins, but I know you're not."

"No, that's our sisters, and they're still in bed. We could be in bed, but we wanted to see Mrs. Bessie," the first girl said.

"And it's a secret. We don't want Mom to know, and we sure don't want the twins finding out," her younger sister added.

Rose looked with amusement at the determined-looking little girls, who, with their small, sturdy figures and dark brown hair in pigtails, could easily pass for twins as she invited them indoors where they found Bessie in the kitchen.

"And who do we have here so early in the morning? Well, good morning, Daisy and Marigold, They are Kate and Robert's youngest girls, Rose," Bessie said with a smile.

"You're right, Mrs. Bessie. And you knows we're not twins, that's Lily and Pansy, and we won't be the youngest soon because Mom is having a baby." Marigold said.

Then turning to Daisy, she said, "See, I told you Mrs. Bessie was smart. She knows us."

"It was me that said Mrs. Bessie was smart, not you. And it was me that said she would be a good cooker," Daisy quickly responded.

"Thank you, girls, for those compliments. And do you know Miss Rose, who is my sister-in-law? She's pretty smart too," Bessie said, laughing.

"We knows Miss Rose. Bobby says she's going to learn him the guitar," Daisy said.

"And we knows Miss Rose plays the organ in church," Marigold added, then turning to Daisy, she said, "Bobby don't know yet if Miss Rose is going to learn him the guitar. He's just hoping."

"And is that why you girls are here? Are you hoping to learn how to play guitar?" Bessie asked.

The girls looked at each other and simultaneously said, "No. You tell her. You ask."

Asking who was the oldest, Rose discovered Marigold was almost seven while Daisy was one year younger. Rose suggested, perhaps Marigold being the oldest, should tell Mrs. Bessie why they were here.

Daisy nodded her agreement, and Marigold began to speak, telling the women her mother's birthday was August 11, and they wanted to make her a birthday cake. They heard Maggie tell the twins Mrs. Bessie had shown her how to make a blueberry pudding and what a good cook Mrs. Bessie was. Lily and Pansy had agreed, saying Maggie's birthday cake had been the best. That's when Marigold and Daisy came up with the idea of asking Bessie to help them make a cake for their mother.

"Mom works in the post office, and she cooks and cleans in our house, and she gets tired. Dad tells the twins and us to help Mom. She's having a baby, and she don't always feel good. Mom makes birthday cakes for all of us, but she don't make one for herself, so we thinks she should have a cake."

Daisy finished talking, letting Marigold continue.

"We wants it to be a surprise, that's why we come here early. Dad and Bobby is out fishing, the twins is still in bed, and Mom is going to the post office soon. We told her we was going for a walk."

"And we brought money to buy stuff for the cake. I've saved up 90 cents, and you've got more, haven't you, Marigold?"

When Marigold proudly announced she had a whole dollar, Daisy anxiously asked was their savings enough money for a good cake because they wanted the cake to be the best one ever.

"It won't cost that much. What about 25 cents each, or is that too expensive?" Bessie asked, looking serious for the girls' benefit.

Two relieved-looking girls said they could afford that and still have enough left over for each of them to buy their mother a birthday card.

"Hopefully, you'll also have enough left over to buy yourselves a treat. Now, do you know what kind of cake your mother likes?"

"Cherry cake," the two voices said in unison.

"I have a good recipe for a cherry cake, so that's not a problem. We'll need to make the cake next Tuesday. We can either decorate it later that day or the following morning on her birthday. How does that sound?"

Two huge smiles greeted Bessie's words before Daisy spoke again.

"You won't tell the twins or nobody, will you, Mrs. Bessie? It's alright you knowing Miss Rose, cos you's a teacher and teachers can keep secrets, just like priests."

"Here's my money Mrs. Bessie," Marigold said, handing over her quarter.

"Give Mrs. Bessie your money, Daisy, and then we'll get out of the way. Mom would be mad if she thought we was bothering you. Thank you, Mrs. Bessie. Daisy, mind your manners and say thank you."

The girls were gone as quickly as they arrived, leaving Bessie and Rose in laughter as they recalled the conversation.

"One thing for sure, there can never be a dull moment in Kate and Robert's house with the four girls and Bobby. Those two little girls are priceless, and they look enough alike to be twins. Well, Bessie, it looks as if you have your work cut out. You were saying earlier how music kept me busy, and now it seems you're getting a reputation for baking."

"I wasn't going to take the girls' money, but then I thought I'd ask them for 25 cents each," Bessie said.

"That way, they not only know they are making their mother's cake but are also paying for it. I remember their father, Robert, as a boy. A more independent young fellow you'd never meet, and it seems he and Kate are bringing their children up the same way."

"Speaking about the Browns, I haven't got back to Bobby and Michael about guitar lessons yet. I spoke to David when I was in St. John's, and he is willing to teach the boys to play guitar. He still hopes to get some sort of youth club on the go."

Bessie was about to reply when the telephone rang. It was Angela asking if the afternoon was convenient for her to come to Martin House. After agreeing, Bessie had just put the receiver down when the phone rang again. Thinking Angela might have forgotten something, she answered with a hello instead of her usual 'Good morning, Martin House, may I help you?'

"Is this the place that offers accommodations?" a female voice asked.

"Yes, this is Martin House. How may I help you?" Bessie replied

"It would help if you announced the name of your business from the beginning, instead of having callers guessing if they have the right place or not. I wish to book accommodation for three nights next week, the 8th to the 10th. Do you have a single en-suite room available?"

Taken aback, Bessie said she could offer a downstairs room with two single beds and an adjoining bathroom. The caller wanted to know were there any en-suite rooms upstairs because she wasn't particular about sleeping on the ground floor. Hearing nothing else was available, the caller reluctantly agreed to take the downstairs room, saying she had no option since she understood Martin House was the only accommodation in the area.

"My name is Penelope Harris, and I don't know what there may be to occupy oneself for three days in such a small place, but because I'm travelling with my brother the Anglican bishop and his wife, I have little choice in the matter. I will therefore arrive with them. Good-bye."

"Who was that? By the look on your face, you're not too impressed." Rose said

"I'm not, and it's left me wondering if we've been too optimistic thinking all our guests will be pleasant and appreciative. Our latest caller doesn't appear to fit in that category at all. She's the Anglican bishop's sister and is travelling with them so that we will have her for three days. She wanted an en-suite room. It's a good thing we discovered an en-suite was a bedroom with an attached bathroom when we travelled around Scotland. Otherwise, I'd have had no idea what she meant. I just hope her brother and his wife don't share her attitude, or it will be three awfully long days."

"You're not usually one to make snap judgements, Bessie. Perhaps the woman was having an off day."

"You may be right. We'll just have to wait and see. Hopefully, the bishop and family will keep busy when they are here. That way, we won't see much of them. In the meantime, two more pairs of sheets are ready to go out on the clothesline."

When the phone rang again, Bessie immediately spoke.

"It's your turn to answer it. It could be the bishop's sister again. I hope you'll get a better response than I did."

Laughing, Rose went to the phone as Bessie stood waiting until she heard Rose speaking and discovered the caller was Sharon Nolan.

Leaving Rose to chat with Sharon, Bessie took the last lot of laundered bedclothes outdoors. As she finished pegging them out, she looked with appreciation at the sheets blowing gently in the fresh breeze and the scenery around her.

Maggie is right. Mark's Point is beautiful. Not much wonder our guests have so many good things to say about it.

Thinking about guests brought her thoughts back to the recent phone call from Penelope Harris.

I hope I'm wrong about the woman, but she sounds like a pain in the neck.

She was still standing in the garden, enjoying the warm breeze and the view when Rose came outdoors.

"Sharon and David are moving some of their things out to the house next Sunday, and they're planning to stay in the house for a few days before going back to St. John's. I've got to call Gabe to ask if he will hook up the water to the house before they come. They've already contacted the power company and put the light bill in their name, and they're having a telephone installed next Tuesday. That's one thing Mother and Father never had because apart from the post office, there was no phone service until after they moved in with you and Alex."

"Did I tell you that Lucy never knew Dave and Sharon rented your house until the other day?" Bessie asked Rose.

"It must be the first thing she didn't know. How did she find out?"

"I had a visit from her when you were in St. John's. Feeling sorry for the way I always give her the brush off, I invited her to stay and have a cup of tea. I soon regretted doing so when she started in with her usual gossip and asking questions. She spoke about Gabe working around the house and wanted to know if you were getting it ready for sale. When I said you were renting it, and Sharon and David were the tenants, she got the surprise of her life. Within a couple of minutes, she was gone, no doubt to spread the news," Bessie said, smiling at the memory of Lucy's speedy departure.

"You probably made her day passing on a bit of news," Rose said.

"I see the first sheets I hung out are already bone dry. What if I put another load of clothes in the washer? It would be a pity not to take advantage of this gorgeous weather and the good water supply. Not many houses in Mark's Point have such a good well. Look at the water we went through this weekend with the house full of guests all having baths and showers."

"We are lucky with our well. Alex used to say we had a natural flow from the hill behind the house and touch wood; even in the hottest summers, the well never did go dry."

The morning went quickly, and before noon, the women had most of the washing done and brought indoors and their bedrooms back to normal. While Bessie prepared lunch, Rose went to the post office to see if they had mail. She was surprised when Kate Brown began apologizing for the behaviour of her youngest daughters.

"Why? What did they do?"

"Lucy was here, and she told me the girls visited you and Bessie this morning. I knew they went for a walk and knowing the trouble they can get into, and, with the pair of them almost as nosy as somebody else I could name, I warned them about bothering people. Now I hear they went to your house. Ever since the twins were at Maggie's birthday party, Marigold and Daisy have been curious about your place. I gave them a telling-off for bothering you this morning, but when I questioned them, they just clammed up. That's unusual for them, and I've been worried they did or said something wrong," Kate said.

"That Lucy! She sees and hears far too much. We had a lovely visit with the girls. I was hanging out clothes when I saw them. We got talking, and I invited them to come in."

"They were very well-behaved guests, and we hope they come again. Bessie invited them over next week. I know she plans to do some baking before then, so she can offer them something sweet to eat. They were so proud, telling us about the new brother or sister they are getting and how hard you work. They're a pair of caring children. Don't let Lucy's talk stop them from visiting us."

"But you are running a business, and the last thing you need is my chatterboxes talking your ears off," Kate said.

"To be truthful, we thoroughly enjoyed their company. We usually see the twins when they're with Maggie, and we also had Bobby visit us. Bessie and I have often said that you and Robert are raising a lovely family, and soon you'll have another baby. You are a lucky couple, and you should be proud of all your children."

Later as they ate lunch, Rose told Bessie about Lucy's gossiping. She said that Lucy could have spoiled the little girls' surprise for their mother because of her need to talk.

"Why would she find it necessary to tell Kate the girls were here? She had to be watching us this morning. It's pretty bad when she starts talking about children. If I ever hear she's been discussing me, I'll give her something to talk about. I can't stand nosy and gossipy people," an indignant Rose said.

It's a good thing Rose doesn't know what our neighbour implied the other night. I'm glad I didn't react or make much of it when Lucy spoke about Rose and Gabe becoming wonderful good friends. If I had, she'd probably think there was something between them, which surely would make matters worse.

Changing the topic, Bessie asked Rose how they would raise the idea of more education to Angela. Rose felt they should come right out and tell her that they and Sister Bernadette agreed she was too intelligent to waste her talents on a minimum wage job.

That afternoon, Maggie arrived unexpectedly with her mother. Knowing Angela wouldn't want to talk in front of her daughter, Rose brought the young girl through to the front room for a piano lesson.

"I'm sorry, Aunt Bessie, but Maggie took it for granted she was coming with me. If I told her I wanted to come here alone, she'd wonder what was wrong. I don't want her worrying about things that have happened. I told her we no longer live in the apartment, but I couldn't tell her about being evicted for not paying rent. She is happy and relaxed here, and I want her to stay that way.

"I found it difficult telling Dad everything that's happened in the last couple of years, but since we talked, it's like a weight lifted from me. I can't believe how understanding he is, and I'm sure it's all thanks to you. You must have talked to him because his whole attitude is changed."

"You have both changed because you're finally willing to treat each other like adults. You've matured over the years, Angela. The difference is you are a mother, and whatever you do now, it's with Maggie in mind. I've said more than once that you are like your father, and that's true, but you are also very much like Meg, your mother. We were great friends, and I still miss her. She was a good mother, and you inherited that trait from her.

"But unlike your mother, Gabe has always found it difficult to show his feelings. I hope you never doubt how much he cares for you and Maggie. He's delighted to have you home, but now he also realizes that you have to make your own decisions."

Although she knew most of Angela's story and how she had fallen in bad times, Bessie still found it difficult to hear how miserable Angela's and Maggie's lives had been in recent years. She let Angela talk without interruption, knowing it was helping the young woman to speak openly. But when Angela started berating herself for her mistakes, Bessie cut her off.

"You've had a difficult time, but now you need to put the past behind you. It's time to think about the future and what is best for you and Maggie. I should tell you that Rose, Sister Bernadette, and I have discussed your situation. We believe you should return to school and upgrade, then go on to postsecondary education. You are smart and capable but working in a minimum wage job is the best you can ever expect with your amount of education."

Bessie looked at Angela almost apprehensively, wondering what was going through her mind and how she would react.

"Fifteen years ago, you said I'd regret leaving school. You were right then, and you're right now. I've realized that I need more education for some time, but I also have to consider Maggie. She may be a teenager, but I won't leave her alone every night while I work or go to classes, but I also know we can't go on the way we were.

Bessie started to respond but stopped when she heard Maggie and Rose talking as they made their way to the kitchen.

"Angela, your daughter, is going to be a great pianist one of these days. She enjoys her lessons, which makes it a pleasure for me to teach her. I just introduced her to a new music book, and you should hear how well she picked up the first song."

Both Angela and Maggie smiled with pleasure at Rose's words. Bessie, who was anxious to continue talking with Angela, congratulated Maggie before asking if the teenager would mind going to Kavanagh's shop for her.

"Of course, I will go, Aunt Bessie. What do you want?"

"I was about to put the kettle on for a cup of tea, and you know how your Aunt Rose likes a biscuit with her tea, but we used up all our sweet stuff over the weekend. I'll just get my purse to give you money for a pack of mixed biscuits. Treat yourself to ice cream or a bar with the change. After such a successful music lesson, you deserve a treat."

With Maggie on her way to the shop, Bessie told Rose that Angela had agreed she needed additional education if she wanted her job prospects and her life to improve.

"However, there are problems to overcome. We know upgrading is available in Toronto, and according to Sister Bernadette, there's the option of day or night classes. But either way, Maggie would spend a great deal of time alone because Angela will have to work to pay their expenses. They need a place to stay and quite a large sum of money to cover a month's rent, a damage deposit, and to buy furniture."

"Where there are problems, there are always solutions, and, if you think about it, there's a simple solution," Rose quickly responded.

"Why not let Maggie stay with your father, Angela. I know it will be hard for both you and Maggie, but in the long run, it's for the best. If you were alone, you could live at the hostel, recommended by Sister Bernadette, which not only offers accommodations, it provides a good environment for studying. Going to day classes and working at weekends and possibly some nights, you would cover your expenses. Meanwhile, Maggie could live with Gabe and go to school with her friends, something I know she would love to do. That way, you won't worry about leaving her alone for long periods."

As Rose spoke, Bessie was nodding in agreement.

"You would miss each other, but in some ways, it would be good for both of you. Without the worry of Maggie spending too much time alone, you'll find it easier to study. Meanwhile, Maggie has been dreading the thought of starting a new high school in Toronto, and Rose is right. Maggie has wished she could go with her friends to school in Murphy's Cove more than once. If she stayed with Gabe, you could phone each other regularly, and of course, you would come home for Christmas. Will you think about it, Angela?" Bessie asked.

Angela was silent for a second, and when she spoke, she took the sisters-in-law by surprise.

"It's something I have thought about quite a bit since I came home, especially since seeing how happy Maggie is now. I know she's been worrying about going to a new high school in Toronto, and although she's never come right out and told me, it's evident she'd love to go to school here. I don't blame her. From what I hear about the high school in Murphy's Cove, it has a great reputation. I might have finished high school if I had a school like that to attend. Instead, I had a teacher who barely passed grade X1 herself, looking after five or six grades. It certainly wasn't a good learning experience. But getting back to Maggie, of course, I'd miss her, but something must change, and I know she would be safe and happy with Dad."

"I thought we might be in for a struggle, but I see you have given this as much thought as we have, and you needed to do that," Bessie said.

Angela said she would never have considered going back to school or letting Maggie stay in Mark's Point a year earlier. However, she now recognized the mistakes she made in the past, and since coming home, she could see a much happier and more relaxed Maggie.

"The best thing that ever happened to me was Maggie. I told myself I was giving her the best opportunities by bringing her to Toronto. But that wasn't true because I was the one who wanted to move away. Maggie always wanted to be home with Dad.

"I know she's hoping we'll stay in Mark's Point, and she'll be upset when she knows I plan to leave. But she is in good hands with Dad, and you both play large roles in her life. It's not going to be easy for either of us at first, but Maggie will look forward to starting school with her friends, and, as you say, we'll talk on the phone once or twice a week."

After discussing it further, the women decided not to mention the plan to Maggie yet. Angela wanted to talk to Gabe and Sister Bernadette, who would begin registering Angela in classes.

A few minutes later, Maggie was back with the biscuits. Looking from her mother to Rose and Bessie, she surprised all three women when she spoke.

"Did you ask Aunt Bessie and Aunt Rose, Mom?"

The adults looked at Maggie in confusion, each wondering what Maggie knew about her mother's plans. Maggie shook her head.

"Mom, you've been here all this time, and you didn't ask Aunt Bessie and Aunt Rose to come to supper tomorrow night. I thought that's why we came here. You haven't much of a memory, have you? So, I guess I'll do the inviting. Mom, Pop, and me all think it's time someone else cooked you a meal, and that's going to be Mom and me. We want you to come to supper tomorrow. Mom's a good cook, and I'm helping make a dessert."

Laughter met Maggie's announcement and agreement from Bessie and Rose that they'd love to sample both Angela's and Maggie's cooking.

"That's great, and Mom, I was just talking to Theresa and Nell Martin. Did you know their grandfather has loads of raspberries growing in his garden? They're leaving now to pick some, and they asked me to go with them. Aunt Bessie, could I borrow a dipper, so I don't have to go all the way home?"

"Of course, you can, and you can also have a small bucket. The girls are not wrong when they say their grandfather, Pat Martin, has loads of raspberries, and he encourages people to pick them. At least once each summer, I pick raspberries in Pat's garden to make jam, and they are always big and sweet."

As Maggie ran down the path, Bessie told Angela that Theresa Martin was Maggie's age, and they would be in the same grade at school while Nell was two years younger.

"It's good to see Maggie has several friends here, and she has the freedom to go to different places. I couldn't allow her to do that in Toronto, but now while she is busy, I'm going home to talk to Dad and tell him what I'd like to do. Thanks for everything you have done, and are still doing, for Maggie and me. One of these days, I'll pay you back," Angela said on her way out.

Later that evening, Rose was surprised to see Angela parking Gabe's truck at the bottom of the driveway. She called out to Bessie, asking if she was expecting Angela to return.

When Angela appeared, and it was evident she had been crying, Bessie's first thought was something was wrong.

"What is it, Angela? I can see you're upset about something. Did you discuss your plans with your father?"

When a still upset-looking Angela answered yes, Bessie thought their talk must have ended in disagreement.

"I came back to tell you I am definitely going to Toronto, and Maggie is staying with Dad. I could have phoned and told you this, but I needed to get out of the house."

Angela said she had been driving around thinking about everything that was happening. In particular, she was mulling over the conversation with her father. Bessie's heart sank. She had believed Gabe would support Angela's decision, and he would also love having Maggie stay in Mark's Point. But it appeared as if something was wrong.

"After I told Dad I needed to make changes and was considering going back to school, he said he was glad I was finally coming to my senses. But it was what he said next that probably brought me to my senses more than anything else," Angela said through her tears.

"He told me whatever money he had was mine, and he would also send me more each month. That way, I wouldn't have to work and could go to school full time, and Maggie and I would have a decent place to stay without worrying about money.

"Can you imagine how I felt? All Dad has ever wanted was for Maggie and me to stay in Mark's Point. Yet, he was willing to give us his savings to go back to Toronto because he believed it was what I wanted. Why would Dad be willing to do this when I have been so thankless and mean to him? I've been so stupid not to realize how much he cares for us. That's why I am upset and why I've been driving around trying to get my head around everything."

Angela went on to say she had no intention of taking her father's hard-earned savings. Still, after much discussion, she and Gabe had finally agreed he would buy her a return air ticket and give her enough money to cover two month's board.

"By that time, I should be in school, have a job, and able to pay my way. You can probably guess that Maggie is beside herself with delight, knowing she can attend school here. More importantly, she understands why I am returning to Toronto alone. I think she's proud I'm going back to school.

"As for Dad, once I told him all my plans, I don't think I ever saw him so happy and contented. He's going to love having Maggie. He also said I should consider going on to university when I get my high school diploma, and in case I didn't know, Memorial University has a wonderful reputation."

"And he is right. MUN is an excellent university, and it offers a wide choice of degree programs. It is certainly something to think about because a high school diploma is only a start. You'll need further education or training to get ahead," Rose said.

"You gave me a fright when you arrived, Angela," Bessie said.

"I thought for a second you had disagreed with your father again and changed your mind. Thank goodness I was wrong. Knowing you and Gabe are finally at peace and in agreement is wonderful news.

"Now, after all this excitement, I need a cup of tea. Why don't you stay and have one with us, Angela? You'll be returning to Toronto soon, so let's take this opportunity to enjoy a cup of tea and a chat together.

CHAPTER 15

Returning Friends

Rose had just left Martin House to attend choir practice in the church when Bessie answered a knock on the door and greeted Mina.

"Come on in, Mina. It's good to see you again," Bessie said.

"The kettle is on, and when I pour up our tea, we'll go out to the sun porch and enjoy this lovely evening. It's only early August, but already we can see the difference in the amount of daylight we have. We should take advantage of it while we can."

"That's for sure. School opens next month, and before we know it, the weather will change. It was good to hear from you this morning. I didn't know if Rose intended having choir practice until yesterday when Father Kiely called the girls saying it was going ahead, and he would pick us up."

"That's why I phoned to make sure you knew I was expecting you. Now let's go through to the front of the house where we can relax. Tell me, how did the girls like their first choir practice?"

Mina smiled as she told Bessie the girls had enjoyed it and were excited about that night's practice.

"They haven't started singing in church yet, but I understand Father is hoping a few more adults and teenagers from St. Peter's Church will show up for practice tonight. He thinks if more people come, they'll get enough confidence to sing without music," Mina replied.

"The girls are also pleased because Maggie phoned, inviting them to meet her mother after choir practice. Isabelle can't wait for school to start since Maggie told her she was staying. They've been on the phone these last two days talking about different school subjects and choosing what activities they want to do during lunch hour. I know Maggie is happy to be going to school here, but it won't be easy for her or her mother to be separated."

Bessie explained Angela was returning to Toronto to improve her education, and although they would be apart, both Angela and Maggie realized how important this was for their future.

"Maggie may only be 13, but she's a wise child. She'll miss her mother, but she's proud of what Angela is doing. You probably know Angela left school when she was in grade 10 and took off for the mainland. Her lack of education meant little chance of decent employment. Now she can upgrade her education with the full support of her father and daughter. Gabe and Maggie have always had a close relationship, and he's a happy man knowing she is staying in Mark's Point."

"I remember hearing about Angela running away, and when Chrissie left, it brought it all back to me. I realized then how Gabe must have felt years earlier. Chrissie left with my blessing, and I knew she was in good hands, but it was still hard letting her go. I often thought of Gabe at that time. It had to be a nightmare for him, not knowing where Angela was or what she was doing."

Mina bringing up Chrissie's name gave Bessie the opening to ask about her oldest daughter. She knew most of Mina's story but didn't understand why Chrissie left home before graduating from high school.

When Bessie voiced this question, Mina said there was plenty of speculation when Chrissie left school and home. Their close friends knew where Chrissie went, but not her grandmother or her family.

"After I had the blazing row with Herbert and his mother, I thought things might improve for the entire family, but as the days passed, I began to worry about Chrissie. My once happy daughter, who loved school, began making excuses to stay at home and didn't want to go outdoors in the evenings or on weekends," Mina recalled.

Unknown to Mina, her mother-in-law was terrorizing Chrissie. When she realized she could no longer intimidate Mina, she decided to target Chrissie instead. She would watch for her granddaughter and threaten her with all kinds of terrible things. Not content with bullying Chrissie, Herbert's mother began telling people that she was a thief.

"I later discovered she was going around saying that anyone who'd steal from their father was capable of cheating in school, that it was no wonder Chrissie kept getting high marks."

Although Mina realized her daughter was unusually quiet, it wasn't until her mother-in-law tried spreading lies to the wrong person that she discovered why.

"Mrs. Abby Lynch, Nan Lynch's sister-in-law, had also been Nan's closest friend. It was Mrs. Abby who witnessed Nan's will, and after Nan's death, she not only was a good friend to me, she always took an interest in my girls. When my mother-in-law visited her and said Chrissie was a thief, Mrs. Abby was furious and told her to leave the house. Then she phoned, asking Chrissie and me to come and see her."

Mina recalled how upset she was to hear what Mrs. Abby had to say and realized why Chrissie was upset and withdrawn.

"How could a woman say such things about any young girl, let alone her granddaughter? When Chrissie broke down, saying she was afraid of her grandmother, I was upset for her and furious at my mother-in-law. Chrissie also worried that her teachers and friends might believe she was a thief and a cheat. To see Chrissie crying so pitifully, saying she couldn't go back to school, was heartbreaking."

The worst thing, Mina recalled, was hearing her say she would do what her grandmother wanted, leave home, and go to work, anything to get out of Murphy's Cove South.

"I knew then I had to do something before Chrissie made herself sick with worry."

Determined to stop the harassment, Mina was ready to do battle with her mother-in-law. It took a great deal of persuasion from Mrs. Abby before Mina agreed to wait until the following day before confronting Herbert's mother. She needed a cool head, Mrs. Abby told her, but unknown to Mina, her elderly neighbour was also looking for ways to help Chrissie. She had already enlisted help from her cousin Millicent Murphy, and they were determined to find a long-term solution to stop the bullying and lies.

"The following morning, Mrs. Abby called, asking if I would come to her house before doing anything else. I was surprised to see Millicent there and remember wondering who was looking after the shop because it was rare to see her outside her business or community. They told me not to worry about Chrissie; her problems would soon be over."

To ensure there would be no more trouble from Herbert or his mother, Millicent had contacted her son Andy, an RCMP officer in Ontario. Andy then called his friend, Constable Jackson, at the local RCMP detachment. When he heard what had been happening, the constable immediately agreed to visit Mina's mother-in-law.

"I'd never have thought of contacting Constable Jackson, but he turned out to be the right person for what needed doing. He not only put the fear of God into my mother-in-law for spreading lies and slander, he laid down the law to Herbert, telling him he had no legal right to Chrissie's wages. I knew Herbert would be furious, and that had me worried because he's the type who would take his rage out on Chrissie, even if it meant waiting for months to do so."

But knowing her mother-in-law must now stay away from Chrissie was a relief, and it gave Mina hope that her daughter would gradually return to her natural happy self. Mrs. Abby and Millicent weren't so sure. They believed Chrissie needed to get away from her father and grandmother and offered a solution that Mina received with mixed feelings.

Mrs. Abby spent winters in Nova Scotia with her widowed daughter Ellen, a nurse. Ellen worked nights and worried about leaving her elderly mother alone in the house when she was nursing. She had considered offering free accommodation to a university student to provide her mother company and be there in an emergency.

"Until then, Mrs. Abby had rejected the idea of sharing the house with a stranger, but Chrissie was like a family member. The elderly woman was leaving for Nova Scotia the following week and wanted Chrissie to go with her. Ellen thought it was a great idea, as did Millicent, who said not only did Chrissie need to get away from home for a while, it would give Ellen peace of mind knowing Chrissie would stay with her mother."

Although Mina knew it was the fresh start Chrissie needed after the weeks of hell she had endured, it was a difficult decision to make. Mrs. Abby suggested Chrissie attend school in Halifax until Christmas. If she enjoyed her new school, she could finish grade X1 in Nova Scotia after spending Christmas at home with her family.

"I was torn, knowing it was a wonderful opportunity for Chrissie. She knew and liked Mrs. Abby and also Ellen, who spent all her holidays at home. I thought about it all that day, and by the time Chrissie came home from school, I was convinced it was the best possible solution. The younger girls and I would miss her, but it was the opportunity Chrissie needed. She would be worry-free, living with people who cared for her and who would provide the peace she needed to live and study," said Mina.

After weeks of stress, Chrissie was only too glad to leave Murphy's Cove South. Once in Halifax, she thrived in her new home and school and was happy to stay. Ellen planned to give her a return airline ticket to go home for Christmas, but when Mrs. Abby suffered a stroke in early December, Chrissie remained in Nova Scotia to help Ellen and the elderly lady.

Mina didn't see Chrissie for almost a year. Mrs. Abby was too feeble to come home the following summer, and Chrissie stayed in Halifax, allowing Ellen to continue working. From the time Chrissie moved to Nova Scotia, Ellen had insisted on giving her a weekly allowance in gratitude for all her help. Unknown to Chrissie, Ellen and her mother were also banking money in the young girl's name to allow her to attend university after high school graduation. That September, Chrissie registered at Dalhousie University. A month later, Mrs. Abby died, leaving enough money to pay all Chrissie's university expenses until graduation. Ellen, who never had children of her own, urged Chrissie to stay with her until she completed her degree.

"Going to Halifax was the best thing that could have happened to Chrissie, but not because of the money. It was because Mrs. Abby and Ellen gave Chrissie a new start. They were wonderful friends to our family."

It was evident just how proud Mina was of her oldest daughter, who would graduate the following May with a Business degree.

"I've been saving my quilt money for over a year to get Chrissie a good graduation present. Maybe I'll get a briefcase or something she might need when she begins work. I want it to be something special because I know

Chrissie won't get anything from her father. He never asks about her, and when she comes home on holiday, he completely ignores her. Meanwhile, my younger girls have never forgotten that he struck Chrissie. They are afraid of him and avoid him when possible. It's a terrible way for children to feel about their father, but he brought it on himself."

"But why didn't you tell people where Chrissie went? Why let her be the topic of rumours?" Bessie asked

It was the same question Rose asked Bessie later that night when the two women discussed the actions that led up to Chrissie going to Nova Scotia.

"Mina told me Chrissie's leaving was never intended to be kept secret. Mrs. Abby's neighbours knew she was returning to Halifax with her daughter Ellen, but at the time, not many may have known Chrissie was going with her. Chrissie was scared her father or grandmother might try to stop her and begged her mother not to tell them. Herbert was fishing the morning they left, and it was three days before he even noticed his daughter was missing. When he asked where she was, and Mina told him Chrissie had left home, he replied, 'Good riddance.' Mina told me she has never spoken Chrissie's name to him since that day."

When Chrissie began writing letters home, she sent her mail to Millicent Murphy, who ran the post office from her shop in Murphy's Cove. She or her niece, who helped in the office and shop, never let Herbert know about the correspondence. In the same way, Mina wouldn't give her sister-in-law, the Murphy's Cove South postmistress, the satisfaction of knowing where Chrissie had gone and never posted mail in the local post office.

"Most people in Murphy's Cove South soon knew where Chrissie was living and attending school, but aware of the treatment she received from her father and his family; it was as if there was an unwritten rule not to discuss Chrissie with any of them. The grandmother and her daughters could only speculate, not knowing where she was, which led to different rumours. They probably didn't realize she was in Halifax until almost a year later when Chrissie accompanied Ellen home for Mrs. Abby's funeral."

"It's good to know Chrissie is doing well. There will be no prouder mother or sisters than Mina and the girls when Chrissie graduates. What about Katy? Is she planning to attend university when she finishes grade X1 next June?" Rose asked.

"No, I asked Mina about Katy's plans, and she wants to be a nurse. She is applying to St. Clare's Hospital and the Grace General, hoping to train as a registered nurse. Ellen offered to pay her way to Halifax for training, but she wants to stay in Newfoundland."

"And what about Mina's brute of a husband? What kind of life do Mina and the girls have with him now? You know, this makes me think of Philly Moss. Although he's an old fool and had all the wrong motives, he had the right idea in one way. There should be annulments for people like Mina. She shouldn't have to live with that man for the rest of her life."

"I completely agree with you, and I asked Mina why she stayed with him. She says she has no intention of leaving her home, but I would say when Isabelle finishes high school, Mina won't stay long in Murphy's Cove South."

Bessie added no doubt that Herbert would love Mina to leave.

"He's told people if Mina moves out, she'll never be able to sell the house because he's no intention of leaving his home. He says she'd have to go to court to evict him. But Mina is no fool, and I'm sure if, or when, she leaves, she'll have taken steps to make sure he doesn't get the house."

"Proper thing," Rose said.

"By the sound of things, Mina and the girls don't have much of a life with him around. What you said about the younger girls being afraid of him is evident. Just look at how they act in their home compared to how relaxed they are here or choir practice. I'm also guessing Mina doesn't want him knowing how many quilts she sells or how much she gets paid for them."

Bessie said Mina apologized for the girls meeting her in the road with the quilt. Herbert had arrived home unexpectedly, and she couldn't use the phone without him knowing what she said or planned. Because she kept her finished quilts in the girls' room, she managed to put the quilt in a pillowcase without him noticing. He was oblivious to Katy and Isabelle leaving the house, carrying the quilt under a folded coat.

Mina said she would never invite anyone into her home if there a chance of Herbert arriving unexpectedly. He was fishing the day Rose and Bessie brought Sue to buy the quilts. Even so, she said, her girls were always nervous when anyone came to their house. They would never think of asking friends to visit.

"What a terrible way to live," Rose said.

"It makes me so mad when I think of that awful man and his mother. I wonder what causes people to be that way, but let's forget about him and talk about something else before I get even more furious.

"You heard Father Kiely say how pleased he was that so many people turned up at choir practice. We had more than two dozen, but of course, almost half were from the Murphy's Cove area. It would be great to have that many in one choir, but I can't complain; we are doing well with numbers and talent for our choir."

Rose went on to say how Maggie met three girls at choir practice who would be in the same grade when she began school. One, Susie Howell, from Mark's Landing, would travel on the same school bus, and the other two lived in Murphy's Cove. However, with two grade eight classes, it was possible that they, Maggie, Isabelle, or Theresa Martin, would be in a separate classroom.

"I also heard the girls saying two school buses will pick up students from here, Mark's Landing, Muddy Brook Cove, and finally Murphy's Cove South. One is for the younger children going to the new elementary school and the other for high school students. The twins said it was a good job that there were two buses, that it was bad enough having Bobby on their bus, without having to put up with their little sisters."

All thoughts of Mina, choir, or school were put on hold when the phone rang. When Bessie went to answer it, Rose began clearing away the dishes. It was several minutes before a smiling Bessie returned, saying someone wanted to speak to Rose. Answering the hall telephone, Rose was pleasantly surprised to hear Sue Newman.

"Hi, Rose. I asked Bessie not to tell you why I'm calling. I wanted to be the one to tell you that Bob and I are returning for another holiday. Bob has never stopped talking about Mark's Point since we left. We told you we would come back, but we're not waiting until next summer. You'll see us next month, and this time we're flying to St. John's and renting a car. We're staying for ten days if I don't drive you crazy before that," an excited Sue said.

Rose barely got a chance to answer, saying it was great news when Sue began talking again. She never thought she'd get Bob to agree to return so soon, but when he finished a large project, he decided it was perfect timing. He planned to phone Gabe with the news after Sue finished her call with Rose.

"I guess Maggie will soon be going back to Toronto. Do you know we got the loveliest letter from her thanking us for the birthday card? You'd have thought we gave her a fortune instead of just $20, but it was so nice to hear from her. It's too bad that we will miss her. Hopefully, we'll see her next summer," said Sue.

When Rose told her Maggie was staying and attending school in Murphy's Cove, Sue was delighted, saying Gabe must be a happy man, but wouldn't Maggie miss her mother? Rose explained that Angela had decided to upgrade her education, and both Maggie and Gabe were pleased and proud of her decision. Sue was glad, saying it appeared to work out well for everyone. She would look forward to seeing Maggie again.

"Fancy Sue and Bob, returning so soon. I knew they planned to return, but I never expected it would be this year. It will be nice seeing them. I also forgot to tell Sue that David and Sharon are going to be living in Mark's Point," Rose said.

"Yes. and moving in some of their furniture in a few days. Gabe plans to hook up their water tomorrow. He says there should be no problems with the pump or water lines because he had the water running before you agreed to rent the house."

"Although they're not staying with us, I'm looking forward to seeing them. I wish I felt the same way about our guests who arrive that day."

"Nonsense Bessie, I'm sure everything will go well. We've worried about guests before now, and things always turned out fine. There's no reason why it should be any different this time."

Famous last words. Rose didn't hear the condescending way the woman spoke.

Deciding not to harp on the subject and worry her sister-in-law, Bessie decided to keep her thoughts to herself.

Three days later, she knew her feeling of unease had been right when Martin House's latest guests arrived. A tall, angular woman was first out of the car and looked at the house with a distinct frown on her face. In contrast, a much shorter and rounder man and woman, beaming with delight, admired their surroundings.

"Wonderful! Doesn't this make a beautiful picture, Beatrice, my dear?" the jolly-looking man, who had to be the bishop, asked.

"Yes, we are so lucky, Clarence, to find ourselves in such delightful surroundings. Good afternoon ladies, how nice to meet you. Are you the lucky people who live here and operate Martin House? I'm Beatrice Harris. This is my husband, Bishop Clarence, and my sister-in-law Penelope Harris. We are all so happy to be here. We've never visited this part of Newfoundland before, and I, for one, am so looking forward to exploring it."

"Welcome to Martin House. We are equally pleased to have you stay with us. I'm Rose Martin, and this is my sister-in-law Bessie who owns this lovely home."

Still apprehensive, although doing her best to appear welcoming, Bessie greeted them and invited them indoors. As they entered the kitchen, she asked her guests if they'd like to have a cup of tea or coffee.

The bishop and his wife beamed and agreed a cup of tea would hit the spot. Penelope, looking disdainful, asked whether they would be drinking their tea in the kitchen? Before Rose or Bessie could reply, Mrs. Harris quickly intervened, saying she couldn't imagine a more homely and welcoming room to enjoy their tea.

Seeing Bessie's expression, Rose decided to take over the conversation.

"You are welcome to have tea here or the sun porch where you can relax and enjoy the view. We also give our guests the choice of eating breakfast in the dining room or the kitchen. Meanwhile, while we are waiting for the kettle to boil, why don't I show you the rooms we have given you?"

Returning from showing the guests to their rooms, Rose managed a quick word with Bessie.

"The bishop and his wife couldn't be any nicer, but if that Penelope sniffs or puts on that superior air one more time, I'll have a fit. Her room wasn't what she expected; she thought the bathroom would be more modern, then she asked if the sheets were linen? And what did Mark's Point or any of the communities around here have to offer?

"Thank goodness Bishop Harris and his wife are completely different. I guess you were right, Bessie; we could very well be in for a rough few days if Penelope Harris doesn't change her attitude," Rose admitted.

"And here was I, thinking it could be worse. We could have had a return visit from Philly Moss. Too bad he wasn't here when she arrived. He might have convinced her to keep house for him while his wife Jean is on holiday," a laughing Bessie said.

"But seriously, I keep reminding myself she's only here for a few days, and now we can stop waiting for a problem guest because it appears as if we finally have one. I've taken out some cake and scones; why don't you set the table."

Bishop and Mrs. Harris came into the kitchen full of appreciation for their accommodations a few minutes later.

"What a beautiful home you have. Thank you for giving us that lovely room at the front with a stunning view. We'll look forward to getting up tomorrow morning and seeing the boats in the harbour, won't we, Beatrice, my love."

"There's no harbour view from my bedroom window," said a querulous voice from the doorway.

Bessie quickly responded to Penelope Harris, feeling it was time to nip any more complaints in the bud.

"Yes, it's too bad you requested the downstairs bedroom. Your room is part of an addition built onto our home to accommodate my in-laws. My husband built the addition at the back because the sun porch took up all the front of the house. However, my husband's parents were always so apprecia-tive, and I never did hear them complain. They enjoyed seeing the hills and church from their bedroom window."

"And speaking of churches, do you think we would be able to visit your beautiful church before we leave? Bishop Clarence and I were admiring it when we drove past. How old is it?" Mrs. Harris asked, quickly changing the subject.

"The first mass held in the church was on 'Lady's Day,' August 15, 1897, making it 74 years old next week. Our parish priest, Father Kiely, thinks we should plan a celebration next year on the 75th anniversary."

"My goodness, that is a milestone. I thought 50 years was good. That's the anniversary St. Michael's Church in Murphy's Cove celebrates on Tuesday. However, this evening, we are travelling to Freeman's Beach for a potluck supper with parishioners of Christ Church. Reverend and Mrs. Paul will stop by and lead us there by car. Is it alright to give him a quick phone call and let him know we are here and what time we should be ready? I'll pay you for the telephone call."

"There's no cost to call Murphy's Cove from here, Bishop. The communities in this area are on the one exchange, so feel free to call whenever you want," Bessie replied.

It was just after four o'clock when a knock came at Martin House's door. Rose, who answered, was taken by surprise when greeted with a question.

"Hello, are you Bessie the wonderful cook, or are you Rose the musical genius? Father Kiely has told us all about Martin House's women. I'm Raymond Paul, and this is my wife, Linda. I hope you don't mind us dropping by. We are here to meet up with Bishop and Mrs. Harris."

Slightly taken aback, Rose replied, "I am Rose, and although I play the organ, I'm sure if you ever heard me, you would soon realize I'm no musical genius."

Inviting them in, Rose led them through to the kitchen, where she introduced the couple to Bessie.

"Before my husband puts his foot in his mouth, as usual, let me tell you it's our pleasure to meet you. Father Kiely is a good friend of ours, and he has great praise for you two ladies. It's thanks to him we heard of Martin House. We have three small children, which made our home not the most suitable place to accommodate the bishop and his wife."

"Why Linda would worry about me putting my foot in my mouth, I'm sure I don't know," the young minister said, trying unsuccessfully to look serious.

Just then, Penelope Harris entered the kitchen. Ignoring the Pauls, she addressed Bessie, asking if she had any other brand of hand soap.

"I find cheaper brands of soap are bad for my skin. I should have brought my soap. I might have known my brand was unavailable in a backward place like this."

"That's the only brand we have in the house, but you can try Kavanagh's shop just up the road and see what they have. Other than that, I am afraid we can't help you, Ms. Harris."

With a disapproving sniff, the demanding guest turned on her heel and marched out of the kitchen, leaving Reverend and Mrs. Paul looking aghast.

"If that is the bishop's wife, I'm glad they are not staying with us. You handled that much better than I could, Mrs. Martin. You didn't seem one bit upset or annoyed," Linda Paul said.

"In our business, we can't afford to get annoyed, but that wasn't Mrs. Harris. The bishop and his wife are lovely people and very appreciative of everything. That was Ms. Harris, the bishop's sister."

The words were no sooner out of her mouth when a voice came from the doorway.

"I'm sorry I couldn't help overhearing you, but truthfully, Penelope is not always so abrasive and insensitive as she is acting recently. I can't discuss her personal business; all I can say is she has been ill and is an unhappy person. Please accept my apologies on behalf of my family. I will have a word with my sister."

Turning to the young minister and his wife, Bishop Harris then introduced himself.

"And you must be Reverend and Mrs. Paul. I have been looking forward to meeting you and the people of your parish. You are lucky people living in such a beautiful part of our province."

Reverend and Mrs. Paul quickly reacted to the bishop's words, welcoming him to the parish and adding how his parishioners were pleased and excited about the visit. By the time Mrs. Harris and her sister-in-law were ready, the two clergymen had their schedule arranged. The women would drive with Mrs. Paul to the church hall where parishioners were preparing supper while the men would first visit an elderly housebound couple.

When the two cars left for Freeman's Beach, Rose sighed with relief.

"They said to expect them back around 9.30, so we can relax for a while. I wonder how many complaints Miss Harris will have by then? Fancy her asking if we had a different soap. I had a mind to produce a bar of Sunlight Soap and tell her to try that. If it's good enough to scrub away dirt, it might remove her sour look. 'An unhappy person' is how Bishop Harris described her. I could think of other descriptions that might fit her better."

As Rose gave vent to her frustration, Bessie suddenly stood up, saying, "Listen, is that them coming back? I'm sure I heard something."

From the back porch came sounds of laughter, and the door opened to reveal Sharon and David.

"We were coming in earlier until we saw you had visitors, and then we saw a minister and a woman stopping by your bottom gate. You must have several guests, but do you have an hour or more to spare before they return?" Sharon asked the women.

"We have three guests, the Anglican Bishop, his wife, and his sister. Reverend and Mrs. Paul were here to guide them to Freeman's Beach, where their parish is hosting a potluck supper tonight," answered Bessie.

With that, Sharon started laughing again.

"That is a coincidence. We're here to invite the pair of you to a potluck supper in your family home. Mother also drove her car and brought a load of our things, and between us, I'm sure we also brought enough cooked food for an army. We want the pair of you to be our first dinner guests. What do you say?"

"I say yes on behalf of both of us. Truthfully, I think it's just what we need. Don't you agree, Rose?" Bessie asked.

"I most certainly do. I not only agree, but I would also say you have perfect timing because right now, we could both use a break from the business."

CHAPTER 16

Baking Lessons

August 10th had been a long time coming for Daisy and Marigold Brown. It was more than a week since their first visit to Martin House, and keeping a secret for all that time was extremely difficult for the young sisters. Today, they would begin making a birthday gift for their mother, one they knew for sure would surprise everyone in their family.

Their long-anticipated baking lesson was finally here, and the two excited girls wearing large aprons rolled up to fit had already helped Bessie measure ingredients and were now ready for the next step.

"Is this it, Mrs. Bessie? Is this the right stuff in the bowl to make the cream? It don't look like the cream I puts on my rolled oats," six-year-old Daisy said, inspecting the contents of her bowl.

"It's not cream like milk, Daisy. You knows what Mom always says, 'Listen and learn,' and Mrs. Bessie already said it's not that kind of cream," Marigold, who was one year older, replied.

"And do you know what my mother used to say," a smiling Bessie asked as she was showing the sisters how to measure ingredients.

"She'd say, there's no such thing as a stupid question. Don't worry about asking questions because that's how you learn. You are two smart young girls, and I can imagine how proud your mother will be when she sees her birthday cake and discovers you made it yourselves."

"Not all by ourselves, Mrs. Bessie. You're helping us a lot. Did your mother show you how to make cakes? You wasn't born in Mark's Point, was you Mrs. Bessie? Did people make cherry cakes where you comes from?" Daisy asked.

"Mrs. Bessie comes from War, that's over the sea. I learned that when Mr. Alex died. I heard Great Uncle Walt say that Mrs. Bessie and Mr. Alex met in War, and he was the best man at your wedding over the sea. Great Uncle Walt and Mr. Alex was sailors. Isn't that right, Mrs. Bessie?"

Rose came into the kitchen in time to hear Bessie explaining to Marigold that war wasn't a place and that she came overseas from Scotland after meeting Alex during World War 11.

"I guess you'll be giving geography and history lessons in addition to baking lessons this morning, Bessie," a smiling Rose said.

"Sorry, I don't want to interrupt your baking. The Bishop and Mrs. Harris finished their breakfast and have gone upstairs, but Ms. Harris was a bit later joining them in the dining room and is still eating. I told her I'd get her a fresh cup of tea," Rose explained as she moved the kettle over on the stove to boil.

"Do you see our stuff for the cake, Miss Rose? We're going to make some cream. Mrs. Bessie said we're doing a good job, didn't you, Mrs.Bessie? Wait 'til we decorates it tomorrow. Mom is going to be some surprised, and so is the twins. The twins thinks we can't do nothing, but we'll show them, won't we, Daisy?"

Just then, a voice came from the doorway.

"Oh, sorry, Mrs. Martin, we didn't realize you had company, but we are on our way outdoors. We decided to take a walk around the community before we leave for lunch in Murphy's Cove. Well, who do you have here? Look at these two busy little bakers, Bishop Clarence. What are you baking, young ladies?"

To Rose and Bessie's surprise, there was absolute silence. The usually talkative youngsters appeared frozen in time as they looked at the bishop and his wife.

"These are the Brown sisters, Daisy and Marigold. Girls, this is Bishop Harris and his wife, Mrs. Harris. Do you think you could tell them what you are baking? I know they won't tell anyone about it."

After Bessie spoke, Daisy and Marigold turned to each other and held a whispered conversation before Daisy finally said.

"It's a cake for our Mom's birthday tomorrow. Our Mom is getting a new baby before Christmas, and she never makes a cake for herself. Mrs. Bessie is helping us, and it's going to be a cherry cake."

"What a wonderful thing to do," Bishop Harris told them.

"You are two good girls to think of your mother. Do you have any more brothers and sisters?"

Marigold looked slightly puzzled as she told him about the twins and Bobby and then decided to ask the question on her mind.

"Is you really a bishop?"

When Bishop Harris smiled and said yes, Marigold had another question for him.

"Then how come you wasn't in our church when the twins got confirmed last year? And how come you're married and priests don't have wives? Father Kiely don't have a wife; he's not allowed to be married. That's what Mom said, right, Daisy?"

The four adults looked at each other, wondering not only how to answer Marigold's questions but who would try to explain the difference between an Anglican and a Catholic bishop.

The answer came from an unexpected source. Penelope Harris had entered the kitchen carrying her cup for a refill when she heard Marigold.

"It also used to confuse me until I learned there were two kinds of bishops, Anglicans and Roman Catholics. Bishop Harris is an Anglican bishop, and Anglican priests and bishops can marry. Your bishop is Roman Catholic, just like you, and he and your priests choose not to marry. Your bishop takes care of Confirmation in your church, and Bishop Harris looks after Confirmation in Anglican churches." Miss Harris said, giving the girls a lovely smile.

Bessie and Rose looked at each other in astonishment. Was this the same woman who had been so ungracious since her arrival?

They had another surprise when their guest walked over to the girls, introduced herself as Penny, and began asking questions about the cake. All thoughts of bishops and priests vanished from the girls' minds as they quickly responded, picking up and showing Miss Harris the ingredients and the cake pan they planned to use while chatting nonstop to their new friend.

Bessie moved away from the table to allow her guest access to the girls but had another surprise when Daisy spoke.

"Mrs. Bessie, Penny don't know how to make cakes, and we told her you could learn her just like us."

When Bessie said Miss Harris had come into the kitchen for a cup of tea and wouldn't want to get flour all over her nice clothes, Daisy was quick to respond.

"You could give her one of your aprons like you gave us."

Bessie smiled, wondering how Miss Harris would get out of this situation, and had another surprise when her guest looked almost wistfully from the girls to the cake ingredients.

"Maybe I could watch. I promise not to get in your way, but I'd love to see the girls make their cake. We won't be leaving yet, will we, Beatrice?"

Her sister-in-law, who appeared to be having difficulty finding words, nodded her head.

"We have all the time in the world, Penny. We planned to take a walk around the community before leaving for Murphy's Cove."

"If that's what you want, Miss Harris. Then not only can you watch, but we could also use your help. But first, we'll take Daisy's advice and get you an apron," Bessie said.

Bessie hadn't noticed their two other guests' reactions, but as they left the kitchen, she wondered if her imagination was playing tricks on her. The Bishop and his wife were smiling, but at the same time, their eyes looked moist.

Shaking her head at her foolishness, she turned to the girls.

"Let's see where we are. Daisy has the butter and sugar in the bowl, ready for creaming. I told the girls earlier that creaming was once hard work. That's because we used a wooden spoon to beat the butter and sugar. Then several years ago, Rose bought me this electric mixer as a birthday gift. It is one of the handiest and most time-saving things I ever had.

"While I use the mixer, the three of you can work together on the most necessary ingredient, the cherries. A cherry cake must have cherries, so why don't you begin cutting them up? I've several knives and, although they're not sharp, they are good enough to cut cherries. If you girls kneel on your chairs by the table and Miss Harris either sits or stands, I'll show you how small the cherries should be, and then the three of you can get to work."

"How come you don't call Penny by her name?" Daisy asked Bessie.

To Bessie's amazement, Miss Harris spoke up.

"Yes, please call me Penny. Do you know I have never made a cake before? This is so much fun."

Bessie, still amazed by the total change in their difficult guest, could only nod in agreement.

The butter and sugar were perfectly creamed a few minutes later, and Bessie shut off the mixer. While the beaters were on high speed, she had been observing the others who, even while chopping away, still managed to keep a conversation going. The mixer's noise prevented her from hearing what was said, and Bessie wondered what they found in common to keep them talking. She soon found out.

"Mrs. Bessie, Penny is some smart. Me and Daisy knowed you since we were babies, but we only learned that you were born in Scotland this morning. Penny guessed you was from Scotland right away, and we never even told her. She says she can tell by the way you talks."

Looking embarrassed, Penny apologized, saying the topic arose when the little girls praised Bessie's baking skills.

"I told them I had a Scottish friend who was also an excellent cook, and perhaps it was a skill many Scottish people had. When the girls asked how I knew you were Scottish, I told them I recognized your accent, explaining that meant the way you talked."

"If your friend was a war bride, I might know her. I came by ship to Halifax and then by train and ferry to Newfoundland with other war brides, and I've kept in touch with several of them," Bessie said.

"Morag is not a war bride. She originally came from Edinburgh but lives in Africa now. We worked there together for more than 20 years," was Penny's surprising reply.

"You was in Africa? There's elephants and a jungle in Africa. Was you really there, Penny?" an amazed-looking Marigold asked.

"I didn't live in the jungle, but I saw lots of wild animals when I travelled through Africa. But I can tell you about it later after you get your mother's cake made."

"That's a good idea. Once we get everything mixed together, and the cake in the oven, Penny and I will enjoy a cup of tea while you girls have a glass of milk. Maybe then you will tell us all about Africa and what kind of work you did. Would you do that, Penny?"

"Certainly, but how many more cherries do we need to chop."

"We need two cups of cut cherries, and you have more than half that amount done. While you continue, I'll beat three eggs."

Half an hour later, the cake was in the oven, while the kitchen and the young helpers were once again flour-free. Rose, who kept busy with chores while the others prepared the cake, was back in the kitchen with the tea ready when Daisy addressed her.

"Miss Rose, did you know Penny lived in Africa, and she's going to tell us all about it, isn't you, Penny?"

Rose laughed, believing Daisy had mixed up her facts when she noticed Bessie standing behind their guest, nodding her head as if warning her not to say anything.

"Yes, and as soon as we pour up tea for the women and milk for the girls, Penny will tell us about her time in Africa. But what about trying some scones or squares that Rose and I baked yesterday. We baked them, especially for you girls coming today."

"We'll be here tomorrow as well, Mrs. Bessie. Don't forget; that's Mom's birthday, and we needs to put the icing on her cake."

Once the girls had their fill of baked goods and milk, they settled back in their chairs, waiting for Penny to start talking. When Penny didn't seem in any hurry to speak, Bessie began to wonder if she was having second thoughts.

Marigold must have had the same idea. After a few minutes of silence, she spoke up.

"Have you finished eating yet, Penny? Will you tell us about Africa now?"

When Penny finally spoke, it wasn't about her life in Africa. Instead, she started talking about her childhood.

"When I was a little girl about the same age as you girls, I loved reading and my favourite stories were about foreign lands. My father was a minister, and I was taught as a child to help others and save my pennies to send to the missions. In Sunday School, I learned all about people who worked in foreign lands helping the people there. That's when I began dreaming of becoming a missionary."

"What's a missing, what's a missing Harry, Penny?" Daisy, struggling with the pronunciation of the strange word, asked her new friend.

"A missionary is someone who travels to foreign countries like Africa and works in faraway places where people need help. I was a missionary and worked as a nurse in African villages. At first, I couldn't speak to my patients without having someone who could speak both English and the villager's language. That person is called an interpreter, and he would tell me what was wrong with my patients. He would also explain to my patients what I said and how I planned to help them. The villagers were hard-working people, assisting the missionaries to build schools and clinics in different parts of the country. And the children had beautiful smiles, just like you two girls."

"Was the children sick? Did they get bitten by monkeys or elephants? Did you see other kinds of animals?" was the first of many questions from Daisy.

"Was you scared of the animals in the jungle, and did you see lions?" Marigold wanted to know.

As Penny patiently answered the girls' questions, Bessie, hearing movement in the porch, opened the kitchen door to find Bishop and Mrs. Harris had returned from their walk. The bishop put a finger to his lips as if he didn't want Bessie to speak as his wife beckoned her outdoors.

"What's wrong?" asked an alarmed Bessie when they were outside.

"Nothing's wrong. In fact, things couldn't be better," said Mrs. Harris, who was smiling yet looked almost teary-eyed.

"There's something wrong, I thought I imagined it earlier, but you and your husband are definitely upset. Did something happen while you were walking?"

"No, and truthfully we haven't felt this happy for such a long time. Do you see how Penny talks to the little girls and how she got involved in making the cake with them? It is the breakthrough Clarence and I have been praying for, one we almost gave up hope of ever happening. I know Penny hasn't been the most gracious of guests since she arrived, but that's not the Penny we once knew. She was always a happy, loving, and kind person who, since she was a child, always wanted to be helping others."

Mrs. Harris went on to tell Bessie that Penny was recovering from an illness that began as an infection while she was nursing in Africa. When she became increasingly ill, failing to respond to local treatment, Penny was air-lifted to a Toronto hospital specializing in tropical and infectious diseases. Over the next three months, there were times when it looked as if she would never get better as she lay drifting in and out of consciousness.

"Penny finally recovered, but she will always have side effects from the tropical disease and will never be able to return to her work in Africa. Apart from training as a nurse and returning to Newfoundland every second year on holiday, she had spent her entire adult life in Africa. When Penny heard she could never work there again, she felt her life was over."

Mrs. Harris said that working and living with the poor and sick in Africa was all Penny ever wanted to do.

"Clarence and I visited her at the mission several years ago, and we couldn't believe the harsh conditions in which she lived and worked. But her happiness was so evident, and everyone we met, patients, medical staff, and missionaries, loved and admired her. She was especially good with children, teaching them songs and hymns in what little free time she had. The thought of giving up the life she loved was too much for Penny, who was still very weak from months of illness," Mrs. Harris recalled.

Penny retreated into herself, causing her brother and his wife to worry she might become mentally ill. They tried to get her involved in various activities and brought her places, but nothing seemed to help. It was as if she had given up.

Bishop Clarence finally decided they weren't helping by doing everything for Penny. He told her off, asking what her patients and fellow missionaries would think of her giving up. He said she would land up in a mental hospi-tal if she didn't start doing things for herself. His words got her out of her passive state.

"Unfortunately, the result was the rude, abrasive Penny you witnessed earlier. What we see this morning has given us hope," said Mrs. Harris.

She explained she and her husband were astonished when Penny began speaking to the girls and explaining the differences between bishops. It was the first time she had shown any interest in anything or anyone since her illness. When she appeared eager to join the baking activity, it was like having the Penny they once knew again. Then on their return from walking, they heard Penny talking about Africa.

"We arrived a few minutes before you saw us and didn't come into the kitchen, thinking she might stop talking if we interrupted her. Seeing Peny so involved and talkative made us so happy, and we let our emotions get the better of us. It is the most wonderful thing."

The two women returned to the porch, where the bishop stood by the partially open kitchen door, smiling and wiping his eyes. When they heard Rose speaking, they decided it was time to go back into the kitchen.

"Where were you, Bessie? I was just saying to Miss Harris she should be going into schools and speaking to students about her time in Africa. Daisy and Marigold agree with me. She's kept us completely enthralled with her adventures."

As Penny shook her head, saying it was nothing and people wouldn't be interested in her stories, the girls and Rose vehemently disagreed.

"Believe me; as a former teacher, I know what's interesting and what children would love to hear. You should be talking to them and adults about your years as a missionary and life in Africa. I could contact some of my teaching friends in St. John's, and I'm sure they'd love to have you come and spend time in their classrooms."

"I think that would be a wonderful idea, Penny. You have so much to offer," her brother said.

"And you seem to love working with children," Rose added.

"I guess you're pretty busy, but did you ever consider volunteering with children in the city? I used to help in an after-school program that gives children a safe place to play and study after school. Some of their parents might be working, and the majority were from poorer homes. They took part in different activities. I helped children with their homework while other adults taught crafts. The coordinator hopes to get adult volunteers to offer music, cooking, and woodworking classes this year. It's a wonderful program to keep children off the streets, and it also provides them with a healthy snack."

"You could teach a singing class, or what about first aid classes? And if you went, I wouldn't mind helping too, perhaps in a cooking class or just working in the kitchen preparing snacks. What about it, Penny?" her sister-in-law asked.

"Do you really think I could help, Miss Martin?"

"Of course; you and Mrs. Harris both could. The coordinator Tom Hammond is a friend of mine. I spoke to him when I was recently in St. John's. He said there's an urgent need for more volunteers. Some of the classes he hoped to start may not get off the ground without additional helpers. I could call him and set up a meeting for both of you."

"Yes, I'd like you to call him. I think we would enjoy helping out, don't you think so, Beatrice?" Penny asked, looking for agreement from her sister-in-law.

Mrs. Harris nodded, and her husband, who by now was beaming with pleasure, said, "You never know, maybe I can also help out in some way, although I can't see myself in the kitchen or teaching woodworking."

"It would be nice to make this a family activity. We could all help, and Clarence, you could easily supervise homework. You used to help me with my homework when I was a child. I think this will be good for us," his sister said.

"Good, and before you change your minds, I'll try and contact Tom today. He'll be so happy to have three new volunteers."

"Miss Rose, could we have that in Mark's Point? We wants to learn good stuff like they has in St. John's, don't we, Daisy?"

"Yes, Mrs. Bessie could learn us more baking, and maybe Bobby and Michael could learn to play their guitars. Please, Miss Rose," said an earnest-looking Daisy.

"You never know what might happen later, but talking about baking, has anyone bothered looking at the cake in the oven. It would be a terrible thing if it burned while we were all talking," Rose said with a laugh.

After lunch, when Rose and Bessie were alone and recalled the morning's activities, Penny was their main topic.

"You know how they talk about miracles Rose, well, according to Bishop Harris and his wife, we witnessed one with Penny this morning. And truthfully, I never saw such a transformation in a person."

"When did you start calling her Penny? I almost choked when I heard you address her as Penny, and then to top that, every second word coming from Daisy and Marigold was Penny."

Laughing, Bessie told Rose that their guest insisted they call her the name her family and friends used.

"She turned out to be a nice, friendly person, and it's thanks to the girls she seems to be like her old self. Mrs. Harris said when they knew they were coming to the 50th anniversary of St. Michael's Church, they invited Penny to travel with them, thinking the trip would do her good, but she refused their invitation. Then out of the blue, she told them she had not only changed her mind, she already called and booked her room."

"And you were on the receiving end of that phone call, Bessie. After talking to her, you were sure she'd be a problem, and you were right, at least at the start. Anyway, all's well that ends well, and it looks as if everything will work out for the Harris family from now on. I spoke to Tom Hammond, who is delighted with the prospect of three new volunteers. The Harris's are certainly enthusiastic about helping and will contact him when they get back to town and see when they can start at the drop-in centre."

"And what about the birthday cake? Penny was every bit as proud of it as Marigold and Daisy were. I was starting to think the Harris's would be late for lunch in Murphy's Cove because Penny wanted to see the finished product come out of the oven," answered Bessie.

"They have reason to be proud because the cake looks delicious, but what excuse do the girls have to return here tomorrow and decorate it," Rose asked.

Bessie had arranged that. She had driven the girls back home, checking on the mail and talking to their mother, Kate. A week earlier, the postmistress had agreed her younger daughters could visit that day, but on hearing guests had still been in Martin House, Kate was concerned the girls may have made pests of themselves.

"I said not only were the girls well behaved, but they also made a great impression on our guests, especially Penny, who wanted to see them again. When Kate heard about Penny's stories and how educational they were, she agreed the girls could return tomorrow morning, but only when I promised to make sure they behaved themselves. It's true, Penny wants to see them again, but I couldn't tell Kate that our guest will be helping the girls decorate a birthday cake for her."

The following morning the decorated cake, placed on one of Bessie's good plates, was the centre of attention as the bakers gazed at their finished masterpiece. Also looking on in admiration were Bishop and Mrs. Harris. They had delayed their departure to allow Penny to assist with the icing and finishing touches on the cake.

"Isn't it beautiful, Penny? I bet you're some glad you helped us and Mrs. Bessie make the cake. It's going to be the best present Mom gets for her birthday. Just wait 'til she sees it," Daisy proudly announced.

"You are wonderful girls. Your mother will be delighted when she sees what you made for her. She's a lucky lady to have daughters like you. Now, Penny, we must get on the road as I have a meeting back in town this evening. Thank you, ladies, for your amazing hospitality. It has been a lovely visit, and we also had the most enjoyable time with the people of this parish, which might not have happened if we couldn't stay in Martin House," Bishop Harris said.

With promises to keep in touch, the family left. Penny also promised to look through her African photos and send some to the girls.

"Penny was some nice, wasn't she? And the bishop and his wife too. When we starts school again, I'm going to tell my teacher about the bishop who had a wife," Marigold said.

"I'll tell my teacher as well, and I'll tell her about Penny and Africa. Did you know I start school soon, Mrs. Bessie and Miss Rose? Mom says I'm some lucky, 'cause I'm starting grade one in a brand-new school," Daisy added.

"You are both lucky girls to attend a new, modern school which has a gym and a library, and you will eat your lunch in a proper cafeteria. And you won't have to share your teacher with other grades of students."

"Yes, and Mom says we'll make lots of new friends from other places like Murphy's Cove and Mossy Brook. It's going to be some good, and we'll get to ride the bus to school," an enthusiastic Marigold added.

"How are the girls getting the cake home, Bessie? I know they're big enough to carry it, but they might drop it or rub against it and spoil the icing and decorations. If we drive the girls over, Kate will see us from the office and wonder what we are doing."

"That's all looked after. Girls, why don't you tell Miss Rose what is happening."

"Dad and the twins are cooking supper for Mom's birthday. Mom knows about it, but she don't know what they're cooking. That's going to be a surprise. When the post office closes at three o'clock, Mom is going to visit Aunt Jean in Mark's Landing to let Dad and the twins do the cooking," Marigold told Rose.

"But it's not going to be as good a surprise as the birthday cake. Mrs. Bessie's bringing it over to our house after Mom goes to Aunt Jean's," her younger sister said.

"That's true, and to make sure nothing happens to the big surprise on the way there, maybe Rose, you'll come with me and hold it on your lap while I drive."

"That's not a problem. After all, we couldn't have anything happen to your masterpiece, could we, girls?"

As Marigold and Daisy agreed with Rose, the outside door opened and David and Sharon came into the kitchen. The girls immediately stopped talking.

"This is a coincidence," Rose told their visitors.

"We were just talking about school opening and the brand-new elementary school and all its benefits. Mr. Nolan, have you met Marigold and Daisy Brown, who will be two of your youngest pupils. Mr. Nolan is your new school principal, and Mrs. Nolan is a high school teacher. They are also your new neighbours because they are now living in Mark's Point."

"Are you celebrating your birthday today, girls? That's a lovely-looking cake you have there.".

Sharon asked the right question. At first, the girls appeared to be struck dumb at being introduced to their new principal but now began speaking together, telling the teachers about their mother's birthday and how Bessie had helped them and Penny make the cake.

When Sharon congratulated them on the beautiful job and asked if Penny was their sister, Daisy explained who she was.

"No, she's not our sister. Penny is a missing Harry from Africa, but she lives in St. John's now, and she's our friend."

"That's not how you say it. Penny's not a missing Harry, is she, Mrs. Bessie? Anyways, Penny's sending us pictures she took of animals in Africa, and we're going to show our teachers. The cake couldn't be for me and Daisy 'cause we don't have the same birthdays. We're not twins like Lily and Pansy.

I'm the biggest, and I'm going into grade 2, and Daisy only starts school this year."

Then addressing Sharon, Marigold continued speaking.

"If you're a teacher in high school, you'll see our sisters, the twins, and our brother Bobby."

"And our Mom is having a new baby before Christmas, and I won't be the youngest in our family then," Daisy added.

With that, Marigold announced it was time they were going home, and with reminders not to forget to bring the cake to their house, the little girls left, leaving Sharon and David laughing behind them.

"Okay, ladies, what is a missing Harry?" a grinning David asked.

"And tell me, are all my students going to be so outgoing and interesting as Daisy and Marigold?"

When Bessie explained that their guest Penny had previously spent many years as a missionary in Africa, the teachers, who had never considered Daisy's mispronunciation as a missionary, had another spell laughing.

"You know, the more we get to know people in Mark's Point, the more certain I am that we made the right decision moving out this way. We've only been here for three days and we not only have the most interesting neighbours, but they are also very friendly. Several have come to the door to welcome us, and we even had gifts of cake and freshly baked bread," David said

Bessie looked at Rose, who was finding it difficult to contain her laughter

"Rose, I am sure, is thinking the same thing as me," Bessie said, smiling.

"Sharon and David, you don't know much about small communities, do you? Although we have friendly people in Mark's Point, I'd say it's nosiness more than anything else that's bringing people to your door. They'll want to know if there are any changes inside the house and what kind of furniture you brought with you. Did Lucy Pearce happen to be one of the people welcoming you?"

There was even more laughter when the couple admitted their first visitor was Lucy.

"But Mother came with us, and she's not used to people she doesn't know walking in and out of her house. We spent most of yesterday at the new school checking out things, and while we were gone, Mother very politely answered the door. She thanked our visitors, telling them she will let us know they called. Lucy was all set to come inside, but Mother very quickly told her we were gone for the day."

"Speaking of Mother, she's in her element getting the house ready. She cleaned all the windows, lined the kitchen drawers and cupboard shelves, put away dishes and pots and pans. In fact, she's hardly stopped since she arrived. She says she'll drop in and say goodbye on the way back this afternoon, but for now, she's too busy to leave. The day we arrived, she gave me a very welcome belated birthday surprise when she insisted on making up our bed. On the top was the beautiful quilt Mrs. Lynch made."

"I'm glad you liked it. One of these days, I might tell you the story behind the transportation of that quilt, but for now, I'm putting the kettle on," said Bessie.

"By the way, don't expect to see us knocking at your door, offering cake as an excuse to see inside the house. Our door, however, is always open for our friends. Mind you, I'm not promising we'll have fresh baked bread and cakes to offer you like some of our neighbours, but one thing for sure, the kettle is always on the stove, and it only takes a few minutes to make a cup of tea."

CHAPTER 17

Friends And Neighbours

It was Saturday night, and Bessie was relaxing in the sun porch when she saw a line of vehicles passing along the road. Knowing it signalled mass in Holy Family Church was over, and Rose would soon be home, Bessie went through to the kitchen to put the kettle on to boil.

A short time later, as the women enjoyed their tea, Rose spoke about the cemetery and how the parish needed posts and rails to replace the old fence.

"I know we don't have fencing material, but there should be something in the church bulletin about accepting donations. Now, where did I put my bulletin when I came in?" Rose asked, looking around the kitchen.

"Perhaps it's in your prayer book. If the parish is looking for donations, I want to help. Alex put his church envelopes in the collection every Sunday, and I've given nothing since he died. I may not be a parishioner, but Holy Family has always been your family's church. Besides that, with Alex and your parents buried in the cemetery, I should contribute."

Thinking she might have left both her prayer book and bulletin in her car, Rose went outside to look and saw a young couple walking up the driveway. Recognizing Maureen Mackey, Rose called out a cheery hello.

"Hello Miss Martin, I hope you don't mind us stopping by," Maureen responded.

"This is Jerome, my fiancé. We thought your mass was at 7.30, but it was almost half over when we got to the church. We decided then to drive down through Muddy Brook Pond and Mark's Landing because it's years since we were down that way."

Inviting them to come indoors, Rose led them through to the kitchen, where Bessie, sitting with her back to the door, asked if she found her prayer book and bulletin.

"I forgot about that, but look who I did find," Rose said.

Introducing Bessie and Jerome, Maureen said they were worried the women might have guests. But, with their wedding in two weeks and all the music still not chosen, they hoped to discuss suitable hymns with Rose. Thinking of catching her after mass, they were disappointed to find everyone had left when they returned to the church.

"Whether we have guests or not, this is still our home, and you are always welcome. You did us a great favour, Maureen, by coming to Maggie's birthday party and doing the girls' hair and make-up. You made the party such a success; the girls are still talking about it," Bessie responded.

"Did you choose the remaining music for your wedding? If you've got the complete list, I'd like to have a look," Rose said

When Maureen produced a list of hymns, she asked if it was possible to hear them before making a final choice. Happy to oblige, Rose invited the couple into the sitting room to listen to the hymns played on the piano.

"While you choose the music, I'll put the kettle on, or would you prefer a bottle of beer? We usually keep a few bottles in the fridge for people dropping in."

"I'd love a cup of tea, but Jerome would probably prefer a bottle of beer, especially on a warm night like this," his bride-to-be answered.

A grinning Jerome wondered aloud if Maureen would be so quick to suggest beer once they were married before agreeing a cold bottle of beer would certainly 'hit the spot.'

Bessie had the tea made and produced a plate of freshly baked squares when Kate and Robert Brown appeared.

"Hi Bessie, are we disturbing you?"

"Not at all, come on in. I told Rose this morning that I rarely see you unless I go to the post office. And I can't remember the last time the pair of you visited us."

"I came to thank you for letting Daisy and Marigold help you make such a delicious birthday cake, but they had some nerve asking you to do it. Goodness knows what kind of torment they were, but I wish you could have seen their faces when they produced the cake. They were so excited, especially when they saw how much I was surprised," Kate recalled.

Kate wasn't the only one to get a surprise, Robert said.

"I believe Lily and Pansy might have been upset that it was their little sisters, not them, who thought of asking you to make a cake. It's not often the little girls get one over on the twins. We love our children equally, but we know the twins often give Bobby and their sisters a hard time by bossing them. It was good to see Marigold and Daisy get the upper hand because their cake was the hit of Kate's birthday. Bobby felt the same way because he kept praising them and the cake, much to their delight."

"I brought back your plate and a piece of cake to share with you and Rose since you never got to try it. I can truthfully say it tastes as good as it looked. I had two happy little girls when I said I was bringing you some cake until they heard their father and I were coming by ourselves."

"We'll try it now with a cup of tea. But what about you, Robert? Would you prefer a cold bottle of beer instead?" Bessie asked.

Nodding happily, Robert thanked Bessie, while Kate laughed, saying as they walked to Martin House, Robert recalled how Alex always kept a few cold beers on hand. However, knowing Bessie and Rose didn't drink beer, he didn't expect to have any that night.

"Kate! Bessie will think I've only got beer on my mind. I do drink tea, you know," said her indignant husband, causing both women to start laughing.

"I thought I heard voices," Rose said as she returned to the kitchen.

"Hello, Kate and Robert. Do you know Maureen and Jerome?"

"I know your parents, but I never met you before. Although ever since Maggie's birthday party, I've heard so much about you, Maureen." Kate said.

"You are quoted all the time in our house. 'Maureen says we should always use conditioner in our hair, Maureen says we should file our fingernails and not cut them with scissors, and many other helpful hints."

"I'm sorry; the last thing I wanted to do was preach to them," Maureen replied.

"Gosh, no! I'm not complaining. I'm delighted to see the girls taking an interest in their appearance. I agree with everything you told them. You made such an impression on the girls that now they're all planning to see you get married. Angela and I promised to bring our girls to the church, and the four girls from Murphy's Cove area, who came to Maggie's party, will also be there."

"Now enough about the girls, when do you expect to open your hairdressing business because I plan to be one of your first customers? Having a hairdresser is the best thing that's happened in this area for a long time."

"Thanks. I hope more people feel that way. I plan to open around the middle of next month. The shop itself is ready, thanks to Jerome, who has done a great job on it. But some of my equipment is coming from the mainland, and it's taking a while to get here. We're getting married in two weeks and will be gone for another two weeks after the wedding. I'm keeping my fingers crossed that the equipment will be here by the time we return."

"I know you're a carpenter, Jerome, and worked in St. John's these past few years. Will you still work in town and come home at weekends?" Robert asked.

"My job's still open with my old boss, but for this next year, I'm going to try working on my own and see how it goes. Coming home to start our businesses is something Maureen and I always planned. We had good jobs in St. John's, but we wanted to live in Mossy Brook after we married."

Bessie said she was glad to see them settling in Mossy Brook, adding too many young people from the area left annually to find work. She was sure both would do well in their respective businesses.

Rose agreed, saying women were excited to know that soon, they would be able to have their hair cut and styled locally. As for Jerome's business, she believed there would be plenty of work for a good carpenter.

"Don't forget, you'll draw business not only from Mossy Brook; but all 14 communities in the area. And speaking of Mossy Brook, how is Philly Moss these days? Do you ever see him?" Rose asked.

When Jerome almost choked on his beer from laughing, Maureen gave him a disapproving look.

"Don't tell me the news spread to Mark's Point," she said

"I suppose I shouldn't be surprised considering Old Philly is the talk of Mossy Brook. His wife Jean has gone on an extended holiday to the mainland. I've heard stories they're either separated or will be, not that I blame her. I even heard they were getting an annulment, although that's hard to believe. I know he took off with his suitcase one morning but came back the same afternoon, and the next morning, Mrs. Jean left on holiday."

"Come on, Maureen, get to the real story," Jerome said, trying to control his mirth.

Giving him a dirty look, Maureen resumed talking.

"A couple of days after Mrs. Jean left, I was home by myself when I heard a loud impatient knocking on the door. Wondering what was wrong, I rushed to open the door, and there was Philly.

"'I've got a good offer for you, girl,' were his first words. I asked him what he was talking about, and he said he heard I wasn't working, so he'd come to help me out. That old so and so only offered me a job as his housekeeper, as if he did me a great favour. Wondering if I understood correctly, I didn't answer him until he informed me that he'd give me a trial run. 'If it works out, I might have a much better offer for you,' he said with a dirty leer on his face."

Seeing Maureen's indignant look, the others joined in Jerome's laughter. Having dealt with Philly Moss, Rose could well imagine the situation Maureen found herself in.

"How did you manage to get rid of him, Maureen? I'm asking because I know it's not the easiest thing to do. The morning he left Mossy Brook, Philly came knocking on our door, looking for a boarding house. He was determined to stay, but thankfully his son Bob came and brought him home. I thought that was the story you were going to tell because with the help of our neighbour, Lucy, it didn't take long to spread the news of Philly arriving with a suitcase on our doorstep."

"So, this is where he went! When Philly came to our house, he seemed determined to stay until he got the answer he wanted. I was even more determined to get rid of him. I told him I was just leaving to check out my new hairdressing shop and that I would be working there permanently. I picked up my car keys and, almost pushing him ahead of me, I closed and locked the house door. He walked away totally disgusted, muttering something about manners and young maids not knowing when they were well off. That's the last I saw of him.

"Jerome thought it was hilarious, but that old man was serious, and I still don't think it was funny. He's weird, and it wasn't until I got into my car that I felt at ease again. Anyway, why are we wasting so much time talking about him? Can we change the subject? I had told Jerome what a lovely house this was. That's why we left our car on the road, so we could admire it while walking up the driveway."

"Who built your home, Mrs. Martin? They did a great job on it. I wouldn't mind seeing the house plans," Jerome said.

Bessie told Jerome she could show him around the house, but there were no plans because her husband Alex built the house, and any plans he had were in his head.

Bessie said Alex loved looking at and inspecting buildings, especially houses. In Scotland, he often walked around the streets, admiring and sizing up different homes. Alex did the same in England before the couple boarded the ship to Nova Scotia on their way to Newfoundland. Every opportunity he had, including the three days they spent in Halifax after their ship docked, her husband walked the streets looking for different styles of houses.

Robert said he remembered when Alex started building the house. He was about 13 and began hanging around Alex when he put down the foundation. He had watched as the house took shape and could see it would be the most prominent house ever built in Mark's Point.

"Every holiday, Saturday, and after school, I was right behind Mr. Alex when he worked on the house. Do you remember Bessie? You should because many a time you brought us a lunch, and you always had something sweet for me." Robert recalled.

"I do indeed. Alex would come home telling his parents and me about his young helper and what he had to say that day. We had many a chuckle at some of the stuff he told us. Alex enjoyed your company, and he'd laugh, saying no one would ever get lonesome when young Robert Brown was around. He'd also say that you might be young, but you were a good worker."

Robert said he was proud when Alex called him his helper, letting him pass the hammer or nails. Gabe O'Brien and Uncle Walt were Alex's buddies, and they'd give him a hand with big projects, like the roof.

"How much did I torment Mr. Alex to let me climb the ladder to the roof, but he'd always say, 'one of these days' Finally, he let me go up, but he stayed right behind me on the ladder. I was so excited I thought I was on top of the world because apart from the church, it's the highest place in Mark's Point."

"And you never stopped bragging about climbing that high either," said Gabe, who arrived as Robert was speaking.

"What a prate box you was. Alex used to say you'd be a politician when you grew up 'cos you never stopped talking. It's easy to see where your youngsters get their gift of gab."

"Thank you, Gabe," Kate said.

"I keep telling Robert the youngsters get their non-stop chatter from him. But oh, no! According to my husband, they take after their mother."

Addressing the others, Kate continued.

"On our walk over here, I was trying to convince Robert to put his tongue to good use. It was in the church bulletin that two parish council members from Mark's Point are wanted, and I'm putting his name forward."

Quickly supporting Kate, Rose spoke up, saying that was a great idea, adding the parish needed someone like Robert, who was a good worker and who would speak up when necessary.

"I'm glad you feel that way, Rose, because you're the second person I want to nominate. We need women on the parish council, who like you said, don't mind speaking up. And if you read this week's bulletin, there's another issue to be discussed, and that's our school."

"What about the school? I haven't read the bulletin yet. I was going to look for it in my car when Maureen and Jerome arrived. I knew Father Kiely spoke about looking for stakes and rails for the cemetery, and I wanted to see what the bulletin said about donations,"

Gabe said that's why he was there. Angela had shown him the notice about rails and stakes for the cemetery, and he had enough of both to give from his home and Martin House. Having also read the church was accepting donations towards the fence, he wondered how much money a person would give.

Kate said that if a parishioner had no posts or rails, they could provide a cash donation to buy additional lumber, nails, and paint.

"And Rose, although you never answered me, I still want you to run for the parish council. It's what's going to happen to the school that has me bothered. I remember Bessie, you saying how the empty school would be ideal for Mark's Point, for socials as well as activities for the youngsters."

Now, Kate said, the school board was passing the former schools back to the parish. According to the bulletin, the parish would have five empty schools for sale unless a committee or group volunteered to accept financial responsibility for the one in its community.

"I'd hate to see our school sold. Where would we have parish or community events then?" Kate asked.

"You're right; we need to keep our school. Men in this community built that school and gave freely of their labour. That's why I took it for granted that it would stay here for the use of the community, but I never considered the upkeep." Rose said.

"You know David and Sharon Nolan, who rent my parents' home. David is keen to start a youth club, and we had discussed using the school for classes such as guitar and crafts. Was there anything in the bulletin about holding meetings in each community to discuss the school issue?" she asked.

Kate said no, but believed the notice was to get people thinking about the schools and ideas for their use.

"I'd love to see a youth club in Mark's Point, and we need a meeting place in the community for all ages. Even as a school, we had the use of it for our annual garden party and occasional Christmas social," Kate said.

"We'll be in the same boat in Mossy Brook. There's nowhere else to hold socials or meetings." Maureen said.

"Maybe it's a sign of the times," a thoughtful-looking Jerome replied.

"It seems everything is getting centred in bigger places, just like the schools. I'd say George Turner was a wise man when he opened his club. It might end up as be the only place in the area where even a meeting can take place."

"His club is already a busy place. Isn't that where your reception is taking place, Maureen? You were saying earlier you'll be gone for two weeks after you're married. Are you and Jerome going away for a honeymoon, or is it a secret?" Bessie asked.

"No, it's not a secret; we're flying to Ontario. My sister Joan, her husband and children are coming home for the wedding and plan to stay an extra two weeks. We'll be using their house in Cornwall. We're also planning to go to Niagara Falls for a couple of nights as we hear it's a popular spot for honeymoons."

"We didn't have a honeymoon, did we, Robert? But we did get as far as Mark's Landing, and what a time we had at the reception," Kate recalled, smiling at the memory.

"When we married in '55, we didn't have much money, so we only planned a small family meal after church. But my Nan Furlong, who lived in Mark's Landing, wasn't having that. She insisted she would host us to a proper wedding 'time' in her house. And did she ever!"

Kate recalled how their families and neighbours helped by bringing food for the meal, which took place in her grandmother's tiny front room. Two tables put together seating a dozen guests took up almost the entire room, and, as one lot of guests finished eating, another group took their places. There was loads of food, according to Kate. She remembered her Nan saying it was like the miracle of the loaves and fishes. Hundreds seemed to eat, and there was still plenty of food remaining.

Robert took up the story, saying it was a good thing the weather was warm and dry because the outside door stayed open all night with people coming and going.

"The house was packed tight. The kitchen was the place for entertainment with singing, dancing, and both accordion and fiddle music, and it went on until the early hours of the morning. People sat or stood in the porch and hall, while dozens more kept up the wedding outside. When the kitchen became too crowded for square dancing, I remember a couple of sets took place in the garden."

As Kate and Robert spoke, Bessie was smiling at her memories of the wedding reception.

"Alex and I were there, and what a great time we had. Your grandmother's house overflowed with guests of all ages. Upstairs was reserved for babies and small children, who, as they got sleepy, were laid on top of beds and covered with coats while they slept. There were foods of every description, and I wouldn't venture to guess how much liquor, home-brewed beer, and wine made the rounds that night. I know Alex brought his share of liquid refreshment with him, and he also drank a fair amount. Although I never saw Alex the worse for drink, he became exceedingly happy as the night went on. However, the next morning was a different story, and, if I recall Gabe, you were in no better shape," Bessie said, laughing at the memory.

Gabe shook his head as he defended his reputation.

"I don't think me or Alex was half as bad as you and Jean made us out to be. I agree we enjoyed ourselves, but we didn't drink too much," he argued.

"Gabe, never argue with a woman when alcohol is involved," Robert said with a grin.

"I got that advice from my grandfather when I was young, and he heard it from his father. He used to say that it was a strange thing how women were experts when it came to liquor, considering most of them spoke as if it was the Devil's own brew."

The women began laughing when Kate quickly responded.

"Huh! It's too bad his advice never included any kind of arguing, but considering the men in your family love an argument, I guess that would be too much to hope for."

"And speaking of the Devil's brew, there's more beer in the fridge. Gabe, why don't you do the honours and pass them around? After Robert's words of wisdom, I won't start an argument on the topic, but my preference is tea. I'll have another cup; what about anyone else?" Bessie said.

An hour later, Maureen and Jerome were first to leave, thanking Bessie and Rose for an enjoyable visit. When they left, Rose asked Kate if the girls were serious about seeing Maureen and Jerome married.

"Why are you asking, Rose?" the postmistress inquired.

Rose said when choosing wedding hymns; Maureen asked for *Hail Queen of Heaven* because it was her grandmother's favourite hymn. The elderly woman had been seriously ill for months and rarely got outdoors, but she was determined to attend the wedding even if it meant using a wheelchair.

"There's no choir at Sacred Heart Church, but Maureen said it would mean a lot to her grandmother to hear it. But, it's a hymn that is better sung, and when you said the girls planned to attend the wedding, I thought it would be a great surprise for Maureen and her grandmother to hear the girls sing it." Rose said.

Kate and Bessie thought it was an excellent idea, but Rose cautioned them that first, the girls had to agree and secondly, it meant practicing, and with four of the girls living in the Murphy's Cove area, it might be not easy getting all of them together.

"I'm sure the girls will be only too happy to sing, and we could practice in both churches by taking turns driving the girls to practices. Knowing Teen Ryan, she wouldn't mind driving her daughter and the other three girls over here. However, my girls will be gone for three days next week."

Kate said she was keeping a promise she made to the twins. When they turned 14 in April, the girls had only one request. They wanted to visit St. John's during their summer holidays and stay in a hotel overnight.

For months, the girl made plans for the birthday treat. Their father would stay home with Bobby and the little girls while Patsy Martin filled in at the Post Office. Looking forward to shopping in the Avalon Mall, the twins scheduled their trip for August, thinking it was the best time to buy new clothes and school supplies.

"But this summer, they stopped talking about the trip. I'm sure they thought I might be too tired to go because of the baby. The twins might appear tough, but they're softies at heart. They hover around me at times, wondering if I'm alright. They might have given up on the idea of a trip to St. John's, but I didn't."

Because the twins had been a great help in the house all summer, Kate showed her appreciation by giving them extra pocket money. That morning, she asked them how much money they had saved?

"When they told me, I said it looked as if they had enough money to buy school supplies and clothes when we go to St. John's next week. They screamed with delight when they realized I was serious. They haven't stopped talking about it all day."

Kate hadn't told her girls yet, but she planned to invite Angela and Maggie to go with them. Robert favoured the trip but said he'd feel better if another woman went with them. Kate liked the idea and immediately thought of Angela and, of course, Maggie.

"We can all fit easily in our station wagon, and with Angela sitting in the front seat, there will be no arguments from the twins about who's sitting where. We have two double beds and a couch in the hotel bedroom I booked, and that gives us lots of sleeping space. What do you think, Gabe? Would Angela be interested? We get along well, and she'd be doing me a great favour. Besides that, the three girls will have the time of their lives."

Gabe thought it was a great idea because he knew Angela and Maggie had been discussing school clothes.

"I'm sure they'll want to go, and I'll help pay for gas and the hotel bill. It will be a treat for them before Angela has to leave for Toronto next month," Gabe said

"And that you won't," Robert broke in.

"I already told Kate this was my treat, and I'm adding a few dollars for meals and treats for the girls. Kate is well on with this baby, and I want someone we trust with her on the trip. I know Angela will make sure Kate doesn't overdo it. Then too, the twins and Maggie get on wonderfully well."

"I'll phone Angela first thing in the morning. I have the hotel booked for three nights starting this coming Wednesday, and we would come back early Saturday morning. I chose that time because Patsy Martin, who fills in for me at the office, will be gone the following week. But the girls can practice a couple of times before we go and again next week."

"I'm glad for the girls; they'll have a great time in St. John's, and so will you and Angela. We have sung the hymn at practice at the request of Mrs. Josie Joy. The girls won't have a problem singing it after practicing a few more times," Rose said.

At Maureen and Jerome's wedding two weeks later, Rose remembered her words as the girls stood in the choir gallery ready to sing. With the wedding mass over, Father Kiely asked the congregation to be seated before the final blessing. He said the bride had requested the playing of her grandmother's favourite hymn at this time.

As Rose started the musical introduction to the hymn, she gave an encouraging smile to her small group of singers. The congregation had little reaction when the music began, but as the girls' voices soared, people turned and looked up to the organ gallery with surprise and appreciation. Maureen and Jerome rose and went to where her grandmother sat in her wheelchair and, turning Mrs. Mackey around to face the choir, stood behind her.

During the first verse, the older woman appeared overcome, looking at the girls through misty eyes. But then she began singing and was quickly joined by Maureen. When the bride and groom's families also stood and sang, the congregation followed. Soon the church resonated with the words and music of *Hail Queen of Heaven*.

Later, outside the church, Rose and the girls received almost as much attention and congratulations as the newlyweds. When they heard they were having their photograph taken with the married couple, Maggie and the twins were delighted they wore new dresses purchased a week earlier in St. John's.

"Smile!" called Bessie and the girls' proud mothers as Rose and her small choir stood with the bride and groom for a photo, then again for another with the senior Mrs. Mackey. While this was taking place, Maureen's mother approached the women.

"While the girls are busy, I need to ask if you would allow them to attend the wedding reception and dance. Maureen says it's the least they can do after that amazing singing. I was at the club this morning, helping make up cold plates for the suppers, and we have extra meals. The only problem is getting the girls to and from the club. That's why Maureen wouldn't mention it until she knew you were willing to let them attend the supper and dance and that they had transportation."

As the mothers looked at each other, Bessie said she and Rose had invitations to the supper, and if their mothers were willing, Maggie and the twins could come with them.

"We can drop them off at the club, and then one of us could come back to Murphy's Cove South and Murphy's Cove and pick up the other four girls. What do you think?"

The women knew the girls would love to attend the reception but wouldn't bother Bessie and Rose with transportation. They talked it over until Teen Ryan came up with the perfect solution.

"Bill and I will pick up all the girls in our car and truck after the dance, and they'll stay with us. Between Martina's room and the other two spare bedrooms, we have lots of space. I know they will enjoy themselves, and to be truthful, so will I. Since my older girls left home, I miss all their noise and giggles."

With the women agreeing, Maureen's mother left to call her daughter aside and give her the decision. Less than a minute later, screams of delight left no doubt about the girls' reaction to Maureen's invitation. Almost immediately, there were more screams.

"I'm guessing by that second lot of screams; the girls just heard they'll all be staying at your house, Teen. Good luck with that. If you're sensible, you'll go home now and enjoy a few hours of sleep because you certainly won't be getting any tonight," Kate said.

It was close to midnight when Rose and Bessie finally left the wedding dance and made their way back to Mark's Point in Rose's car.

"Well, for two people who intended being home by 10 o'clock, I'd say we lost track of time."

"You're right. Bessie, but wasn't it a lovely wedding and reception. Maureen looked beautiful; she and Jerome make a fine-looking couple. And what do you think of the girls? They are having a ball. I don't think any of them came off the dance floor after the music started."

"I know we offered to bring the girls home tonight, but I'm glad they're staying with Teen because the dance will probably go on for hours. I'm getting too old to stay up until the early hours. and I would have hated to drag the girls away." Bessie said, stifling a yawn.

"I don't think I could have stayed much later either," Rose admitted.

"It has been a good day, but the thought of home is very inviting. The first thing I plan to do when I get there is put the kettle on and relax with a good cup of tea before I hit my bed."

CHAPTER 18

Summer's Over

It was the first week in September and an exciting time for students in Mark's Point and its neighbouring communities. Not only was it the beginning of the school year, but for primary and elementary age children, it was the first time they would ride in school buses to attend a large school with multiple classrooms.

An unofficial count of Mark's Point residents was 114, but the community covered quite a large area. The main road stretched almost two miles from the entrance sign, with several lanes leading down to the lower beach road. The two buses, one picking up high school students and the other for children in the new grade 1-6 school, would each make five stops in the community.

Parents weren't the only adults waiting to see the students board the buses. Bessie and Rose had decided to drink their tea in the sun porch, hoping to see the children, particularly Marigold and Dasy, line up at a nearby bus stop.

"I'm just thinking about Kate having to pack lunches for all five of her youngsters. I'd say the Brown home was a busy spot this morning," Bessie said.

"According to Kate, all Marigold and Daisy talk about now is starting school. I sometimes wonder if they are more excited about the new school or travelling by bus for the first time. But it isn't only the small ones who are looking forward to this morning. Look how pleased Maggie was when she and Angela returned after registering for school yesterday. I think it's a smart idea to have new high school students register a day early, meeting staff and letting them get acquainted with the layout of the building before classes start," Rose replied.

"Yes, they were impressed with the high school and the staff they met. I think their visit laid to rest any doubts Angela might have had about leaving Maggie when she returns to Toronto next week.

"Now, what did you do with the grocery lists you started to make up last night? I want to add a jar of marmalade to the things we need from Murphy's shop. After all these years, I've given up trying to convince the Kavanaghs to stock marmalade. They complain about people going outside the community to buy groceries, but when I said one time it could be because there was more choice elsewhere, they were highly offended," Bessie recalled.

Oscar had pointed out the extension he built to his shop three years earlier, saying it held everything a person would ever need. He then itemized products, or as he called them, necessities in a well-stocked general store that he always kept on hand.

"And true enough, he had a large variety of goods. Rubber overshoes, batteries, ammunition, kerosene, flannelette and thread were only a tiny sample of the products Oscar recited, almost like a long poem. I remember he ended by saying he always stocked plenty of the ever-popular Beef Iron Wine because it was a favourite of older men in the community."

Bessie said Flo joined the conversation, pointing to the well-stocked grocery shelves in the middle of the shop and behind the counter, plus the many household goods on shelves along the back wall.

"When I said I could never find marmalade on the shelves, Flo righteously replied that Oscar preferred to stock good Newfoundland food. I felt like telling her marmalade was made in the same place as the jam on Oscar's shelves, and it wasn't Newfoundland, but I'd have been wasting my breath."

Rose laughed, saying Flo had never heard the saying, 'The customer is always right.'

"According to Flo, it's Oscar who is always right. She's well known as a contrary soul, but she's intensely loyal to her brother, and in her opinion, whatever he says is gospel."

"Loyalty is a good trait, but it would be nice to go into the shop and see a smile on Flo's face occasionally. Anyway, I'll leave the things we need from Oscar's until tomorrow and go over to Murphy's Cove this morning," Bessie said.

"I think I'll come with you. We've nothing else planned, and the room is ready for the Porters when they arrive tomorrow. If any unexpected guests show up, everything is in place to accommodate them."

Bessie had a better idea, saying it was such a gorgeous morning; why didn't they take the entire day off and enjoy themselves.

"We won't have too many more days like this. Summer is over, and apart from a few times berry-picking, I haven't spent much time away from Martin House. When we drove to the wedding reception in Freeman's Beach, I was trying to remember the last time I was out that way.

"It got me thinking about a pool and a small sandy beach, where Alex and I often took a picnic lunch and spent an afternoon. I know you're not much of an outdoor person, but what if we took a run out that way. Then maybe we could come back through Murphy's Cove, Basket Cove, and Fisherman's Creek. We could pack a lunch, and if you don't want to eat outdoors, we can have it in the car," Bessie said persuasively.

"I guess I could eat outdoors for once. Hopefully, there are no black flies around now, and it would be nice to have a car run for pleasure. These days, it's rare for us to travel outside Mark's Point and Murphy's Cove. I was surprised to see the changes in Mossy Brook when we went there for the wedding."

"Would you mind if I phoned Mina and invited her to come along? I don't think she gets the opportunity to go far as she doesn't have a vehicle. Then too, the girls are in school today, and she's probably missing their company."

"That's a good idea, Bessie. Give her a call and see if she wants to come. While you're doing that, I'll hard boil some eggs for sandwiches. We've got roast beef left from yesterday; did you want to keep it for supper, or can we use it for sandwiches too?"

After agreeing to use the roast beef, Bessie called a surprised Mina. Delighted to be included in the plans, she immediately accepted the invitation, saying she would see what she had to add to the picnic lunch.

Just over an hour later, the three women were relaxing in a small cove outside Freeman's Beach West, where a brook ran into a good-sized pool before emptying into the sea. Looking around the pool and the sandy beach in appreciation, Mina expressed surprise at not knowing it existed. She wasn't alone, Bessie told her; not many people knew about the sheltered cove.

"Alex heard about it from Joe Stamp, who served with him in the Royal Navy. After my first unfortunate swimming experience in Newfoundland, Alex brought me here and made me promise this would be the only place I would swim from then on."

"What unfortunate swimming experience?" Rose and Mina asked in unison.

"Did you never hear about it, Rose? It happened the first summer I was in Mark's Point. I always loved swimming and grew up on Scotland's north-east coast where there were many sandy beaches to enjoy a picnic and swimming. I was looking forward to my first swim in Newfoundland, but I wasn't interested when Alex suggested a local pond. I couldn't see why I'd swim in a pond when the sea was on our doorstep."

And as much as Alex and his parents tried to change her mind, saying the water was too cold, Bessie recalled how determined she was to test the ocean. She argued that if she could swim in the North Sea, she could undoubtedly swim in the local ocean.

"I should have listened to them. It was a hot sunny afternoon when I walked over to Old Man's Cove for my first dip in Newfoundland waters. I had thrown a dress on over my swimming costume and quickly shed it before running into the water. The icy cold water took away my breath, but stupidly, I took another few steps before ducking my head under the water, ready to swim. Never before in my life did I get such a shock. I believe I froze when my head went under the water, and for a minute, I thought I'd never move again.

"I've heard the expression icy cold, but until that day, I had never experienced that degree of coldness. It left me absolutely shaking yet almost frozen on the spot. How I got out of the water, I don't know. If it wasn't for Alex, I doubt I'd have made it home."

Unknown to Bessie, Mrs. Martin had insisted that Alex follow Bessie, and he was sitting in his truck up on the road keeping an eye on her. Realizing something was wrong, he ran down to the cove, where he grabbed her towel and began to dry her roughly. Putting her sandals on her feet and grabbing her clothes, he half carried, half led her up the bank to his truck where he wrapped her in an old blanket used to cover the seat, then drove rapidly home.

"Alex seemed furious, but later, he told me he was scared stiff I might not make it because I appeared in shock. Your mother was so good, Rose. Instead of calling me all kinds of a fool for not listening, she had Alex bring me upstairs and get me into bed while she filled up a couple of hot water bottles. Even then, I couldn't stop shaking. The hot water bottles were good, but it wasn't until she produced a 'hot toddy' of rum, and I drank it, that I knew I was going to be alright. She or Alex never once said, 'I told you so,' and I never again tried swimming in the sea."

Bessie's story had Mina recalling how she, too, had considered swimming in the local sea only to be ridiculed by her in-laws at the idea of a grown woman swimming.

"I loved swimming, and growing up, I went weekly to the 'baths,' as we called our local indoor pool. Listening to your story Bessie, I'd say the only good thing Herbert's family ever did was mock me when I spoke about swimming in the sea. It stopped me from trying to do so. If I had an experience like yours, I doubt if any of them would have bothered looking for me no matter how long I was gone."

Several hours later, following a relaxed lunch and lots of talking and reminiscing before the women packed up and left the beach to head in the direction of Murphy's Cove. They travelled slowly back through Freeman's Beach and Indian Spring before entering Murphy's Cove on the way to Basket Cove and Fisherman's Creek, noting the changes since their last visits. As they entered Mossy Brook, Bessie suggested stopping and treating themselves to ice cream at the local shop.

"Yes, and maybe we could park the car and stroll around the community. Here's the shop now. Wait! Don't tell me; isn't that Philly Moss standing outside talking to those two men? Don't stop, Bessie. Keep driving; I'm not going in there!" Rose exclaimed.

"The next thing Old Philly will be telling people we came to Mossy Brook to see him and, I'm certainly not having my name bandied around with his."

"Why don't you want to see Philly Moss?" Mina asked.

"Although looking at who he's talking to, I'd say he probably won't even notice you because he's got bigger fish to fry. That's the PC candidate for our district with his campaign manager, and I've no doubt Philly's giving them an earful. Everyone seems to think the Progressive Conservative party has a good chance of winning next month's provincial election, and this candidate is certainly doing a lot of campaigning. He was at my door and probably every other house in Murphy's Cove South on Tuesday. He seems to be a nice, sensible fellow. In all the years I've lived here, I never heard of a politician visiting these communities," Mina said.

Bessie drove past the shop, saying she would turn near the church and get ice cream on their way back through Fishermen's Creek. On their return, they saw Philly was still talking to the politician and didn't notice the car or its passengers.

"You don't have to worry about Philly seeing you now, Rose. I know the man is a pain in the neck, but what did he do to annoy you?" Mina asked as they left Mossy Brook.

Rose's tale of Philly's visit to Martin House kept the other two women entertained until they reached a tiny shop attached to a house in Fishermen's Creek. After buying vanilla Dixie Cups, they parked the car and walked along the community's lower road towards the harbour.

"This is only the second time I've actually stopped in Fishermen's Creek. I came with Alex to buy lobster pots from Nora Moss shortly after her husband died. Alex also bought most of Peter's nets because Mrs. Moss was selling everything off and moving to St. John's to stay with her daughter. I must say this is a beautiful community. Not many places have such a sheltered harbour." Bessie said as the women strolled along the gravel road enjoying their ice cream.

"I'm having such a good time. I can't remember when I enjoyed a day out or even relaxing with other women. I enjoy being with my girls, but apart from Nan Lynch and Mrs. Abby, I never had any close friends in Murphy's Cove South. Not that there's anything wrong with my neighbours, most are nice people, but with my in-laws living practically on my doorstep and watching my every move, it's better to keep to myself," Mina said.

"It's too bad you don't live a bit closer to us. Apart from one nosy person, I've always found the folks in Mark's Point to be good neighbours. I never did get into the habit of just dropping into people's houses, but I know if I want help, all I need to do is ask a neighbour. Don't you agree, Rose?"

"You are right. I guess growing up in Mark's Point, I took our neighbours for granted, but since moving back home, I've come to realize how lucky we are to have such friendly folk around us. And we're not the only ones who feel that way; our guests tell us they thoroughly enjoy strolling around the community and meeting local people who always make them feel welcome. It's certainly a plus for our business."

"That's true, and although there are people who thought I only stayed in Mark's Point because of Alex, I've always enjoyed living there. I love returning to Scotland for a holiday, but Mark's Point is my home. I also know some people expected me to leave after Alex died, but I couldn't see myself living anywhere else," Bessie said.

It didn't take the women long to walk around the small fishing community, enjoying their ice cream as they went. Once back in the car, they made their way to Murphy's Cove to pick up the supplies needed for Martin House.

"Are you expecting guests this weekend?" Mina asked.

"We have one couple arriving for two nights from St. John's. They heard about our bed and breakfast from one of the wedding guests who stayed with us. We don't know anything about them, whether they are young or old. We also never know when an unexpected guest or two will show up. That's why we try and keep a fair stock of groceries and supplies on hand and why we are stopping at Murphy's now. Rose, you have our list, right?" Bessie asked as she parked in front of the shop.

Unfortunately, the women soon realized the shopping list was still lying on the kitchen table back in Martin House, resulting in them trying to remember what they needed when they entered the shop.

"Hello, Mina, and fancy seeing Bessie and Rose with you. I know now why I couldn't get an answer when I called Martin House," Millicent Murphy remarked from behind the counter.

"I've been trying to phone you for hours because I know two men who are looking for a place to stay next week and hoping you will help them. They are Albert and Jack Matthews. And they want to stay in this area for at least three days. Before you make up your mind, I should tell you Albert is the Progressive Conservative, or as some people still call them, Tory candidate, for this district, and Jack is his brother and campaign manager."

"What difference does that make?" Bessie asked.

"Well, some people take politics seriously, and if they support the Liberals, they wouldn't speak to a PC, let alone have them stay in their house. It's the same the other way around. I know Tory supporters who would walk across the road rather than speak to a Liberal," the shopkeeper answered.

"Politics, race, or religion makes no difference to us. But what else do you know about this aspiring politician?"

"I have a personal connection to him in a way, through my son Andy. You know Andy is in the Mounties; well, Albert, the candidate, is retired from the RCMP. He was Andy's commanding officer in Ontario, and Andy has a lot of respect for him. He believes he will make an excellent member of the House of Assembly. Albert now lives in St. John's, where he grew up, but he's running in this district because apparently, his grandmother was from this area."

Millicent went on to say the men left St. John's at seven that morning to travel through the district. Their trip that week was their second one, but the long car ride meant they lost about six hours of potential campaigning each time they made the return trip. Until she told the men about Martin House, they had no idea there was anywhere to stay in the area and immediately asked how they could contact the owners.

"They were disappointed when I called your place, and there was no answer. They wondered since it was now September if you had closed, but I was sure I'd have heard if you had and promised to continue trying to reach you. Meanwhile, they are campaigning in Mossy Brook, hoping to meet voters, but they'll be back here before leaving for St. John's to see if I got hold of you. They're going home for the long weekend and coming back to the district on Monday," Millicent said.

She had barely finished speaking when the door opened, and the two men the women saw earlier in conversation with Philly Moss entered the shop.

"Speak of angels! I was just saying you'd be dropping in before returning to St. John's, but I wasn't expecting to see you yet. Albert and Jack meet Bessie and Rose Martin of Mark's Point, the owners/operators of Martin House Bed and Breakfast. I think you already met Mina when you were campaigning in Murphy's Cove South," Millicent said.

"This is a pleasure and, hopefully, good for us. We stopped to see what news you had and instead meet the women we are looking for," the smiling candidate said.

"It's nice meeting you. It will be even better if you say you can put us up next week because travelling to and from St. John's every day is just not working. We'll never be able to cover the district if we continue this way. If we could stay with you next week, it would allow us to campaign longer and meet more voters while visiting all the communities in this part of the district."

"That's not a problem, Mr. Matthews. We can accommodate you. We have rooms with one double bed, and we also have rooms with two single beds. Which would you prefer?"

The candidate and his brother started to laugh, and Albert spoke,

"We'll share a room with the two beds. At least we will have a bed each. Growing up, not only did we share a bedroom, but in a family of 11 children, we considered ourselves lucky when only two of us shared a bed."

"Great, you can have the downstairs room. It's a nice-sized room and has its own bathroom. Have you visited Mark's Point yet? You shouldn't have any problem finding Martin House."

"No, not yet. Today we were in Mossy Brook and spoke to quite a few people and found most are receptive. Although we did run into one old fellow who told me I didn't have a chance against Joey Smallwood, who sends him the pension every month."

"Yes," his brother said in agreement.

"And it was no good trying to tell him that pensions come from the federal, not the provincial, government, and have nothing to do with the premier. He believes Joey is Newfoundland's saviour and is personally responsible for providing old-age pensions. Thank goodness, not everyone feels that way."

"Maybe so, but he's not alone in his opinion. Many older people still believe without Joey as premier, there would be no pension," Millicent said.

"There's an old lady I visit once a week to deliver her mail and groceries. I enjoy my visits and stop to have a chat because she's always interesting. But it's the month-end visits I enjoy most because of the ritual she follows when I pass over her pension. First, she opens the envelope, looks at the cheque before she thanks me for delivering it, goes over to a large framed picture of

Joey, kisses it, and says, 'Thank you for my pension, Mr. Smallwood, you're a lovely, lovely man.' Next to Joey is a picture of King William on his horse at the Battle of the Boyne. She then stands in front of it and very seriously says, 'And thank you, King Billy, for saving Ireland from the Catholics.'

"I don't know what Joey and King William have in common, but she holds them both in high esteem. I was sure I misheard her the first time she addressed King Billy's picture and said nothing. When the same ritual happened the following month, I asked her if she forgot I was a Catholic. She quickly said, 'But you is different, my child. You wouldn't try and drive the Orangemen out of Ireland, would you? I'm still trying to think of an answer to that."

Millicent's story was met with laughter, and turning to Albert; she continued speaking.

"And regardless of religious denomination, Joey's picture is on display in quite a few homes. I visited an elderly couple one night and found them kneeling, saying the rosary. There's nothing unusual about that, but seeing two large framed pictures, one of the Sacred Heart and the other of Premier Smallwood, hanging side by side on the wall above their heads is. It was almost as if they were keeping watch over the praying couple. It struck me as the oddest combination."

"I guess I'll just have to be on my P's and Q's when I speak to voters and not mention Mr. Smallwood," the candidate said.

"So far, we've had a good reception, and no one has told us outright that they wouldn't vote for me. As a matter of fact, people have said it's time for a change that Mr. Smallwood has been premier for too long, and I'm not going to argue with them. Anyway, now that we have our accommodation problem solved, I think we have time for another couple of hours of campaigning before we hit the road. Great to meet you, ladies; we'll see you on Monday."

"I never considered politicians when I imagined the guests we might host in Martin House, but the Matthews appear to be nice men. Now let's see what we need and get it all into the car. What about you, Mina, is there anything you have to pick up?" asked Bessie.

"I just have to get a few of those lovely-looking apples. Did Dave bring out any oranges from St. John's on this trip, Millicent?"

"No, but the wholesaler will have some tomorrow, and he's also hoping to have bananas. Whatever fresh fruit and vegetables Dave manages to get will be in the shop on Saturday. I know you'll want me to save oranges for the girls, but what about bananas? Millicent asked.

"Keep me four if you get them; they'll be a treat for the girls as it's not often they get bananas. The mass schedule changes for September this weekend, and I'll pick them up after church on Saturday night. The girls like having apples in their lunch tins. Speaking of the girls, they will soon be home with lots of talk about new teachers and the different courses they'll be taking this year."

Back in the car and heading towards Murphy's Cove South, Bessie spoke about the fresh produce selection Millicent carried in her shop compared to Kavanagh's Store.

"Oscar could have much fresher vegetables, and it's seldom he has fruit at all. I heard Dave Murphy approached all the shops in this area a few years ago, offering to bring out supplies from his St. John's wholesaler. Dave goes in and out of town three times a week, and he brings fresh fruit and vegetables for Millicent's customers. I understand several shops took advantage of Dave's offer but not Oscar. He said he had enough trucks delivering to his shop."

When they reached Murphy's Cove South, Bessie and Rose declined Mina's offer to come in for tea, saying the purchased meats, including ham and bacon, needed to be refrigerated as soon as possible.

"We'll stop for a cup of tea the next time we have a day out, and hopefully, that won't be too far in the future," Rose promised

Back in Mark's Point, the women were unpacking groceries from the car when they heard another vehicle stop behind them.

"Now I see why you aren't answering your phone. By the look of things, you've been shopping in Murphy's Cove. I phoned you a couple of times, and so did Father Kiely without getting an answer," Robert Brown said.

"With politicians, priests, and fishermen looking for us, it appears we are in great demand today, Rose. What can we do for you, Robert? For sure, you're not looking for accommodation," Bessie said with a smile.

"No, no, nothing like that. We need to talk about the parish council. It seems, Rose, that me and you are members of the council because no one else was foolish enough to agree to try for it. I feel like killing Kate. I let her put my name in after she tormented the life out of me. Even then, I only said yes because I thought other people would get elected. Now Father Kiely says, you and me, Rose, are the members representing this part of the parish, and he wants us to set up a meeting as soon as possible to discuss our school."

"I know the school board wants to get rid of the small schools, but what's the big rush to have a meeting?" Rose asked.

Robert told them Father Kiely had received a letter that morning from the School Board informing him the parish would get ownership of the schools on September 30. All electricity and building insurance costs would then become the responsibility of the parish. Although the priest had known this would happen, he thought the parish would have several months to consider its options.

"Father wants the residents of each community to meet and discuss whether the parish should keep their school. If a community decides to keep its school, residents need to form a committee to look after it and pay the bills. He plans to attend each meeting, but first, he wants a parish council meeting next Tuesday. Our community meeting will be a week tonight, but he's hoping we will talk to people now, encouraging them to attend and get them thinking about what's happening," Robert said.

"That makes good sense," Bessie said.

"If the community wants a meeting place, the school has to stay. If I belonged to the parish, I'd vote to keep it."

"You live here, and this is about what's good for the community, so you should come," said an indignant sounding Robert.

"I thought we could count on you coming to the meeting and giving your ideas. You belong here, and that's what's important."

"Robert's right. This has to do with what the entire community wants. I'd like to see everyone making use of the school. Just think of the different classes we could have for men, women, and children. I'm sure we could raise money to pay the bills through card games and socials. Having a proper community meeting place might be the best thing that ever happened to Mark's Point."

"Not much wonder Kate wanted you on the parish council. Talk like that at the meeting. Rose, and I'm sure everyone will be in favour of keeping the old school in the community," Robert spoke admiringly.

"They would need to know there's more to keeping the school as a community centre than paying light bills and insurance," Bessie said.

"The school board removed everything from the school after it closed, which means there's no tables or even chairs to sit on. You can't have a card game or social in an empty building. There's nobody better than you, Rose, for making lists. I suggest you have one done before the meeting to include things such as tables, chairs, and maybe a stove and kitchen equipment like kettles and dishes."

"With your help, we can easily do that. And Robert, you should do the same, and we could get together and compare our lists before the meeting," Rose responded

"No problem, I'll get Kate to give me a hand. Boys, oh boys, it looks like it's going to be a busy time if we're going to try and raise money for everything we need."

"Well, now the pair of you have that settled, we need to get the meat and other groceries into the house before they start to spoil on a warm day like this," Bessie said, opening the porch door, only to be greeted by the sound of the telephone ringing.

"Rose, you should answer that as it could be Father Kiely looking for you again. Robert, if you want to give me a hand with the groceries, I'm sure you'll find a cold bottle of beer in the fridge. As for me, the first thing I'm going to do is put the kettle on and enjoy a good cup of tea."

The groceries were soon out of the car, refrigerated, or stored in the cupboards. While Robert drank a beer and Bessie steeped tea, Rose was still talking on the phone. When she finally came back into the kitchen, she was smiling.

'It looks as if we are going to be busy next week, Bessie. That was Sue on the phone. She and Bob are flying into St. John's on Monday night, renting a car, and then driving out here on Tuesday. Bob just finished his work project and has another big construction job starting in a couple of weeks that will keep him busy until Christmas. He had promised Sue if a slow down of work happened, they would return to Newfoundland. Sue's like a small child, so excited about returning. She had all kinds of questions, whether Mina had any more quilts for sale, could she go berry picking, was Gabe still fishing, and was there anything we wanted that she could bring," Rose said

"I told her about the politician we have staying here next week. She says politics are right up Bob's alley, that he'll have all kinds of questions when he meets him. Knowing Bob, I'd say we might hear some interesting conversations when they get together."

"Who's the politician you've got coming? I heard the PC candidate has been visiting Murphy's Cove. Is it him?" Bob asked.

"Yes, his name is Albert Matthews. He is travelling with his brother Jack who is also his campaign manager. We met them in Murphy's shop, and they seem to be nice men. So do you think he has a chance of getting elected? There's been a Liberal in this district for as long as I can remember."

"And that's as good a reason as any for voting PC this time. Joey Smallwood has run things too long. It's time for a change. I'll look forward to meeting this fellow Matthews and see what he says for himself. Meanwhile, I was fishing when Daisy and Marigold left for their first day at the new school. I promised to be waiting at the bus stop when they got home, so I better get a move on," Robert said.

"I'm sure they'll have lots to tell you, and no doubt it will be entertaining. Tell them we are looking forward to hearing all about their first day. Now, Rose, the tea's made. Let's enjoy our cuppa. As you said, we have a busy week ahead of us so let's relax and take advantage of this quiet time."

CHAPTER 19

Busy Times

Albert Matthews had less than two months to make himself known to the people in the district he hoped to represent after the October 28th Newfoundland provincial election. But as he arrived in Mark's Point, his thoughts were not on the campaign but on the beauty of the community and the house where he and his brother Jack would stay for the next four days.

"What a lovely home you have, Mrs. Martin. It's one of the nicest I've seen. Have you looked at the view, Jack; isn't it grand? Some people would pay a fortune to have a view like this."

"Although most politicians tend to exaggerate, I have to agree with my brother. You have a beautiful spot, but I'm sure you hear that all the time from your guests," Jack Matthews said to Bessie and Rose.

"We do get a lot of compliments. The view was the reason Alex, my husband, built the sun porch onto our house. We always called it the sun porch, not a sunroom, because Alex originally planned to have an open porch the entire length of the house. As he was building and admiring the view, he decided to enclose it as a room with many windows. That way we could appreciate the view all the year round from indoors. We often sat here, but our favourite time to enjoy it was in the evening when the sun began to go down and the sky and the ocean often turned a multitude of different colours.

"Now, I'll show you to your room. It's at the back of the house, but feel free to relax in the sun porch any time. We're having dinner at six o'clock. Are you going out campaigning before then?" Bessie asked the men.

The candidate said they should because it would give him and his brother two hours to meet Mark's Point residents before returning for the meal.

"We can also continue for an hour or more after dinner. Perhaps we'll drive to the end of the community and gradually return this way, making sure we're back in lots of time to eat. It's so good of you providing a meal each night when this is a Bed and Breakfast establishment," Albert said.

His brother agreed, saying they thought themselves fortunate to find a place to stay without providing meals.

"We imagined we'd be buying slices of baloney and tins of sausages or beans from the local shops and eating in our car. When Albert's wife heard the cost included breakfast and dinner, she thought we must have heard wrong because your rates are so reasonable," Jack said.

Later, when the men had gone campaigning, Bessie spoke about the prices they were charging at Martin House.

"It's not that our rates are too cheap. I just think most of our guests compare them to city prices. We're far from St. John's, and we still make a reasonable profit. The one thing I don't want to get into is cooking meals full-time. It's something we'll be doing this week, and while Sue and Bob are here, but we won't be preparing meals for guests staying only one or two nights."

"I completely agree. The idea that we would be serving meals, apart from breakfast, never entered my mind before we opened. We provided a few meals to Sue and Bob when they were here before, but the Kennedys had friends and relatives who invited them for dinner, and most of our guests stay only one, or at the most, two nights. I know Sue felt she was imposing on us when we provided meals, but we couldn't let them starve or eat take-out food all the time, and we both enjoyed their company. It's too bad that there's not a restaurant in the area. It would do good business and relieve us of feeling responsible for providing meals."

As Rose talked, the phone began to ring. Bessie went to answer it and discovered Sue on the other end of the line.

"Hi Bessie, we arrived an hour ago and checked into our hotel room. It's wonderful to be back in Newfoundland. We're going out soon, but I needed to ask you something first. I believe you have a freezer apart from the one in your refrigerator. Am I right?"

Bessie replied they had a large freezer and asked why? Instead of answering, Sue had another question.

"When we were here before, you spoke about going berry picking. Are there berries around now because it's something I'd love to try."

"Yes, there are still lots of blueberries. In fact, Maggie and I have planned to go berry picking on Saturday with the Lynches, and you're certainly welcome to join us. And who knows, perhaps the partridgeberries will be ripe enough to pick before you leave Mark's Point."

"That sounds great, but tell me, do you have any extra space in your freezer?"

"Yes, there's lots of space, especially if you want to freeze your berries or some of the fish Bob catches and pack them in ice for the air journey home," Bessie replied.

"That's a great idea; I'll mention it to Bob. I'll hang up now and see you tomorrow afternoon. Are you sure it's not too much for you and Rose preparing dinner for us and your other guests?"

"Not at all. You're only here for a short time, and it's the least we can do. Rose or I don't profess to be restaurant quality chefs, but if you and Bob can put up with our meals, we're more than happy to have you join us."

Returning to the kitchen, Bessie related her conversation to Rose, who asked whether she still planned to go berry picking with Maggie the following Saturday.

"Yes, Maggie enjoys going berry picking, and I thought she'd not only look forward to the outing, but it might take her mind off Angela leaving to go back to Toronto on Friday. Instead of going to our usual berry grounds, we're picking up Mina and the girls and heading to a place they know. It's supposed to be a good spot, but they don't often go there because it's almost two miles outside Murphy's Cove South. We are leaving early and packing our lunch. Sue can come with us, and we'll be back in lots of time to prepare dinner at night."

"Don't worry about that. You go and enjoy your day out. With Albert and Jack leaving on Friday, only Bob will be here. I'll get him and Gabe something to eat when they come back from fishing. I'll also prepare our main meal, so there's no need to rush back. Speaking about fishing, Sue must be expecting Bob to catch lots of fish, with her wanting to know how much room we had in our freezer," Rose said.

But when the Newmans arrived the following day, it became evident Sue didn't have fish on her mind when she asked about freezer space. Rose and Bessie watched with astonishment as their guests made several trips to and from their rented car carrying bags and cartons into the kitchen.

"Bessie and Rose, before you say anything, Bob and I wanted to thank you for agreeing to have us as guests again. We know it's difficult to get fresh meat locally, so we went to a butcher shop in St. John's yesterday to place an order and then picked it up this morning before we left the city. I noticed too that your local store has little in the way of fruit and vegetables, so we thought we'd get a small selection for you. Your rates are so low, and we believe we should be paying more, but we know you and figured that wouldn't happen. This way, we feel we are making a fair contribution," Sue said.

"A fair contribution!" Bessie exclaimed.

"You've brought that much stuff we could feed an army. There was no need to do this. What do you think, Rose?"

"Looking at all these meats, fruits, and vegetables, I would say we have more fresh supplies than Oscar has in his shop. Sue and Bob, you shouldn't be doing this. Bessie and I have looked forward to your visit, not only as guests, but as our friends, and so have Gabe and Maggie," Rose replied.

"There's another reason we brought meat and some other groceries. If you don't mind us using your kitchen, Sue and I would love to cook dinner for you one night and invite Gabe and Maggie, as well as David and Sharon. Would that be okay?"

"Of course, that's alright, Bob, but you don't need to cook. Rose and I will look after the meal. It's bad enough you providing all this food without having to cook it," Bessie said.

"But we want to do this, although we are also looking forward to your cooking some of the delicious meals you gave us the last time," Sue said.

"Which reminds me, I asked the butcher to mince some steak, Bessie, so you can cook some of the lovely Scottish mince and tatties you made when we were here before. I remember you said it starts with good quality minced steak, so I had the butcher make up three packages with two pounds in each one. Is that okay?"

"Okay! It's more than okay. I don't know how we can ever thank you for all this. We'll be eating like royalty for a long time. There's pea soup for dinner tonight, but perhaps we should decide what we will have for the next two nights and put the rest of the meat into the freezer," Bessie said.

"There's also a surprise gift for you, Bessie, and it's not from us. When I asked if they would mince the steak, one butcher said I should buy a cheaper meat cut if I planned to make hamburgers. I told him I wanted the steak for mince and tatties, and he asked who in Newfoundland cooked mince and tatties? When I told him about you, he said if you were Scottish, he was sure you would appreciate good pork sausages just like those he made as a young butcher in Aberdeen. He wouldn't take money for them. Instead, he said the next time you're in St. John's, drop in and let him know how you enjoyed the sausages and the mince."

"Aberdeen, that's not too far from my town. I didn't know there was a Scottish butcher in St. John's, but for sure, I'll drop by his shop the next time I go to the city. I haven't had any tasty pork sausages since I was home with Alex and Rose."

"And I also remember how good they were. But Sue and Bob, you have brought such a variety of meat, it will be difficult trying to decide what, and when, to eat." Rose said.

"I did tell you we had two other guests didn't I," Bessie asked the Newmans later as the four of them sat around the kitchen table enjoying tea or coffee.

"Yes, and I'm looking forward to talking to the politician," Bob said.

"I'm sure he will be interesting. I guess having Martin House open this year was mighty convenient for him. Do you plan on staying open to guests during the winter?"

"We do, not that we expect to do much business. We'll be living here, so taking guests, perhaps an occasional salesman or someone from the school board, won't be a problem," Bessie replied.

Bob rose, saying he wouldn't be gone long that he wanted to see Gabe. Sue wanted to know whether he was taking the rubber clothes.

"Yes, I have both sets in the car. I know mine fits well. I just hope I picked the right size for Gabe. Are you coming with me?"

"Knowing Gabe and how independent he is, I'm sure he's going to have something to say about bringing him a gift, so I'll leave you to go alone. I'm going to relax and enjoy Bessie and Rose's company. I'll see him and Maggie later."

For the next half-hour, the three women sat and chatted until a quick knock on the door and the sound of footsteps from the porch interrupted them.

"Hi Miss Rose, Hi Mrs. Bessie, it's me and Marigold. Guess what we got today!" said an excited-sounding Daisy as she entered the kitchen before abruptly stopping when she saw Sue.

Behind her, Marigold gave a small gasp.

"Oh, Daisy, Mom's going to be some mad. We're not supposed to come to Mrs. Bessie's when she's got company."

"But Mom looked over to make sure the polishes weren't here before she let us come. And there's no car here," Daisy said, looking accusingly at Sue as if wondering how she managed to get there when there was no vehicle outside.

Rose began laughing.

"That's alright girls, Mrs. Bessie and I are always pleased to have you visit. Come and meet our friend Mrs. Newman who is on holiday from the United States. And don't worry, the politicians won't be back for hours."

But the two girls looked undecided until Sue spoke, asking them if they liked fruit, that perhaps Mrs. Bessie or Miss Rose wouldn't mind sharing some of their fruit.

"That's a great idea. Come over, girls, and choose what you'd like to have. We have apples, oranges, bananas, and even grapes," said Bessie.

That was enough to move the girls who came to the kitchen counter to admire the variety of fruit.

When both girls chose bananas, Sue remarked it looked like they had the same taste and asked whether they were twins.

"Grown-ups is always asking us that, but I'm a year older than Daisy. I'm nearly seven years old and in grade two, and she just started school. It's our sisters, Lily and Pansy, who are twins, not us," Marigold said.

"You have such beautiful names. I'm guessing your mother must love flowers. Do you have any more sisters with lovely names?"

"No, only a brother and his name is Bobby," Daisy broke into the conversation.

"But our Mom is having a new baby before Christmas, and it might be a baby girl, and if it is, I think she should be called Poppy. Though Bobby says it better be a boy because there's enough girls in our house now. He says the baby should be called Ken, like the goalie of his favourite hockey team, the Montreal Canadiens."

When the adults started laughing, Marigold very seriously said that her Mom and Dad told Bobby they didn't care if the new baby was a boy or girl as long as it was healthy.

"But it don't stop Bobby wishing for a brother," she added.

"One thing for sure, your parents can never be lonely with five children in the house. They are lucky people," Sue said.

Meanwhile, Bessie had picked up an envelope put down on the counter by one of the girls when they chose their fruit.

"What do we have here? This envelope is addressed to Misses Marigold and Daisy Brown, so it must belong to you girls. Now, who would be writing to you? It's a big envelope, and it looks important. Would it be from your school? Or perhaps it's from the government," Bessie said, trying hard to look serious.

By now, both girls were hopping with excitement, and Marigold spoke up.

"It's from Penny. She said she would write, and she did. She sent us photos, and we brought them to show you and Miss Rose. Mam gave us the letter as soon as we got off the school bus. She said if we weren't pests, we could come over and show it to you. Read it, Mrs. Bessie and Miss Rose; your friend can read it too if she wants."

"Penny never forgot us, and tomorrow we're bringing the photos to school to show our teachers," Daisy added.

"See the cute, little babies with Penny, and there's a photo of children in school, and there's even a giraffe photo. And Penny says she'll look through more photos and see if there are any other wild animals. Isn't it great?"

Turning to Sue, she said, "I bet you didn't think that Mrs. Bessie, Miss Rose and us, knew a missing Harry from Africa, and that is Penny, and she is our friend."

"No, I'd never guess you knew anyone from Africa. How did you meet your friend?" a bewildered-looking Sue asked.

"She was here and helped us make a cake for our Mom's birthday. It was a surprise, wasn't it, Mrs. Bessie? But it was some good cake. It was a cherry cake, Mom's favourite kind. Mom loved it, and Bobby says it was the best birthday surprise ever, even though the twins helped cook dinner on Mom's birthday. Can you bake? One of these days, Mrs. Bessie is going to learn us more baking. And Miss Rose, or Mr. Nolan, our principal, they're goin' to learn Bobby and Michael to play the guitar. They really wants to play the guitar. Michael is Bobby's friend, but he don't like Bobby's favourite hockey team; he likes the Maple Leafs. Michael don't have any sisters, only big brothers. Isn't that right, Mrs. Bessie and Miss Rose?"

By now, Rose and Bessie were both laughing at Sue's expression. Their American friend appeared to be having trouble keeping up with Daisy's non-stop conversation, so Rose decided to step in.

"Girls, how would you like milk with your bananas? And I'm sure Mrs. Newman wouldn't mind us sending some fruit over to the twins and Bobby."

When the girls enthusiastically agreed on milk while beaming with pleasure at the thought of bringing treats home with them, Rose got out glasses and milk, suggesting perhaps Bessie would tell their guest more about Penny the missionary and how they all met her.

The two young girls sat with proud smiles while Bessie told Sue about their friend Penny, Bishop Harris, and Beatrice, his wife. When Bessie finished talking, Sue said she had told her friends about Bessie and Rose's fascinating lives.

"You meet the most interesting people and don't have to go out of your home to do so. And I'm hoping to meet more of your neighbours, especially if they are friendly like these two young ladies. Perhaps you girls might join me for a walk after school one day and show me the sights of Mark's Point. What do you think? If you agree, perhaps Mrs. Bessie or Miss Rose could check it out with your mother to see what she says."

Nods and smiles from the girls showed their pleasure with Sue's invitation. They were in the middle of telling her where they might walk when the door opened, and Bob came into the kitchen, putting a halt to their excited conversation.

"Bob, come and meet Marigold and Daisy, who have agreed to be my guides after school one afternoon. They're going to take me for a walk and show me everything there is to see in Mark's Point. Girls, this is my husband, Bob."

"It's nice meeting you, young ladies. Sue loves walking and meeting people, so I know she will enjoy the walk around the community, especially having such good company," Bob said with a big smile to the girls.

But Bob's smiles were lost on Marigold, who, jumping up, informed Daisy it was time to go home. Despite Bob's protests that he didn't want to drive them away, Marigold was adamant it was time to leave.

"Mom will be looking for us, and Bobby and the twins should be home from high school by now. Mom said we should only stay a few minutes, but she didn't know you had company, Mrs. Bessie. She always tells us if you and Miss Rose got company, we're not allowed to bother you, so we've got to go. Come on, Daisy," and with those final words, the two girls prepared to leave.

"What about your fruit," asked Sue.

"Let's get a bag, and you pick out some fruit for your sisters and brother before you leave. Tomorrow we'll check with your mother to see about our walk. Is that okay?"

A few minutes later, the girls were on their way with Daisy clutching Penny's letter and Marigold carrying bananas to share with her family. Once they were gone, Bob turned to the three women saying it looked like it was his day to meet people.

"Gabe just introduced me to his daughter, Angela. What a friendly young woman she is. However, she's leaving for Toronto on Friday, so I was thinking on the way back that perhaps Sue and I could cook our meal this Thursday to let Angela attend. What do you think, ladies?"

"There's only one problem, Albert and Jack, our other guests, will still be here."

"We don't mind cooking for them too, do we Sue?" Bob said.

Sue was in complete agreement, saying it would be nice to cook for a crowd instead of two.

"Now, all we need to do is invite everyone. Four of us, plus the politicians, Gabe, Angela and Maggie, and David and Sharon, make 11 people. Do you think we could also invite Father Kiely to make a round dozen? He was so nice to us when we met him. Would that be okay with you, or is it too much of a crowd to accommodate?" Sue asked.

"It's okay with us, and we'll make enough space for everyone in the dining room. If you have your dinner on Thursday, it would be convenient for Father Kiely. He has a community meeting in the church. Do you think we might have dinner early, say about five o'clock, because the meeting starts at seven, and both Bessie and I will be attending? I'd say Sharon and David will also want to go to the meeting and who knows, Maggie and Angela might convince Gabe to come," Rose said.

Bob and Sue had no problem with the time, adding they would ask the politicians and any guests from Mark's Point but would leave Rose or Bessie to invite Father Kiely.

"I can do that tonight as I have a parish council meeting in Murphy's Cove. Meanwhile, David and Sharon intend dropping in later so you can invite them then," Rose replied.

"Weren't Sharon and David lucky finding a house near you? And to think it belongs to you. I knew they wanted to live in Mark's Point but thought there were no houses available. I didn't realize you had a home. Rose, until Sharon wrote saying it was your house and how delighted she and David are with it," Sue said.

"It was a surprise to me to know the house was ready to be occupied because it was empty since my parents came to live with Bessie and Alex. I never knew Alex had been renovating it in his spare time to surprise me, but he died before he had it quite finished. Unknown to me, Bessie arranged with Gabe to continue the work and do some painting. It's a cozy home now and completely up to date, and I'm happy to see it used again, especially by a young couple. Having them live in Mark's Point is good for the parish and the community because they plan to get involved in both."

"They'll be an asset to Mark's Point," Bessie added.

"You heard us speaking about the meeting on Thursday. It's to see if there is enough support to use our former school as a parish and community centre. We'd have to raise money to maintain and equip it, but it could be an ideal place for card games, socials, and meetings. David heard there was no organization for students outside school, and he is interested in starting a youth club, which I think would go over well in this area, but we need somewhere to hold the activities."

"Will the school need any renovations? If so, I might be able to give you some ideas as my company not only constructs buildings but also renovates older homes and hotels," Bob said.

"Depending on how the meeting goes, we might be glad of your help. But, if we want to use the school, we will need equipment like tables and chairs. Our priority will be to raise money because, in addition to buying supplies, the community will be responsible for electricity and insurance on the building, plus any repairs that may arise." Rose said.

As Rose was speaking, Bessie saw Bob and Sue appeared to be looking at each other and nodding, almost as if they were having a silent conversation. When neither of them spoke, she laughed inwardly, believing it was a figment of her imagination. Thinking they might be bored by talk of the old school, she was about to change the topic when Bob spoke.

"Bessie and Rose, when you have some time to spare, Sue and I hope to discuss something important to us. Between meetings and your guests, it looks as if you have a busy week ahead. We hoped you might give us some input or advice and wondered when it might be a good time to talk."

"What about now. With the soup simmering away, we only need to cook potatoes, which means we don't have much to do for the next hour or more."

Rose agreed, suggesting they go into the sun porch to be comfortable and see anyone approaching the house.

Once they were seated, Bob said he didn't know if Bessie and Rose realized the impression Newfoundland, especially Mark's Point, made on Sue and him

"We told you that I was considering retirement. Since returning to New York, Sue and I have given serious thought to the idea. We feel the time is right to do so, and we also agree Mark's Point is where we want to spend our retirement years. If we can find land for sale, we would build our home here.

"When we first thought of retiring to a new community, our biggest concern was that residents wouldn't accept newcomers. We know that won't be a problem in Mark's Point because it didn't take us long to discover how friendly local people are to strangers. We're sure we'd be happy here and already feel we have good friends in the two of you, Gabe, and of course, David and Sharon. Do you think we are crazy or what?"

"Of course not. I think it's wonderful news, and anything I can do to help, just let me know," said a delighted Bessie.

"At one time, I might have thought you crazy because apart from my family, I couldn't see anything to bring me back here. Not now, because I am completely content in my new life, and I believe you'll be happy living in Mark's Point. Like Bessie, I think it's great news. However, you might find the winters hard," Rose said

But Sue said they had considered the weather during their many discussions. They agreed they could always rent a place in Florida for a few months if it got too bad.

"Apart from good friends, who can always visit us, we have no family. My parents are deceased, and I only had one sister who died young, while Bob has no relatives. We had always hoped for children, but it never happened, and by the time we considered adoption, we were too old. But Bob and I have had good lives together. Our only disagreements were about how hard he worked," Sue said.

"What Sue didn't tell you, and I don't talk about it much, not that I'm ashamed of my background, but I was a foundling. As an infant, I was left unclaimed and unidentified in a hospital waiting room. I was never adopted and grew up in a children's home, but nothing was wrong with my life. I was happy, and one thing I loved as a boy was woodworking and the classes offered to us. I began to learn the carpentry trade while still a teenager, and I always thank the orphanage for my love of making things.

"Sue talks about me working long hours," Bob continued speaking.

"That's because I was determined to never be in want or to see Sue in need of anything. But I neglected her over the years by spending too much time on the job. It was when she got sick last year, and I thought I might lose her, that I realized everything I had worked for was worth nothing if I lost Sue."

Bessie and Rose had not known about Sue's illness, and now they questioned her about it, only to be told that it had been a heart problem, but now she was 100 percent better.

"What Sue isn't saying is she had major surgery, and it was touch and go for a time," Bob said, putting his arm fondly around his wife.

"Thankfully, Sue is now well, and like me, she is ready for a new life in Newfoundland. Making our home here is not a whim as we have given it lots of thought. When we first left New York to travel across the States and Canada, the possibility of finding a place to retire was in our minds. We count our lucky stars that we met the Kennedys when we got off the ferry in Newfoundland. We would never have heard about you or Mark's Point without them. Our time in your home and this community turned that possibility into a determination to move because nowhere else did we find the friendship and sense of belonging we found here."

"That's quite the compliment to the people of Mark's Point. And although this community isn't large in population or homes, it's surprising how much land there is. There has to be some for sale. We have a fair-sized piece of land on the main road outside the community, but that's no good because it doesn't have a view. If you're going to live here, and I am delighted you plan to do so, you need land with a view that you can enjoy each day from your home," Bessie said.

"I agree with Bessie. I'm still getting used to the idea you will be our neighbours, but it's welcome news. All we need to do is find land to get you started on your plans and be ready to move in next year. We will ask around to see what land is available. Gabe might know as he sees most of the men down by the wharf. Just think, Bessie, if we hadn't started our business, this would never have happened."

Later that night in the living room of Martin House, Sue and Bob shared their news with Gabe, Sharon, and David, who expressed surprise and pleasure.

"Well, it looks as if I'll have a full-time fishing buddy and, if you're planning on becoming a permanent resident, you better be prepared for the woods in the winter. I'm sure you'll enjoy cutting logs with me and Nell. I can see us having some great boil-ups in the woods," Gabe said with a chuckle.

"Who's Nell?" four voices asked in chorus.

"Nell? Did you never meet her? She's a wonderful companion. We've spent some long days in the woods together, 'though I must say Nell does most of the heavy work."

"Stop tormenting them, Gabe," Bessie said.

"Like most men in this area, Gabe uses a horse to haul out his logs, and Nell is his horse. Alex and Gabe always cut logs together and used Nell when it was time to haul them out."

"We'd load the logs on a sled Alex and his father made years ago that's still as sturdy as it was the day they finished it. Bessie insisted I take it after Alex died. I used it by myself in February, but it was some lonesome without Alex. I probably could have got someone else to come with me, but it didn't seem right. Even having a boil-up in the woods wasn't the same without Alex. But if you feel you'd like to come in the woods once you move here, I'm sure Alex would be glad to know I had a buddy once more."

When Bob wholeheartedly agreed to accompany Gabe in the woods, David spoke.

"Would you consider taking a townie in the woods some weekends? I should tell you I've never spent any time in the woods, but I'd love to try."

Sharon laughed when Gabe said he would be glad to have David along, saying it should be an interesting experience.

"Especially for you, Gabe, taking two novices into the woods. It almost sounds like a Newfoundland joke. There was a Bayman, an American, and a Townie who went into the woods together. I guess we'll have to wait and see how it ends," Sharon said, laughing at the idea.

"When I catch a brace of rabbits and bring them home for you to clean and cook, we'll see who's laughing then," David retorted.

"You can catch all the rabbits in the world, but you'll never get me to skin or cook one, so if I were you, I'd stick to cutting logs or having a boil-up if you ever go in the woods," his wife replied.

The group was still laughing at the young couple when Rose and Angela came into the living room.

"Look who I met as Bob was dropping me off at the gate. Isn't this a fine crowd, and it will soon get bigger because Albert and Jack are just parking their car," Rose said

"I never knew you were coming here, Angela. I could have waited for you. Come and meet Sue, Bob's wife."

Gabe introduced the two women and then asked Angela if Maggie was alright.

"Of course, she is, Dad," Angela replied.

"It was Maggie's idea that I come over. When you phoned to tell us Sue and Bob had invited us to dinner on Thursday, she got excited thinking that she and I could provide dessert. We won't do it unless it's okay with you, Sue and Bob. You see, Bessie recently taught Maggie to make blueberry pudding, and she wants to show off her skills. She says it works out perfectly because the high school is closing at noon on Thursday because of a teachers' meeting, and we would make it that afternoon. What do you think?"

"It sounds delicious. I'm sure everyone will look forward to blueberry pudding. I know I will," Sue said.

"Who's making blueberry pudding? It's my favourite dessert, and Albert loves it too. Don't you, Albert?" said Jack from the doorway.

"That's good because we'll be having it for dessert on Thursday, thanks to Angela and Maggie," Bessie said.

"Albert and Jack, you've met Gabe and got to know Bob and Sue at dinner, but what about Angela, Sharon, and David?"

With introductions over, the talk centred around Thursday and the upcoming dinner and meeting.

"You mean everyone here is coming to dinner on Thursday?" Albert asked.

"Cooking a meal for ten people is too much. It's nice of you to ask us Sue and Bob, but Jack and I won't intrude on your dinner. We can get something to eat elsewhere."

"Nonsense!" Bob replied.

"We're looking forward to your company, and there will be 12, not ten of us, for dinner. Maggie, Angela's daughter, as well as Father Kiely, will be here. Sue and I consider all of you as friends."

"And you know what the next best thing to friends sharing a meal?" asked Bessie.

"In this house, it's sharing a cup of tea. Say no more, Bessie; I'm on my way to the kitchen to put on the kettle. Since we are short of places to sit, perhaps a couple of you men can come with me and bring in a few chairs from the kitchen, so we can all sit as we enjoy our tea," said Rose.

CHAPTER 20

Eating And Meeting

Rose had just finished hanging a load of newly laundered towels outdoors when she spotted Gabe's boat coming into the harbour. Returning indoors, her hands cold from the wet laundry, she was glad Bessie lit the kitchen's large oil stove earlier that morning. Standing by the stove, she rubbed her hands, enjoying the warmth, while Bessie poured up tea from the big teapot for Rose, Sue, and herself.

"There's a real nip in the air this morning. It's probably why Gabe's boat is headed into the harbour this early. I'd say the men, especially Bob, found it chilly on the water. I wonder if Angela saw them coming in. She's probably not expecting them yet, so I'll give her a call," Rose said.

"It sure was nice of Gabe inviting Bob this morning and Angela cooking Gabe's favourite breakfast for them," Sue said, then looked curiously at Rose, who was grinning.

"Don't mind me, Sue. I was just thinking you should be glad you weren't invited to breakfast, considering roast capelin and homemade beans are on the menu. Poor Bob doesn't know what he's in for, sitting down to a meal of salty old capelin this morning."

"Just because we don't like it doesn't mean Bob won't enjoy his breakfast. Your father and Alex always enjoyed a meal of capelin," Bessie reminded Rose.

"I had never tasted or even heard of capelin until I came to Newfoundland, and any beans I ate before that time came from a can," Bessie told Sue.

"I learned to enjoy homemade beans, but I never did acquire a taste for capelin. But Bob might well enjoy his breakfast, and if Angela is anything like her mother, Jean, she'll probably have something else on hand in case he doesn't."

After phoning Angela, Rose spoke about taking a run over to Murphy's Cove that morning, asking if Bessie or Sue wanted to go with her.

Sue said she would go along as she knew Bob planned to go fishing later with Gabe.

"There are a couple of items I need for the Italian meal we are making. Do you like Italian food? We have Italian friends who prepare the most delicious meals and, although our cooking won't come up to their standard, we are hoping you'll enjoy it," Sue said.

"Sounds great, and it will be a new kind of food for me. I love macaroni and quite like tinned spaghetti, but I've never tried real home-cooked Italian food. What about you, Rose? Have you eaten an Italian meal?" Bessie asked.

"Yes. I love cheese and tomatoes, which seem to be staples in many Italian meals, and I like all kinds of pasta. I'm looking forward to our meal tomorrow."

Bessie was reminded of their conversation the following afternoon as smells from their American guests' cooking wafted throughout the house. Banned from the kitchen for the afternoon, she relaxed in the sun porch while Rose practiced organ music in church.

She was reading her most recent Scottish magazines and newspapers when Sue came looking for her.

"Bessie, I'm sorry to bother you, but is it possible to use a loaf of your homemade bread. I completely forgot to buy any. I'm just hoping I haven't forgotten anything else."

"No problem, Sue, there's plenty of bread. I have a couple of loaves in the bread bin. Use as much as you want because there's more in the freezer. I don't know what you're cooking, but by the wonderful smells coming from the kitchen, I know it's going to be tasty. I've been trying to read, but my mind is on tonight's meal. I'm certainly looking forward to it," Bessie replied.

"It's nice to see you sitting down and relaxing, Bessie. Rose should be back soon, and when she does, we will bring you both a cup of tea and a treat that I'm hoping you will enjoy," Sue said as she left the room.

Rose had no sooner arrived back from church when Bob, wearing one of Bessie's aprons, came into the living room carrying a tray with tea, sugar, and milk before returning with a plate of Scottish shortbread fingers.

"Sue discovered these in a supermarket at home and picked up several packs, especially for you. We hope you both enjoy them," he said.

"This is a treat, not only being served afternoon tea, but I never imagined I'd be enjoying shortbread made in Scotland and brought to Newfoundland from the United States," Bessie said smiling.

"Thanks, Bob. I'd go through and thank Sue, but she's got us banned from the kitchen until dinner time. Let us know when you're ready to have the table set. We are using our best dinner service and cutlery because tonight's a special occasion and calls for something better than the dishes we use every day."

Rose asked the last time Bessie had the table extended right out and used her china dinner service?

"I can remember helping you put the extra piece on the table and taking out your best dishes when Mother and Father celebrated their 55th wedding anniversary. We had Gabe, Uncle Walter, and Aunt Floss and a few older friends of Mother and Father to dinner, as well as Father Walsh, who celebrated Mass here in the house." Rose recalled.

"The dining room was pretty well full a couple of weeks ago when we cooked brunch for the wedding crowd, but we never used the china dinner service. I remember thinking that Alex was crazy when he wanted to buy the large dining room set. But he said there was no sense in having a big dining room with a small table and only six chairs in the set. It certainly came in handy for the anniversary and a few more times over the years," Bessie said.

"Wasn't that a happy time for Mother and Father, Bessie? Father Walsh knew they'd like an anniversary mass but would find it difficult to go to church, so he celebrated Mass here. It made the day extra special for them."

"Those were good times, Rose. When I think of Mina's life, it makes me realize how lucky we are to have so many good memories of your parents and Alex. I'm sure in a few years, we'll be just as happy when we remember today's gathering because it marks a new period in our lives."

"I'll tell you what's making me happy right now, and that's the smells coming from the kitchen. I can't wait to taste Sue and Bob's Italian meal," Rose said.

Rose's opinion was shared by the other guests, who began sniffing with appreciation as they came into the house. First to arrive were Albert and Jack, saying they finished campaigning early so they could wash and change before the 'dinner party.'

"And a dinner party is just what this feels like because it's certainly different. How is your campaign going?" Bessie asked.

"We think it's going well. The reception is good as we go door to door. When someone answers our knock, they are often surprised. Most say I'm the first candidate they have ever met. People usually invite us inside, and I must admit I enjoy meeting so many of them. The one problem we have is turning down all the food and drink they seem determined we should try."

"I was just saying to Jack the other day that I'm glad I decided to try for the seat out this way. I thought of seeking a nomination in one of the St. John's districts, but I wanted to try my luck here because of my grandmother's connection. If I do get elected, and I feel more confident about the possibility, I plan on spending a lot of time in this part of the district," Albert said.

"Not only are you the first candidate who has gone door to door, but I'd also say you're the only politician who has done any campaigning in the district. The only time I remember our member visiting this area was when the premier came to Murphy's Cove and officially opened the high school. That was ten years ago," Bessie recalled.

"What was ten years ago?" Gabe asked as he arrived with Father Kiely in time to hear the tail end of the conversation.

"I was just telling Albert and Jack that the first and only time I knew of our member coming to this district was when he arrived with Joey Smallwood for the opening of the high school in 1961," Bessie answered.

"It may have taken ten years, but the Liberal member is back in his district. He was in Murphy's Cove this morning," Father Kiely remarked.

"He was? Maybe we'll meet up. Were you talking to him?" Albert asked

"No, I was just getting into my car after leaving the shop when a station wagon, with a loudspeaker on its roof and Liberal signs on the doors, stopped alongside me. I waited a couple of minutes to see if anyone was getting out of it and when nobody did, I left and went on to Mossy Brook. Even then, I didn't know who was inside the car."

However, on arriving in Mossy Brook, the priest discovered the Liberal member was campaigning in the area and had travelled through that community earlier without stopping.

"How can he let people know what he stands for or intends doing for this district if he doesn't stop and talk to at least a few people," Rose asked.

"According to Bob Moss, he plays his message over a loudspeaker. Bob said it blared so loud; it scared his chickens and had all the dogs in the community barking and going crazy. His father was mad because the candidate never stopped to speak to him, especially since Philly is an ardent Liberal and Joey supporter. You never know, Albert; you just might get old Philly's vote. He told Bob that at least that young PC whippersnapper stopped and spoke to him," Father Kiely said, laughing.

David and Sharon joined the group in the living room in time to hear the end of Father Kiely's comments.

"Don't go talking about the Liberal candidate. He disrupted our classes by parking outside our school this morning. For almost 10 minutes, he was blaring over that loudspeaker of his. The students had never heard one before, and what an excitement it caused. I had most of the teachers complaining that their students rushed to the windows to see what was happening," David said.

"It was the same at our school, but he wasn't content with just one tirade. He then moved to the main entrance of the high school and started up again. When one of the teachers asked the principal if he was going outside to tell the candidate to stop, Mr. Smith said no. He felt it would give the candidate the attention he wanted. Tell me why he would get on a loudspeaker outside schools? It's not like students can vote for him," Sharon said.

"Maggie was telling Angela and me about it. She said he was kicking up a racket. She's picking up a lot of Newfoundland expressions since she came home," Gabe spoke fondly.

"Where is your granddaughter and Angela, Gabe? I thought they were coming to dinner," Jack asked.

"They are, but they're making a boiled pudding for dessert, and Maggie tells me they've got it timed to come out of the pot at exactly quarter to five. They're bringing it here in the pudding bag when it's ready. When I left the house, Angela was making some sort of sauce in a dipper on the stove, while Maggie was beating tinned cream which, according to her, is also perfect with blueberry pudding."

"Maggie's going to make a great cook because she's interested in knowing how different foods taste and how they are made. Wait until she finds out it's an Italian meal we are having. I'm sure she'll have all kinds of questions for Bob and Sue," Bessie said.

"Who's taking our names in vain?" Bob asked, coming into the living room.

"I hope you're all hungry as we have loads of food. Bessie, we thought you or Rose might like to check the dining room and see everything is the way you like it. Sue was also looking for more serving dishes. Do you think one of you could come and see what she can use?"

Glad to help, Bessie and Rose followed Bob out of the living room while Albert and Jack excused themselves to freshen up before dinner.

"The more I talk to Albert, the more I think he'll make a good member for this district," David said when the candidate left the room.

"From what I hear, it's a rare occurrence when the current member shows his face in these communities. I've also heard he's difficult to get a hold of when people are looking for help or information."

Gabe agreed with David, saying, according to Bessie, the last time the member showed his face was at the opening of the high school ten years earlier.

"And I'd say he only come then because he knew the premier was attending. He and his fellow Liberals have taken things for granted for too long. I don't know much about this Frank Moores fellow that's leading the Tories, but if he's got more candidates like Albert, I think we should give him a chance to see what he can do."

The living room began to fill up again when Maggie and Angela arrived. Bessie then appeared from the kitchen, full of admiration for the upcoming dinner.

"We're in for a great meal according to everything I've seen. Not only has Bob and Sue made a variety of Italian dishes, Angela and Maggie brought in a boiled blueberry pudding, and it smells delicious. Sue says to give her and Bob five minutes then take seats in the dining room. I can hardly wait."

When called through to the dining room, the guests were amazed by the spread, which saw the large table practically covered with colourful food dishes.

"Bessie and Rose, we'll leave the seating arrangements to you, but before we sit, Sue and I wondered Father Kiely if you wouldn't mind giving a blessing. We're so glad to have this opportunity to share our meal with people we consider friends and soon to be our neighbours. Would you do this, Father Kiely?"

"I'd be happy to do so, Bob," the priest replied.

"Dear Father, bless this abundance of food that we share today and bless those who prepared the meal. Thank You for bringing us here, not only to enjoy the meal but for the opportunity to spend time together and to realize that regardless of where we live, we are all neighbours. Father, let us always be willing to share our blessings and keep us safe in our travels until we can be together again. Amen."

When Father Kiely's 'Amen' was repeated by everyone, Sue's eyes became misty as she thanked the priest for the blessing, saying it was lovely and made everyone feel so welcome.

"Now it's time to eat," Bessie said,

"And as hosts Bob and Sue, you should each take an end of the table while the rest of us will just grab a chair anywhere in between. But before we start eating, why don't you tell us what we are having. I'm probably the only one here who's never tasted real Italian food, and the smells have my taste buds watering."

"We have meatballs in a tomato sauce, spaghetti, and also lasagna. There are two dishes of each, and lots of spaghetti still on the stove. Remember, Bessie, I asked for a loaf of bread from you. That was for the garlic bread you see in the baskets. Now everyone, start serving yourselves. There's also more sauce if it's needed," Sue told her dinner guests.

Her guests didn't need any more encouragement, and soon, the sounds of serving spoons or cutlery touching plates filled the dining room as everyone began eating. Apart from requests to pass food, it appeared everyone was too busy enjoying the meal to talk.

Bessie was the first to break the silence.

"To think I've never tasted Italian food before! These dishes of food are delicious. Before you leave, you have to show me how to make them."

"Me too," Maggie said.

"I've had meatballs and spaghetti before, but not as good as these. I'd love to be able to make them. And the lasagna and garlic bread are some good too. Can I get all the recipes?"

When Sharon said she also wanted the recipes, Bob and Sue began smiling.

"Well, that's a relief. If you want the recipes, the food couldn't have been too bad," Bob said.

"We were afraid it might be too spicy, not spicy enough, or that you might not like any of it. We're happy the meal went over well, and of course, you can have the recipes."

As Angela and the men began complimenting the couple on the meal, Sue spoke up, saying she always felt the best part of any meal was the dessert, and she was looking forward to the blueberry pudding.

It was Angela and Maggie's cue to get the pudding. When the other women started removing the dinner plates, Albert and Jack stood up quickly, telling them to stay seated.

"Sit down, ladies; this is where we come in. We grew up in a large family, and in our home, the rule was if the females cooked, the males cleaned up. Our parents believed boys and girls should equally share tasks. We made our beds and learned the basics of cooking and cleaning while our sisters took their turn at outdoor chores. My wife and I brought our children up the same way," Albert said.

With David giving them a hand, the brothers soon had the table cleared and the dirty dishes brought into the kitchen, where they rinsed and stacked them ready to be washed when the meal was over.

"And tonight, we'll do the dishes when you go to your meeting. Now I don't know about the rest of you, but I can't wait to try Maggie and Angela's blueberry pudding," Jack said.

According to Father Kiely, the pudding put the finishing touch to the meal, who said it was a perfectly successful dinner that would be difficult to top.

Then remembering how often he had eaten in Martin House, he added, "Just like all the meals I've eaten here."

"That's right, Father, don't go putting your foot in your mouth. You wouldn't want to miss out on an invitation to any more of Rose and Bessie's Sunday dinners," Gabe said, which made Angela shake her head and utter a reproving 'Dad.'

Seeing this, Father Kiely laughed, telling Angela she should pay no heed to her father.

"I never mind him, but I do notice he never turns down an invitation to Bessie and Rose's Sunday dinners either, and although he never comes to church, he always manages to arrive here just as mass finishes."

"Knowing your appetite, I have to arrive then in case you get to it first and leave nothing on the table," Gabe retorted.

"And that's just where we'll end this conversation," Bessie intervened.

"Remember what I said about the two of you going on with your nonsense in front of Maggie? Let's take our tea or coffee into the sun porch and relax for a while. We have plenty of time before the meeting."

As they sat in the sun porch enjoying their refreshments, Rose asked Father Kiely if he had heard about Sue and Bob's plans to move to Mark's Point.

"Yes, I did, and I'm delighted for them. You'll feel right at home, Sue and Bob. Look at how Sharon and David have settled in and become part of the community."

"Thanks, Father Kiely. We're sure it will be a good move considering the friends we've already made in Mark's Point," Bob said.

"If you plan to live here, you should come to the meeting tonight. Sharon and I thought it was for long-time residents only, but Father said everyone should come and give their input. Isn't that right, Father?" David asked.

"Certainly, the pair of you should come; you probably have some good ideas we could use," the priest agreed.

"What about my friends and me?" Maggie asked.

"We've got ideas. Everyone was talking about it on the bus, and if the school gets turned into a hall, we will want to use it."

"Why not? I completely agree with you. Young people should be at the meeting and have their say. I'm sorry I never thought about this, but you are welcome to attend," Father Kiely told Maggie.

"We can? Aunt Bessie can I use your phone and phone the twins and Michael, and they can spread the news that students can come to the meeting," a delighted Maggie asked.

When Bessie gave her the go-ahead, Maggie quickly scampered off to make the calls, but she addressed her mother on her return.

"I forgot for a minute that this is your last night before you go back to Toronto, so I'm not bothering about going to the meeting."

"You go to the meeting. It will give me a chance to finish packing. I need to have everything ready tonight because the taxi picks me up at eight o'clock tomorrow morning. You won't be that long at the meeting," Angela said.

"You're taking a taxi?" Jack asked in surprise.

"Albert and I are going to town tomorrow. You could come with us; couldn't she, Albert?"

"Of course. We would be happy to take you, Angela, and it would save you having to pay the taxi fare."

"I appreciate the offer, but I have the taxi booked, and Ted Brown, the driver, who makes the trip to St. John's every day except Saturday, is bringing me directly to the airport. Driving a taxi is Ted's living, and I wouldn't cancel my trip once I had my passage booked with him, but thank you anyway," Angela said.

"I wished we'd known before you booked the taxi," said Jack.

"It wouldn't have been any problem for us to take you to the airport and help you with your luggage too, but you never know; perhaps we can help you some other time."

"So, you're also leaving tomorrow. Will you be back next week?" David asked the brothers.

"No. We're going to concentrate on the other side of the district for the next few weeks, but we'll be back for at least a week before the October 28 election. We have already booked our room with Bessie and Rose. We'll be looking forward to seeing you all again then. I also promised Ellen, my wife, to bring her out this way, and we're coming the last weekend of this month," Albert said.

"What about your wife, Jack? Is she interested in coming to Mark's Point?" Sharon inquired.

"Jack isn't married. He's the confirmed bachelor in our family. I think my mother has given up hope of her youngest son ever getting married. She says he's too particular, but she prays every night that he'll find a good woman who will have him," Albert said, laughing.

"You're lucky you found Ellen, who wasn't one bit particular when she agreed to marry you. You're also lucky I'm not married and can afford to take time off work to drive you around. That way, the voters know there is at least one sensible person in our family," Jack retorted.

The next hour went quickly as the group chatted among themselves, enjoying each other's company. It came as a surprise when Father Kiely, looking at his watch, jumped up, saying it was time to go to the church for the meeting.

"The church! Why not the school?" Gabe asked.

"David, Sharon, Bob and Sue have never been inside the school, so it would be a good opportunity for them to see it."

"And pray tell me what we would use for seats?" Rose sarcastically asked.

"The building is empty. In fact, that's one of the first things we're going to need. We can't have fundraising events like card games or socials without some chairs and tables."

"It looks as if the community has its work cut out if it hopes to use the school for events then," Albert said.

"But I guess that's why you are having the meeting. I hope you get a good turnout of people willing to work to keep the school as a centre for the parish and community."

An hour later, it was evident there was plenty of interest in the former school when every teenager and most adults from the community attended the meeting. Even when Father Kiely explained how their community would be responsible for maintenance and all ongoing expenses, there was no negative feedback.

Pat Martin, one of the oldest men in the community, shared the opinion of others addressing the crowd when he spoke about the importance of keeping the school, noting it had always played a role in the lives of Mark's Point residents

"The men in this community built that school, and I was one of them. We was all so proud when it opened, and the old one-roomed building that was long past its prime could be closed. Our youngsters finally had two warm, comfortable classrooms where they could get their education. That was 1952, and the school is just as sturdy as it was then. Then, when the high school opened ten years ago, we knocked down the middle wall to make the school bigger. Now everyone has a chance to use it as a hall."

"Mr. Pat's right, and so is everyone who spoke here tonight. However, it's easy to say keep the school, but we need to raise money to pay the bills and to do that, we need a committee to put some plans into action," Robert Brown said.

Father Kiely, pleased to see the positive comments for keeping the school, agreed with Robert that forming a group was the way to begin.

"People have to be committed, not only to raise money for the school's upkeep but for buying necessities such as tables and chairs or even kitchen equipment. The committee would also be responsible for groups wanting to use the building. I've heard ideas tonight such as darts, card games, crafts for adults, and a club for our young people. All these ideas are excellent, but someone has to arrange a schedule letting people know when the school would be available."

Father Kiely added that as parish council members, Robert and Rose should be on the committee before asking for nominations for at least four more people to work with them.

Pat Martin was one of the first to be nominated. Although he declined, he promised to help in any way he could.

"Instead of an old fella like me, I'd like to see one of these young ones here take a hand in making the decisions," Pat said

"Just 'cause they's still in school, don't mean they don't have good ideas, and I knows they wants to be using the school. I think they should figure out among themselves what one of them should go on the committee. While they does that, I'd like to see our new principal go on the committee as well. From what I'm hearing, he wants to get some kind of club on the go for the youngsters."

Pat was still talking when loud music from outdoors had everyone wondering what was happening. The music continued to get louder, making hearing almost impossible. Because it was a warm night, the church doors had been left open, and Dan Ryan, who was sitting near the back of the church with his wife Nora, got up to close them. Looking outside, he saw a large vehicle, with a loudspeaker on its roof, parked in the middle of the road.

Closing the church doors, Dan ran down the steps and out through the gate before stopping at the car and knocking on the front passenger window. At his knock, the music stopped, and the window lowered to reveal a man's smiling face.

"Good evening, I'm your Liberal Member of the House of Assembly, and I'll be looking for your vote next month. I'm going through every community in my district, letting people know they can count on me again. I've been your member for over 15 years, and I'm proud of what I have accomplished. Now my man, is there anything I can do for you?" the member asked.

"You certainly can. You can turn off that blasted music. What do you think you're doing, kicking up a racket outside a church?" an indignant Dan asked.

"But it's not like it's a service; it's only a meeting. That's what some children playing on the road told me. They said everyone had gone to the church for a meeting. Until I saw them, I was beginning to think this had become a ghost town. There wasn't a soul around. Even the shop was closed. When I heard what was going on, I thought, what better place to let everyone hear my message? I'll stop the music and address my constituents over my loudspeaker. It's a great way to get out important messages."

"And that's what you won't. Everyone's talking about the upset you caused outside the two schools in Murphy's Cove today. You're certainly not going to spoil our meeting with your noise. If you wants to talk to people, why don't you do the same as the PC candidate, Albert Matthews? He's going door to door through all the communities."

"I'm a busy man. I don't have time to go to people's doors. I suppose I'll just wait here until your meeting is over and then address everyone at one time. Anyway, why would people complain about me being outside the schools? If it wasn't for my Liberal party, there would be no new schools in this district. People would have something to complain about then."

"You're full of bull!" Dan exclaimed, shaking his head.

"If I was you, I wouldn't be saying stuff like that around here, not if you're looking for votes. Now I'm going back inside. I can't stop you from parking here, but you might have a long wait and don't go playing any music while we're still inside. I can guarantee you won't get any votes that way."

Once back in the church, Dan slipped into the pew beside Nora, who excitedly told him their youngest son Michael's friends, choose him to be the youth member. Another of their sons, Sean, and his girlfriend, Kelly Pearce, were also on the committee.

"Who else is on it?" Dan asked.

"Mr. Nolan, the principal of the elementary school, has agreed to be a member, and I'm trying to get a chance to nominate Bessie. I knows she's not a Catholic, but this building is going to be for everyone. She's always been a hard worker, and I think she'd be good on the committee. What do you think, Dan?"

Before Dan could agree or disagree, Lucy Pearce jumped up.

"Bessie Martin should be on the committee. She's not only my good neighbour; she's got good ideas. Who else would think of opening a Bed and Breakfast in Mark's Point?"

Nora was on her feet before a surprised Bessie could react, saying Lucy had taken the words out of her mouth.

"Bessie should be on the committee. It never mattered that she didn't belong to our church; she always worked as hard as any parishioner when doing things for the parish. And Lucy's right, Bessie. You've got good ideas, and when it comes to raising money, we needs people with ideas on how to do it."

Applause broke out, and when Father Kiely asked if she would serve, her neighbours began encouraging her to say yes, until a red-faced Bessie agreed to do so. The last person to accept a position was Oscar Kavanagh, bringing the committee membership to eight.

"Wonderful; I believe we have a great group of people to represent the residents of Mark's Point. Now it's up to them to start making plans. It will mean a lot of work, and everything won't get done at once but give your committee a chance, and I'm sure your former school will become a vibrant part of the community. I would suggest the eight members stay behind for a few minutes and decide when and where they can get together for a meeting," Father Keely announced.

"And before we leave, just a reminder to all our male parishioners that work on the graveyard fence will continue this Saturday. You've done a great job so far with all the old fencing down and removed. Robert tells me he has been in contact with men from Muddy Brook Cove and Mark's Landing, and the plan is for everyone to gather here at eight on Saturday morning to start putting up the new fence."

As the crowd began streaming out of the church, the politician, fearing people would ignore him, began addressing his constituents by loudspeaker, startling some of them.

"Good God!" bawled Dan Ryan, almost as loud as the candidate. Going over to the car door, he jerked it open.

"Get out, man, and talk to people properly. Carrying on this way will scare everyone to death. Another thing, there's still some people meeting inside."

Later, back at Martin House, Bob enjoyed telling Albert and Jack what happened when Dan almost pulled the candidate out of his vehicle.

"I've met Dan several times around his boat or on the wharf, and he always seemed to be the mildest sort of man. But I think he scared that politician and his manager half to death. The candidate didn't seem to know what he should be doing or saying. We never waited as Bessie and Rose are on the new committee, and the members, including David, stayed behind for a short meeting."

"We never heard any loudspeaker here, or I would have gone out and introduced myself to the candidate," Albert said.

"But I'm not going looking for him now. He probably got more than he bargained for when he decided to campaign outside the church. Getting back to the meeting, it's great that both Bessie and Rose are on the committee, and you said David is also a member. They will be excellent representatives, and I've no doubt we'll see a community centre up and running soon. Now I know what Bessie would do if she expected any of us back soon. She'd put on the kettle, ready to make a cup of tea. So that's what I'm going to do right now, and when she and Rose come in, they'll be happy to relax with a cuppa."

"Great idea Albert. I'll get some Scottish shortbread from the cupboard that they can enjoy with their tea. We'd better take out the biggest teapot. Although Gabe will be home with Angela tonight, I wouldn't be surprised to see Father Kiely, and maybe even David and Sharon, come back here," Sue said as she bustled around the kitchen helping Albert.

CHAPTER 21

Goodbyes And Good Buys!

It was the morning of Angela's departure, and in Martin House, Bessie, Rose and Sue were preparing to go to Gabe's house to say their goodbyes. Bessie felt guilty, leaving Albert and Jack, who had not yet eaten breakfast, but promised she would be back soon to cook it.

"Are you sure you don't mind us going? You'll find boxes of cereal on the counter, and the coffee is ready. Could you make do with that until we return in about 15 or 20 minutes?" Bessie asked

"You go on and say goodbye to Angela. There's no need to worry about us. We're used to fending for ourselves but be sure to wish Angela good luck from us," Jack replied.

"And that goes double from Jack," his brother said with a mischievous grin.

"I'm surprised you're not going over to say goodbye to Angela yourself, considering how disappointed you were when she didn't accept your offer of a trip to town. Then at dinner, although everyone agreed the blueberry pudding was delicious, you praised it up at least a dozen times."

"I did not," a red-faced Jack answered.

"I did say it was good because I thought Maggie deserved to know what a great job she did. However, I do admire Angela going back to school to upgrade. She's doing the best thing for herself and Maggie."

Seeing Jack getting embarrassed with the conversation, Bessie broke in, telling Sue that Rose had gone outside to start the car. Sue told the men not to expect her husband back because Robert Brown, knowing Gabe would stay home to see Angela leave, had invited Bob out in his boat.

"It will probably be afternoon before Bob returns," Bessie told Sue as they walked out to the car, adding Robert fished with his brother-in-law, Tim Furlong, from Mark's Landing.

She told Sue the two men were the first in the area to take a chance and invest in a longliner. The fibreglass vessel, equipped with the most modern equipment, was about 40 feet long compared to Gabe's wooden skiff at half its size. Its size and powerful diesel engine let them fish much farther out than most local fishermen. Equipped with bunks, the men could even stay out fishing overnight.

"That's not happening today, but Kate did say that Robert planned to cook a meal of freshly caught fish for Bob while out fishing," Bessie told Sue.

"Bob's sure to enjoy that as he loves all kinds of seafood. He even liked the capelin he had for breakfast at Gabe's; although Rose, you didn't think he would," Sue replied as she got into the car.

Arriving at Gabe's house, they walked into the kitchen to hear Maggie doing her best to convince her grandfather she should carry her mother's suitcase to the gate. However, Gabe had no intention of letting her do so, saying he wasn't having her hurt herself.

"Aren't you going to school today, Maggie?" Rose asked.

"Yes, the taxi should be here before my bus leaves, but just in case it isn't, Pop says he'll drive me to school because I don't want to leave before Mom goes."

When Sue asked Maggie how she was enjoying school, her enthusiastic reply left no doubt in the women's minds.

"I love it. I have the best teachers, and my classes are excellent. I was a bit worried I might be behind in some courses like Newfoundland History, but my homeroom teacher says everyone is starting grade eight courses together, which means I won't be behind. Next week, intramural sports begin at lunchtime, and Mrs. Nolan and Miss Mills are even talking about getting basketball and volleyball teams together to compete with other schools. Everything about high school is wonderful."

"And she's not just saying that, so I won't worry. One look at her beaming face is enough to know how she feels," Angela said.

"I've never seen her so happy as she is each morning leaving to catch the bus. Then when she comes home, she's full of stories about what happened that day or what she and her friends are planning. I'm going to miss all her news, but she and Dad will be phoning me, and she's also promised to write once a week."

"You've got to answer me. And Mom. I know you'll have to study, but you can't be at your books all the time. Pop and me will keep each other company, but you'll be alone. Go out, maybe to a movie sometime and enjoy yourself."

"I sometimes wonder who the mother is around here," said Angela, which made everyone, even Gabe, laugh.

When Rose and Sue handed her envelopes, Angela asked what they were.

"It's just a card from Bessie and me to wish you good luck and a little something to help you get a few supplies for your classes," Rose said.

"Yes, and as Maggie said, you need to relax sometimes, not spend all your time studying. Bob and I had the same idea, and we want you to have this gift to allow you to do so," Sue added.

"We've enjoyed getting to know you. We knew we would, considering the great job you did raising a lovely girl like Maggie and having Gabe as your father."

Seeing Angela looking misty-eyed as she thanked them, Rose broke in, saying Sue was right; Maggie was indeed a credit to her mother; however, having Gabe for a father was a different kettle of fish. Her typical response regarding Gabe had the females laughing, causing Gabe to shake his head in exasperation.

"Well, Saint Rose, now you're done commenting on my character, perhaps you'd be kind enough to move your arse and let me get past with Angela's suitcase."

"Pop! You wouldn't want me talking like that," Maggie said.

Angela shook her head but couldn't refrain from smiling.

"Dad, you're supposed to be showing a good example to your granddaughter. Maggie, you'll find there will be times when you need to close your ears to what your grandfather says, especially when he and your Aunt Rose butt heads."

"We're going to get out of your way now, Angela. We just wanted to wish you the best of luck, although we know you'll do well. We'll see you at Christmas," Bessie said as she hugged Angela.

"And I'll see you next summer when hopefully, we will at least be building our new home. Bessie and Rose already know our good news, but I'm delighted to tell you that it looks as if we have a piece of land here in Mark's Point. Once the sale is legal, we can start building next spring," Sue said excitedly.

"Where's the land, and who did you get it from?" Gabe asked.

Sue answered that Mr. Martin was selling them the land, asking Bessie or Rose to explain where it was.

"It's Pat Martin's land and includes the raspberry garden, so hopefully, we'll still be able to pick berries there," Bessie said with a smile directed at Sue.

"Both his sons have enough land, and his daughters are married and living outside Mark's Point. With none of them wanting the garden, Pat offered it at a good price to Bob and Sue. It's a perfect piece of land."

"It is indeed," Gabe agreed.

"I'd say you're lucky to get it. I bet if others knew Pat was selling it, he would have had more people interested."

But Bessie said that Pat had no intention of selling it until he heard Bob wanted land to build a home. Knowing someone wanted to put a house there and not just acquire more land to lie vacant, he was happy to let it go.

"And speaking of going, we need to leave as we have Albert and Jack waiting for their breakfast," Bessie said.

After a final goodbye to Angela, the three women left, arriving back at Martin House to smell frying bacon and Albert and Jack making breakfast.

"Come on, ladies, you're just in time. We have bacon and scrambled eggs ready and a stack of toast on the table. Seat yourselves and be served for a change," Albert instructed them.

"It seems you weren't bragging about being handy around the kitchen," Bessie said.

"Although I don't usually have a cooked breakfast, I think being outdoors has given me an appetite because the food certainly smells good."

Bessie wasn't the only one to find her appetite, and soon all three women were tucking into the tasty breakfast prepared by the brothers.

"What's on your agenda today," Albert asked the women as they sat back, enjoying their tea and coffee following the meal.

"I'm going to be one of the first customers at the newest business in Mossy Brook. I have an appointment at two this afternoon to get my hair cut. Maureen Maloney opens her hairdressing salon today. It's a first for this area, and her husband Jerome is also starting his carpentry and construction business. Although they trained in St. John's, they're going to live and work full-time in their community," Rose told the men.

When Albert asked if all three of the women were getting their hair done, Bessie said she and Sue planned to have their hair done the following week.

"Later this afternoon, I'm going sightseeing in Mark's Point with two tour guides," Sue said with a twinkle in her eye.

"Tour guides? There are tour guides in Mark's Point?" the brothers wanted to know.

"Yes, and from what I've heard, it's going to be a fascinating experience. My guides are two little girls, the daughters of postmistress Kate Brown and they plan to show me the sights of the community when they get home from school. Their father is Robert, the fisherman who invited Bob out in his big boat this morning. They are delightful children with beautiful names, Marigold and Lily, isn't that right, Bessie?" Sue asked

"You are half right. It's Marigold and Daisy who will be walking with you. Lily is their older sister, and her twin is Pansy." Bessie replied.

When Jack remarked Kate must be a nature lover to call her daughters after flowers, Bessie recalled how Kate was determined to give uncommon names to her daughters.

"I've heard Kate say several times that growing up; she always wished she had a different name. Many girls were called Kate, and other common names were Mary, Meg, and Jane. It resulted in them having nicknames to identify them. She was called 'Kate in the Lane' (that's where she lived). Her cousin was 'Jack's Kate,' while Kate Martin was always referred to as 'Kate Fox' because of her red hair.

"And these were nice names compared to some. Kate swore she would give any daughters she had names unlike any other in the area. She called the twins Lily and Pansy and continued the tradition with Marigold and Daisy. Bobby is, of course, named after his father."

"I'm looking forward to my walk with the girls, and then tomorrow, I'll have another new experience when I go berry picking," Sue said.

"Are your tour guides taking you berry picking?" Jack asked.

"No, I'm going with Bessie, Maggie, and Mina Lynch and her two daughters. We also plan on having a picnic lunch. Gabe says it's going to be perfect weather for berry picking, and I'm getting excited about it all."

"I suppose if Gabe says the weather is going to be good, we have to take that as gospel," Rose said.

"Maybe not gospel Rose, but you know as well as I do that Gabe is usually spot on when it comes to weather, but let's change the subject because I know after your encounter this morning, you're not in the mood to agree with anything Gabe said. Albert, do you plan to go campaigning today before returning to St. John's?" Bessie asked.

Although Albert looked curious on hearing Bessie's comment regarding Gabe, he let it pass, saying he and Jack didn't plan to stop anywhere.

"I have a meeting in town later this afternoon, and once we pack our bags, we'll be getting on our way. You'll be glad to see us gone so you can sit back and relax."

"Not at all. We're going to miss having the two of you around," Rose said.

"If there's a downside to running a Bed and Breakfast, it's seeing our guests leave just as we get to know them."

"If I'm elected, you might get fed up seeing me. And don't forget, I'll be back with my wife Ellen in a couple of weeks, and later, Jack and I plan to finish off the campaign in this area, which means you'll have to put up with us for another week." the candidate said.

"By then, we hope you have your community centre open. When is your committee having its first meeting?" Jack asked.

The meeting was taking place on Sunday afternoon at Martin House, Rose told him. Having a dining room with a large table to accommodate all the committee members, the Bed and Breakfast seemed the best option for their first official meeting.

"Hopefully, we'll soon get some chairs and tables for the school and be able to have our meetings there. That's one of the main topics we need to discuss because without chairs, there's not much can take place in the school."

"Buying a whole bunch of chairs is not going to be cheap, and you'll also need tables. Do you have any idea how much this will cost?" Jack asked.

"Not a clue, and we don't even know how many we need or where to buy stacking chairs and tables," Rose answered.

"Maybe I could help by asking around when I get back in town. I'll check with a couple of organizations and see where they got their tables and chairs. Albert's not starting campaigning again until Tuesday, which gives me all weekend and Monday to come up with some answers for you."

Later that night, as Rose sat relaxing in the living room with Bessie, Sue, and Bob, she mentioned Jack's offer.

"I think if we had chairs and tables sorted out, everything else would fall in place, and we would soon have the school up and running as a community centre."

"It's going to be good for Mark's Point," Sue said.

"Marigold and Daisy were telling me all about it when we were walking. However, they're worried the youth club will only be for older students, which, as they indignantly said, would be wrong considering they, not the twins and their friends, were the last ones to use the school."

Sue told the women that her walk with Marigold and Daisy was as good as a tonic, remarking how comical the girls were at times, yet so serious in some ways.

"I thoroughly enjoyed our time together, and we plan to walk again before we leave. However, I didn't fully understand what the girls meant about fishing for capelin on the beach. Isn't that what you had for breakfast at Angela's, Bob? Is it possible children can catch them and do so on the beach?"

Bessie and Rose laughed and explained how most of the community got involved in the caplin fishery, and no doubt, the girls shared in the excitement.

"It happens about once a year and usually only for a couple of days. The capelin roll onto the beaches to spawn. People catch and dry them to roast later, while some use the tiny fish as fertilizer on gardens. Did the girls mention the whales that often come into the harbour following the small fish?" asked Rose.

"Don't tell me that was true? When they said whales played in the harbour, making loud noises and jumping up in the air, I thought it was their imagination. I didn't think there were whales anywhere near here. Oh, my goodness, how I would have loved to see them."

"You never know, you might as we often have whales in the harbour, and they are entertaining to watch as they jump up in the water with lots of splashing and noise, which some people say is singing and others crying," said Rose.

"The little girls must get their chatter from their father, Robert," Bob remarked.

"I found him excellent company as well as being a good cook. He stewed codfish with potatoes, onions, and turnip, and it was delicious. I ate two big servings. There's a big difference between Robert and Tim's boat and the one belonging to Gabe. Their boat is much bigger, and they told me they've stayed out fishing overnight at times.

"I enjoyed my day, but it wasn't the same as fishing with Gabe. Don't get me wrong; today was a great experience and one I wouldn't want to miss. But when I go out in the boat with Gabe, whether I'm helping haul pots or nets or just jigging for fish, it's such a satisfying feeling, and for someone like me, it's a perfect way to relax. Having Gabe as a fishing buddy is a big part of that. He's easy to get along with, and although we are not big talkers, we do enjoy each other's company."

Thinking Rose might consider responding negatively to Bob's opinion of Gabe, Bessie quickly asked Bob what his plans were for the following day when Sue went berry picking.

"I'm working with the men on the cemetery fence. If we plan to be part of the community, I should do my part by helping out in projects benefitting the church or community."

"Bob's right. We both want to become involved in Mark's Point activities. I would like to help in some way, maybe in fundraising for hall equipment. I know we're leaving in another week, but perhaps if your committee has a sweepstake or raffle, I could supply some prizes. I'll wait until after your meeting and see what the plans are before deciding what I can do to help," Sue said.

"I've been thinking of different ideas to make money since last night's meeting, and one I remember from years ago in Scotland is the Parcel Post Stall. It was always a good fundraiser, and I'm sure we could adapt the poem to use here," Bessie said.

"What poem? Why do you need a poem?" Sue and Rose questioned.

Bessie explained the fundraiser started with a poem, which people gave or mailed to friends and relatives. It invited them to buy, donate, and wrap a gift and address it to The Parcel Post Stall, Mark's Point. The parcels were left unopened until sold at the fundraising event. The poem also explained the minimum amount the donor should spend on the gift, the same price when bought at the stall.

"I've been trying to remember the poem we used at home, and I know it went something like this:

Have you ever heard of a parcel-post stall?
Then read this letter, one and all.
And you will see how with your aid,
Lots of money can be made."

"Gosh, that sounds like a real winner, Bessie. Do you think you'll have a parcel-post stall here? I could bring letters back home with me and pass them out to my friends if you did. I know they would be only too happy to help," Sue said.

"Yes, and knowing how good you are at writing, Bessie, I'm sure you could easily make up more verses to tell people about our proposed hall in Mark's Point," Rose enthusiastically added.

"Hold on. We might think it's a good idea, but the rest of the committee might have a different opinion, although I wouldn't mind speaking about it at Sunday's meeting."

"I've got a better idea. Why don't you put a few verses together before then and let the committee hear them? I'm sure if they heard your idea and the poem, the members would love it."

"I don't know when you think I'll have the time Rose. I'm going berry picking tomorrow; we have Father Kiely, Gabe, and Maggie coming for dinner on Sunday, and the meeting takes place that afternoon."

"Knowing you, Bessie, I'm sure you'll come up with a few verses before then. When you set your mind to something, it's as good as done."

Bessie remembered Rose's words the following day as she sat on a rock in the middle of a blueberry patch. With a gallon bucket almost filled with berries and several more gallons in the freezer back in Martin House, she had more than enough for the Bed and Breakfast. As she rested, she tried to think of new verses for the parcel-post stall poem.

"A penny for them," Mina said as she came and sat on the rock beside Bessie.

"You look deep in thought. There's nothing wrong, is there?"

"No, not at all. I'm trying to be creative and getting nowhere fast. Maybe you can help me. What do you know about a parcel-post stall?"

"My goodness, Bessie! It's years and years since I heard those words. It brings me back to the annual Sales of Work we used to have at home in Scotland. The Parcel Post and the Tombola stalls were two of the most popular attractions and guaranteed to make money. Why are you asking?"

"I had forgotten about the Tombola stall, but you're right, Mina, those two stalls were always big attractions and money-makers at home. Our committee has to raise money to make the old school into a parish and community centre. but before that happens, we need money to furnish the empty building with at least chairs and tables."

Mina thought having the community use the school was a great idea, and if fundraising was necessary, a parcel-post stall made good sense.

"Do you have a poem ready to mail out for the Parcel Post Stall?" she asked.

"That's the problem. I have the first verse, but that's all. Now Rose thinks I can have a complete poem ready for tomorrow's committee meeting, but my brain is blank. Have you any ideas?"

"You need to decide what information is going in the poem. I remember we would ask the sender to write on the outside whether the parcel was for a boy, girl, man, or woman. If you list what information you want people to know, it might make it easier to write the poem. Give me the first lines you remember."

When Bessie recited the first verse, Mina thought for a while.

"What about something like this?

Mark's Point school lies empty and bare,
Our children are no longer educated there,
But we're making plans to benefit all,
By using it as a community hall.

That tells the reader why you are fundraising. Maybe you could add another verse to say what you need to buy before it can open as a community centre, then give instructions on how the stall works."

Sue, who brought the berries she collected to where the two women were sitting, arrived in time to hear Mina's verse.

"Gosh, you and Bessie are a great pair to make up poems. It must be a Scottish trait," she said, causing Bessie and Mina to break into laughter.

"Move over, Robbie Burns, here we come," Mina said through her laughter.

"Sue, I don't know about Bessie, but I'm going to get a big head if you keep giving me compliments. The first thing today, you were praising my quilts and telling me how much your friends loved them. Now you're praising my skills as a poet. That's too many compliments in one day for me," she said, wiping tears of laughter from her eyes.

"I might not be much of an expert on poetry, but it sounded good to me," Sue said, sounding slightly put out.

"However, I do know quality work when I see it, and so do my friends."

"She does make lovely quilts," a voice said from behind Mina and Bessie.

"But Mom's not used to getting compliments. She doesn't realize how smart she is and what a good mother she is to my sisters and me."

"Well said, Katy. I couldn't put it any better myself. We all know she makes beautiful quilts, and she's certainly done a great job raising you and your two sisters. She also has another skill, which I hope Maggie hasn't noticed; she's a champion berry picker. I well believe she filled her bucket faster than me, and I have the reputation of being the fastest berry picker in Mark's Point, or so Maggie believes. And speaking of Maggie, why don't we give her and Isabelle a shout. I think this would make a great spot to have our lunch. I don't know about the rest of you, but I'm starting to get hungry," Bessie said.

Soon the women and girls were enjoying a variety of sandwiches and drinks. Earlier, when Katy and Isabelle promised Millicent Murphy a gallon of berries, she had given them bananas and apples, which they now happily shared. Bessie also produced a container of homemade squares.

"Rose contributed these to our picnic lunch. She doesn't like picking berries but enjoys eating them, so last night, she baked these squares, and in return, she's hoping we bring home lots of blueberries. I've got my bucket filled, Sue, and when we finish eating, I'm going to pick more and freeze them for you to take home to the States. You can share them with your friends and show them what they are missing. Maggie also wrote out our recipe for blueberry pudding, so when you're back home and enjoying the pudding, you will remember Newfoundland and your first berry picking experience."

But Sue didn't need to wait until she returned to the States to remember her first berry-picking excursion. The following morning, when she woke up with every bone and muscle in her body aching, she remembered Bessie's warnings about slowing down and taking it easy when picking berries. Bob, who was still in bed because it was Sunday, and nobody went fishing on the Sabbath, jumped up in alarm when he heard Sue groaning.

"Sue, are you in pain? What's wrong? Is it your heart? What can I do to help you?" he asked her frantically, then got a shock when Sue ruefully started laughing.

"I've got the berry picking blues; that's what's wrong with me. Bessie warned me to take it easy when we picked berries, and even Maggie said I might be sore and stiff. Boy, were they ever right!" she said with another groan.

"I feel as if I just finished 24 hours of back-breaking labour. If you want to help me, what about running a hot bath so I can try soaking some of these aches away."

A few hours later, when Sue slowly eased onto a chair in the dining room, she felt as if everyone's eyes were on her.

"My goodness, Sue, what's wrong?" Father Kiely asked.

"Nothing to worry about, Father. I guess I don't listen too well. We went berry picking yesterday, and I forgot I was a grown woman. Instead, I acted like I was Maggie's age and went clambering all over the hills bending up and down like a yo-yo. I should have listened to Bessie and Mina and watched how they stayed in one spot until they had a bush picked clean. I'm paying up for it today, but it hasn't put me off berry picking. We still had a great day. Don't you agree, Maggie?"

Maggie gave a relieved smile as she said, "I do, Mrs. Sue, and I hope you soon feel better. Before I forget, here's Aunt Bessie's recipe for blueberry pudding that I wrote out for you."

"Thanks, Maggie, but now let's forget about my aches and pains and enjoy our dinner. As usual, Bessie and Rose have done a wonderful job on the meal. Bob and I are going to miss being catered to when we get back to New York. We'd better make the most of it because we only have a few days left in Mark's Point."

"But at least this time, we know for sure you'll be returning. Rose and I are looking forward to having you as neighbours, and I'm sure Gabe is happy to have a buddy again," Bessie said.

"I'll be glad to see you come back, and so will Daisy and Marigold," Maggie added.

"The twins told me their little sisters were all talk about their new friend Mrs. Sue, who lives in New York where the buildings go up to the sky."

When the others started laughing at this, Sue said, "Well, I did tell them we had skyscrapers, and I guess they took me at my word."

When Father Kiely asked when they were leaving, Bob replied they originally planned to stay until Wednesday and fly out Thursday. But since buying land in Mark's Point, he and Sue wanted to get the sale legalized, which meant they had to leave a day earlier to meet with the lawyer Rose had recommended. Before leaving, he hoped to arrange to have the land cleared in the coming weeks to allow construction to start on their home the following Spring.

"Later today, we are meeting Pat Martin and one of his friends who will be a witness to the sale of the land. I guess this is a busy afternoon here in Martin House with the community hall meeting. Are you staying for the meeting Father?" Bob asked.

"No, we have a committed group here, one that is more than capable of looking after things. I'm meeting with residents of Mossy Brook to discuss the future of their school. I believe they also want to keep it for their community, which is good. I'm hoping they get some good volunteers to work together. Rose or Bessie, if one of you gets a chance, I'd appreciate a call to let me know what happens at your meeting and if I can help in any way."

Later that afternoon, as Bessie considered the people seated around Martin House's dining room table, she thought Father Kiely was correct about the committee members. It hadn't taken long to elect an executive and for each person to accept a specific responsibility. Robert became chairman and Bessie secretary, while David and Michael volunteered to be responsible for youth activities. Oscar agreed to look after publicity, saying he would put notices in his shop, the post office, and send them to nearby communities. Rose accepted the treasurer's position, while Kelly Pearce and her boyfriend Sean Ryan were enthusiastic about taking charge of scheduling and entertainment.

"I've agreed to go co-chair of fund-raising with Rose, but I hope this committee will also have ideas. Before we can use the school, we need chairs and tables. That means a good fundraiser is necessary to start things off. What about a fair with different booths such as hoopla, a bake good or craft stall, penny toss, and other games? We could ask the men of the community to make up some stalls inside the school. I think Rose that we have a few sheets of plywood and some board that might do a couple of stalls," Bessie said.

"Me and my friends have something we'd like to try, Mrs. Bessie. It's something Maggie says is done in Toronto. It's a bottle drive where we'd go door to door to ask people for their beer and drink bottles and then sell them back to the shop. We figured we could hire someone to play for a teenage dance from the money we get for the bottles. We could make even more money that way 'cause all the high school students will come."

The adults sat amazed by Michael's plans. Robert was the first to respond, saying Pat Martin knew what he was talking about when he said a young person should be on the committee.

"I don't know about the others, but I think that's two great ideas you youngsters have already. The only problem I could see is getting someone to play for the dance," he said.

But just as quickly, David had a solution, saying his sound system would be perfect for a building the size of the school. He was sure Michael and his friends had favourite records they could bring along to the dance. That way, the music would be free.

Michael's beaming face at this news quickly changed when David said he thought the elementary school students would also love the idea of a dance.

"I don't mean all of you together. We could have two dances on a Friday night, probably from seven until nine o'clock for the younger children and from 9:30 to midnight for high school students. What do you think of that," David asked?

Everyone, Michael included, thought it was a great idea. David agreed to coordinate the bottle drive with Michael, and the two of them would set a date for the dances.

Ideas continued to flow from there. When the meeting finished, each committee member was committed to a six-week campaign, ending on the weekend of October 29-30 with a fair and adult dance.

Rose would have tickets on a box of groceries printed. Oscar agreed to put a box in his shop for grocery donations and make posters for his shop and the post office asking all residents to donate to the prize, while Kelly and Sean volunteered to go door to door selling the tickets. Meanwhile, Robert, Bessie and Rose would investigate different games and stall ideas for the fair before the next meeting in two weeks. Rose then insisted Bessie talk about the Parcel Post and Tombola stalls. When everyone enthusiastically said they would be great attractions at the fair, Bessie and Rose agreed to look after getting them ready for the event.

When the women sat down with Sue and Bob later that night, the conversation was about the upcoming fundraiser. Rose had already set the ball rolling for the grocery draw by arranging the ticket printing for the following day.

"I figure we could get ten tickets on a long sheet of paper. I spoke to Father Kiely, and he is asking the parish secretary to type and copy them up for us. The parish office has a cutter like a guillotine to separate them and plenty of staples to put them into books. When you have your hair appointments at Maureen's tomorrow morning, I'll go to the parish house and get the tickets copied, also the Parcel Post stall letters. I knew you would get the poem finished, Bessie, and didn't I tell you the committee would like the idea. And Sue, you'll be able to bring back a few letters to your friends; that's if you're sure you still want to do so."

"Of course, I do, but it's not much good me bringing tickets on groceries to sell in New York. Bob and I will come up with some other way we can help with the fundraising," Sue said.

Bob was all alone in Martin House the following morning when the women left for their appointments. He and Gabe had gone out in boat much earlier, but when the wind increased to the point where the small vessel was bobbing around on waves that continued to get higher, they called it a day and made their way back to shore. Bob planned to go to Gabe's shed, where his fishing buddy would introduce him to the art of mending nets. He was about to leave when the telephone rang. On answering, he was greeted by Jack Matthews looking for Bessie or Rose.

"I was hoping to speak to one of them as I've been checking out the prices of tables and chairs. According to the local supplier, new ones are not cheap and are no less expensive if ordered from the mainland. But I need to talk to Bessie and Rose because if we act right away, there's a club owner who shut down his business and is now selling everything, and that includes tables and chairs. I called him this morning, and he had already sold 100 chairs and a dozen tables, but he still has several dozen stacking chairs and about eight tables left. He is asking $100 for the entire lot, and it's a case of first come, first served because he wants clear of everything."

There was only one problem, Jack said. He could pay for the tables and chairs and be repaid later by the committee, but as Albert's brother and campaign manager, people might accuse him of buying votes.

Bob, however, had another idea, and he asked Jack for the seller's phone number.

"Sue and I will be in the city tomorrow, and we've wanted to do something for the new community centre. We'll pay for the tables and chairs and donate them to the community. This is perfect because they'll have them in lots of time for the fair at the end of October. Give me the seller's phone number Jack, and I'll call him, then go see him tomorrow."

A phone call later, Bob and the club owner had agreed to hold the tables and chairs until they met the following day. Bob then phoned Jack telling him about his purchase and asking him not to tell Bessie or Rose yet.

"If it's alright with you, I'd like to keep this just between us for now. I'll say you called and are checking out some prices. Once I see if the tables and chairs are worth buying and pay for them, I'll see about contacting the trucker in Murphy's Cove and have them shipped to Mark's Point."

Bob said the lack of tables and chairs was the main stumbling block to opening the centre, adding the committee would appreciate Jack finding the club owner.

"They can get more chairs and tables later. I know the hall will need other things in the future, but this will give the community a start if everything works out. It's a good buy and one we need to grab fast; that's why the club will be our first stop when we get to town tomorrow. Thanks a million, Jack, and good luck with the upcoming election. I know Albert will make a good member."

CHAPTER 22

Activity Plus

The Newmans were on the outskirts of Mark's Point on their way to St. John's when Bob told Sue about bargaining for chairs and tables.

"What! Why didn't you tell me this before? More to the point, why didn't you tell Bessie and Rose?" Sue asked her husband.

"For two reasons. They are second-hand tables and chairs, and although the owner says they are in good condition, I want to see them for myself. We wouldn't want Bessie and Rose getting their hopes up only to have them dashed if the chairs and tables are not fit to use, would we?" Bob explained

Sue reluctantly agreed, but then asked about the second reason.

"You know as well as I do how proud and stubborn our friends in Mark's Point can be. Look at the last time we were here and left money for the women and Gabe. Didn't they tell us in no uncertain terms not to consider doing it again? If Bessie and Rose knew what we intended doing, they might insist on giving us the money."

"Okay, I can see why you didn't tell Bessie and Rose, but why didn't you tell me?"

Bob grinned, saying, "Just think about it. You'd have been so happy you would have a hard time keeping the news to yourself."

"You're probably right. Oh, I do hope the tables and chairs are in good condition. Getting them would mean the community centre could open that much sooner."

When the couple reached their destination almost three hours later, they found Steve Marsh, the club owner, inside. Inviting them to look at the chairs and tables, he asked if there were any other items they might be interested in buying.

"The new owner plans on converting this building into apartments, and I have to clear everything out before he takes over next week. I sold all the bar and kitchen equipment, such as dishes, glasses, stove, and fridge, but I still have a large cooler left, and it's in good condition."

As Bob and the owner went to look at the big upright cooler, Sue spotted an electric bingo machine as well as several dartboards on one wall.

"This must have been a busy spot, Mr. Marsh. I see you have a bingo machine and dartboards," she said.

"Yes, this was a popular and profitable business. My wife and I worked hard to succeed, but now it's time to retire while we are in good health and can do some travelling. There's also a big club opening not far away, which helped us make the decision.

"The bingo machine is just over a year old and for sale. There are also a few hundred bingo cards. If you're interested in buying the machine, I will sell it at a good price. Bingo is always a good money maker. I tell you what; you said this was for a new but empty community centre, and I'd like to help. If you take the bingo machine, cards, plus the cooler, chairs, and tables, I'll sell the works for $150, and that's a good deal."

"What about the dart and scoreboards; are they for sale?" Sue asked.

"They were, but now they are sold. The fellow is coming tomorrow to get them. I had no trouble selling them because dart leagues are popular."

"Sue, I see by your face what you're thinking. You want to buy it all and even more," Bob said.

"I've no problem with that, but what about the committee? Last night, you heard Bessie say how much the community had come together because the residents have a common purpose, equipping the hall and seeing it opened. By getting all these things, they might think their work is over."

"I'm sure you're wrong, Bob. I think this will give the residents even more of an incentive to move ahead. They still need other equipment and probably renovations. I heard Bessie and Rose saying the women would love to have a separate kitchen at some time. Building one and buying a stove, dishes, and other kitchen equipment will be costly. I think we should go for this."

"Okay, Steve, you have a deal, and it's a good one, which we appreciate. I have enough cash here to pay for this stuff, but how soon do you need it removed because now I have to see about getting it all back to Mark's Point?"

Once the sale was complete, Father Kiely was the first to learn the community centre was getting chairs and tables. Knowing there was a trucker in Murphy's Cove, Bob contacted the priest for information on how to get in touch with him. Father Kiely listened in amazement when Bob told him the extent of his purchases.

"This is unbelievable. I'm sure the committee thought it would take ages to get any of it. What are the members saying about this windfall? They must be over the moon," he said.

"They don't know yet, and I'm hoping this doesn't stop the residents from continuing to fundraise. Bessie and Rose were so delighted to see everyone working together, saying the idea of getting the school opened as a community centre was the best thing that could have happened to Mark's Point. I'll leave you to tell the committee, contact Murphy's Trucking and arrange to have everything picked up.

"The cooler is the biggest thing to be moved while the chairs and tables are stackable, but Steve Marsh, the owner, says he has two young fellows coming in to clean the place, who can help load the truck. If you would pay the trucker and let me know the cost, I'll send you the money," Bob told the priest.

But Father Kelley insisted the parish pay for the trucking, saying it was little enough to do. Once Bob gave him the club owner's phone number, the priest said he would contact Dave Murphy to pick up and transport the equipment.

"Bob, I can't thank you and Sue enough for all you are doing. What a boost this will be for Mark's Point. With all this equipment, I fully expect to see the centre up and running soon. I believe this will make the residents work even harder to make the upcoming fair a success."

Knowing Dave was probably on the road somewhere, the priest left to check with Millicent at the store. Millicent said his timing was perfect when he mentioned he had a load of equipment for Dave to bring out from St. John's.

"Dave will be calling in about five minutes Father. He always phones around two o'clock to see if anyone has contacted me to pick up items in town. Do you want to wait until he calls, or can I give him the message?"

"I probably should talk to him myself because I don't know how much room he has to bring a big load. Once I know when he can pick it up, I'll have to make arrangements in St. John's and out here."

Millicent, a parish council member, asked what the parish was having trucked. When she heard how Sue and Bob were donating equipment to Mark's Point, she was delighted.

"I said to Dave the other day that the best thing that's happened in this area lately is Bessie and Rose opening their Bed and Breakfast. We are seeing all kinds of positive things happening and just think of the visitors coming this way now.

"Without Martin House, Bob and Sue would never have heard of Mark's Point. And, with Bessie deciding to stay and Rose moving home, there have been many other benefits. Mina is a good example. Since Bessie first called her to see if she had any quilts for sale, they have renewed their friendship, and it's doing Mina and the girls so much good. Besides that, Sue has now arranged a well-paying market for Mina's quilts."

"You are right, Millicent. Mina and the girls do appear happier and more relaxed. But getting back to the chairs and tables, I need you to keep this news to yourself. Bob asked me to tell the committee, which I will do, but not yet."

"Don't you worry, Father, I won't mention it, but as a parish council member and having many friends in Mark's Point, I see this benefiting everyone. I hear Mossy Brook people also decided to keep their school. We're lucky in Murphy's Cove because we have the use of the high school, and, with the Fishermen's Committee buying our two-room school, we'll never be short of a place to hold events."

When Dave called, he agreed to pick up the goods the following day. Taking Steve Marsh's phone number, he promised to call him and get back to the priest. Father Kiely had just returned to the parish house when, true to his word, Dave called.

"Everything is in place, Father. I'll be home in Murphy's Cove around six o'clock tomorrow with the chairs and tables. If you want to come with me to Mark's Point, I could pick you up after I have supper. Maybe you could arrange for a couple of men to be there at 7:30 to help me unload. How does that sound?"

"That's perfect, Dave. Wait until the committee members see what Bob and Sue bought. I'm not telling any of them about this. I plan to call a committee meeting, saying it's important to meet me at the school. What a surprise they will get. Apart from us, only Millicent knows, and she won't mention it."

The following night, every Mark's Point committee member was waiting inside the old school, wondering why Father Kiely called the meeting in an empty building.

"I hope this isn't going to take long. With nowhere to sit, it won't be easy trying to write minutes. Did Father give you any idea what the meeting is about, Robert?" Bessie asked.

"No, he just said it was important to the future of our hall. I suppose the school board hasn't changed its mind and now plans to keep our school?"

The heated discussion following Robert's words was interrupted by Michael, the youngest committee member, who stood by the open porch door.

"Dave Murphy just stopped outside and is backing in here in his big truck. There's someone else with him. It looks like Father Kiely. I'm right, it is Father Kiely, and he's getting out of the truck. Now he's waving to Dave to back it up to the school door," Michael called out in excitement.

The young boy's play-by-play stopped when the priest came to the door inviting the committee members outside, saying he had something to show them. Wondering what was going on, Bessie followed the group and watched as Dave pulled open the truck's back doors.

The first items to be revealed were stacks of chairs, bringing all kinds of questions from the members about where they came from and whether they were for the centre.

"Why don't the women go back inside the school and allow the men to unload the truck. But yes, the contents are for your community, and once we get them everything inside, I'll tell you where they came from," Father Kiely told the group.

Before long, the men had the chairs into the school and began unloading tables. Meanwhile, Bessie, Rose, and Kelly were counting, and when Robert and Sean carried in the first table, they could tell them there were 86 chairs.

"And it looks as if there are eight or nine tables. I know there are five long ones like this one and a few smaller ones. But I bet you will never guess what else there is!" an excited Robert exclaimed.

"There's a great big cooler and an electric bingo machine as well as boxes of bingo cards. I don't know where this stuff came from, but I can tell you it will more than give us a head start in opening our community centre. Now we have to wait for Father to tell us about these things and what they will cost."

With the truck unloaded, and everyone seated, Father Kiely asked Bessie, who had been busy jotting down numbers, did she have a final count.

"Yes, Father, there are 86 chairs, five long tables, four shorter tables, one big cooler, a bingo machine complete with bingo balls, and at least 600 bingo cards. It's an amazing lot of stuff, but is it ours? If so, how much do we have to pay for it?" Bessie asked the questions on everyone's mind.

Father Kiely told them that yes, everything now placed in the former school belonged to the community.

"Better still, all of this is a gift, a very generous gift, from Sue and Bob Newman. All these things were originally in a St. John's club that recently closed. Bob and Sue saw the club owner yesterday and purchased everything you see. They hope this will allow the centre to begin operating much sooner. However, they don't want this gift to put a stop to the efforts of your committee. They think it's wonderful to see everyone working to improve this community where they plan to make their home."

"This is so like Bob and Sue," Bessie said.

"They're a very generous couple and interested in what's happening here. Bob and Sue say it's the people of Mark's Point who make this the place they want to call home, which is a huge compliment. We must write and thank them."

"We also need to thank Dave for bringing these things here. I was going to have the parish pay for the transportation, but Dave has refused payment," Father Kiely said.

When the group began to clap, an embarrassed Dave said they should thank his wife.

"Millicent said it's the least we can do. When she heard about the bingo machine and cards, she said to let her know when you start bingo, and she'll be over with a carload of women. She thinks you'll do well with the bingo, especially since there's none anywhere else in this area."

As a happy Robert looked around the school and its new furnishings, he said the committee would need to meet.

"Now we have chairs and tables; let's see where to go from here. We've already made a good start advertising our fair next month, and the tickets and the parcel-post stall letters are getting out around the community. What do you people say about having a meeting sometime this weekend?" Robert asked.

After talking it over, the group agreed to meet on Friday night. Before they left the school, Robert reminded them to be prepared to report on each of their committee's progress at the next meeting. An excited group then left the school, eager to spread the news of the new furnishings.

That night as Rose was taking stock of the parcel post letters and checking her list of who still had to get them, she spoke about the help received from the parish secretary.

"Joan started with 50, but then we decided to double that amount because people would be sending them to their friends and relatives. We also printed 200 books of tickets, five in a book at a quarter each or five tickets for a dollar."

"Don't you think that's too many tickets to sell in a community this size?" Bessie asked.

But Rose said Sean and Kelly, responsible for ticket sales, planned to go door to door selling them in neighbouring communities and expected to sell at least that amount.

"And if more tickets are needed, I'll be leaving Sean and Kelly to get them. It's a dirty job getting the tickets printed and put into books. Joan and I both had black ink all over our hands from the office duplicating machine."

Rose had almost 30 letters given out now, she told Bessie, including the six Sue took with her to New York. Kate had offered to distribute others in the post office to people collecting their mail. She was sure Millicent Murphy would take some letters, while Mina had asked for a couple to send to Halifax.

"Things are certainly moving forward. I'm still trying to get my head around all those chairs and tables in our school. Then there's the bingo machine and cards; that could be an ongoing fundraiser if we can get it organized. I could see us having a weekly bingo and people coming from different communities to attend. What do you think, Rose?"

"From what I've heard, it's extremely popular in some places and a good way of making a steady income for fundraising groups. But David says if we start a weekly bingo, we need a start-up fund to cover prizes for the first few weeks until we build regular attendance. Maybe if we do well at the fair, the committee should think about it. We could also try a game or two during the fair."

How popular Bingo could be was evident the following day when Bessie and Rose, accompanied by Mina, who they picked up at her home, walked into Murphy's Store. They were greeted by Millicent, asking when bingo was starting in Mark's Point.

"I love bingo. Whenever I get a chance to spend a few days with my sister Abigail in St. John's, we always go to bingo. She plays at the Legion and the Knights of Columbus every week, and you should see the crowds. Some people even go to bingo every night. I'm sure your committee will want to run a weekly bingo. After all, you are not going to waste a good machine and all those cards," Millicent said.

Assuring Millicent nothing would be wasted, Rose asked her if she would take a parcel post letter.

"Yes, for sure. Mina told me how popular a fundraiser the parcel-post stall was in Scotland and how it works. The more I hear about the things happening at this upcoming fair, the more I look forward to it. I'll have a dozen letters, do up at least a couple of parcels, and send others to my family. I have customers who won't mind doing the same. I'll put these out on the counter," the shop owner said.

The following night when the committee members sat around a large table in the old school, they came prepared to work with scribblers and pens. Michael was first to report and proudly related how he and David had organized the bottle drive, which would go ahead the following morning.

"And we're getting loads of help. When we told the students from Muddy Brook Cove and Mark's Landing that we're having a teenage dance once we have the bottle drive, they all wanted to help. They're doing the same in their communities, and my dad is going to pick up the bottles collected in Mark's Landing and Sean's picking them up in Muddy Brook Cove; aren't you, Sean?"

When Sean agreed, Michael continued talking, explaining that Mark's Point students would bring their bottles to the former school and put them in empty beer and drink cases supplied by Oscar.

"Mr. Nolan and me will bring them to the shop after. That's right, isn't it, Mr. Nolan?"

Agreeing with his young co-chair, David said how proud he was to see Michael and his friends working together on the bottle drive. Because of their efforts and the hall now having chairs, he felt they could hold the first youth dances the following Friday, leading to a cheer from an exuberant Michael and laughter and agreement from the remaining committee members.

"Sean and Kelly have already agreed to chaperone our first dances, and Sharon and I will also be there. Oscar, I know you're in charge of publicity, but I can help you when it comes to advertising these first dances. It would be a good art project for my grade six students to draw posters for both dances and then bring them to stores and post offices in their communities. It's no problem for the older students to spread the word about their dance, but parents need to know when both dances start and stop."

David and Michael's positive report was the first of many. It appeared everyone was taking their committee responsibilities seriously. Oscar was the last member to speak, saying he had little to report on publicity, but he wondered when the committee would decide what stalls to have at the fair and would they offer suppers or teas? His customers asked these questions, and almost all wanted to know what they could do to help.

"Oscar's right; people are excited. They want to know more, and it seems everyone wants to help. My Aunt Lucy wants to know if there's going to be a baked goods stall. She enjoys baking and says if there's one planned, she'll start making a couple of fruit cakes now," Kelly said.

"Lucy makes delicious cakes and cookies. I think she might be the ideal person to look after a baked goods stall. Not only would Lucy make cakes or cookies, but I'm also sure she wouldn't mind contacting the women in the community and asking them to help," Bessie said.

After the meeting, Kelly approached Bessie.

"I know for sure that Aunt Lucy would love to help. If you asked her to look after the bake stall, she'd be so proud. I know she loves to gossip, but she is good to my family and me, and I know she'd do a fine job."

Bessie was thinking over Kelly's words the following morning. The committee members had not only agreed a baked goods stall would be a crowd-pleaser but decided to draw up a complete list of stalls at the next meeting.

"I should call Lucy now and ask her about looking after the baked goods stall. Didn't you think it was nice to hear Kelly talk about Lucy that way? Too often, people, including us, just think about Lucy's tendency to gossip and forget she has good points," she said to Rose.

"Yes, Kelly is a nice girl, and I know by her actions at choir that she's also fond of her Uncle Jim. I've seen her leaving choir practice with one arm looped through Sean's and the other through Jim's as they walk him home," Rose answered.

"She's so happy she got the job as the secretary at the elementary school when it opened. She told me after finishing the course at trade school, she was sure she'd have to move to St. John's for work, but then the school position came up. Kelly also mentioned although Sean is fishing with his father and brother, he actually wants to work at his trade as a mechanic, and sometime in the future, he's hoping to open a garage in or near Mark's Point."

"That's something we need around here," Bessie responded.

"The nearest garage is over an hour and a half's drive away, which is not one bit convenient. Alex always told Sean that he could have the land on the main road if he ever decided to open a garage.

"A combined garage and restaurant business like those springing up on the Trans Canada Highway would be perfect for this area. Maybe if Sean approached an oil company, they might consider putting one in this area. It would certainly help us out if a restaurant opened. And thinking about food, I must make that phone call to Lucy."

Lucy was delighted to hear about the baked good stall, saying she couldn't wait to start baking. When Bessie asked her if she would consider taking charge of it and contact the women in Mark's Point asking for baked donations, there was dead silence.

"Lucy, are you there?" Bessie asked.

When there was no response, she thought something was wrong with the phone and was about to hang up when Lucy answered, asking Bessie what she had said. When Bessie repeated her request, there was another silence for a few seconds.

"Bessie, is you really asking me to do this? I'm not smart like you and Rose. Our Kelly is the one you should ask. Not that I mind helping, not one bit. Like I said to my Jim, anything I can do to help Bessie and Rose and their committee, I'll do it. I also told our Kelly I'd bake fruit cakes because I'm thinking they'd be good sellers."

"Lucy, I spoke about this with Kelly and the committee. We all agreed you should look after this stall. We're sure you'll do a great job getting other women to help when you tell them there will be a sale of baked goods. Don't you think so? I hope you do this. I know it's a big responsibility, but you are certainly capable of doing it. As for your fruit cakes, everyone knows how delicious they are. I'll be looking forward to buying one."

"If you really thinks I can do it, Bessie, then I'll try. In fact, I'll get on the phone right away and start calling all the women. I'll get a piece of paper and pen and write down everyone's name as I gets hold of them. I don't want to miss nobody out. Oh Bessie, wait 'til I tells my Jim. He was wondering what he could do to help the fair. If you thinks of something, just let him know. Now I must hang up and start making my phone calls. Bye, Bessie, and thank you, thank you so much."

As Bessie turned away from the phone, she heard Rose speaking to someone in the kitchen and went through to find Daisy and Marigold, who, she discovered, were taking part in the bottle drive.

"The twins said we was too little to be collecting bottles, but we wanted to help. Dad asked Mr. Nolan if we could do a couple of houses, and the twins was mad when Sir said we could. We've got our wagon to put the bottles in, and Dad is at the bottom of your garden in his pickup, and he's going to take the bottles from us and then put our wagon in the back of the truck, and then we goes to the next house for more bottles," Daisy said in one long breath.

"And Mr. Nolan said we could pick the houses that we wanted to collect bottles, and we picked you. He told us we could also do Mr. Jim and Mrs. Lucy's house 'cos they lives close to you. Do you have lots of bottles?" Marigold asked.

"I'm sorry, girls, we don't have many bottles. There's less than a case of beer bottles and about half a dozen drink bottles, but Mrs. Bessie and I decided to help with a donation of five dollars. It's great to see the two of you doing this, and of course, Mrs. Bessie and I always enjoy seeing you. Here's the money, and if you come out to the shed, I'll give you what bottles we have. Is that alright?"

The girls were more than delighted with the money and bottles. They wondered if anyone else would get a donation and couldn't wait to give it to Mr. Nolan.

"Just wait until the twins hears we got money. I bet they don't get any. Mom told all of us to ask people nicely, smile, and thank them for the bottles. I don't remember if we smiled, but we did ask nicely, didn't we, Miss Rose and Mrs. Bessie?" Daisy asked, looking anxiously at the women.

"You did indeed, and you both had beautiful smiles. When you go home, tell your mother that Miss Rose and I said we couldn't have asked for better bottle collectors, that you smiled all the time, and your manners were perfect," Bessie told the girls as they prepared to leave.

The girls had the bottles in their wagon when Robert walked up the garden to see how they managed. His daughters quickly informed him to go back to his truck, that bringing the bottles down to the road was their job.

"What an independent pair," Robert said with a laugh.

"Anyway, I didn't come to take the bottles. I just walked up to see what was keeping you. Knowing how the two of you can chatter, I figured you'd be here all day if I didn't remind you that we still have another house to visit."

"We're coming, but I needs to tell Mrs. Bessie and Miss Rose something first. Did you know there's a dance for us next Friday in our old school? It's our very first dance, and a lot of our friends from school are coming; isn't that right, Marigold?"

"Yes, and we have lots of friends now, and guess what! Sir, our principal, is going to be playing the music for the dance. Isn't that good?"

After agreeing with the girls that the dance would be perfect, Bessie and Rose watched as Marigold slowly and carefully pulled the wagon down the garden path while Daisy held on to the back so that the bottles wouldn't fall out.

"Bye, Mrs. Bessie and Miss Rose. We'll come and see you another time," shouted Daisy.

"We'll be wanting to hear all about your first dance, so the two of you make sure you do visit us," Rose answered, while at the bottom of the garden, Robert shook his head at their exchange.

Once indoors, Bessie told Rose about Lucy's reaction when asked to look after the baked goods stall.

"I felt awful because she thought she wasn't good enough to do it, but when I finally convinced her, she was so happy to help. I'm glad Kelly brought up the idea and that we asked Lucy. I'm betting she'll make sure it's one of the best stalls and money makers at the fair. She also said Jim is willing to help, so we should try and find something for him to do."

Rose said she might have something for Jim to do. She recalled seeing a hoopla stall at a garden party and how it was a big attraction. Although hoops were available at a city store specializing in games and carnival supplies, wooden blocks were not. Rose thought Jim would have the patience to cut the blocks needed for the game.

Rose said the hoop had to be just wide enough to pass over the prize and the block but said they would need to know what size the blocks were before asking Jim to cut them out.

"I'll call Jerry Molloy in town; he should know as he's usually in charge of games at his parish's garden party."

While it was still in her mind, Rose got on the phone with Jerry, who had taken over her position as principal when she retired. It was a long phone call as Jerry not only had ideas for the upcoming fair, but he also had plenty of school news for Rose. When the phone call was over, she told Bessie calling Jerry was a good idea.

He planned to phone the supply company and get them to mail their catalogue to the women. It included a wide selection of games to be bought or rented, plus prizes and hoops. Jerry suggested buying stuffed animals, which he said, were always popular prizes on tickets.

"This company sells everything from tickets to large and small prizes. If the catalogue goes in the mail Monday, we should have it later in the week and bring it to our next meeting. I almost forgot, the blocks need to be cut five by five inches and two inches high," Rose said

Bessie knew there was lumber of differing sizes in Alex's store and said she would ask Gabe to look when he and Maggie came for dinner the following day. With Sharon, David, and Father Kiely joining them, it would make seven at the Sunday meal.

"That reminds me, I need to go and pick some apples because I'm making apple pies for tomorrow's dessert. Mina and I are going partridgeberry picking next Wednesday, and I promised her a bag of apples to stew up with her berries. Imagine, neither Mina nor I ever saw or heard of a partridgeberry until we come to Newfoundland. Now we think there's no better jam than partridgeberry and apple, especially on freshly baked bread," Bessie said.

The next day, when everyone enjoyed apple pie and ice cream, Rose spoke about Bessie picking the apples just outside the back door and how the apple tree originated from shoots taken from her mother's tree, which was still growing in Sharon and David's garden.

"Is that right?" Sharon asked.

"The one in our garden is full of apples, and I was going to ask you if it was okay to pick a few. Mother saw all the apples when she was here and wished she also had partridgeberries. She will be here on Monday, and she asked me to find out if partridgeberries grew out this way."

Bessie told Sharon that she and Mina planned to go partridgeberry picking on Wednesday and Mrs. Dawson was welcome to join them,

"That would be a relief. I've had visions of Mother going over the hills by herself, looking for berries that weren't there and getting lost. Once she gets something in her mind, there's no stopping her."

"So that's where you get it from," David said, laughing.

"I told Sharon yesterday there was no need of her sorting out bottles, but oh no! Even though we had every high school student in Mark's Point there to help, she insisted on helping."

"I had to show my students a good example, and I enjoyed myself. What about you and your friends Maggie; did you have a good time?"

"It was great. Even the twins enjoyed themselves, although they grumbled when they heard Marigold and Daisy were taking part. But they were the first ones to help the little girls unload their bottles, and Mr. Nolan, when the little ones handed you the five dollars, the twins were every bit as proud as their sisters."

"I'm not too sure about their feelings for Bobby because he won't take orders from them. I like Bobby, he's in my class, and he and Isabelle are always ready to help me. I was glad they were there when I started school."

"Everyone worked hard yesterday, and we even had Robert giving us a hand. I still can't get over how much money came from the bottle drive. Thanks, Father, for announcing it after mass because everyone was interested in knowing the result," David said.

"I could hardly believe the amount either when you told me. It's hard to imagine raising almost $140 from empty bottles. It was a wonderful effort by everyone," the priest said.

David agreed and again praised the students' efforts. When he asked the students if their dance should be free, considering how well the bottle drive went, their answer was an overwhelming no. They said the money raised from the dances would help buy things for the former school.

"By the way Rose, about those guitar lessons for Michael and Bobby. The boys and I spoke about it, and we are starting on Tuesday night at the old school. I also agreed to take two of their friends from Muddy Brook Pond," David said.

"The boys must be happy considering how long they've waited to learn guitar. Guitar lessons are a first for this area and one more positive thing that's happened recently. Millicent Murphy and I were talking about this the other day, and Millicent says opening Martin House as a Bed and Breakfast has had a positive, umbrella effect on the area," Father Kiely said.

When Rose and Bessie appeared puzzled, and Bessie asked what their business had to do with anything, the priest smiled.

"Opening Martin House brought people to this part of the province who would never have visited, let alone stayed in this area. Your guests are bringing business, not only to you but to local stores and people. Just look at

Mina, for example. You brought Sue Newman to see her, and now Mina has a regular, well-paying market for her quilts. Through that visit, you and Mina renewed your friendship, and it's made a positive difference in her life."

Sharon began nodding as the priest spoke and said she had to agree with him about Martin House's impact.

"If we had made a rushed visit in one day, I doubt if the schools alone would have enticed us to stay. Schools are only buildings, and there's plenty of them in St. John's. What made us decide were the people we met by staying a couple of days in Martin House. You were not only wonderful hosts, Bessie and Rose, but you also became our friends, as did you, Father, Gabe, and Maggie. We knew this was the place we wanted to live and to work. Then actually finding a home in Mark's Point was a bonus."

"Sharon, you couldn't have put it better," Father Kiely said.

"And by deciding to stay, you and David contribute to the schools, the community and the parish. You are involved in the choir and the youth in Mark's Point, and I'm expecting great things from both of you in this regard. Besides this, a little bird told me that two things are planned for the high school that never happened before, thanks to you, Sharon. I hear a grade 11 graduation dinner and dance will take place next year and that sports teams will travel to compete with other schools."

"That's what we are hoping, Father. I couldn't believe the school didn't compete in sports with other schools. Miss Mills is coaching girls' basketball, and I'm coaching volleyball. We have friends teaching in rural areas with school enrollments close to that of Sacred Heart High, and we hope to do an exchange with them later, for both girls and boys."

"Everyone is right excited about it too, Mrs. Nolan, especially the grade 11 class. Katy will be graduating, and that means Mrs. Mina will have two graduates next year as Katy's sister Christine is graduating from university in Halifax. Isabelle, the twins, and me are trying out for all the teams as we love sports. Now we're having a competition to find a name and mascot for our school teams. Isn't our school the best?" Maggie asked enthusiastically.

"And Aunt Bessie and Aunt Rose, I know what Father Kiely means about Martin House. Mark's Point wouldn't be the same without it because it means you both stay here. Who would go berry picking with me or teach me to bake except you, Aunt Bessie? And Aunt Rose, who else would give me piano lessons or play the organ in our church if you weren't here? Pop and me would be lost without the two of you, and not only because you feed us a lot. Isn't that right, Pop?"

Gabe, looking slightly embarrassed at being called upon, nodded at Maggie's words.

"You're right, as usual, Maggie. I knows your mother wouldn't be as easy-minded about letting you stay with me if she didn't know Bessie and Rose were here if you needed them. It's like I said when I heard Alex and Bessie's house would be open for visitors to stay. The Martin family was always helping people. Many a meal they gave away and many a favour they did for anyone in need. Bessie and Rose is just carrying on like the Martins always done."

"Thank you all, but I think that's just about enough about the Martins for one day," Bessie said.

"It's good to see new things happening, and it's all due to what Rose and I were saying the other day. When a community has a common purpose, good things begin to happen, And now, since everyone has their dessert finished, I think it's time to put the kettle back on to boil because the best part of a meal is always the cup of tea that finishes it off."

CHAPTER 23

Celebrating

B essie and Rose were in the kitchen, clearing up from supper, when Kate Brown phoned, asking if they had any guests and were they busy. Hearing the women were alone and never too busy for a Brown family member, Kate had a question for them.

"Do you remember the dances are tonight? You wouldn't have a chance to forget if you lived in our house because that's all our youngsters have talked about this week. To make a long story short, Marigold and Daisy are leaving soon to go to their dance, and they're almost as bad as the twins, taking ages to decide what to wear. They finally decided, and now they want to show you and Rose what they're wearing. Is it alright to drop in on our way to the dance?"

"You don't even have to ask. We're always happy to see any of you, although Marigold and Daisy are by far the Brown family's most entertaining members. We love having them visit. We'll be waiting to see them."

About 10 minutes later, Bessie and Rose watched from the sun porch as the two youngest members of the Brown family ran up the garden, with Kate coming behind them at a slower pace.

As the women made their way to the kitchen to welcome the girls, Bessie suggested they try and get Kate to stay and relax for a while. If she drove the girls to the dance, it would allow Kate to rest for a short time.

Rose just had time to say it was a good idea when a knock and shrill voices heralded the arrival of Marigold and Daisy.

"Mrs. Bessie, Miss Rose, it's our dance tonight. We want to show you our dresses. Mom bought them when she and the twins were in St. John's before school started, and this is the first time we've worn them. Mine is blue," said Marigold.

"And look at my green one. See how the skirt goes out. It will be a good one for dancing," Daisy said, twirling around.

"You girls look lovely, and your dresses are perfect. For sure, there will be no shortage of boys asking you to dance," Rose said with a smile.

"We don't want boys asking us to dance. We'll be dancing with our friends. We've lots of friends in our new school," Marigold replied.

Kate entered the kitchen in time to hear Marigold's comment and reminded her daughters not to be rude by refusing to dance with a boy.

"Do we have to dance with boys?" Marigold plaintively asked while Daisy grimaced as if the thought of dancing with the opposite sex had to be the worst thing in the world.

"If asked to dance, you should be polite and say yes, whether it's a girl or boy. How would you feel if you asked someone to dance, and they said no?" Kate asked in a stern voice.

"But all our friends are coming, and we said we'd dance together, and our bestest friend, Beverly Turner, is bringing a record of *Raindrops Keep Falling on my Head* for Mr. Nolan to play. Her dad got it from the jukebox in his club because it's her favourite song. I wish our Dad had a jukebox," Marigold said with a sigh.

"There is no such word as bestest; the word is best. And we might not have a jukebox, but we do have a record player. It does the same job because the twins and Bobby are always playing records. I might be mistaken, but I'm sure *Raindrops Keep Falling on my Head* is one of them."

It was evident by Marigold's expression that a record player was not in the same category as a jukebox, but before she could argue, Bessie cut in.

"Girls, what if I drive you over to the school and your mother stays here with Miss Rose. I'd love to drive you to your first dance. Is that alright?"

When both girls immediately asked if they could sit in the front seat, Bessie replied she was sure they both could fit in the front. The next rapid-fire question about who would get the window seat quickly led to an argument between the girls.

"Marigold and Daisy, do you realize how rude you are? Instead of thanking Mrs. Bessie for offering to drive you to the dance, the pair of you start arguing about where you want to sit. Well, that's easily settled. I'll drive, and you'll each get to sit next to a window, but it will be in the back of the car. You're lucky you are still going to the dance after this fuss."

The girls' cries of disappointment that they'd behave, please let Mrs. Bessie drive, and they'd sit in the back seat, had Kate shaking her head.

"I don't know about the two of you at all. You are not acting like girls who go to school each day on a bus. Your new baby brother or sister will soon be here, and all this time, I've been thinking about the help I'll get from my children. Instead, I have my two youngest daughters behaving like babies," Kate said to the girls.

It was a very subdued pair who promised to behave, then apologized to all three women.

"We'll help you with the new baby, Mom. We'll act like big sisters instead of just being little girls like everyone calls us," Marigold said.

Daisy not only added her apology but also had a solution to the car seating problem. Because they were getting bigger, she said she and Marigold would walk to the dance. That way, Kate and Bessie could both take a rest.

Looking at Bessie and Rose, who were trying to keep from smiling, Kate answered Daisy.

"Your very first dance is special, so I think you should go by car. Mrs. Bessie has kindly offered to drive you, but I want both of you to sit in the back seat and not move out of the car until Mrs. Bessie says you can open your doors. When your dance is over, stay in the school until Dad picks you up. Now, is that understood and do you have your money to get into the dance?"

With smiles and choruses of 'Yes Mom' and 'Thanks Mom.' the girls left with Bessie while Kate accepted Rose's offer of a cold glass of lemonade.

"What a pair of monkeys they are. Fancy them not wanting to dance with boys. I don't have that problem with the twins; they're the complete opposite. All they talk about is boys, who will be there and who will ask them to dance. They don't think I hear them, but it's difficult not to. I probably was the same when I was their age.

"This drink certainly hits the spot, Rose. I could easily get used to this life, being served cold drinks without having five youngsters arguing in the background," Kate added with a grin.

As the women relaxed, they spoke about the community activities that had happened or were in the planning stages.

Rose said she returned to Mark's Point, thinking she would have a more relaxed lifestyle, but wondered if she might get bored.

"After all, I took early retirement, but it seems I'm as busy, if not busier, than when I was teaching full time. And you know something Kate, I love it.

"Remember when you said something needed doing with the school, that we couldn't let it be sold or removed and residents should use it? And it's happening, and even quicker than anyone imagined."

Kate agreed with Rose, adding the early opening was mainly due to Sue and Bob's generous gift. Just then, Bessie came back accompanied by Agnes Dawson.

"I met Agnes walking along the road. Agnes, I'm not sure if you met Kate Brown, our postmistress. And Kate, this is Sharon's mother, Agnes Dawson, who is visiting Sharon and David. Agnes came berry picking with Mina and me on Wednesday, and now she says she's ready for another day at the partridgeberries before she goes back to St. John's."

"Although I haven't met you before, Kate, I know you have four daughters with lovely names. I met your twin girls when they and Maggie were out walking, and Sharon says you also have a son and two younger daughters. Bessie tells me I missed seeing the two little ones; she just dropped them off at the dance. That's where Sharon and David are, so I decided to take a walk until Bessie stopped and invited me here," said Agnes.

"It's nice meeting you, Agnes, but you're probably better off not meeting Marigold and Daisy today. All they can think about is the dance, and their manners tend to fly out the window when they get excited."

Rose told Agnes not to mind what Kate said, that she was actually a proud mother, who tended to judge her children a bit hard at times. She added that the Brown children were all well mannered and, like their parents, were always willing to help people.

"However, they're also like their mother and father in another way, they all enjoy talking, and when it comes to Marigold and Daisy, some of the things they say are hilarious. They have no idea how amusing they are. You should have been here when the pair of them helped Bessie make a birthday cake for Kate and met their 'missing Harry' friend."

Time flew past as the four women talked. They were enjoying each other's company and cold drinks when they heard someone calling from the kitchen. When Rose returned from seeing who it was, Robert was by her side.

"I didn't know where you were, Kate, until I saw our station wagon on the road below. Did you forget I'm supposed to pick up Marigold and Daisy? I know they wouldn't mind coming back in the truck, but your older daughters are having a fit at the idea of being driven to the dance in what they describe as a 'smelly old fish truck,' so I need the wagon. Bobby asked why they couldn't do the same as him and walk to the dance, but your daughters scorned that idea."

"Do you notice how Robert calls Lily and Pansy my daughters? It's a strange thing, but when our children do something he isn't happy with, they become my children. When they do something good, my husband suddenly remembers he's their father."

The other women had a great chuckle at Kate's words, while Robert just shook his head, saying it would take someone far smarter than him to try arguing with Kate.

"While I'm here, Rose and Bessie, don't forget we have a meeting on Wednesday night to make a final decision on what attractions we're having at the fair. Rose, will you bring the catalogue? I glanced through it, and I think it will give us some different ideas for the fair.

"Come on, Kate. Let's get going and pick up one lot of girls, and hopefully, the oldest two will be ready to go to their dance when we get back. I never saw such excitement in all my life as over these dances. According to the carloads of young ones arriving, every student attending school in Murphy's Cove must be in Mark's Point tonight."

It appeared Robert wasn't far wrong in his estimation. When the newly named Mark's Point Hall Committee met on the following Wednesday, David said the dances and the bottle drive were highly successful and asked Michael to report on the attendance figures and the amount of money raised from both events.

"We had 78 little ones at the first dance. They paid 50 cents each, so we raised $39. There were 145 students at our dance, and we all paid a dollar, bringing in $145. Add the dance money to what we brought in from the bottle drive, and altogether we have just over $323," Michael proudly announced to applause from the rest of the committee members.

"Our young people are doing a marvellous job," David said.

"But getting back to the dances, the one thing we never thought about was a canteen. Our rule was once students were inside the hall, they couldn't leave until the dance was over. But they soon got thirsty and wanted to know why they couldn't go to the shop. Sean went to the shop and saw Oscar, who then brought over drinks and chips and sold them in the hall, making him the most popular man at the dances."

"If you have another dance, I can supply you with drinks and chips for the canteen at a price to make a small profit. We can probably get parents to take turns looking after it, and now we have a big cooler, the drinks will stay cold. What do you folks think?" Oscar asked.

When everyone agreed, Sean asked whether the dances would become regular events and what kind of music they had for the fair's adult dance.

"The feedback I got, both from students and parents who picked up their children, was all positive, with everyone hoping the dances would become a regular occurrence. However, I should tell you that both schools are looking to raise money for different projects and one of the ideas discussed was dances. I maybe spoke out of turn, but at a staff meeting of both schools, I said if our dances were successful, we would be looking to have them again. I think there's room for both the schools and us to take turns. Is it alright if I arrange some sort of schedule that would be fair for everyone?" David asked.

David got the committee's support to look after a schedule for youth dances. Following discussion, the committee decided on a variety of Newfoundland and popular music for the adult dance. With David looking after taped music, Robert said he would contact Pat Martin, who played the accordion, hoping Pat would get a couple of his talented friends to help him provide Newfoundland dance music.

As each committee member updated their responsibility, it was clear plans were well in hand. Sean and Kelly had already visited every home in Mark's Point and Muddy Brook Cove and had all their tickets sold for a total of $200. They now planned to have more tickets printed and canvas Mark's Landing and Murphy's Cove. They suggested having a ticket wheel at the fair and asked that strips of tickets, stuffed toys, and other prizes, be ordered. They also volunteered to look after bingo during the fair and have at least a couple of games, selling cards at 25 cents each.

By the time the meeting concluded, ten fundraising activities were in place for the big event. Hoopla, parcel post, tombola, a baked goods table, and bingo were the first to be approved, followed by the 120-ticket wheel with draws continuing throughout the afternoon. There would be grab bags for children, and a dart game, advertised in the catalogue, would be purchased. Oscar liked the idea of a bean bag throw, saying it should do well at the fair. He was sure his sister, Flo, would make the bean bags, and he would look at different ideas for targets.

When it came to what type of food or meal to serve at the fair, suggestions included cold plates, afternoon teas, beans, and soup. With the women in the community already asked to bake and help on stalls, everyone agreed it would be easiest to serve soup and sandwiches. Before the meeting closed, Bessie, Rose, and Kelly arranged to meet the following Sunday to order supplies from the distributor's catalogue.

As the Bessie and Rose left the school, David caught up to them, asking how they got on with their guests from the school district, saying he heard positive remarks from the superintendent and business manager about their stay at Martin House earlier in the week.

"They were full of praise about their rooms and meals, as well as the beauty of the area. Not that I was one bit surprised."

"You might not be surprised, but I am," Rose said.

"I've known Dan Power, the Board business manager, for years, and we butted heads many a time. As a principal, I objected to what I felt was his constant penny pinching, especially when it came to resource material. He complained I thought his office had an unlimited budget. I can tell you we had many a battle over finances. However, I had never met the new superintendent, Harold Kelly."

"I think Mr. Kelly will do well in the position, and I'm sure you'll be getting more business from him. There are plans to have all district elementary and high school students tested in English and Mathematics. He spoke of sending two specialists to our schools for several days and hopes they can stay with you. Did he mention it?" David asked.

"Yes, he did, and we have them booked for the week of October 11 for four nights. Rose had me slightly anxious about Mr. Power, saying he'd probably find something to complain about, but I found both men to be excellent guests for the two nights they stayed with us. Speaking of guests, we have Albert and his wife coming on Friday for the weekend, and then he and Jack are coming back on October 18 for a week to finish campaigning in this area," Bessie added.

"Time is certainly flying," David said.

"We're almost into October, and voting takes place in a few weeks. I have a feeling Albert will do well, and so do most people. They say voters in this district are finally able to put a politician's face to a name because, unlike his opponent, Albert made himself visible to the constituents."

Bessie repeated this conversation to Albert and Ellen the following Friday night as they sat in the sunroom drinking tea with her and Rose. Ellen had immediately made herself at home, saying she had heard so much about Martin House and the women that she felt they were already friends.

"Albert loves this part of the province, and if we could find a place to rent next summer, it would be wonderful to have all our family, especially our grandchild, spend a few weeks here. Our daughter Julia, and her husband Mark, had a little girl earlier this year, and it's such a lovely feeling to be a grandmother. I can't wait until our sons are married and have children."

"Now Ellen, there's lots of time for grandchildren. I'm hoping it will be years before anyone else in our family looks at getting married unless, of course, it's Jack. He might be the baby in my family, but he's getting up there. He turned 34 just a couple of months ago, and I'd love to see him settle down. His job might be well paying, but it means a lot of travelling, and it doesn't give him much opportunity to meet marriageable females."

"I wish you'd leave Jack alone. He'll settle down when he finds the right person. He loves his job, and instead of complaining, you should be thanking him for taking time off to run your campaign," Ellen said.

"I thought Jack worked in St. John's as a bookkeeper," Rose said

"He might have described himself that way to you, but Jack's the chief financial officer of a national company. He chooses to make St. John's his base because the company has branches in this province," Albert replied.

"As the company's troubleshooter, he travels across Canada sorting out financial problems. He's been in Ontario for the past few days. We decided to take a break from campaigning this week, and with his company opening a new branch, Jack decided to go and check out its bookkeeping system. I was expecting him back yesterday, but he called saying it would be Monday before he returns."

When Ellen said it was good for Albert to take a week off from campaigning since it gave him time to relax, her husband snorted with disbelief.

"Relax, she says, and her with a list of jobs as long as my arm for me to do. I tell you, Rose and Bessie, I'm glad we booked this weekend here or else she'd have me working. Since retiring from the RCMP, I've been busier than I ever was in my job. Even campaigning is more relaxing than trying to keep up with all the maintenance Ellen finds for me to do around our house and garden," Albert said, laughing at his wife's horrified expression.

"Albert Matthews, you'll have Bessie and Rose thinking I'm a slave driver."

"Not at all, Ellen. Jack tells us you are a saint to put up with his brother, and I'm starting to think he was right. But truthfully, Albert is just tormenting you because he's always praising you and his children."

Rose agreed with Bessie, then changing the topic, she asked what the couple's plans were for the following day.

"We're going to Murphy's Cove for lunch with Millicent and Dave. Their son Andy and his wife and children are home on holiday. I haven't seen Andy since we served together as RCMP officers almost ten years ago. He wasn't married then and spent quite a lot of time in our home. According to Millicent, the weekend is the only time she gets to do any real cooking. She says it's time she cooked for us because Andy ate many a meal in our home. We're looking forward to seeing him and meeting his wife and children."

Albert also planned to take Ellen to Fisherman's Creek to show her the community where his grandmother lived as a child. When her mother died and her father having drowned several years earlier, an aunt in St. John's raised the little girl and her sister. She was nine and her sister seven years old when they left Fisherman's Creek.

"Grandmother's aunt was good to her and her sister, but the sad thing was, she had two brothers who she never saw again. A relative came from Boston and took them to the States. That was the last she ever heard of them. Over the years, my father and his brothers tried tracing them for grandmother, who dearly wanted to see them again, especially since her sister died as a teenager. They had no luck, and they wondered if the brothers were adopted and given new surnames. Before grandmother died, she begged my father not to stop looking for them."

Rose agreed it was a sad story but recalled how it wasn't uncommon for relatives or friends to take orphans into their homes to raise. Unfortunately, brothers and sisters often grew up in separate homes.

"Pat Martin and his brother Joe were orphans when their aunt and uncle, who already had six children, brought them to Mark's Point from Sydney, Nova Scotia, and raised them as their own. From the day Pat arrived here, he and Father were the best of friends, a friendship that lasted until Father's death," Rose recalled.

"I've been here over 25 years, and that's the first time I heard that story. I always thought Pat and Joe Martin were born and raised in Mark's Point," Bessie said.

"Their father was born here, but like many men, he left Newfoundland to find work. He was a miner in Sydney, and it was a mining accident that claimed his life. Several years later, when Pat's mother was dying, she wrote asking her brother-in-law to find a good home for her boys. Mr. Jerry Martin went to Sydney and was with the boys' mother when she died. He promised her both boys would be looked after by him and his wife."

"Well, you learn something new every day, and that was news to me. I couldn't imagine Mark's Point without Mr. Pat," Bessie said.

The following afternoon, the politician and his wife were in Murphy's Cove. After a delicious meal and an enjoyable time reminiscing with Andy

Murphy and chatting with Andy's wife and parents, Albert and Ellen prepared to leave for their visit to Fisherman's Creek.

"That's right; I remember you saying your relatives came from Fisherman's Creek. Who were they?" Millicent asked.

When Albert said his grandmother Alice Fleming was born in the community but moved to St. John's as a child following her mother's death, Millicent and Dave looked at each other in astonishment.

"Are you serious? Don't tell me Father Kiely and the parish secretary have been searching through decades of parish baptism, wedding, and death records as well as questioning older residents from different communities for information on Flemings, and you've been here almost all summer. Do you know if your grandmother had any sisters or brothers?"

When Albert said yes, and related his grandmother's history, Millicent said he needed to see Father Kiely as soon as possible and read a letter the priest received from the States.

"Much earlier this summer, the letter I'm talking about came addressed to the Parish Priest, Fisherman's Creek, from a woman in Boston. She wrote that her father always said he was born in Newfoundland. But, because he was only four when he left, he didn't remember the community name, only that it had something to do with fish. I don't know her father's surname now, but growing up, his brother, who was two years older, would tell him never to forget his real name was Fleming, and he was born in Newfoundland."

"According to Father Kielly, this woman found a list of Newfoundland communities. She wrote to the priest in each place that had fish, or anything related to fish, in its name. We knew of no Flemings in Fisherman's Beach, but as Father said, this took place almost 90 years ago. He asked Ted Best, the community's oldest resident and Ted recalled hearing about a family of orphans who were separated when their parents died, and he thought their name might have been Fleming,"

Albert had been listening to Millicent in astonishment and excitedly questioned her.

"My God, is it possible that her father is my grandmother's brother? I'm sure it must be because my grandmother's name was Alice Fleming. How wonderful if this woman is related to our family. I must go and see Father Kiely. Do you think he would be home now, Millicent?"

The shopkeeper didn't know if the priest was home but knew for sure he would be in Mark's Point that night for 7 o'clock mass. She suggested Albert try phoning him, and if there was no answer, he could speak to the priest after mass.

Later in Mark's Point, after an unsuccessful attempt to reach the priest, Albert told Bessie and Rose about the surprising news.

"It has to be grandmother's brother this woman is talking about, and that would make her Dad's first cousin. Once I speak to Father Kiely and know for sure, I'll call Dad. He will be over the moon and want to contact her right away. It's just too bad that my grandmother never lived long enough to know this."

"What about this woman's father and his brother. Are they still alive?" Bessie asked.

Albert doubted they would be living as his grandmother would have been 98 by now, which would make both brothers well up in their 90's.

"Just to know he has relatives on his mother's side will mean so much to Dad because his Aunt Sue died without having children. I can't wait to tell him and to speak to Father Kiely."

"You'll have that opportunity soon. With the mass schedule changed for October, we have mass tonight. You should invite Father over here for a cup of tea after mass, instead of talking to him in the church. That way, you can speak privately in the sitting room or sun porch," Rose said.

A few hours later, Albert showed Bessie and Rose the letter from Boston, that thanks to Millicent, Father Kiely, brought with him to Mark's Point.

"The most amazing thing about this is that my grandmother's brother is still alive. He is 93, and according to his daughter, he's determined to discover his family history before he dies. I haven't called Dad. Instead, I'm bringing him this letter with his cousin's address and phone number. I'm betting. Dad will be on the phone to her five minutes after he reads the letter."

Ellen smiled at her husband's words and said by listening to her husband and Jack about their travels around the district, she had known she would enjoy her visit.

"They told me how much they enjoyed the area and their stay here in Martin House, and I knew I would too. But the last thing I expected was to find an answer to the family puzzle. Mr. Matthews is going to be over the moon with the news. The only downside is that I know Albert will want to leave at the crack of dawn to get back and tell him."

Ellen wasn't wrong, Bessie thought, as she and Rose waved them goodbye just before nine the following morning. Albert would have left even earlier if his wife hadn't put her foot down, insisting he relax and let her enjoy breakfast.

"This is a change for us, having no guests on a Sunday and not cooking a big Sunday dinner. What are we going to do with ourselves?" Rose asked.

The words were hardly out of her mouth when the phone rang. On answering it, Bessie was surprised to hear Maggie.

"Aunt Bessie, the twins and me are going partridgeberry picking, and we wanted to know if you'd like to come with us. Mrs. Kate always makes jam at this time of year, but she can't go berry picking herself. She says if we pick the berries, she'll show us how to make jam to share between our families, and you know Pop loves partridgeberry jam. There's no mass today, and I just saw Mr. and Mrs. Matthews drive out of the community, so we thought you might have time to come with us; that's if you want to come." Maggie said.

"You know Maggie, that's a great idea. Rose and I were just wondering what we would do with ourselves all day, with no big Sunday dinner to cook and no guests. The only thing I have planned is a meeting with Kelly and Rose to make out an order from the game store catalogue. That's not until tonight, so yes, I'd love to go berry picking with you."

An hour later, Bessie and the three girls were climbing the hill behind the church on their way to the partridgeberry grounds.

"Mom was some glad when she knew you were coming with us, Mrs. Bessie. We told her we knew the way, but I heard her telling Dad that you would make sure we didn't take off over the hills. I think she's afraid we might get lost. Mrs. Bessie, did you ever hear about a man from Muddy Brook Cove who got lost while berry picking and never returned? Do you think that's true, or is it just something Mom tells us so we don't go too far? What do think, Mrs. Bessie?" Lily asked.

"There must be some truth to it because I heard the same story the first time I went berry picking, and each year when the blueberries begin to ripen, the story is told again. I heard it from my mother-in-law, and she'd never pass the story on unless she believed it. It must have happened many years ago, but to make sure none of us get lost, let's always keep in sight of each other. Okay?"

The girls agreed and began talking about how many berries they would pick.

"For sure, none of us will pick as much as Aunt Bessie because she's a champion berry picker. How much did you pick Aunt Bessie when you went with Mrs. Mina and Mrs. Nolan's mother?" Maggie asked.

"Enough for what Rose and I are going to need and still have plenty of jam for our guests. If we each pick a gallon today, I'll add mine to yours. When you stew them up this afternoon, you can split the jam between your families. Come to my place for apples when we get back. I have almost a barrel full in our cellar, and we're not going to use all of them. The apples put a great taste on jam, and by adding them, you'll get even more jam," Bessie told the girls.

Just after noon, three proud teenagers, each carrying a gallon bucket filled with partridgeberries, arrived back at Martin House with Bessie to collect their apples. They were greeted by Rose, telling them they were staying for brunch, which she started preparing when she saw them walking down behind the church.

"I already spoke to your mother Lily and Pansy, and it's fine with her, and Maggie, your grandfather, also knows. He dropped in here on his way to Nolans, where he's having dinner. So, it's just us five females for brunch. I have ham and bologna fried, hashed up potatoes, and I'm also making eggs. I've started the toast, and now all I need to know is how you like your eggs cooked," Rose told the girls.

"Why don't you use the downstairs bathroom to wash up, and after we finish eating, Rose and I will get your thoughts on suitable prizes for the fair. We're meeting with Kelly tonight to make out the catalogue order, and having your ideas will help us decide. We'd like to know what different ages might like. What do you think?" Bessie asked.

One look at the girls' faces was answer enough. They were positively beaming with pleasure as all three excitedly agreed to help choose prizes.

After brunch, Bessie brought the girls into the dining room and sat them down with pencils, paper, and the catalogue. Asking them to chose prizes in three different categories, high school students, elementary students and small children, she left them alone. She and Rose would relax with their tea, clean up, then drive the girls home with their berries and apples.

As the women drank their tea, they could hear the girls' voices rising with excitement as they discovered something else new in the catalogue.

"The girls are happy to get to choose prizes. I'd say every student on their bus will soon know, and it will make them even more eager to come to the fair," Bessie said.

"And I'm guessing Michael and Bobby will be the first to hear about this. The girls will be only too pleased to let Michael know he's not the only one involved in getting the hall up and running," Rose answered.

Just then, Maggie came to the kitchen doorway with a question.

"What about prizes for men and women. We were saying the fair is for all ages, that it wouldn't be right just to get prizes for the young."

"Maybe so, but we can leave the adult prizes until tonight when Kelly comes over. I think most adults will want to see the children enjoying themselves and won't care too much about prizes for themselves," Rose answered.

A short time later, the girls presented the women with a page full of prize suggestions. Pansy also had a question for the women.

"Maggie, Lily and me, wondered if we can help at the fair. We asked Dad, and he said he thought we were too young, but Michael says he's helping, and Michael is only the same age as Lily and me."

It wasn't a decision that she or Bessie could make, Rose told the girls, but she promised they would raise the topic at the next committee meeting.

On the way over to the Browns by car, Lily spoke again about helping at the fair.

"We wouldn't want to work at the fair for the whole afternoon because we want to try the games. But I'm sure Mrs. Bessie, you don't want to be on your feet, working all the time. Wouldn't you and Miss Rose like the thought of having a break now and then? We could help you by taking a turn at your stalls. What do you think?"

"I'm thinking, Lily, that not only did you and Pansy inherit the Brown's gift of the gab, you also have your parents' thoughtfulness. But as Miss Rose said, we'll talk about this at the next meeting. I'm sure it's not that your father thinks you are too young to help at the fair, but because he wants to see you enjoying yourselves."

Later, when Robert walked out with Bessie to the car, she told him about the twins' request and how she and Rose handled it.

"I'll write it down to discuss at our next meeting. I know the girls are able and want to help, but as you said, I want them to enjoy our first-ever fair. Hopefully, we'll work out something when we meet. You did a great thing letting them pick out prizes. I guess you saw the looks on Marigold and Daisy's faces, who aren't impressed by their sisters spending time with you and Rose. Since you made Kate's cake, they seem to consider the pair of you their personal property.

"Meanwhile, Kate tells me you're planning a party for Rose's birthday in a couple of weeks. What can we do to help?" Robert asked.

"In Kate's condition, and her working all day and you on the water, there's no need for the pair of you to do anything. However, knowing you won't be satisfied unless you contribute something, why don't you bring a case of beer. I've asked Dave Murphy to pick me up some wine and liquor in St. John's. I haven't mentioned the party to Rose yet, although I'd better do it soon because she doesn't like surprises. Her birthday is the 25th, but celebrating it a few days earlier won't matter. With the election and the fair happening the following week, it's going to be hectic."

When Bessie finally told Rose about the planned party, she was surprised to find her sister-in-law had only one objection.

"I don't want any presents."

"But Rose, you know people are not coming to your party without a birthday gift," Bessie said.

"I don't want any gifts. I have everything I need, and I can't see the sense of people spending money on unnecessary things. Did you forget my parents' home, which was the best birthday gift ever? I can't get anything to compare with that. So please tell our friends they are welcome to come, but no presents for me, please," Rose emphatically stated.

The women's conversation was interrupted when the telephone rang, and Rose went to answer it. On her return, she said Albert called with good news that he wanted her to share with Bessie, the Murphy's, and Father Kiely.

"His father talked to the woman who sent the letter, and true enough, her father is Albert's great uncle. Albert said he's never seen his father so excited and happy, and he's been calling his siblings and children to tell them. His cousin, Madeline Wallace, now has to tell her father, and when she does, she expects he's going to want to call his newly found relatives in St. John's. Albert said she was laughing and crying, and before she hung up, she said her father would most likely want to visit Newfoundland."

When Rose went to call Father Kiely and Millicent, Bessie thought about the upcoming birthday party. She knew their friends would want to bring gifts, but Rose was adamant she didn't want anything. All she could do pass the message on.

With Rose's party planned for the 23rd, just a week before the fair, and the provincial election on the 28th, she knew it would be a busy week.

Then we will be into November. I've been talking about a trip to St. John's for a few months. Before we know it, it will be time to prepare for Christmas, and Kate and Robert's baby will be here. I need to get into town and stock up on wool to knit some baby clothes and look for Christmas gifts. But for now, it's time to put the kettle on. Once Rose finishes her phone calls, we'll have a cup of tea.

CHAPTER 24

So Much To Do

W hen Rose went to the church for choir practice, Bessie paid a surprise visit to the Brown's home. She carried a large bag, which she began to open when Kate called Daisy and Marigold, saying they could take a short break from their homework.

"Who are they for?" Daisy asked, gazing longingly at two black dresses and cone-shaped hats that Bessie removed from the bag.

When Bessie said the costumes were for her and Marigold, the youngest Brown daughter squealed with delight.

"Marigold, they're for us! We're going to be witches; we're really going to be witches. Just wait 'til Halloween, and everyone sees us. I can't wait for our school party to wear mine."

Marigold was too busy admiring the Halloween costumes to answer her younger sister but quickly agreed when Bessie suggested the girls try them on for size.

Bessie thoroughly enjoyed Daisy and Marigold's reactions to the costumes she and Rose had made for their school's Halloween party. When the girls came running back into the kitchen dressed in black dresses and long pointed hats, they were positively beaming.

"Just look at us, Mom. Nobody else will have near as good costumes as me and Daisy, even though Lorna Moss and Elsie Maloney said theirs came from St. John's. Just wait until we tells them you made ours, Mrs. Bessie, and you come from Scotland, which is farther than St. John's. That's right, isn't it, Mrs. Bessie?" Marigold asked.

"I think you girls have forgotten something. What do you say to Mrs. Bessie for making your witch outfits?" Kate rebuked her daughters.

"I only made the dresses. Rose had the bright idea of the long black hats, and although she says she is hopeless at crafts, she did a great job with them. We both thoroughly enjoyed making the costumes."

"Miss Rose would be here if she didn't have choir practice, but she says she's looking forward to seeing you wear them when you come trick or treating to our house. Now all you need to be perfect witches is for each of you to find an old broom," Bessie told the girls.

Squeals of thanks and talk of going door to door looking for treats flowed from the girls until Daisy suddenly had a thought.

"Mrs. Bessie, is you soon going to learn me and Marigold some more baking like you said you would?"

"Daisy!" Kate said, giving her youngest daughter a disapproving look.

"Don't you think Mrs. Bessie and Miss Rose have done quite enough for you and Marigold? You expect too much. The pair of you go and get changed, put away your costumes, then get back to your homework. Tomorrow is Friday, and Marigold, you have a spelling test and need to study your words."

When the girls went to their bedroom, Kate shook her head, saying Bessie and Rose were spoiling them.

"Don't be foolish. It didn't take long to make the costumes. It was a first for us, but knowing the girls had their hearts set on being Halloween witches, we thought we'd give it a try. It might make up for them not being invited with the twins for brunch at our place. I'll be baking for Rose's birthday party this Saturday and for the fair all next week, but once this month is over, I intend to have them come to the house to make cookies."

"There's no need. You've enough to do without baking with Marigold and Daisy and having them make a mess of your kitchen," Kate said.

"Nonsense, things should be pretty quiet from now on at Martin House. We have no guests booked in for November, which means Rose and I should have lots of time on our hands. Albert and Jack are staying with us this week, making a final push on the election campaign. Albert should do well in this area, and, according to Jack, he's also getting good reception on the other side of the district. They're leaving tomorrow because Jack is flying to the mainland on Saturday for some work emergency. He will be back in St. John's on Tuesday, two days before the election. And talking about time, yours is getting shorter. When exactly is the baby due?" Bessie asked.

"It's supposed to be December 11, but apart from the twins, my babies were lazy and weren't born until a week or more after my due date. I hope this one is different because I don't want to be in the hospital just before Christmas. It's bad enough having to go to a hospital in St. John's since the cottage hospital no longer has a maternity ward, without having to wait in town for days," Kate replied.

Later that night, Bessie told Rose how pleased Marigold and Daisy were with their witch costumes and the chat she had with Kate about her upcoming birth.

"It's times like this that Kate must miss her mother. With Marie living in Ontario, it's not like she can pop in to see her daughters. I know Kate and Jean were pleased to see their mother happily remarried, but when she moved with Gus to the mainland, it wasn't easy for them adjusting to life without her. Knowing Jean has her hands full with her young family and Kate having no other female relatives around, I offered to look after the children to allow Robert to stay with her in St. John's, but Rob has volunteered to move in with the children." Bessie said.

"Rob is as good as any woman when it comes to looking after a home. He did a fine job raising Robert alone from the time he was a baby," Rose replied

"Your parents often said the same thing. Although I also heard Rob was too independent by far. There were women in Mark's Point who would have gladly provided meals for him and Robert after his wife died, but he made it quite plain he needed no help. I guess that's where the Browns get their independent streak. I know Kate thinks there's no one like him. She jokes with Robert that she only married him to get Rob as her father-in-law," Bessie said.

"Kate never really knew her father. She and Jean were only about Marigold's and Daisy's ages when he died, leaving Marie on her own to raise the girls. The only good thing was her in-laws lived next door to them in

Muddy Brook Cove and were a great support. Gus, who is now married to Marie, grew up in Mark's Landing, but he was a young man when he left for work on the mainland. But wasn't he back living in Mark's Landing before they got married?" Rose asked.

"Yes, that was almost seven years ago when he took early retirement. Two years later, he and Marie married, and no one could have happier for them than her daughters. But then, Gus's former boss expanded his business and began calling him, asking him to return to work. He even visited Mark's Landing to convince Gus to come back to the mainland and help him. Gus and Marie talked it over and decided to accept the job for five years. Kate tells me her mother is enjoying her new life, and although they are happy for her, she and Jean will be even happier when she returns home for good. They've been gone three years, so there are two more years to go."

"Talking about time, your birthday party is in two days. You keep telling me not to make a fuss, but are you sure there's nothing we are forgetting?"

But Rose was sure everything was in place. Her only concern was whether Bessie remembered to tell guests not to bring birthday gifts. Bessie assured her everyone got the message, as Rose muttered how it was foolish for a woman of her age to have a birthday party.

Rose was even more sure having a party was a bad idea two nights later when her friends began arriving with wrapped parcels. It was only when Robert, Gabe, and Dave Murphy came in, each carrying large boxes filled with wrapped gifts, that Rose finally learned about the surprise Bessie and her friends had planned for her birthday.

"Happy birthday Rose. We know you insisted you didn't want birthday gifts, and we respected your wishes. But ever since we decided to hold the fair, you've worked hard and long to make it a success. Bessie told us that you pushed her to write a poem for the Parcel Post stall with the promise you would look after it. So, instead of giving you presents, we decided to donate parcels to your stall. In addition to our own, we have two boxes filled with parcels that arrived at the post office. Kate kept them until now, and that box Dave is carrying comes from Murphy's Cove, thanks to Millicent who has been collecting parcels in her shop," Robert announced.

"There are a few more in my bedroom that I've been trying to sneak out without success. When Bob and Sue phoned the other day, she told me she collected about 20 with her friends' help. Her parcels should arrive at the beginning of the week. So happy birthday Rose, you'll be glad to know you are going to have plenty of mail to give out at the fair," Bessie said.

Once she got over the surprise, Rose was delighted and thanked everyone.

"This makes me even more certain our fair will be a success. You couldn't have given me any better gifts. Now I'm stocked and ready to roll; the rest of you are going to have your work cut out to equal the money my stall will bring in."

"You'll do good, Rose, but I knows the cake stall will give you a run for your money. All the wimen in Mark's Point is baking, and even my Jim is helping. He's been cutting up fruit for me for the cakes I'm making. Next week I'm starting on cookies and sponges. I tells my Jim that if Bessie thought me good enough to look after the cake stall, I have to do a real good job. Don't I?" Lucy asked her husband, who gave a quick nod in agreement.

Much later that night, when the guests had gone following a night of music, singing and plenty of good food and refreshments, Bessie and Rose reflected on the party and how everyone appeared to enjoy themselves.

"I'm glad we invited Jim and Lucy. Jim doesn't say much, but I know Lucy was delighted when I asked them. And look how proud she is of the baked goods stall. I doubt if anyone in Mark's Point will donate half as much as she does to it," Bessie said.

"You're probably right. I was looking at Lucy tonight and wondering if I was imagining it or had she mellowed recently? Maybe it's because I'm getting used to her, but it seems to me that Lucy's not gossiping much these days," Rose replied

Bessie agreed with Rose, saying perhaps Lucy's responsibility to look after the baked goods stall, which meant she had to call all the women in the community, kept her too busy to think about gossiping.

"And she could be like me, never really getting involved in community activities until now, and it's keeping both her and Jim occupied."

"You may be right, Bessie. I know she supervised Jim cutting out the hoopla blocks and made sure he did a good job painting them. Did you see the blocks? I don't know where he got the paint, but he made 24 blocks and used four different bright colours to paint them. He and Lucy were so pleased to show them to me. Lucy also said Jim wouldn't mind looking after the hoopla game but thought he might need help. I told her we would make sure we had a helper in his stall," Rose said.

"It looks like everything is falling into place for the fair. Let's bring all your parcels to the school on Monday afternoon, Rose, then divide them into adult and children's categories. We should get that done before Dave delivers the games and prizes from St. John's at night. I also need to start picking up prizes from people and make out tickets for the Tombola stall. For every 20 tickets, there will be a prize and, with each prize numbered and on display, anyone buying a ticket will know right away if they won and what prize they'll get."

During the next few days, Bessie and Rose began to wonder if there would ever again be time to relax. It seemed there were endless meetings at the school, whether it was deciding on a floor plan for the stalls, sorting out prizes for games, or just working to ensure everything was in place for the fair. They also took turns in the kitchen baking cakes and cookies for Lucy's stall. When Bessie visited homes in Mark's Point collecting items for her Tombola stall, Rose would be counting ticket proceeds, dividing the money into floats, or making out signs for the Parcel Post stall. She had already changed paper money for coins at Kavanagh's and the post office, but she decided to see if Millicent could help when she still needed additional small change on Wednesday morning.

"Bessie, do you feel like taking a break from fair business and going over to Murphy's Cove this morning. I need more coins for the floats on each stall, and I thought I'd see if Millicent has more she would exchange for paper money. If not, I'll check at the parish house to see if I can get some from the church collection."

"I wouldn't mind at all. Getting away from Mark's Point right now would do both of us good. We could also stop at Mina's to pick up a prize she has for my stall. I'll give her a call and see if she's home," Bessie said.

Not only was Mina home, but she insisted Bessie and Rose come for lunch.

"Herbert has taken his mother to St. John's and won't be back until tomorrow night. I'm baking, and just this minute finished putting a blueberry cake in the oven, so come for lunch, and we'll have cake for our dessert," Mina said with a chuckle.

Later, as Bessie and Rose enjoyed lunch with Mina, she told them of her plans in the Murphy's Cove South polling station the following day.

"It's being held in Clara Maloney's house. She's in charge, and I'm her poll clerk. Clara's an old hand at this, working at provincial and federal elections, but it's my first time, and I'm a bit nervous. We had training in Murphy's Cove last week with people from all the communities in this district. I talked to Kate's sister Jean from Mark's Landing, and it's also her first time working in the booth. We were both glad there was someone else who hadn't worked in a polling station before," Mina said.

She spoke about getting everything ready to take with her the next day because it would be late before getting home. She had planned to have the girls' dinner cooked so they would only have to heat it on their arrival from school, but they insisted they were old enough to get a meal on their own.

"Although I haven't worked in the booth before, I'm looking forward to it, but 12 hours is a long time. That's why I not only need lunches; I'm taking my embroidery with me so when the booth isn't busy, I can do some needlework. Meanwhile, Bessie, I promised you a prize for your Tombola stall," Mina said, producing a pair of handmade cushions.

"These are beautiful, Mina. When people see them, they'll be wanting to know who made them. I wouldn't be surprised if you get orders for them after the fair," Bessie said.

"I'm glad you like them too, Rose, because I put a pair of cushion covers in one of the parcels I brought to your party. The other parcel had a table runner I made and embroidered."

"Mina, that's far too much from you. It's not even your community or school, and it's far from cheap making these things!" Rose exclaimed.

"It might not be my community or hall, but I'm sure my girls will spend time there once the youth club gets going. But that's not my only reason. It's because you and Bessie have been wonderful friends, doing so much for the girls and me. You might not know it, but I feel like a new person this year. Katy and Isabelle see the difference, and it's making them happy, and, goodness knows, they deserve to be happy. Now, let's not hear any more about it. What about another piece of cake?"

Changing the subject, Bessie asked if Katy and Isabelle enjoyed themselves at the twins' house on Saturday night.

"Yes, it was a great idea of Kate's to let them have a girls' night," Mina answered.

"With the twins babysitting their younger sisters to let her and Robert go to your birthday party, Kate said they could invite their friends over. There were about ten girls. Katy, Isabelle, Martina, and Jenny, came to mass with Father Kiely and stayed until after your party. According to the girls, everyone had a great time."

"Yes, Maggie said the same thing. I asked about Bobby, but he stayed at Michael's that night because it was a girls-only party. Maggie doubts if he or Michael would have come even if asked, and I had to agree with her," Bessie said, laughing.

As Bessie and Rose drove to the Mark's Point polling station held in Patsy and Jim Martin's home, Rose wondered how Mina was getting on the following day.

"It's good to see Mina accepting the position in the polling station. When I was in Murphy's Store getting change, Millicent said Mina would have refused the polling booth job a year ago, but she has more confidence these days, and that's good to hear. You know, when we were having lunch with Mina, I got to thinking that I've been home all year, and I've still never seen sight nor sound of that husband of hers."

"Which could be a good thing because you have a tendency not only to show your feelings but to tell people exactly how you feel. If you came face to face with Herbert Lynch, I wouldn't want to imagine what might happen."

"Nonsense Bessie. I may consider him an ignoramus, and I would never be able to talk civilly to him. However, there are many ways to show disdain for a contemptible individual without getting into a verbal battle."

"I sometimes think you forget you are no longer a nun or a high school principal, Rose. And for sure, if you used words like that, Herbert wouldn't have a clue what you were saying. Now let's change the topic because we are almost at the polling station. Albert will be on pins and needles today. When we phoned last night to wish him well, I thought he sounded nervous. But I'll be surprised if he doesn't win this seat. I can hardly wait for the results, although I know Jack will keep his promise to phone as soon as they know. We're here now, and I should stop talking about Albert because anyone hearing me might think I'm trying to influence their vote."

Later that night, there was no doubt that voters in the district had been influenced by their PC candidate when Albert won the seat by an overwhelming majority. Almost two hours after the polls closed, Jack phoned and gleefully announced it was official; Albert would be their new member in the House of Assembly.

"The decision hasn't been announced yet on radio or television, but I'm at PC Party headquarters, and they just announced the official count. Not only has Albert won, but the Progressive Conservatives might also form the next government. Right now, 20 of our candidates are leading in their districts.

"It's a great night for the Conservatives, and I'm so proud of Albert. He'll be calling you himself when he gets a chance to come down to earth. I'll also be talking to you again soon because Dad and our American relatives are in constant touch these days and are coming to Newfoundland. I will let you know more once their plans are final, but one thing for sure, Dad's uncle wants to visit Fisherman's Creek and of course, we'll want to stay with you if that's alright."

Bessie was relating the news about the election results to Rose when the phone rang again from someone else anxious to know how Albert did in the election.

"Bessie, are the election results in yet? Bob's on the other line, and we couldn't wait any longer because we've been wondering all day about Albert," Sue said.

When Bessie told the American couple about Albert's victory, Rose could hear their cheering from where she sat. Bob cheered again on hearing that Jack believed the PC party might have as many as 20 seats.

"Bob or I were never so excited about our elections. But of course, we never knew any of our politicians personally like we know Albert, and we both feel he'll be an excellent member. When you talk to him, tell him how pleased we are and give him our congratulations.

"I guess these are exciting and busy times for you all, what with Rose's birthday party and your fair this weekend. I just wish I could be there. Hopefully, the next fair you have, Bob and I will be residents and work at it. Did our boxes with the parcels arrive yet?" Sue asked.

Bessie passed the phone to Rose, who wanted to thank Sue for the many donations she and her friends collected.

"We knew the Parcel Post stall would do well, but I don't think anyone ever thought we'd get as many parcels as we have. It's close to 200 now, and I still have people telling me they have parcels to pass in," Rose told Sue.

When Sue asked about the Tombola stall, which Bessie was looking after, Rose passed the phone back to Bessie.

"Between the Parcel Post, Tombola, and the Baked Goods stalls, we should raise a good amount of money. We also have other attractions, including bingo, thanks to you and Bob. Once the fair is over and things settle down, our committee is looking at starting a weekly bingo. You'd be surprised how many people have been asking when it will begin," Bessie said.

When Sue finally hung up, Rose and Bessie began calling their friends, sharing the good news about Albert's win. When Rose relayed the results to Sharon, the young teacher wasn't surprised.

"I was sure Albert would do well, and our high school students did too. Our school organized a mock campaign to show students how our democratic system works. Today, each student received a ballot and voted for who they believed should win. Albert won by a landslide. Young people are pretty smart. They may have heard their parents talk about the candidates, but they also know much more about politics than we think."

Sharon then apologized for not being available to help the following night when everything would be put in place for the fair because she was one of the chaperones at the high school Halloween dance.

"David will be at the hall to help prepare for the fair because the elementary school is having its Halloween party and dance tomorrow afternoon. With buses picking up high school students for the dance, I'm sure parents will also turn up to help. But I'll be there bright and early on Saturday. Mom and Dad are coming tomorrow, and Mom says she's available to help serving soup. She's also bringing my contributions to Lucy's stall because she knows I'm not much of a baker."

Ending her telephone conversation, Rose remarked how Sharon's father was making his first visit to Mark's Point at a time when people might be too busy to talk to him.

"You're probably right, but I think he and Agnes are staying for a few days, and he'll have an opportunity to meet everyone when things calm down. Sharon last saw her father in April before he went back to work on the Lake boats. I heard her say he had a month's holiday and wanted to come out and see where she and David lived after hearing so much about Mark's Point."

But it didn't take long for Sharon's father, Jerry Dawson, to get to know local people. He showed up with David and cheerfully worked alongside the many volunteers who turned up at the former school on Friday night to get it ready for the fair. After putting out chairs and tables with the men, he helped Bessie set up the Tombola stall.

Later that night, Bessie and Rose, tired after spending almost three hours at the old school, thankfully relaxed with cups of tea and chatted about the nights' activities.

"Wasn't it great to see so many people turn up to help? Even Sharon's father pitched in, and he came up with a solution for my stall. I wondered how to deal with prizes like beer and spirits because if a child won alcohol, I couldn't give it to them. But I knew they would want to try for the prizes, especially the ones from the catalogue. Jerry suggested dividing the prizes into two categories."

Bessie went on to tell Rose how they put all prizes for children on one table, while a second table held those suitable only for adults.

"I spoke to Robert about it, and we changed the price of the tickets. Children won't be allowed to try for adult prizes but will only pay 10 cents for their Tombola tickets. Meanwhile, adults can try both sides of the stall, but their tickets will cost 25 cents. I had numbers for the prizes and tickets made out, and while I divided them between the two parts of the stall, Sharon's father cut the original sign in half and made out two new price signs on the blank sides. Thanks to him, I'm ready for tomorrow. Meanwhile, Robert said Patsy didn't have any specific place to help tomorrow, and he will ask her to look after the children's table."

Rose was in complete agreement with cheaper ticket prices for children. When she agreed to look after the Parcel Post stall, she asked the committee to put a one-dollar price on children's parcels, while those intended for adults would cost two dollars.

"I know this is a fundraiser, but we don't want to charge too much, and we certainly want the fair to be a fun time for children. Not many children will have a lot of money to spend. I'm glad the committee agreed to two prices before we put out the letters. That way, people donating parcels knew how much they should pay when buying gifts to put in a parcel. However, I know the parcels from the United States are worth much more. Each one required a label to go through Customs, with the value of the item included."

Rose said it was one of the reasons she looked for sacks. The parcels were in six categories: small boys, small girls, older boys and girls, women, and men, with a sack for each group. She said people would not be rummaging through the burlap bags looking for what they think is a 'good' parcel. Instead, Rose, or whoever was working on the stall, would always pass out the top package. When a sack began to empty, there were spares to refill them.

Some attractions, including hoopla, grab bags, and the beanbag toss, would be held outside if the weather permitted.

"I hope the weather is as good tomorrow as it was the past two days. Gabe and Pat Martin say it should be a fine day, but I'm glad our stalls are inside. I know Lucy is happy to be next to the area set aside for a kitchen. She has the big stand-up cooler filled up with baked goods, and with a little help, she'll quickly get everything set up in the morning. Did you see the two tables Jim made with legs that fold under when not being used? Lucy says he made the first one for his hoopla stand, and when she saw what a good job he did, she got him to make a longer one for her baked goods. I don't think there was a prouder or happier woman in Mark's Point than Lucy when everyone began to admire Jim's work," Bessie said, smiling at the memory.

"Yes, Lucy and Jim are certainly coming into their own these days. Before now, I think Jim only opened his mouth when he sang in church, but I saw him talking to people several times last night. As for Lucy, she's in her element. Did you see all the cakes she baked herself? If every woman in Mark's Point made that many cakes, Jim would need to make at least a dozen tables to accommodate them," Rose replied.

"Talking of the fair, I was going to put a five-dollar bill in envelopes for Maggie and Mina's girls to spend. I would give Kate and Bob's crowd something, but they might be offended knowing how independent their parents are. However, if I see the children and it looks as if they have spent what money they had, I'll pass them a couple of dollars," Bessie said.

Rose laughed, saying she had the same idea and had put aside one and two-dollar bills for that reason.

"Working on the stalls, we're not likely to have an opportunity to spend much money. By giving it to the youngsters, we're helping the cause and also making them happy. I'll probably buy something from the baked goods stall and tickets, but I can't get parcels if I'm running it. Here's $15 to put in the girls' envelopes to go with your money. They'll be delighted with $10 each to spend. Now that's looked after, I'm going to bed. We have a long, busy day ahead of us."

The following day, even before the fair started, the women had soup to make and a container of sandwiches. Bessie had cooked an extra-large roast for supper the night before, intending to use the remainder for sandwiches.

"We have to bring our soup to the fair at four o'clock. That's the worst about having no stove in the school; we can't keep several pots of soup warm at one time. The hotplates can heat something fast but not much good for low heat to keep the soup warm. Robert's idea of having the soup brought to the school at staggered times was good, and with Gabe offering to come here and get ours, we don't have to worry about transporting a big hot boiler. If we leave it sitting at the back of the oil stove, it will be ready to serve when Gabe brings it to the school," Bessie said.

Saturday morning lived up to the weather forecast issued by Gabe and Pat Martin. It was a bright day as Bessie and Rose cleared up after breakfast. Already, they could see signs of activity around the community.

"People are not usually up and on the go this early on Saturday mornings. Isn't that Gabe's truck that just went by with a couple of men in the back? Where would they be going at this time of the morning? And look, I'm sure that's Dan Ryan's truck with somebody sitting in the back holding a long ladder. I hope there's nothing wrong."

As Bessie spoke, the telephone rang. After listening to the caller for a minute, Rose began to laugh.

"Well, that is a relief. Bessie and I were beginning to think something was wrong. Just wait a minute, and I'll ask her. Bessie, do you still have Alex's Union Jack?

"That's Robert on the phone. He and some men are putting up strings of bunting that Father Kiely unearthed from the parish house basement, thinking it would give the fair a festive look. Gabe, Dan, and others will put it up outside the community while Robert, David, and some boys decorate around the school. Robert thought it would be fitting to hoist a flag once again on the pole in the school grounds, and the only flag he knows about is Alex's Union Jack."

"Tell him he's welcome to use it. I'll bring it over, although I'll probably need to iron it first," Bessie replied.

It was just after nine o'clock when Bessie and Rose brought the newly ironed flag over to the school, but the building and grounds were already a hive of activity.

"My goodness Robert, we have almost three hours before the fair opens and just look at how busy everyone is. Rose and I thought we'd take a quick look at our stalls to see if there was anything we had forgotten to do. I see we're not the only ones checking up on things. Jim is setting up the hoopla stall, and it's so colourful and welcoming," Bessie said.

Jim wasn't the only one with his game set up. Oscar had been busy with the bean bag toss, and he had two different ways to play the game. Anyone trying for a prize could either throw a bean bag through a clown's big mouth or have a go at knocking down sets of cans.

"Oscar has done a great job, and just wait till you go inside the school. Lucy has her table filled with baked goods of every kind, and then she tells me that there's still lots more in the cooler. While I have you here, let me check my list. Yes, you both have help with your stalls, and you're down to bring your soup at four o'clock; is that okay?" Robert asked.

"Yes, it's simmering away now, and Gabe will go to the house this afternoon and bring it here. I have Patsy with me on Tombola, and Sharon will help Rose with the Parcel Post. It's a good idea to have lists, especially a schedule for bringing soup when we only have hotplates. Too bad we don't have a big stove in the school for events like this," Bessie said.

"You never know; if we do well today, we might just be able to buy one," Robert replied.

"But I'm in the doghouse at home because of these lists. I have one very unhappy wife who went off the head when she looked at them to see where she would be working. Kate didn't mind when her name wasn't on the list to serve soup because she thought she might be working in a stall. When she discovered her name wasn't on any list, that's when she got mad. She's told me not to come home until I found a place for her to help.

"What am I going to do? Kate shouldn't be on her feet for hours at a time. She's got less than six weeks to go before the baby is born, but it's no good talking to her. At least in the post office, she has a chair to sit on or else go into the house and take a spell. Can you help me, Bessie or Rose? Can you think of anything Kate can do where she can take things easy and still help?" Robert asked.

"I can," Rose quickly replied.

"And Kate is the ideal person for the job. I should have thought of her before now. I've been wondering how I was going to manage all the money today. I have the parcel post-stall to run, and as treasurer, I'm supposed to be looking after the main float and changing money for each stall when needed.

Rose said Kate could sit at a table, look after money from the stalls, and change people's money. Stall workers knew not to keep a lot of cash on hand but to return some to the main float periodically. It would avoid rummaging through a pile of paper money in cash cans looking for change while customers were waiting or have so much paper money it might fall out of the can.

"I have an exercise book with a page made out for every attraction starting with its cash float. Kate can keep up the book up to date as she gets in money. Now, don't you think Kate is the best one for the job?"

"That's wonderful, Rose. I know she will be happy with that. She's used to handling money, but the best thing of all, she'll be able to do it sitting down. I had visions of her in the kitchen area, trying to lift big boilers of soup. Now when I go home, this news should get me out of the doghouse. I'm leaving here before eleven to get washed and dressed and will be back at 11:30 when the workers arrive. David is staying when I leave to keep an eye on things. Now, ladies, I guess I'll see the pair of you when I return. Thanks again, Rose, for making my life much easier."

Laughing, Rose and Bessie left Robert and went to check on their stalls. Once they were sure everything was in place, they walked over to see if Lucy needed any help.

"Thanks, Rose and Bessie, but everything's good. I've got the cakes in one place, pies next to them, then loaves of bread, between the pies, and just look at all those cookies. And guess what? The table's full, and we still has lots more stuff in the cooler. Nora starts serving tables at three o'clock, but she's working with me in the stall 'til then. Last night the two of us priced everything, and Robert says when it's Nora's turn serving soup, some young girls is willing to take her place. But right now, I've got to find Jim and go home. I must finish making my soup and see what kind of sandwiches I'll make. I'm some excited with all this. I thinks we're going to do real good at the fair, don't you?"

After agreeing with Lucy and saying they also had to go home and get ready, Bessie and Rose took one last look around the school and then went outdoors in time to see Robert raising Alex's flag.

"I think this is a good place for Alex's flag to fly, don't you, Bessie?" Rose asked.

"He would be proud to see it here," Bessie replied.

"When I go Christmas shopping in St. John's next month, I will buy two Canadian Maple Leaf flags. When Canada officially adopted the Maple Leaf flag as the national flag in 1965, Alex often spoke about getting one, but he never did get around to buying it."

When Rose asked her why she would want two flags alike, Bessie said she'd like to erect one on the school grounds in memory of Alex, who was proud of his Newfoundland roots and a proud Canadian.

"The other one will fly alongside the Union Jack in our garden. Alex always took the flag down in the winter and put it up again in the spring. I never put it up this year, but next spring both flags will fly proudly in our garden. What do you think?"

"It's a great idea, but now we should be getting home. We've been here chatting and looking at things, and it's almost 10 o'clock. The fair will open before we know it. We still have things to do before we get dressed and get back here. I don't know about you, but I'll want something to eat before I leave, so come on, Bessie, let's get home."

CHAPTER 25

All The Fun Of The Fair

T he unofficial count of Mark's Point residents was 114, but when Bessie and Rose arrived at the former school, it appeared that number had at the least tripled. Vehicles were parked end to end along the main road while groups of people stood outside the fence.

"My goodness Bessie, there's a crowd here already, and the fair doesn't open for another half hour. I'd say the best place to park your car is probably by the church."

Bessie wondered where everyone was coming from as she finally found a place to park her car. As they approached the school on foot, they saw David and Sean standing at the gate like a pair of guards. Bessie laughingly asked whether they were allowed entrance to the school grounds.

"You are, but only committee members and stall workers will be allowed in for now. Everyone else must wait until we open at noon. Father Kiely should be here by then to officially begin the fun. If not, we have another surprise guest who will probably be only too happy to do so, and by the way, our guest or I should say guests, are inside the school," David said.

Wondering who the unexpected guests could be, Bessie and Rose walked into the school, where they got their first surprise. Every volunteer wore a boater hat while stall workers were also sporting waist aprons with lots of pockets.

"Where did the hats and aprons come from?" Rose asked.

"From your new member of the House of Assembly," a voice said, and with a great deal of laughter, Albert, Ellen, and Jack appeared from a corner of the school.

"You can't have a fair without hats, and although these are only Styrofoam, we thought they'd add to the look and fun of the fair. The money aprons were Ellen's idea. She said the pockets would be handy for people working on stalls," Albert said.

"This is my first official appearance as your district MHA, but Jack and I planned to come to the fair, elected or not. And once Ellen knew about it, there was no keeping her in town. We can only stay a few hours because Jack is flying to Ontario in the morning, and I have a meeting in the afternoon, but we mean to make the most of our time here. I've been watching Ellen eyeing up all those cakes and cookies and knowing her; our car will be carrying more than its share of sweet stuff back to St. John's."

Jack, who had a good look at the outdoor games, said he was eager to try them, boasting he was once a dab hand on hoopla and the bean bag throw.

Once the sisters-in-law got over their surprise and had a few words with Ellen and the men, it was time to give their stalls a final check. Rose seated Kate at a table near the lunch area, where she would also take payment from people having soup and sandwiches. She spent a few minutes showing Kate how she set up an exercise book to track money coming from each fundraising activity.

Meanwhile, Robert taped a notice to the front of Kate's table, letting people know to pay for their meal there. Before leaving, he asked Kate if her chair was comfortable and reminded her that he would relieve her if she got tired.

"Go away, Robert, you're clucking around me like a mother hen. I'm sitting down, and Rose is close by if I want to know anything. What else do I need? Go and do what you have to do. Look, Father Kiely is here now; you'd better go and meet him," Kate said, dismissing her husband with an irritated look.

"Honestly, Rose, if Robert doesn't stop fussing around me, I'll have a fit. The way he carries on lately, you'd think this was our first child, not our sixth. Do you know Robert expected me to come here and do nothing today? It's bad enough sitting down all afternoon, but at least I feel I'm helping," Kate said, giving her husband another irritated look as he walked away.

"Kate, if Robert didn't care, he wouldn't worry about you. Some women hear nothing but abuse from their husbands, but I'm sure you've never heard Robert say one unkind word to you or your children. You're a lucky woman, and likewise, Robert is a lucky man, and I think you both know it. So now, with that spiel off your chest, can you please smile at your husband? I know he's upset because he keeps giving you worried glances, and we can't have him out of sorts today."

Hearing Rose speaking this way was so unusual, a surprised Kate nodded in agreement. She looked over and smiled at Robert, who gave her a huge grin in return before turning to greet Father Kiely.

"Sorry, Rose, I didn't mean to take out my frustration on you. I know Robert worries, but I keep telling him I'm fine. I know I couldn't ask for a better husband or a more caring father for our children, but I wish he'd stop his endless fussing around me."

Before Rose could respond, Robert was in the middle of the hall, calling for everyone's attention.

"It will be noon in a few minutes and time to open this event. Before we go outside, where Father will offer a prayer, I want to thank our committee and all the people who've worked so hard to make this happen. That's all I'll say for now, but hopefully, there will be far more to say and even more to be thankful for once the fair and dance are over, and we count all the money we make," Robert said, joining in the laughter from his audience.

"So now, even if your stall is inside, it would be nice if we all went outdoors and let Father Kiely get this fair started. Best of luck, everybody. Have a great afternoon."

With those words, Robert led the workers outdoors. Then, shouting at the top of his voice, he asked everyone to be silent to allow Father Kiely to say a few words.

Bessie, looking beyond the fence to the crowd, which appeared to have multiplied since she and Rose arrived, said it was a good thing many of the attractions were outdoors. She doubted if the old school would have accom-modated the games and the number of people waiting for the fair to begin.

"Welcome to Mark's Point's first, but hopefully not its last, fair. It's been wonderful to see the efforts of the people who worked tirelessly to make this possible. There are all kinds of games and attractions, the biggest selection of baked goods I've ever seen and later, the women will be serving delicious homemade soup. Have a great time. I'll ask you now to take a minute as we thank God for making events like these possible," Father Kiely said.

"Heavenly Father, bless all those gathered here today to work and play together in a spirit of community and giving. Thank You for this beautiful weather, which allows us to hold this event outdoors. We also thank You for the many blessings You continue to give us and pray that You always look with favour on us as we work to strengthen our parish and communities. Amen."

"Thank you, Father Kiely. Now people, give us a couple of minutes to allow the volunteers to get to their stations and then the fair will begin."

Loud applause and cheering greeted Robert's announcement as the vol-unteers left to man the games and attractions.

"At least we have a few minutes so you can explain to me how the prizes work, but I pity David and Sean trying to hold back that crowd," Patsy said to Bessie as they made their way indoors.

"Why don't you go on the children's side of the Tombola? The tickets and float are here, and although everyone will pick a number, there are only certain numbers in multiples of 20, such as 40, 60, 80, that will be winners."

Bessie continued to instruct Patsy, showing her how each prize had a number corresponding to a winning ticket. Children not picking a winning ticket would receive a lollipop as a consolation prize. She had just finished showing Patsy the big bag of lollipops when the school started filling up with prospective customers.

"Before we get overwhelmed with the crowd, tickets on your side of the stall cost 10 cents each. Good luck, Patsy!"

By the time Bessie finished speaking, Patsy had four or five children lined up, all eager to try their luck. Marigold and Daisy, who were among the first to arrive in the school, quickly made their way over to Rose at the Parcel Post stall.

"Hello, girls. Mrs. Nolan has the children's parcels," Rose told the sisters.

"It's big people's parcels we wants, one for a mother and one for a father, and we have lots of money to buy them. We're getting parcels for us after, but the first ones are for Mom and Dad. But don't tell them Miss Rose; it's a surprise," Marigold said.

"Guess what, Miss Rose, Pop's got gout, and he can't come, but he gave all of us five dollars to spend. It's the most money we ever had. The twins said they was buying him a parcel to thank him, and we wants to thank Mom and Dad. They always buy us things, and Dad gave us extra money 'cause he and Mom is going to be too busy to get anything," Daisy added.

"You are generous girls, and your parents will love whatever you get them. Now, Daisy, this is the postbag for men, and the first parcel out of it will go to your dad," Rose said.

Taking a parcel the size of a shoebox out of the sack, she gave it to Daisy. Then going to the brin bag marked WOMEN, she took out a package and gave it to Marigold, telling her Kate was getting the first woman's parcel.

"I wonder what's inside them. I hope it's something real nice. What do you think, Miss Rose; did we get good parcels?" Marigold asked.

Assuring the girls the parcels were sure to please their parents regardless of what was inside, Rose suggested they try Sharon's side of the stall.

"If you want to give me the parcels you bought, I'll write your names on them and put them under the table until you're ready to leave. It will save you from carrying them around. Now look at those children getting toys from Mrs. Nolan's table; go get yourselves something."

Rose's words were enough for the girls to pass over the parcels and make their way to Sharon. From then on, she was kept busy with adults eager to see what they would get.

"I'm enjoying this," she said to Ellen and Albert when they stopped at her stall to buy four parcels.

"I knew people would like the novelty of buying a parcel sight unseen, and I'm enjoying watching their reaction when they open the packages. Let's see what the pair of you get."

She passed over two parcels from the men's sack to Albert and two from the women's bag for Ellen, who told Albert to open his first. She was like Rose, she said, preferring to watch others open their gifts.

Encouraged by Ellen, Albert tore the paper off the first one. Discovering a pair of hand-knit mitts, he gave a whoop of pleasure, saying he couldn't have asked for anything better.

"Now, if I could only get another pair for Dad. Since Mother's hands got so bad with arthritis and she had to give up knitting, we haven't had hand-knit mitts or socks for ages, and I certainly miss them."

"Since I never learned to knit, maybe I should be buying men's parcels to see if I can get another pair of mitts. But open your other one, and let's see what else you have," Ellen said.

Albert's second parcel held a wallet, which Rose recognized as one of Bessie's donations. When Ellen opened hers, she had bath soap and face-cloths in one and a pair of pillowcases in the second.

"These are excellent gifts. I'm going to buy a couple more parcels for men. Even if they don't have mitts, I'm sure they won't go astray; someone will use what is inside."

On saying that, Ellen passed over a five-dollar bill telling Rose she didn't want change and accepted two more items from the men's sack. She gave a sound of delight when she discovered not one but two pairs of hand-knit socks in the first parcel. The second held a framed picture of Mark's Point, which Albert instantly claimed for his office, asking Rose if she knew who took the photo.

"Whoever it is, did a great job. I can see Martin House, the church, and the school, yet the photographer still managed to get a full harbour view. It's a beautiful picture."

"I not only know who took it, but you've met the photographer several times. There's a lovely photo of Martin House in the living room, and the same person took the photo. You probably won't guess, so I'll put you out of your misery. Father Kiely is the photographer, and I've seen some great photos he took of other communities in the parish."

"Is that right? Didn't I hear Father Kiely say the parish needs a good fundraiser next Spring before painting the churches? If he had a dozen scenic photos of this area, the parish could easily have calendars printed and put on sale. Not only would parishioners buy one, but I am sure former residents and visitors would appreciate calendars with local photos."

Rose told Albert it was a great idea. She told him to talk to her later as people were waiting for parcels, or better still, she added, he should speak to Father or Robert.

With those words, Rose turned to serve another group of prospective customers. Glancing across at the Tombola stall, she barely saw Bessie and Patsy behind the crowd gathered around waiting to purchase tickets.

"Miss Rose, are you interested in buying some tickets on a bucket of salt beef? They're 10 cents each, and with only a few tickets left, we'll be spinning the wheel soon," Sean called out to her.

Reaching under the table for her purse, Rose handed him a dollar for salt beef tickets and then a second one, telling him she'd also have more on the next draw, regardless of the prize. Then taking advantage of a quiet few minutes, she asked Sharon if she would keep an eye on her part of the stall to allow her to get money changed from Kate.

"No problem, and would you take these two $20 bills and get one and two-dollar bills for me. The children's parcels are going like wildfire. I had an older man from Fisherman's Creek buy ten and insisted on giving me two dollars for each one. I wonder what he planned to do with them," Sharon said.

Rose arrived at Kate's table in time to see David getting rolls of change for the bean bag throw.

"Have you been outside since this started?" he asked Rose.

"The grounds are packed. John Maloney came over with a full busload of adults and children from Murphy's Cove and Murphy's Cove South, and vehicles are stretched along the road as far as the eye can see. It's a good job that it's such a beautiful day because there's no way everyone would get into the school. As for the games, they are going non-stop. Jack Martin is with Oscar on the bean bag throw, and Sharon's dad is with Jim on hoopla. Jerry picks up hoops from the ground and table, so Jim won't have to be bending up and down. We also have Michael and Bobby on standby to help with the games."

"The young ones are having a wonderful time," Kate said.

"The twins and their friends were here, and I never saw a happier group. According to Lily, this is the most exciting thing that has ever happened in Mark's Point. And you want to hear Marigold and Daisy. They came to show me the parcels and prizes they have. They have a doll's tea set from the parcel post, which they say is the 'bestest prize in the world.' Their choice of a word to describe the tea set may be poor, but it's a perfect prize for them. Mrs. Newman sent it from the States, and according to the Customs label, it's worth almost $10 in American money."

Sean appeared at the open door, shouting out the winning number on the pail of salt beef.

"Number 87, number 87. Has anyone here got 87? If so, you've won a bucket of salt beef."

Reaching into one of the many pockets in her apron, Rose took out her tickets, and to her surprise, 87 was one of her numbers. Holding it up in the air, she called out to Sean, who came over to get it.

"You're the winner, Miss Rose. I'll bring the salt beef to you. I still have your money for the next lot of tickets, but we're stopping selling tickets for a while because there's a big demand for bingo. We might try a 50/50 game, selling bingo cards for 25 cents each, then splitting the proceeds in half between the winner and the fair. How does that sound?"

"You and Kelly are in charge of bingo, Sean, so whatever you think will work, just go ahead and do it, but it sounds like a good idea. Who is calling bingo?"

"Father Kiely volunteered, and it should be great fun hearing him call the numbers. If we do well, and we should, according to those waiting to play, we'll have more games later."

Saying this, Sean went on his way accompanied by David, while Rose, knowing Millicent was a bingo fan, wondered aloud to Kate whether she had arrived yet.

"I just got here," said a voice behind her.

"The first thing I asked was where the Parcel Post stall was, and my second question was when is bingo starting? Why are you standing here? Don't tell me all the parcels are gone already," Millicent said.

"No, I just came over to get change from Kate, and I'm on my way back. Come on, I'll get you a parcel," Rose said as they made their way across the school.

Millicent was looking for multiple parcels, having received money from some elderly Murphy's Cove residents who could not attend the fair. Handing Rose $20, she said she wanted ten, seven for women and three for men and would write a recipient's name on the outside of each one. After putting names on eight parcels, she said the final two were for her and Dave.

"I brought these two bags for the parcels. Can I leave them with you, maybe under your table? I don't want to be carrying them around all afternoon. If you have any parcels left when I come back, I'll buy another couple. Right now, I'm going over to the Tombola and see if I can win a prize."

Millicent waited in line at Bessie's stall and watched as Teen Ryan won a bottle of wine and then had the winning number on a set of bath towels. It had her sister Peggy complaining that some people had all the luck.

"I bought a dozen tickets and didn't get a thing. Teen passes over a dollar for four tickets and wins twice. Where's the justice in that? Although maybe if I'm nice to her, she might consider sharing with her younger sister," Peggy said.

The women around the Tombola stall were still laughing at Peggy when Robert appeared at the door to announce bingo would start outside in five minutes. In double-quick time, the indoor attractions lost most of their customers, all eager to try their luck at bingo.

"Patsy, do you want to try for a parcel or look at the baked goods stall while things have slacked off a bit? I can easily look after both sides of our stall," Bessie asked.

"I gave my girls money to buy parcels for Jack and me. As for Lucy's stall, my mother came over from Murphy's Cove on the bus, and between her and the girls, they've picked up a variety of baked goods. Why don't you take a break and see what you want? It's mostly children around now. We won't see many adults until the bingo is over," Patsy replied.

"I wouldn't mind getting over to Lucy's stall before all her baked goods are gone. I'm hoping one of the cakes she made is still available," Bessie said

She was on her way to check out the baked goods when Gabe stopped her, asking if she was going to Lucy's stall would she take his money and buy a couple of cakes.

"Maggie bought some squares and took them home already, but I was hoping to get a light fruit cake. That's Angela's favourite, and Maggie says she knows you baked a couple for sale. You didn't happen to bake a dark fruit one as well?"

"No, I didn't make a dark fruit cake, but Lucy made several, and I can tell you no one makes better dark fruit cakes than her. Why don't you come with me and we'll see what's left on the stall? Angela won't be home until Christmas, and Maggie already asked me to show her how to make a cake so that Angela will have a light fruit cake. Look for a dark fruit one instead because I know that's your favourite kind. Haven't I made one for your birthday and Christmas every year since Jean died? Come on, and we'll see what you can get."

Reluctantly, Gabe followed Bessie to a much-diminished baked goods stall.

"Goodness, Lucy, you've sold a lot. Gabe and I are hoping you don't have all your dark fruit cakes gone."

"We have one dark fruit cake left. Everything went so fast. It was amazing. It's a good job that Nora was with me as I'd never been able to keep up with the rush. And guess what, Bessie, we put aside our start-up money and counted the paper money we have, and it's over $200. Did you ever think we could make that much money on baked stuff?"

"I'm not one bit surprised with you at the helm. Rose and I knew you were the right one to put in charge of this stall. Now Gabe, are you having this dark fruit cake or not?"

When Gabe paid for the cake, a beaming Lucy told him she made it and hoped he enjoyed it.

"I was hoping to buy one of Bessie's cakes, but your baking hasn't killed Jim yet, so I suppose it's alright," Gabe told Lucy.

"Gabe!" Bessie exclaimed.

"If I were Lucy, I'd take the cake back after that remark. Don't mind him, Lucy; he's just tormenting you. I've told him you're a wonderful baker and he came to your stall intending to buy one of your cakes. Now he's looked after. I see there's one of my cherry cakes left. I think I might buy it."

But the words were scarcely out of her mouth when a plaintive voice at her side asked if she seriously wanted to buy back her cake.

"Bessie, you know you don't want to buy it. I was hoping to get here earlier, but I was busy. Kate loves your cherry cake. What if you buy something else and let me have the cherry cake for her?" Robert asked.

Bessie started laughing, saying when she saw the cake, it made her think of Kate, and she had intended to share it with her.

"You go ahead and buy it. There's still lots of goodies I can get. While you're serving Robert, Lucy, I'll go and buy a couple of parcels from Rose, but I'll be right back."

Arriving at the Parcel Post table, she heard Pat Martin ask Rose if he could change his parcel because he had donated it.

"I can tell you what it is. Inside a shoebox and wrapped in newspapers is a flask of Screech. Knowing it was mostly women doing up these parcels, I figured a man wouldn't have much chance of getting something he wanted. Now, if one of your male customers was to get the Screech, I knows he'll walk away a happy man," Pat said.

"And if he drank it, he'd probably be too drunk to walk. Did you think of that, Pat?" a laughing Bessie asked her old friend.

"Give it back to me," Rose said,

"Now I know what's in that parcel; I'll put it aside and give it to someone I think will appreciate it, like this next customer I see approaching. Are you looking to buy a parcel for a man, Gabe?"

"Well, I'm sure not looking for one to give to some woman. I'm going to Sharon's side to get a parcel for Maggie."

"You should buy yourself a parcel, Gabe. Rose was just about to give me mine, wasn't you, Rose?" Pat said.

Bessie stood back watching as Rose gave Pat a new package, which he opened to reveal a razor, shaving cream and aftershave lotion.

"Now, just look at this, Gabe; it's well worth two dollars. Come on, man, try your luck. You never know what you might get."

"I don't know why you're not working on this stall, Pat. You're trying some hard to sell me a parcel, but I guess it's for a good cause. I suppose I'll buy one."

With that, Gabe handed Rose two dollars, and she passed him out the box donated by Pat, who urged him to open it up. When Gabe eventually got through all the newspapers and uncovered the Screech, his face lit up.

"Guess who got the best parcel, Pat? Don't you wish you got this one instead of shaving stuff? I tell you what, why don't you come over to the house later and we'll have a drink together? What do you say?"

"I'd say you're a good friend Gabe. I'll surely take you up on your offer, although it might be tomorrow afternoon before I make it to your place. Don't forget we have the dance tonight and I wouldn't miss it for anything. And speaking about dances, I'll be expecting a dance from you ladies," Pat said as he moved on.

"Now, if I could just get as good a parcel for Maggie, I'd be happy. Here, Sharon, I spent two dollars on myself, so I'll spend that much on Maggie and get her two parcels. I'll drop this stuff at home, Bessie and then go and pick up your soup. Robert asked me to have it here half an hour earlier. He thinks once this first lot of bingo is over, people will be looking to sit down and eat," Gabe said.

"What did you get from the post, Gabe and are you leaving soon to pick up Bessie's soup?" Robert said, arriving at the Parcel Post.

"If you'd been here one second earlier, you would have heard me saying I was going to get the soup. As for my parcel, I got a flask of Screech."

"Go on, you never did! That cost far more than two dollars."

When Gabe showed him the flask, proving he did get Screech, Robert, who had intended buying only one parcel for Kate, said he might have one for himself. Opening it up, he discovered a fishing reel and a box of trouting flies.

"Well, it's not Screech, but I can sure use these. What do you think, Gabe? Fine-looking flies, aren't they? I'll surely catch lots of trout with them."

Leaving Gabe and Robert to inspect the fishing equipment, Bessie gave Rose four dollars for two parcels.

"Sharon, would you come and pick out two parcels for Bessie? And here are four dollar bills from me because I'll also have two parcels. I won't open mine now, but if I give you a bag, Bessie, will you bring them back with your lot. I'd keep them here, but I've already got a pile of them under my table that people bought and didn't want to be carrying around. And Sharon, why don't you have a break while things have calmed down."

"If you're sure, I wouldn't mind trying the Tombola and having a look at the baked goods, but first I'll buy four parcels, one each for my parents, David and me. I'll pay you and put them under my side of the table," Sharon said before following Bessie over to the baked goods.

Outside, bingo was proving exceedingly popular. All chairs and tables were occupied, including those intended for the inside eating area and brought outdoors for bingo. Even then, some people had to stand to play. Maggie and a group of her friends were seated on the school steps while other teenagers and children sat on the ground, leaning against the school or fence, as they played their cards.

When Sean, Kelly and David saw how many people were buying bingo cards and the amount of money brought in, they decided to give players extra chances to win by letting them play five games on the same card. With a prize of $20, the first game was won by Mrs. Josie Bennett from Freeman's Cove, much to her delight. The winners of the following three games had a choice of large stuffed toys, while the last game had a prize of $30.

"I just took a quick count, and we have about 150 people playing bingo, and apart from a few youngsters, most people are playing several cards. Did you see Millicent Murphy; she's playing eight cards? I don't know how she manages to play them all. Kelly counted the money brought in, and guess what; there's $146. Apart from the stuffed toys, we pay out $50, which gives us a $96 profit. Can you believe it, David?" an excited Sean asked.

David was every bit as pleased as Sean and suggested they take a break after the fifth game but announce bingo would start again in an hour.

"That way, people can go and eat or try other attractions. I've had women asking me how many times we'll play bingo today and asking if it's true that we're starting a weekly bingo in Mark's Point? It's something our committee will have to discuss at our next meeting. Here comes Robert; I wonder did he get the cake he wanted for Kate," David said.

Just then, a teenage girl sitting alongside Maggie shouted 'BINGO.' When Sean called it back then announced it was a correct bingo, there was great excitement on the school steps. Not sure what stuffed toy she should pick, the winner pulled Maggie and Theresa Martin behind her to the prize table, where after much laughter and talk, they decided to choose a large pink teddy bear.

"It's unusual to see young children, teenagers and adults all finding enjoyment from the same thing," a voice said from behind Robert.

"How are you, Robert? It's ages since I saw you last. I guess you're getting too old to be playing sports these days. But boy, we had some wonderful games of hockey on Old Cliff Pond, didn't we?"

A grinning Robert enthusiastically shook George Turner's hand while agreeing they had some great times playing hockey.

"But you must be forgetting the thrashing we Mark's Point boys always gave your team. It was a rare thing for you lot to win a game," Robert said.

"I'll admit you had a good hockey team, but it was too bad your softball team never learned how to hit a ball. Talk about thrashings. You could never win over our Freeman's Beach crowd," George retorted.

The two men laughingly argued and reminisced for a while before a woman walked up to them and reminded George why he came looking for Robert.

"I'm not sure if you know Beth, my wife, and Beth; this is Robert. Beth wants to talk to Kate about your girls coming over to our place next weekend for Beverly's birthday party."

"Is your wife here, Robert? Beverly tells me you are having a baby soon, so she's probably resting at home," Beth said

"You've got to be joking if you think Kate ever rests. She's still working every day in the post office, and today, she's taking in money for meals and keeping a record of money coming in from all the attractions. She's inside; come in and meet her."

A few minutes later, the two women were chatting away as if they had always known each other. When Daisy and Marigold came into the school, accompanied by George and Beth's daughter, they were surprised to discover their parents together.

"We didn't know you knew Beverly's Mom, did we, Marigold?" Daisy said with a puzzled look.

When the girls heard the mothers had just met, and Mrs. Turner had invited Daisy and Marigold to Beverly's birthday party, all three girls became loudly excited. But when they heard Kate agree the sisters could stay overnight at Beverly's home, the cheers erupting from the trio were enough to make everyone in the school look to see what was happening.

Then, spotting the Tombola stall, the sisters each grabbed one of Beverly's hands and almost dragged her over to meet their friend Mrs. Bessie. Not only did Bessie get to meet Beverly, but she also heard all about the invitation to the upcoming birthday party. They had just finished telling her about the planned sleep-over when Beverly's parents joined them.

"Hello Bessie, you've met our daughter, but I'm not sure if anyone ever introduced you and Beth," George Turner said before handing the girls some money to spend on games.

"It seems I've always known you, George, but I've never been introduced to you, Beth, although I've seen you at different places. The last time was at Maureen and Jerome's wedding reception when you were bustling around the club, serving tea and coffee. And, of course, I've heard all about Beverly from Daisy and Marigold."

"Probably not as much as we've heard about 'Mrs. Bessie' We know you're a woman of many talents who made wonderful witches costumes for Halloween with Miss Rose. Even though I bought Beverly an expensive fairy costume in Gander, she preferred to be a witch. We were just telling Robert and Kate how great this friendship is for Beverly because there are no little girls near her age in Freeman's Beach. We have three boys aged from 10 to 15, but I'm her only female company."

Beth said Beverly was like a different child since starting school, and although there were at least another ten girls in her class, it seemed as if she and Daisy immediately became friends, which led to her friendship with Marigold.

"At first, I thought Marigold was Daisy's twin and in the same class because Beverly rarely mentions one without the other. I discovered Marigold is a year older, but it seems as if she and Daisy are inseparable. Now, according to Beverly, she has not one but two 'bestest friends.' She knows everything that happens in Mark's Point through them, and she couldn't wait to come here today. Our boys cycled to Murphy's Cove to catch the bus to the fair, and she would have done the same if I allowed her."

As Beth spoke, the school began to fill up, signifying that bingo was over for a while. Among those coming in were Maggie, Theresa, and the twins, all eager to help with the stalls.

"Are you ready for us, Mrs. Bessie," Lily asked. "Theresa and I are going to work on your stall, and Maggie and Pansy are going to the Parcel Post."

"Yes, and maybe you and Mrs. Bessie should try bingo when it starts up again, Mom. It's fun, and we're big enough to look after the stall for you," Theresa said.

But Patsy wasn't so sure, saying perhaps she or Bessie should stay to look after things.

"Why don't you and I look after the adults' side now, Patsy, and let the girls take care of the children's side until we see they have the hang of it. When they do, we'll leave them and maybe check on them now and then. If they need help, they can easily find one of us."

Bessie and Patsy stayed long enough to watch the girls get comfortable with the stall's workings. Patsy then decided to line up for soup while Bessie went to see if Lucy would like a break.

"If you're sure you don't mind, Bessie, Nora's gone serving soup, and I'd like to check on my Jim and see how he's doing. He's not as young as he used to be, but he dearly wanted to work on the hoopla stall to help this good cause. I'm just hoping Jim's not trying to do too much. Robert tells me the young schoolteacher's father was helping Jim, and that was a relief, but I'll feel better if I sees for myself that he's not overdoing things," Lucy told Bessie.

With Bessie in agreement, Lucy went off to check on her husband and was delighted to see him seated inside the stall taking in the money while Bobby was looking after the hoops, passing them out and picking them off the table and from the ground.

"I'm wonderful grand, Lucy," Jim replied to Lucy when she inquired how he was doing.

"I figured you'd be too busy at your stall to be out here worrying about me. Don't tell me you have all those cakes and sweet stuff sold already? We've been busy here, and Jerry, the young woman teacher's father, was a great help. I couldn't have done it without him. He wouldn't let me go stooping down or running around to pick up the hoops. Jerry said that's why he was here, that my job was to take in the money, and Lucy, we surely brought in a lot of money. Young Bobby is helping me now, and he's as good as any man. So how did you get on, my dear?"

Father Kiely, who was at the hoopla stall, and heard the conversation between Jim and Lucy, told Bessie about it. With the fair winding down, he and Bessie had returned to Martin House to let him freshen up and have a light supper before going to mass.

"It's the most I have ever heard Jim say since I arrived in this parish. You should have heard him, Bessie. He was so happy that he and Lucy were part of everything. Then, when David finally convinced him to take a break and come with me to have a bowl of soup, it was like talking to a different man. He spoke about how wonderful the fair was for the people in Mark's Point, and especially for Lucy.

"Jim is so proud of Lucy and all she did for the fair. He said she loves to help people, but no one ever asked her to do anything until you. She always thought no one would want her help. Jim says she's a much happier woman, and it's all thanks to you and the fair. Then, when he spoke about the hoopla stall, I could see how proud he was of its success and how pleased he was to have helped."

Jim was only one of many who spoke positively to the priest about the fair and its success.

"The enthusiasm and community spirit shown today was overwhelming. I know the fair is going to be a financial success even before the dance starts. But even more important is the effect it has had on residents of Mark's Point and this entire area. Your committee brought people, regardless of age or religion, together for a day of fun and fellowship, and it was great to see," Father Kiely said.

People appeared reluctant to leave the fair scheduled to finish at five o'clock, and it was almost six before the last of the crowd left the old school. By then, every pot of soup was scraped clean, the baked goods and parcel post stalls were empty, while only a couple of unclaimed items remained in the Tombola booth. Before leaving, volunteers cleared the school and grounds and dismantled the stalls leaving the hall ready for the dance that night.

Robert related all this to Bessie and Father Kiely when he accompanied Rose back to Martin House. When Bessie asked him how much money they made, a smiling Robert said she asked the wrong person.

"You'll have to ask the treasurer that question. I just helped Rose carry all these bags of coins and money. What about it Rose, are you going to tell them or not?" Robert asked.

"I don't know if you'll believe it, but we've made about $2,600. It's not an exact figure because so many coins still need to be rolled. That includes everything, the ticket sales on the grocery box, the bottle drive, and children's dances, but it's clear money because we've paid every bill we had," Rose proudly related.

"That's amazing! I'm sure no one expected to make anything near that amount, and you still have the dance tonight," Father Kelley said.

"Yes, and tomorrow afternoon we'll make a final tally. Oscar is bringing paper rollers, and we'll roll all the coins. It's hard to believe we made so much when the best we ever did at a garden party was $1,360, and we thought that was wonderful. But enough about money, I best be getting home to get ready for mass. I'll see you at the dance. What about you, Father; are you coming to the dance?" Robert asked.

"I am for a short time. My first mass tomorrow is at nine in Mossy Brook, so I don't want to go home too late. I've also got four or five girls to bring back to the Murphy's Cove area who are staying here for mass and then going to Maggie's house. I told them I'd pick them up at 10.30."

"That reminds me, Rose, did you see any sign of Mina after I left the school. I had a quick word with her when she came to try the Tombola stall, but after that, she seemed to disappear," Bessie said.

"That's because she was out back serving soup and keeping the eating area clean. She wasn't the only person outside Mark's Point to help because we had Sharon's parents and women from Mark's Landing, including Kate's sister Jean. Mina went home on the bus, and I heard her telling her girls to be sure to be ready at 10.30 when Father plans to leave," Robert said on his way out.

When Robert left, Bessie told Rose to take a rest, and she'd get her something to eat.

"Would you like an omelet? That's what Father and I had. You must be tired as you were on your feet all day. At least I can relax for a few hours before the dance while you not only have mass, you're playing the organ. Sit down, and I'll get you something to eat."

"Thanks, Bessie; an omelet sounds great. That and a good cup of tea will hit the spot. I only ate a couple of sandwiches with a soft drink at the fair. I went to get a bowl of soup, but who was there waving for me to come and sit beside him but old Philly Moss. Telling him I didn't have time for the soup and had to get back to my stall, I took my sandwiches and drink and left. I couldn't sit down with that old reprobate and be civil. It was better for me to leave, even when it meant doing without soup."

Father Kiely began laughing, saying Philly made up for Rose not having soup because he had at least three bowlfuls in addition to a large pile of sandwiches.

"I was standing near the serving area talking to Dave and Millicent, who had just finished eating when Dave said he never saw anyone put away as much food as Philly. 'Yes,' says Millicent, 'Philly could eat the legs off a table.'

"Mina came along in time to hear Millicent and agreed, saying she had served him and for a skinny little man, she didn't know where he put all the food. Her next comment had us all in a fit of laughing when she said Philly, and his appetite reminded her of a story her aunt used to tell. The aunt had invited a man to dinner, and she thought he would never stop eating. Afterward, Mina's aunt said, 'That man could eat bite by bite with an elephant. The next time he hints about needing a meal, I'll be showing him the way to the zoo."

A short time later, when Father Kiely and Rose were in mass, Bessie sat relaxed in the sitting room when the phone rang.

"No, Sue, this is not a bad time," she said, answering the phone to her American friend.

"I was half expecting you to phone to find out how we got on with the fair. It was a great success, but just wait till I bring over my tea, and I'll tell you all about it. Hope you're not in a hurry; this might take a while."

CHAPTER 26

Helping Lucy

It was the last day of October, and in Mark's Point, children were excited, waiting for darkness to come, to go door to door, trick or treating.

A group of adults in the community were every bit as excited, but for a different reason. The Mark's Point Hall Committee members were eager to discover the final total raised from the fair and planned on meeting that afternoon.

In Martin House, Bessie spoke about the upcoming meeting and how, with the fair over, they could now concentrate on other things.

"It's hard to believe it's Halloween already, and tomorrow we are into November. Christmas will be here before we know it. I keep putting off my trip to St. John's, but I need to go soon to do some shopping," Bessie said.

"Let's get the fair finalized before talking about Christmas. But thinking of Halloween, we should get our treats ready before going to the meeting. With the time going back last night, we'll likely see small children out trick or treating early," Rose replied

She spoke of the money raised at the fair, saying she was glad it was mostly all paper money brought in at the dance.

"Look at all the coins we collected at the fair, and they are heavy. Now they've got to be carried back to the school this afternoon for rolling and counting. I know that's the meeting's purpose, but we also need to talk about opening a bank account. As treasurer, I don't want all this money lying around this or any other house. What do you think, Bessie?"

Bessie agreed, suggesting that the money could go in the parish's big safe until deposited in the bank. When Rose brought up this idea during the afternoon meeting, everyone agreed it was the best short-term solution. By then, the last coin had been counted and rolled, and the committee members were still coming down to earth after discovering their fundraising efforts brought in a total of $2,923.39.

"It's almost too much to take in right now. We've all had a busy weekend, so I think we should go home and think about this money. We know we're responsible for the school's insurance and electricity. Rose as treasurer, do you think you can find out what that will cost us either monthly or annually?" Robert asked.

"I've also been getting suggestions from residents of the community about how to improve the school and different things they'd like to see happening. We need to talk to people during the next few days, get their ideas, and meet next Sunday. For now, we should go home and get ready for a night of trick or treating. I've two young and extremely excited witches at home who can't wait to go door to door."

With the meeting over early, Bessie suggested phoning Father Kiely, and if he was home, she and Rose could take the money to Murphy's Cove that afternoon.

"That way, we can relax knowing the money is in a safe place. It's not quite three o'clock, and we'd still be home in lots of time for the youngsters going door to door. But first, let's drop into Lucy's and let her and Jim know how much money we raised. They deserve to know, and Robert did say to pass the word around."

Arriving at Lucy and Jim's house, they were surprised to find it quiet and no sign of Lucy bustling around to welcome them. They called out from the kitchen but got no answer and were about to leave when they heard someone coming downstairs. It was Jim who appeared.

"I'm sorry, Jim, we didn't want to disturb you. I guess you and Lucy are tired and probably taking a nap after the full day you had yesterday. We're on our way over to Murphy's Cove to put the fair's proceeds into the parish safe, but we wanted to let you know how well we did. We cleared over $2,900."

"That's wonderful news, Bessie, and I'll tell our Lucy, but she's not feeling that good today. That's why I was upstairs, bringing her a glass of water. I don't know what's wrong, but it's like she's got a fever. She says she's fine, but something's not right. It's not like our Lucy to lie down during the day. She's always worrying about me, and she was the same with our boys when they was growing up, but she never speaks about being sick herself. The news about the fair money might be the very thing to make her feel better. It's good of ye coming here to let us know."

Telling him they would be back home in just over an hour and call if he or Lucy needed anything, Bessie and Rose left to contact Father Kiely.

"Jim's right about Lucy never being sick. I can't remember a time when I heard she was poorly. On the other hand, Lucy was always worrying about Jim and the twins. When I said that to your mother one time, she told me it was because of Lucy's three stillborn babies. Until then, I hadn't known she lost three babies at birth, but it made me understand why she was so protective over her boys," Bessie said.

"How old are the twins, and where are they now? I know they weren't born when I left for the convent."

"They were babies when I came to Mark's Point, which would make them at least 26 now. It's a coincidence you asked because when Lucy came back to the baked good stall yesterday after checking on Jim, she said Leonard and Lawrence would be some proud to see their father working on the hoopla stall. They're both miners in Northern Ontario, and they called last week to say they'll be home for Christmas. I'm glad for Lucy and Jim because the boys never got home last year. Lucy said it was the most lonesome Christmas she and Jim ever spent."

Over in Murphy's Cove, Father Kiely was full of praise for the committee's work when he heard the final fundraising total from the women. While she remembered, Rose asked if the priest could determine how much the hall insurance and electricity would cost sometime during the week.

"I should have all that information for the parish council meeting on Tuesday. I contacted the parish insurance company, and they promised to give me quotes for all the schools by tomorrow. The school board already sent me copies of the light bills for the past year, so you'll get the figures at the meeting and then bring them back to your committee. So, ladies, what's next for Mark's Point's school; have you any plans in place?" the priest asked.

Telling him they were open to suggestions and that committee members were asking residents for ideas, Rose added that the school was already in use.

"David began guitar lessons on Tuesday nights with four high school boys. Several other high school boys and girls have shown an interest in joining, but he says the four he has, Bobby, Michael and two of their friends, did so well; he wants to continue instructing them as a group until after Christmas. He plans to start another class then and have the four boys help him with the newcomers.

"I know Pat Martin and Rob Brown want to start weekly card games next Wednesday, and since introducing bingo at the fair, it's amazing how many people have asked to have it as a weekly event. I've also heard some women would like to have crafts, and that's something I'd be interested in doing. We'll be discussing all ideas at next Sunday's meeting when hopefully we'll get a list of events and put a schedule in place," Bessie added.

Before returning home, the women drove over to Murphy's Store, where Millicent greeted them with questions about the fair.

"I thought you two would be resting today after a full day on your feet. How did you make out with the money? For sure, you did well. Do you know when your committee will start weekly Bingo?

Millicent wasn't surprised when she heard how much money the event raised, saying she told Dave the fair would be the most successful fundraiser ever held in the area.

"There was never anything like it around here before. I know we've had garden parties and times, but you went all out to make this different, and it certainly attracted people. Then too, you were lucky the weather was so good because you'd never get everyone into the school at one time. If you plan on a fair next year, maybe you should have it earlier. But enough about the fair, you never answered me about when you are starting bingo," Millicent said.

Hearing a bingo decision would be made the following week, and it looked as if it would go ahead, Millicent said she'd be a regular player, bringing a carload of her friends each week. She then asked Bessie and Rose if they were ready for trick or treaters?

"That's why we dropped in. We have enough treats, but we know a couple of little girls who love Crackerjacks, and we stopped by to see if you had any," Bessie said.

Just before six o'clock that evening, the first knock on the door of Martin House announced trick or treating had begun, and two young witches gleefully modelled their costumes for the women.

"Nobody had as good costumes at the school Halloween party as we did. Isn't that right, Marigold?"

"Yes, and when we was asked if we got them in St. John's, we told them that you made them. We said you come from Scotland, Mrs. Bessie and that you was a nun principal Miss Rose, and you made us the costumes 'cos; you're our friends. Beverly said we would have won if there was prizes for the bestest costumes. That's what she said, isn't it, Daisy?"

"And you know what your mother would say if she heard you using that word bestest. How many times are you told that it is best, not bestest? You also need to slow down and take a breath when you're speaking," their father said.

Quickly changing the topic, Rose asked if the girls had visited any other houses. When she heard they had just come from Lucy and Jim's home, she wondered if Lucy liked their costumes.

"We never saw Mrs. Lucy, and she told us yesterday she wanted to see us dressed up, but Mrs. Lucy wasn't there, was she Dad?" Daisy asked.

"You girls go back down the garden and get in the car, and I'll be right behind you. I just need to talk to Mrs. Bessie and Miss Rose for a second."

When the girls left with a flurry of thanks, Robert said the girls were right; Lucy wasn't around. An upset and worried Jim had answered the door.

"I've been taking my youngsters trick or treating for years, and Lucy was always waiting for them with treats. She loves seeing their costumes and would talk to them all night if they didn't have to go to other houses. I used to say to Kate that it was like there was two Lucy's. The gossipy one who loves spreading news and the Lucy who can't do enough for youngsters. But tonight, there's no sign of her and Jim is worried out of his mind, because she's sick. I asked if I could do something, but I don't think Jim even heard me."

"Lucy must be ill because I know she'd never miss Halloween. Yesterday we spoke about it, and she told me about the treats she had for the youngsters.

Rose, what if I go over and see how she is, and you stay here and pass out our treats?"

With Rose in agreement, Bessie left behind Robert, who continued trick or treating with the girls. Arriving at Lucy's house, she was alarmed to see a distraught Jim.

"Oh, Bessie! I'm some glad you're here. Our Lucy's that sick. She won't let me call the nurse or take her to the doctor at the cottage hospital. Will you talk to her?"

Following Jim upstairs into a bedroom, Bessie was alarmed when she saw Lucy. It was evident from her colour and the sweat pouring down her face she was far from well. On seeing Bessie, she unsuccessfully tried to sit up.

"Oh my, Bessie, just look at me. You've come to visit us, and here's me lying in bed at this time of day. Jim, you needs to help me up. Bessie's here, and the next thing trick or treaters will be knocking at the door." Lucy said in a weak voice.

But Bessie wouldn't hear of Lucy moving. Instead, she asked Jim to get her a bowl of cold water, a washcloth, and a towel. When he left, she asked Lucy if she was in pain and what other symptoms she might have.

"I'm alright, Bessie, but I'm worried about my Jim because he's really upset. It's no good me telling him that this is nothing, just a bit of heartburn and a stitch, and there's no need to be worrying. Once I get downstairs, I'll be fine."

"Number one, you are not fine, and two, you are not going down-stairs. Now, where do you have the stitch, and how bad is the heartburn?" Bessie asked.

"It's just a small stitch in my chest, but it's nothing to worry about, and as for the heartburn, I has that all the time. I was just going to ask Jim to get me some water and baking soda. That usually fixes the old heartburn. Here he is now. I'm sure he hasn't had any supper yet. Are you hungry, Jim?" Lucy asked her husband.

Telling Jim to go downstairs and put the kettle on, and she would be down after she saw to Lucy, Bessie rinsed out the washcloth in the water and carefully bathed Lucy's face, neck, and hands. She then re-rinsed the cloth, folded it and laid it on her forehead.

"That's some good. I feels much better already, Bessie. You go on down-stairs, and will you make sure Jim has something to eat?"

To prove she felt better, Lucy made another effort to sit up before dou-bling over with pain.

"That's it. I'm calling Nurse Holland in Murphy's Cove, and I'll not argue about it. You are ill and need help, and the nurse will know what to do. Now lie down until I use the phone," Bessie ordered her neighbour.

But by now, it was evident Lucy was too sick to argue and running down-stairs, Bessie told a worried Jim she was calling the Public Health nurse. Thankfully, Nurse Holland was home, and once she heard Lucy's symptoms, she promised to get there as soon as possible. Bessie's next phone call was to Rose to tell her what was happening and stop any youngsters coming to Lucy and Jim's house. She tried phoning Jim's brother, Edmund, but then remem-bered Kelly said at the meeting that her parents left for Gander that morning.

Instructing Jim to get himself something to eat or Lucy would be even more upset, Bessie returned upstairs. With Lucy no longer masking her pain as she lay half doubled over on the bed, Bessie was thankful the nurse was on her way. Until Nurse Holland arrived, Bessie continued bathing Lucy's face and hands, trying to cool her down.

"It's a good thing you called me," the nurse said after thoroughly examin-ing Lucy. She was back downstairs, explaining to an agitated Jim why it was necessary to call the ambulance.

"It's on its way, and Lucy is going to a hospital in St. John's. I thought it might be her heart, but I'm more inclined to believe it is a severe gall bladder attack after examining and talking to her. Lucy admits to having these attacks for some time, but never one this bad. She may need surgery, and that's why I'm not sending her to the cottage hospital. It takes over an hour to get there, and if she needs surgery, the doctor will then transfer her to St. John's. It might take almost three hours to get to town, but at least she'll be in the proper place with specialists and surgeons."

Later that night, as she recalled what happened at the Pearce home to Rose, Sharon and David, Bessie said Nurse Holland soon had everything under control.

"I don't know how I would have dealt with Jim because he was a wreck and completely lost without Lucy to guide him. But Nurse Holland soon got him moving, saying Lucy would need clothes and toilet items and show me where to get everything. When Jim insisted he was going with Lucy, I thought I might have to follow the ambulance in my car just to make sure he was alright. I couldn't imagine him in St. John's alone," Bessie recalled

When she phoned Rose telling her this and asking if she would accompany her to town, Rose immediately agreed, saying she would get overnight bags ready for the two of them.

"I wasn't looking forward to the drive, but Jim couldn't go alone, and I knew as sick as Lucy was, she'd worry more about him than herself. When you showed up, Sharon, saying there was no need for Rose and me to drive to St. John's, that your parents would go with Jim, it was such a relief. It was so good they changed their plans, going back to town tonight instead of tomorrow and having Jim stay with them. Jim's such a shy man and, although he only met your Dad yesterday, it seems they got on well together. I know he'll be fine with your parents; let's just hope Lucy will be alright."

"Dad's off work for a few weeks, so he'll drive Jim to and from the hospital, and mother enjoys having company. As sick as Lucy was when they lifted her stretcher onto the ambulance, she was still worried about Jim until you told her he'd be staying with Mom and Dad. She was much more content when she heard that," Sharon said.

"She certainly was," Bessie told Rose.

"We also made sure Jim packed some clothes for himself. After the ambulance left, Sharon and I washed up the few dishes and tidied up the kitchen. Kelly and Sean arrived as we were leaving Lucy's house. They had just returned from Mark's Landing when they heard about Lucy. Kelly was worried about them both and relieved when she found out Agnes and Jerry had gone with Jim.

"We are some lucky having Nurse Holland. I don't know what we'll do without her when she retires. The Health Department advertised her job almost two months ago, but there have been no applications. Meanwhile, Rose, with all the excitement, I forgot to ask you how you got on with trick or treating and how many youngsters did we have?"

Rose was telling her they had 17, plus Daisy and Marigold, as the phone rang. When Bessie answered, Father Kiely asked how bad Jim's heart attack was and whether the ambulance took him to the cottage hospital or St John's?

After Bessie explained what happened to the priest, she returned to the sitting room, shaking her head over how fast news travelled when the facts were wrong.

"Father heard from an old lady in Mossy Brook that Jim was at death's door. It's all bad enough with Lucy sick, but why do people repeat stories without knowing the facts," she asked.

Bessie couldn't believe her ears when Rose started to laugh.

"What's funny about that?" she asked.

"Bessie, you're talking about Lucy, and there's no one more likely to mix up facts than Lucy. I just thought it was comical that someone else is spreading news concerning Lucy."

Bessie said maybe so, but there was nothing comical about seeing the pain Lucy was in that night, and she hoped everything would work out for the best.

Changing the subject, Sharon asked if anyone had planned a baby shower for Kate and, if so, when it was taking place. Bessie had never heard of anyone in Mark's Point having a baby shower, although she remembered making a baby's quilt for a shower Rose attended.

"That's right. I wanted something special when there was a baby shower for one of our teachers. I've gone to several baby and bridal showers. It would be nice to do something like that for Kate, although I wouldn't know how to start planning it." Rose said

But Sharon said that wouldn't be a problem, that she would be only too happy to help, and they could maybe hold it in the old school. She added that it should be a surprise for Kate, but it would be nice to tell Lily and Pansy and let them help with the planning.

"I'm sure the girls would love to see their mother have a baby shower. If we are going to do it, we should set a date before your committee meeting on Sunday, and that way, we could book the school in advance."

With Rose and Bessie enthusiastic about the shower and agreeing to help Sharon, they decided to plan it for Sunday, November 21. Before leaving, Sharon said she would talk to the twins the following day. She also promised to let the women know if she heard any news about Lucy. However, when the phone rang at eleven o'clock, it was Agnes on the line.

"Bessie, I know it's late, but I thought you and Rose were probably wondering about Lucy. After seeing a doctor and having several tests, a specialist examined Lucy. She is now in surgery and having her gall bladder removed.

"Poor Jim was scared to death by the specialist saying he had an extremely ill wife, who should have had the surgery long before now. Jim broke down, and I had to get Jerry to bring him outdoors. I'm using the hospital payphone, and I won't call you anymore tonight because it will be late before she comes out of surgery, but I'll let you know in the morning."

"Poor Lucy, fancy her going right into surgery. If it's not too much trouble, Agnes, please phone as soon as she gets out of surgery. I had a phone extension put in my bedroom, but I'll probably stay up anyway, worrying about her," Bessie replied.

It was well after one the following morning when a tired-sounding Agnes phoned to say Lucy was out of surgery and in recovery. She or Jim hadn't spoken to the surgeon, but the nurse on duty told them the surgery was successful.

The nurse also told Jim to go and get some sleep and not return until tomorrow afternoon during visiting hours. According to the nurse, Lucy wouldn't feel like visitors very soon.

"Jim is one relieved man. I told Jerry if anything happened to Lucy, we'd have another patient on our hands because he looked as if he'd collapse at any time," Agnes told Bessie.

Thanking Agnes, Bessie hung up the phone then relayed the news to Rose, who also waited to hear what was happening with Lucy.

"It's good of Agnes and Jerry staying with Jim, and now we know Lucy has successfully come through her surgery, we should be able to sleep. I was worried she had left these attacks too long, and she never mentioned them to anybody. She'd have spread it all over the place if someone else was sick. Oh well, I don't think I will ever understand Lucy, but for now, I'm going to bed," Rose said.

The following morning Bessie called Agnes to ask what news she had of Lucy and how Jim was coping. Agnes had telephoned the hospital on Jim's behalf early that morning and heard Lucy was resting comfortably. He would be visiting Lucy in the afternoon, but Agnes warned him it might hinder Lucy from getting well if she saw him worried and upset. Trying to keep

Jim's mind off Lucy, Jerry had taken him out walking when Agnes was on the phone.

After passing on the news to Rose, Bessie called the elementary school, knowing Kelly, being the school secretary, would be the one to answer. Telling her Lucy's surgery was successful, she added that he was in good hands although Jim was still worried.

"Thank you, Mrs. Bessie, for letting me know. You'll probably get a call from Mum or Dad this morning. They were so upset by the news, especially since they weren't home when Aunt Lucy took ill, but they're so glad that Uncle Jim has Mr. and Mrs. Dawson looking after him. Dad knows that Uncle Jim would be completely lost if anything happened to Aunt Lucy. I'm just glad she didn't have the attack a day earlier because she was so looking forward to the fair," Kelly said.

"I had to agree with Kelly because Lucy had a wonderful day at the fair," Bessie was telling Kate later that morning. She had dropped into the post office to pick up the mail, and the women were discussing Lucy's sudden surgery. Kate agreed, adding Lucy did a great job with the baked goods stall, going all out to make it a success by contacting every woman in the community for donations.

When Bessie asked if Marigold and Daisy were excited about their upcoming weekend party with Beverly in Freeman's Beach, Kate said it was all she expected to hear for the rest of the week.

"But it's working out well for me. I've wanted to go to St. John's to do some Christmas shopping. It's November already, and it seems I haven't had a minute to think about buying gifts for the youngsters, and once the baby is here, I won't get a chance to shop. Robert and I will leave early Friday morning and come back on Saturday. Patsy is looking after the post office, and Mr. Rob is happy to stay at our house with the twins and Bobby. If Daisy or Marigold get homesick, which I doubt, their grandfather will go and get them. They've instructed us not to pick them up until late Sunday afternoon. I'm sure we'll hear lots of stories then," Kate said, smiling at the thought.

"I promised the girls I'd have them over for baking. What do you think about the following Saturday? I'll be going into town myself in a couple of weeks, and I'd like to have them over before I go," Bessie said.

"I hope Marigold and Daisy haven't been tormenting you about baking because I know they're always talking about it. They were playing with the tea set they got from the parcel-post stall, and their talk was all about the cookies they plan to serve once you show them how to make them."

"Kate, you worry too much about things. If I didn't want Marigold and Daisy over to bake, I'd have never asked them. They're a tonic to have around. Just look how well they got on with Penny. The Bishop and Mrs. Harris won't soon forget how the girls charmed Penny back to her old self. Are they still getting mail from her?" Bessie asked.

Kate started to laugh, saying Penny had phoned the girls the week earlier.

"I thought my pair would have told you already, but maybe they're waiting until you set a date for baking."

When Bessie asked why Kate replied the girls had informed Penny they were going baking soon and that Penny, who enjoyed it so much the first time, should join them.

"Marigold told her that. Then Daisy spoke up, saying how Miss Rose said she should visit schools. She asked Penny to come to their school and tell their friends about being a missionary in Africa; only that's not the word she used."

Bessie smiled broadly, saying no doubt Daisy called Penny a missing Harry because she couldn't seem to remember the word missionary.

"That's quite likely. My youngest daughters seem to enjoy making up their own words. I don't know how many times I've told them there's no such word as bestest, but they still keep saying it," Kate said, smiling and shaking her head.

Meanwhile, as Bessie and Kate chatted, Rose was busy in Martin House answering the telephone. Father Kiely and Millicent were the first two callers, followed by Jim's brother, all of them inquiring about Lucy. Answering the fourth call, she thought it was probably someone else looking for news about Lucy but discovered Ellen Matthews on the line.

Ellen was all talk about Albert's newly-found American relatives. His great uncle and son-in-law would arrive in Newfoundland the following week, and Ellen wanted to book rooms for them at Martin House.

"Albert and I were wondering how many of us you could put up for three nights. There's the two of us, plus Uncle Thomas, his son-in-law Gary and of course, Albert's father. He has heard so much from Albert and Jack that I don't know if he's more eager to visit Fisherman's Creek or Mark's Point and Martin House. There's also a chance Jack might want to come too."

"Do you think the great uncle and his son-in-law would mind sharing a room with two beds? We could give them the downstairs room to save the uncle climbing stairs," Rose said.

"They probably wouldn't mind sharing a room, and considering Uncle Thomas is in his 90's, I think he'd be better off downstairs," Ellen replied.

"There's also the room with two single beds in a room upstairs that Jack could share with his father, so there's plenty of space for everyone. When are you planning to come?" Rose asked.

They hoped to come on Thursday the 11th, but it would be late when they arrived because the Matthews' family always attended the Remembrance Day parade and service, which meant they wouldn't be leaving town until later that afternoon.

Rose had ended her conversation with Ellen and was back in the kitchen when the phone rang again. Answering, she was surprised to hear Penny Harris.

"Hello Rose, how are you and Bessie? You probably didn't expect to hear from me. How are things in the beautiful community of Mark's Point? I've been thinking about everyone, and I wondered if it was possible to book a room in Martin House for a few days."

"It's lovely to speak to you again, Penny. I've heard some great things about you, the Bishop and Mrs. Harris, from my friend Tom. He says the three of you are faithful volunteers at the after-school program, and I also hear you brought in a couple more people to help. Bessie and I would love to see you. When do you plan to visit?"

Rose repeated the conversation to Bessie a short time later, adding that it was up to Bessie when Penny came to stay. Rose grinned when Bessie asked what she meant before saying the date of Penny's visit depended not only on her but also on Daisy and Marigold.

"The girls told her you would be teaching them to make cookies and invited her to join them. Remembering her first baking lesson, she's eager for another and wondered if she could join your baking class."

Bessie laughed, saying she and Kate had just been talking about the very same thing. With Daisy and Marigold in Freeman's Beach for Beverly's party this weekend, she had arranged the lesson for the following Saturday.

"It will be nice to see Penny again, and the girls will also love to see her. I'll phone Penny right away and let her know," Bessie said.

"Hold on a minute; we have a full house next weekend. Ellen phoned and booked rooms for herself, Albert, his father, and their American relatives, which means there will be no room for Penny. Can you change your baking date because I confirmed everything with Ellen?"

"That won't be a problem. I'll let Kate know not to mention baking to the girls yet. I don't want to do it the following weekend because we have Kate's shower on the 21st, and I'll be baking for that. Weather permitting, I thought I'd go to St. John's the day after the shower. I'd be back by that Thursday, which means we could bake the following Saturday. Did Penny leave a phone number for me to reach her?" Bessie asked.

After making calls to Penny, who was delighted to come the weekend of the 27th, and then to Kate telling her about the change, Bessie mentioned how Marigold and Daisy weren't the only ones looking for a baking lesson. She had promised to show Maggie how to make both a light and a dark fruit. Gabe knew she was making a light one for Angela but had no idea Maggie planned on making a dark fruit cake for him."

"Maggie's becoming a girl of many talents. She is doing so well with her piano lessons that I'm thinking of having her try the church organ. I'd like to see how she gets on playing a couple of hymns, maybe even a Christmas carol," Rose said.

Later that night, Sharon dropped into Martin House, telling the women she spoke to Lily and Pansy about having a baby shower for their mother.

"The girls are super excited about the idea. I suggested having a meeting Saturday afternoon to discuss it. I said I'd check with you first, and they suggested Maggie and Theresa would probably like to help. What do you think?"

The time worked well for Bessie and Rose, who suggested meeting at Martin House. Rose had coloured writing paper, which she said the girls might like for making invitations.

"That would be a good idea, and with Kate in St. John's on Saturday, she won't know the girls are here. If we get together early and make out invitations, the four girls can deliver them around the community," Bessie said.

Sharon then spoke about a telephone call she had from her mother. According to Agnes, Lucy was sitting up in her hospital bed, more concerned about Jim than about her surgery. After her discharge from the hospital at the end of the week, Agnes and Jerry planned to drive Lucy and Jim home to Mark's Point.

"When Lucy heard this, she kept saying no that it was too much to expect, but Mom said they already planned to come here this weekend because Dad is showing David how to build a garbage box. When Lucy said she would pay Dad for bringing them home, Mom put her off by saying they would talk about payment when they returned to Mark's Point. However, I know Mom or Dad would never take a penny from them."

"Knowing Lucy, she'll find some way to repay your parents. I think she and your mother may be alike in that way. Lucy loves helping people but finds it hard to accept help for herself," Bessie said.

Bessie was proven right the following Saturday morning when she visited Lucy, who arrived home the day earlier. Lucy wasn't interested in talking about her illness or surgery but couldn't say enough about all the help she received during the past week.

"Bessie, I don't know what Jim and me would have done without you. Jim tells me I was too stubborn to admit I was sick, and if it wasn't for you, I'd be even sicker. I always said you was the best neighbour a body could have, and it proves I'm right. And then there's Agnes and Jerry, who were total strangers to my Jim and me until last Saturday. Now just look at everything they have done for us! Bessie, how's I going to pay them for all they did? They wouldn't take any money for what they did for me and Jim in St. John's or for bringing the two of us home, but I've got to do something. I don't expect them to do it for nothing."

Bessie, who knew Lucy would feel she had to repay Agnes and Jerry, had an answer ready for her neighbour.

"I heard you say you made far too many pickles and beets last month and wondered what you'd do with all of them. Agnes was disappointed there were none for sale at the fair. She told me she didn't know how to make pickles or bottled beets but would love to learn. I have a couple of bottles I intended to give her, and maybe you could also give her some. But better still, why don't you tell Agnes that you'll show her how to make them next year. I'm sure she would love that."

Lucy was delighted with the suggestion, saying Bessie must keep her beets and pickles for her guests because she had had plenty of both to supply the Dawson's for the entire winter.

"I knows Agnes made blueberry as well as partridgeberry and apple jam, but I'm sure she's got no bakeapple jam. My friends Marge and Ron on the Southern Shore sent me a gallon of them by taxi, and I've several bottles made into jam, so Agnes and Jim can have some of that. Oh, Bessie, I'm some glad you told me this. Jim will be happy too as he don't like taking things for nothing, And I knows what else we can give them. Jim has a sack of potatoes for you because he knows with Alex gone, you never planted any this year; we'll give Agnes and Jerry a sack too," Lucy said.

"Now, while you are here, tell me about this baby bath party you're having for Kate. Agnes told me about it and how Sharon, you, and Rose have it in the old school. She said it was a surprise party where Kate gets presents for her baby. I'd like to get something for the baby. If I had some baby wool, I'd knit something nice for the little darling."

"I can help you with that because I called Agnes and asked her to pick me up some baby wool as well as material for a baby's quilt. I wasn't sure if I would knit or sew something for the baby. I'll give you the wool, and that way, you can sit and knit without exerting yourself too much because you're supposed to be taking it easy. And before you start in about paying me for the wool, let's call it a fair trade for the sack of potatoes Jim is giving me and which Rose and I appreciate. I'll make a baby quilt, and when I find out more about the shower, I'll let you know. Kate is in St. John's and won't be back until later tonight, so Rose, Sharon, Agnes, and I will meet with the twins, Maggie, and Theresa, to make plans for it. We need to get the invitations out this afternoon to give everyone at least two week's notice about the shower." Bessie said.

That afternoon, the women and girls met at Martin House to plan the first-ever Mark's Point baby shower. Agnes, who was well used to attending showers in St. John's, was full of ideas, and she and Sharon came well prepared.

"Mom and I made out a list of things to be done if we want to make Kate's shower a success," said Sharon.

"We'll be writing out and delivering invitations today, and we also need to talk about decorations, food, a cake, and entertainment or games. I'm sure there are other things, but first, we should find out how many we want to invite and use Miss Rose's nice paper to make a start on the invitations."

By the time they compiled a list of the women in Mark's Point, plus Kate's sister Jean and some friends in Mark's Landing, adding a few in Murphy's Cove and finally Mina and her girls, the list had grown to over 40.

"I already told your Aunt Jean about the shower, and she'll look after inviting her friends in Mark's Landing. I'll contact Millicent and Mina to ask friends over their way. We only need written invitations for the women in Mark's Point. If we take ourselves off the list, I think if we each wrote out two invitations giving us 16, that would be enough," Bessie concluded after making a quick count.

The next hour passed quickly as the girls and women got down to business. Agnes showed them some wall and table decorations she brought from St. John's and volunteered to bake and decorate the cake. Much to the girls' delight, she showed them a miniature stork holding a baby, which she planned to use as a cake topper.

"About the decorations; do you think we could decorate the school the day before the shower?" Sharon asked.

"The mass schedule has changed to Sundays for November, and we won't have much time that day once we come from mass and have dinner. The other thing is, we didn't discuss getting Kate to the school without her getting suspicious."

But the girls had that part of the shower well planned.

"You know how we might be having a weekend exchange trip with students in St. Mary's to play basketball and volleyball, Mrs. Nolan? We thought if we told Mom that you and Miss Mills were having a student and mother meeting here in Mark's Point to discuss the exchange, she'd want to come. We'd walk to the meeting with Theresa and Maggie and get Mrs. Patsy to stop by and pick Mom up in her car. When Mom sees cars by the school, she'll just think it's mothers and girls from other communities. What do you think?" Pansy asked

"I think you girls are quite the bunch of schemers," a laughing Sharon said.

"I will be watching the four of you in school from now on, especially when it comes to excuses for not doing homework or missing classes."

"As a former principal, I know what you mean, Sharon, but I can also see Kate believing their story. Now we have all our plans in place, let's fold the handwritten invitations so you can get them delivered before dark. Be sure to tell the women that we don't want Kate to know about it. If they have any questions that you can't answer, tell them to call one of us," Rose instructed the girls.

A short while later, the girls were on their way, eager to distribute the invitations. When Sharon and her mother spoke about leaving, Bessie asked them to hold on.

"You've lots of time. Rose is putting the kettle on, and I'm sure you know why. Relax for a while and have a chat and a cup of tea with us."

CHAPTER 27

Changing Weather

I t was Sunday morning, and Rose was getting her music ready for mass when Bessie spoke of the meeting scheduled for that afternoon.

"It seems all we do these days is attend meetings. Hopefully, when our committee gets together this afternoon, we will get a few things settled. With the fair over, the real work begins. If we're going to do what residents want, we must put plans in place and get work started. That's this afternoon, but for now, you need to get ready for mass. I'm going to call Lucy, and if she hasn't started cooking, I'll bring dinner over for her and Jim later. We have a large roast, and even with Father Kiely, Gabe and Maggie coming for dinner, two more mouths to feed won't make much difference."

But Jim had the Sunday meal well in hand, Lucy complained, telling Bessie that her husband treated her like an invalid. She said it was no good telling him she wasn't sick.

"The doctor wouldn't let me out of the hospital if I wasn't better, but Jim won't listen. And Bessie, Jim never misses mass and loves singing in the choir, and he's not even going to church this morning. He wants to make sure I'm resting. Jim tells me the doctor says I can't be lifting anything heavy for at least six weeks. I'm not going lifting sacks of potatoes, but peeling a few vegetables wouldn't hurt me. Jim pays me no heed; he's got a chicken roasting in

355

the oven and some salt meat on. We'll be eating good, but I'm worried he is doing too much," Lucy said.

Rose looked up when Bessie returned to the kitchen, saying Lucy must be feeling better for Bessie to be smiling.

"She says she's fine, although she thinks Jim is doing too much. He's determined she'll rest, but you know Lucy as well as I do. The word rest is not in her vocabulary and not her style at all. I can see her and Jim having their first real disagreement over this. He's worried about Lucy while she's equally worried about him. You know she's like a mother hen where Jim is concerned," Bessie said.

Kelly voiced the same concern that afternoon, just before the meeting started in the school.

"It's not like Aunt Lucy would ever let Uncle Jim lift a hand in the house before this. Now she has to watch as he cooks and cleans, and it's not sitting well with her at all. Mom, Dad, and I went to see her yesterday, and we're wondering how long Aunt Lucy will last watching Uncle Jim do all these things. Uncle Jim says the doctor wants her to rest, and she definitely can't go lifting anything, but getting her to listen to what anyone tells her is next to impossible," Kelly said.

Bessie said the right person might not have talked with Lucy. When Father Kiely was at Martin House for dinner, Bessie mentioned Lucy's impatience. Knowing what the surgeon advised, the priest planned to emphasize the importance of rest when he visited her that afternoon. Bessie was sure Lucy would listen to Father Kiely since he intended to tell her that by turning down Jim's help, she could cause more harm than good by making him even more stressed.

All conversation about Lucy ended when Robert called the meeting to order. The committee members discussed improvements and possible events in the former school they had received from residents.

Oscar was one of the first speakers. Being in the shop every day, he heard lots of talk, especially from women who thought there should be a proper kitchen with a stove, cupboards, dishes, and sinks. They also wanted to see running water and decent bathrooms instead of one old chemical toilet.

"And I agree with them. Just think how much easier it would be to hold socials and serve food if we had a kitchen, and it's time to get rid of that old toilet," Oscar said.

There was plenty of support for Oscar's suggestions, while Sean said it seemed improvements to the old school were the community's main topics.

"Folks think we should use the money to make improvements to the school. And I've heard it said that it's time to remove the two pot-bellied stoves. If we had a furnace, the heat could be put on and left. With wood stoves, someone needs to bring splits and junks, light them and then keep going back to add more firewood, and they're not the safest either," said Sean.

The discussion continued as the members weighed up the pros and cons of a furnace, bathrooms, a kitchen, additional tables and chairs, and what should be done first? These were questions no one at the meeting could answer without having the prices of each suggested improvement.

Robert agreed to call a couple of oil companies for quotes, while Jerome Maloney, the newly married carpenter from Mossy Brook, would be asked to give the committee an idea of how much it would cost to build a kitchen. Robert also said he would try to get quotes on a water and septic system.

"Rose, with you being treasurer, what about us getting together and doing up some figures once I talk to the oil companies and Jerome and get some prices. That way, we can see what we can afford to do. We'll have another meeting to decide what improvements we should start with then. And thanks, Rose, for the financial statement you presented showing what we paid out and brought in since we began. I think we should put copies of it in the shop and the post office so everyone can see where we stand right now."

Robert said one major topic they had not yet discussed was one that he had heard more about than anything else was Bingo, and when was it starting? However, he said, unless we have volunteers, there will be no bingo.

In St. John's, teams of people take turns working at bingo, and that's what their committee would need. A weekly bingo would also have a jackpot, which meant the committee would put money aside and a cash float for a few weeks until the bingo got established.

"I wouldn't mind helping out in a group; we'd probably need about a dozen or more volunteers, so the same people don't have to work every week," Robert concluded.

By the end of the meeting, several decisions were in place. A weekly card game of 120s would start the following Wednesday. Oscar and Pat Martin were eager to see the card games begin and were only too happy to look after them. Ordering more tables and chairs was the next decision, and when they were delivered, a weekly Bingo would start.

David then spoke about the proposed youth club, asking what members thought about having adult volunteers pass on traditional skills such as woodworking, knitting or mat hooking to the young people.

"I'd also like to see dances once a month for both the elementary and high school students and, maybe later we can have a recreation program, but it would be good to see our young people learning traditional skills."

David had plenty of support for his idea, resulting in a decision to put notices in the shop and post office, looking for adults willing to help and asking what skills they might be interested in teaching. The final item, a request to book the hall for the 22nd, was not on Robert's list of discussion topics, and it took him by surprise. It was the first he'd heard about the upcoming baby shower for Kate.

Once the women explained it to Robert, they swore him to secrecy. He had another surprise when he heard the twins were involved in the planning and wondered how they would keep the secret from their mother.

"Don't you worry about that, Robert. They can probably keep a secret better than you. They went door to door in Mark's Point with invitations to all the women, telling them it was a surprise for Kate. Maggie and Theresa helped them, while Sharon and her mother Agnes are showing us how to organize and run a shower." Rose told Robert.

"If it's a surprise, how are you getting Kate to the school?" Robert asked.

"That's also looked after. All you need to do is to make sure Kate has nothing else planned for that Sunday afternoon and keep her from becoming suspicious," Rose replied.

The following week went by in a flurry, with many activities taking place. On Wednesday, when Rose and Bessie showed up for the first community card game, they were pleasantly surprised to see about two dozen people, including a few from Muddy Brook Pond and Mark's Landing, already in the school.

"Unlike Bessie, I'm not much of a card player. I'll go back home if you have enough to fill the tables," Rose informed Pat, who was seated by the door taking money from the players and handing them scorecards.

"You're not the first one to say that tonight. What's wrong with you all? Here's Bessie, all ready to play, and she never learned the game until she came to Newfoundland. The rest of you grew up playing 120s and 45s. Is you all losing your memories or something?" Pat asked.

Rose said she wouldn't mind playing at home with Bessie and friends. Nobody would care too much if she made a mistake there, but she had heard stories about card games where players got mad at others for making mistakes. Rose said that some people like Bessie have a natural ability for card playing, but she wasn't one of them.

"I've told Rose not to be so foolish. I'm sure she is as good as most people here. There may be an occasional person who takes cards too seriously, but do what I do, just ignore them." Bessie said.

That night after the card game, Rose was glad Bessie convinced her to attend. A crowd of 28 people showed up, making up four tables with six players and one of four. She was far from being the best player, but she didn't have the lowest score, and no one told her off for her lack of card knowledge. Back in Martin House, enjoying her bedtime cup of tea, she contemplated how lately their outside activities, more than their business, seemed to be keeping them occupied.

"From now to the weekend, we'll be kept busy. I'm having choir practice tomorrow night to start practicing Christmas carols, and don't forget we agreed to chaperone the dance for Marigold and Daisy's age group on Friday. We also have the Matthews and their American relatives arriving tomorrow."

"I might make a pot of soup and have it ready for them arriving. What do you think? Bessie asked her sister-in-law.

"Sounds good to me. It's starting to get chilly, and from now on, it's going to get colder. I just hope the weather stays fine while our visitors are here because Albert says his great uncle can't wait to explore every inch of Fisherman's Creek. When I spoke about the weather to Albert, he said Mr. Kearney is so excited; he probably won't notice the temperature."

Albert was right, Rose later remarked to Bessie after observing their elderly visitor. The weather didn't seem to bother his great uncle, who kept praising everything he saw.

"I have friends back in Boston who pay a fortune to go to Europe and other places when they could be spending time in this paradise. Wait until I go back and tell them about Newfoundland. They don't know what they've been missing. No, sir!" Thomas Kearney passionately declared.

It was Albert's great uncle's final night in Mark's Point. During the past three days, he and his son-in-law Gary Wallace explored and fell in love with the area. Although he was 93 years old and despite the chilly November weather, Mr. Kearney walked all around Fisherman's Creek, determined to see every nook and cranny of his boyhood home. His only regret was his brother and sisters weren't alive to be with him.

"Growing up, Anthony always spoke to me about Newfoundland. It was our father's cousin, Genevieve Kearney, who came from Boston when our mother died. She and Greg, her husband, had no children, and they adopted us. If not for Anthony, I'd have thought my surname had always been Kearney, but he never wanted me to forget who I was or that I was born in Newfoundland. I wish he got back to see our home, but he died before retiring from the railroad. That's where both of us worked, just like our adopted father."

Gary Wallace was impressed by everything he saw and experienced and planned to return the following year with his wife. They were both retired, but Madeline Wallace cared for her grandchildren after school while their parents worked.

"Our two daughters will just have to find another babysitter next year, so their mother and I can visit her Dad's place of birth. Ever since she began searching for information on Newfoundland and the Fleming family, I know she's dearly wanted to visit. The main thing is my father-in-law was able to make this trip. At his age, Madeline didn't want him to wait any longer to see his homeland and to meet his Fleming relatives," Wallace said.

"My mother always wondered what happened to her brothers," Albert's father, Jack Matthews, told Bessie and Rose.

"She said she used to have nightmares about them, remembering Uncle Thomas crying and clinging to her as a woman pulled him away. Her last memory of her brothers was Thomas screaming and kicking as the woman carried him under an arm and dragged Anthony, who had tears running down his face, by the other hand."

"Anthony would tell me it was well over a year after we left Newfoundland before I spoke again," Mr. Kearney recalled.

"My aunt brought me to doctors to see what was wrong. I guess my mother's death and then forced to leave my sisters, and my home was just too much of a shock for me. As you can hear, I eventually spoke, but I have no memory of leaving Fishermen's Creek or sailing to Boston. I must have started calling my aunt and her husband, Mom and Dad when I began to speak again, but Anthony never would."

The Matthews and their American relatives planned to leave Martin House in two cars about nine on Sunday morning. But much earlier, even before preparing breakfast, Bessie was surprised when Jack appeared in the kitchen.

"My goodness Jack, you're up early this morning. You must be eager to get back to town, and here's me not started making breakfast. Rose and I usually relax with a cup of tea at this time, but she isn't downstairs yet. Can I get you tea or coffee to tide you over until breakfast is ready?"

"You stay seated; I'll make my tea. I came down before anyone else because there's something I wanted to ask you or Rose in private. I know it's a lot to ask, but would you consider having a guest stay over New Year. I'll be with my family for Christmas, but I'd like to spend a few days in Mark's Point during the holidays," Jack said.

"Of course; we'd be happy to see you, but there's not much in the way of New Year celebrations taking place in this area. Why would a young man like you want to spend the New Year in Mark's Point?"

"That's the other thing I wanted to tell you," Jack said, looking slightly embarrassed,

"You probably know I've been working in Ontario quite often recently. When I was in Toronto in September, I called Angela and invited her out for a meal. We got on well, and since then, we've been seeing each other regularly and talking by phone. We haven't said anything to our families about our friendship and prefer not to do so yet, but we'd like to see each other during Christmas. That's why I asked if I may stay here. You're sure I won't be spoiling your plans by doing so, Bessie?"

But Bessie was delighted to hear of Jack's friendship with Angela, saying she could understand them getting on well together. Angela had become a mature young woman, and Bessie said she was pleased for them. Jack was welcome to stay at Martin House any time, she added.

"Another thing Bessie, I heard you say you were planning a visit to town soon. Why don't you make it this week because my apartment will be empty, and you could stay there? I fly to Alberta tomorrow afternoon, and depending on how long my business takes me, I may stop off in Toronto for a day and see Angela. I'll be gone until the weekend at least, and with Rose's house rented, you are both welcome to use my apartment. It has two bedrooms and, if you wait until Tuesday, it should be tidy. That's because I have a woman who comes in every Monday to clean," Jack said with a grin.

Although Bessie longed to tell Rose the news about Angela and Jack, she had to wait until their guests left for St. John's. But the group had no sooner left the driveway when Rose asked her what Jack's apartment had to do with them?

Bessie explained how Jack had offered the use of his apartment for the week while he was gone to the mainland, and she hoped Rose would accompany her.

"But that's not the biggest news, and it's something Jack wants only you and me to know for now. He and Angela have seen each other regularly during his business visits to Ontario. They also keep in touch by phone. He came downstairs before breakfast this morning to ask if we would consider letting him stay here over New Year because he wants to be able to see Angela while she is home for the holidays."

"What? That is a surprise, but it's a good one. I'm happy for them. I think they make a good match. You say they haven't told their families; they'll need to do so soon if Jack plans to visit Angela."

"And they plan to do so next month. I can't see Maggie and Gabe objecting to their friendship. They know Jack, and they all got on well. But what about his offer to let us stay in his apartment? If we accept, all we need to do is call Albert, who has Jack's spare keys. I had intended to go to town, so why don't both of us go? We've no guests booked this week, and I know

Gabe won't mind keeping an eye on the house. Didn't you say you still had to get a gift for Kate? Coming with me would be a good opportunity to get it," Bessie said.

"You are right. I had no idea what Jack was talking about when he said he spent more time on the mainland than in St. John's, and I should talk to you about his apartment being available. Yes, I'd like to come. If we leave on Tuesday and come back on Friday, we'd have two full days to shop. We should make up a list of things we want, and maybe we could get together to buy some Christmas gifts. What do you think, Bessie?"

With Bessie agreeing it would be a good idea, Rose went upstairs to get ready for mass, leaving her sister-in-law to relax with a cup of tea before continuing her preparations for dinner.

Following mass, Maggie, Father Kiely and Rose returned together from the church. About ten minutes later, when Gabe appeared, the priest tormented him about almost arriving late for dinner.

"It's not like you to wait until the last minute when there is a meal waiting. Don't tell me you overslept? Although with you not attending church, I suppose there's no reason for you to get out of your bed on a Sunday morning," he said with a laugh.

"But Pop was out of bed early this morning to go to church. He went there at 6.30 to put the furnace on so it would be nice and warm for us during mass," Maggie said in defence of her grandfather.

When Father Kiely and Rose looked surprised, Bessie asked if they weren't aware that men in the community took turns looking after the church.

"If not for Gabe and volunteers like him, the church would be pretty cold. It must be your month, Gabe, to look after the heating and any necessary snow clearing."

An embarrassed-looking Gabe muttered it wasn't much to do, adding he didn't want Maggie getting her death of cold in an unheated church.

"Father, I noticed you looked surprised when Maggie said Gabe put on the furnace. Although Gabe spoke as though he only did it because of Maggie, he's taken his turn to look after the church for years. Gabe likes to pretend he's got no interest in his church or community, but if help is needed, he's sure to be among the first ones to respond."

Seeing Gabe's discomfort at being the topic of conversation, Bessie changed the subject by saying it was time to eat and telling the men to sit at the dining room table while she, Rose and Maggie brought through the food.

Later as they finished their apple crumble dessert and custard, Rose spoke of the upcoming trip to St. John's.

"The twins asked if we could look for a shower gift for Kate from their father and all the children. Robert came to me afterwards and said the girls wanted something special for their mother, and he will pay for it."

"What about you, Maggie? Don't you need to get a gift too? Weren't you going to speak to your mother about it last night?" Gabe asked his granddaughter.

"I did, but she won't have enough time to buy something and get it sent in time to arrive for the shower. She said she'll get a gift once the baby is born and bring it home with her. Mom says Mrs. Kate will understand I couldn't get her a gift now."

However, Gabe wasn't satisfied with this and asked if Rose and Bessie would also pick up a gift from Maggie.

"We can't have you being the only one there without a gift. Bessie and Rose, buy whatever you think is suitable, and I'll settle with you when you get home. It will be your gift for the baby Maggie, and the one your mother buys in Toronto will be from her."

It was Wednesday morning when the sisters-in-law made their way to the Avalon Mall. First on their list to do was buy shower gifts for Kate. However, trying to decide what baby gifts to buy for the Brown girls and Maggie, as well as one from Rose, wasn't going to be easy. The Baby and Child Speciality Shop appeared to be packed from wall to wall and ceiling to floor. With so much choice, Bessie wondered where to start.

"It would help if we knew whether Kate was having a boy or girl. How are we going to choose from all this? I can see us spending all morning in this one shop just looking at everything," Rose said, appearing at Bessie's elbow.

"The gifts don't have to be baby clothes, do they? I just saw something I believe the twins and Kate would love. It's musical, has different animals hanging down from ribbons and turns around as it plays music. Come over and see what you think."

When a sales assistant saw their interest, she explained it was a mobile designed to hang over a crib and not only would the motion and music soothe a baby, it was educational. Listening to Brahms's Lullaby and watching the colourful little animal figures rotate, Rose was as convinced as Bessie that the mobile would make the perfect baby shower gift from the twins and their family.

"I was looking at crib sets of sheets and a blanket. Would that be suitable, I wonder, Bessie?"

"That would work out well with the baby quilt I finished making yesterday. That way, we know Kate will have one set of new bedding for the baby. Now, if we could only find something for Maggie, we could finish up here."

On hearing this, the assistant asked did they have anything in mind. Bessie explained that the baby shower gift was from a teenage girl.

"Would you consider a toy, such as a teddy bear? I've gone to many baby showers, and because most people give clothes, I often give a teddy bear, and the mother-to-be always tells me she loves it. We have bears in different sizes and colours, so there is a choice."

Rose nodded and smiled when Bessie said she thought it was something that not only Maggie would enjoy giving, but one Kate and the twins would love. About 10 minutes later, the happy pair left the store with the three gifts, wrapping paper, and cards.

They shopped together in the Avalon Mall for the next two hours, picking up gifts for Gabe, Maggie, Angela, and the Brown children. They also bought items for baby shower prizes.

"I'd like to get something for Mina and the girls, and what about Father Kiely. I saw the sweater he had on the other day, and it was pretty bare looking around the elbows. If I had thought about it earlier, I could have knit him one, but what if we buy it instead?"

With Rose agreeing and saying she would also go on the halves for Mina and the girls' gifts, they decided to get lunch before shopping again. While Bessie sat at a table looking after their purchases, Rose went to one of the many food outlets and bought bowls of piping hot vegetable soup and sandwiches made with fresh crusty rolls.

"I'll go back and get tea when we finish our soup. If I bought our tea now, it would be cold when we were ready to eat our sandwiches. Waiting to be served, I thought maybe we should go to the supermarket here in the mall before we leave. That way, we could pick up something for our supper and a few other things. I don't know about you, but once we get back to Jack's apartment with all our shopping, I don't think I'll feel like going out again."

"That sounds like a good idea. I didn't realize how tiring shopping was until I sat down. I'm glad it's not tonight that we go to Ellen and Albert's house for supper, because like you, I'm sure I'll want to stay put," Bessie answered.

Later that night, they went through their purchases as Rose checked names off their Christmas gift list. Looking at the second list for Martin House, she asked Bessie when they should go to the butcher's shop.

"I thought we might make that our last stop here in town before we go home on Friday. Although it won't go bad at this time of year, we don't want to buy meat until the last minute. I'm looking forward to getting steak mince and pork sausages. I'm also hoping to buy suet while I'm there as it's perfect in Christmas puddings."

After dropping off Jack's keys to Ellen early on Friday morning, the women made their way to the butcher shop.

"This reminds me so much of home," Bessie said when they entered the butcher shop.

"Just look at all those trays of meat and different kinds of sausages. I could spend a morning here admiring it all. I know you made a list, Rose, but I see liver over there and kidneys too, which I haven't seen in years. I love calf's liver, and if we get kidneys, I could make steak and kidney pie. I wonder if the butcher who gave Sue the sausages is here."

Bessie no sooner had the words out of her mouth when Rose approached one of the butchers and asked whether the Scottish butcher was working today.

"That's the boss you want. He's out in the back. Hey Boss, you're wanted out here," the young butcher shouted.

When a tall, sandy-haired man appeared in a butcher's apron, his younger colleague pointed out Bessie and Rose. As he approached them, he asked with a strong Scottish accent how he could assist them.

"I came to thank you for the gift of sausages you gave my American friends in September and to tell you they were the best sausages I've eaten since I left

Scotland. I'm Bessie Martin, and this is my sister-in-law Rose Martin, and we live in Mark's Point," Bessie told him.

"I'm Archie Leiper, and I'm delighted to meet you. I remember your friend, and when I heard her asking for some good steak to make mince and tatties, I knew she had to have a Scottish connection. She told me you were a war bride, which means you must be living here for at least 25 years. You haven't lost your accent."

"And neither have you. How long have you been in Newfoundland, and what brought you here," Bessie asked.

"Almost six years now, but let's not talk in the shop. The two of you come through to my office in the back. I've got a kettle and teapot there, and we can have a cup of tea while we chat. Wait 'til I tell Shona, my wife, about meeting you."

For the next half hour, the women enjoyed Archie's company. They discovered he came to the province after successfully replying to an advertisement in an Aberdeen newspaper for an experienced butcher to manage the shop in St. John's. The advertiser had visited Aberdeen and was so impressed by Scottish butcher shops; he decided to open one in St. John's.

"I have a wonderful employer who, after my first year working, began giving me shares in the business, and he's letting me buy more each year. In 10 years, I hope to own the business outright. I couldn't be happier, and neither could Shona and our children. We have two sons, Colin in elementary school and Neil in high school, while our daughter Cathie began her first year at Memorial University in September. We consider Newfoundland our home. My boys play hockey instead of playing football, and now we are all hockey fans," Archie told the women.

It was almost an hour later before Bessie and Rose left with a large order of meat. They had made a new friend, and now, with a source of good quality meat available, they intended to ask Dave Murphy to pick up a monthly order. Archie was disappointed they were returning to Mark's Point that day. He wanted to know whether they could return for the St. Andrew's Ball the following week on November 30 or the annual Burns' Supper on January 25th. The events, celebrating Scottish heritage, had gone on for many years and were a big attraction for recent immigrants from Scotland, people claiming Scottish ancestry, and Newfoundlanders alike.

Although they couldn't return the following week, Bessie promised that weather permitting, she and Rose would try and make it to the Burns' Supper in January.

"I was only ever to one Burns' Supper, and that was in 1939, the year I turned 19. The war started that September, and there were none held during the war years. Then, of course, I came to Newfoundland in 1945, where I never imagined anyone held a Burns' Supper. It would bring back some good memories if I could get to the one in St John's," she told Rose as she drove her heavily laden car out of the city limits.

"Hopefully, the weather will co-operate, and we can go, Bessie. It would be a new experience for me. We can book a hotel room for a couple of nights, and it would make a nice change."

The women had been driving for almost two hours when light snow began falling. About 15 minutes later, the snow was coming down thick and fast. Even with the windshield wipers working overtime, Bessie found it increasingly difficult to see the road ahead.

"Where did this come from so suddenly? There was no mention of snow on the radio weather forecast this morning, and now we are in the middle of a storm. At least we are off the main highway, but by the look of things, it's going to be a long slow journey home."

"Do you want me to take a turn driving Bessie? Keeping your eyes glued to the road has to be nerve-racking."

"If we change places, we'll both get cold and wet. I'm good for now, but as I said, it will be slow going. But unless it starts blowing hard, we'll get there. Meanwhile, let's stop for a few minutes to relax and have one of those sandwiches we made before leaving. The worst about this is that I know Gabe will be worrying. I told him we should be home by two or two-thirty at the latest, and it's well past two o'clock now."

It was closer to four o'clock when the women reached the outskirts of Lower Penny's Cove after thankfully coming upon a slow-moving plough and trailing it for almost ten miles.

"We'll make it home now, Bessie, because it's straight going from here. By the looks of things, another plough has already gone through the community. Let's stop at Mason's shop and see if I can use the phone. I'll call Gabe and tell him where we are. If he knows we are this far, it will stop him worrying."

"Goodness me, is that you, Rose? Where have you come from on a day like this?" a shocked Grace Mason asked when a snow-covered Rose entered her shop.

When Rose explained she and Bessie were on their way home from St. John's, Grace wanted them to come into her house and stay until the weather improved.

"You can at least get something hot to eat. You look frozen stiff and shouldn't go out on the road again in weather like this. If the snow don't stop, you can stay overnight."

When Rose made the telephone call to Gabe, Maggie answered, saying her grandfather and Mr. Nolan had left Mark's Point in Gabe's truck to look for them. When they didn't appear by three o'clock, Gabe called Ellen Matthews, who said she'd check with the butcher shop to see if someone there knew when they left. When she called Gabe back, saying the women left St. John's by 11 that morning, he and the young principal decided to look for them.

"That was about half an hour ago. Are you and Aunt Bessie alright, Aunt Rose? I know Pop is some worried, and so is the twins' father and mother. Mrs. Lucy called too, wondering if there was any news from you.

After talking to Maggie, Rose thanked Grace Mason for her hospitality offer but said she and Bessie better make their way home as it appeared there was a search party looking for them. She was just leaving the shop when Gabe's pick-up truck drew up beside Bessie's car, and Gabe and David jumped out.

"Thank God, you're alright! Everyone in Mark's Point is worried stiff, wondering if you were stuck in a snowstorm somewhere on the highway or in an accident. Why don't I drive your car, and David can take my truck?"

But after getting that far, Bessie wanted to continue driving and said they would follow if Gabe went ahead in his truck. Once back on the road, Rose told Bessie about Grace Mason's offer of a meal and accommodation.

"It's good to have people like Grace and our neighbours. Fancy Gabe and David, coming all the way here, and they were ready to keep going until they found us. It won't take us long before we're home, but given all this weather, we're going to have a long walk up through the garden as it's sure to be filled with snow."

On their arrival at Martin House, Rose discovered she was wrong. They met Robert, Bobby, Michael, and Jim, all carrying shovels after clearing the entire driveway of snow.

"We've got your driveway cleared, and if you give me your car keys, we'll unpack your car. Sharon and Maggie arrived a short while ago and said they'd put the kettle on. But even better than that, Jim brought over a pot of soup that Lucy made, and it's keeping hot on the back of your stove. Lucy knew you were coming home this afternoon and figured you wouldn't have much time to cook," Robert informed the women.

Bessie managed to drag herself from behind her car's wheel and almost staggered into her house, to be greeted by a delighted Maggie and Sharon.

"Aunt Bessie, Aunt Rose, we were all worried about you. People have been phoning to see if you got home yet. We got out of school at lunch when the weather started. Mrs. Nolan came over to see if I was okay after Mr. Nolan went with Pop to look for you, and she suggested we come here to get something ready for you to eat. Look at what Mrs. Nolan's mother, Mrs. Dawson, made. It's fishcakes and fresh-baked bread, and Mrs. Lucy sent over soup. I'm so glad you are home," Maggie said, giving each of them a hug,

"Not much wonder it took you so long to come from St. John's," Robert said, as he, Gabe, David, and the boys came into the house with their second load of bags and boxes.

"Your car was so overloaded it's a wonder it moved at all. The pair of you must have cleaned out the Avalon Mall, considering the pile of bags and boxes you have. I don't think you would have got another thing in the car, let alone a passenger. Even the back seat and floor were packed full."

"That's because most of the trunk has meat from the Scottish butcher. Leave the two boxes of meat out in the porch for now. Rose and I will decide what's in the fridge and what needs to go in the freezer later. But first, let's have some of this wonderful-smelling food. Thank you, Maggie and Sharon, for heating the food and be sure and thank your mother, Sharon. Where is Jim?"

"He's gone to tell Lucy you got home safely. He said she was some upset at the thought of you travelling in this weather, although she was sure you'd be alright because she prayed all afternoon to St. Christopher, the patron saint of travellers, to guide you safely home. And speaking about home, it's time we were heading back, Bobby. What about you Michael, I've got the truck, and I can drop you off."

"Okay, Mr. Robert. Mom and Dad will want to know if you got home all right, Mrs. Bessie and Miss Rose, so I'll let them know. Me and Bobby was talking, and we'll come back tomorrow and clear away the rest of your snow. Like we said, you does stuff for us all the time, and this way, we can do something for you. Isn't that right, Bobby?"

"That's right, and Mr. Gabe, we knows that you usually clears the snow for Mrs. Bessie, but tomorrow is Saturday, and we've got no school, so we'll do it. That's okay, isn't it, Mrs. Bessie?"

"It's more than okay, Bobby. We are grateful to you, your Dad and Mr. Jim for clearing our snow. As for you, Gabe and David, although I'm sure we would have eventually made it back, it was a relief to see you and to know you were ahead of us when we left Lower Penny's Cove to drive home. Of course, getting home to a warm house and the smell of good food, we were more than happy to have such caring friends and neighbours."

"You couldn't have said it better, Bessie. It's times like this that make me glad I returned home to stay. We certainly have good friends and neighbours, and now I think we should put all this great food to the test and sit down and eat. Robert, there's plenty of food here. Why don't you all stay and share it with us."

Robert and the boys said they had to leave, but Sharon called her mother to let her know the women were home and that she and David planned to eat there. When Gabe also agreed to stay, Maggie sprang into action.

"That's great, Pop. I'll set more places at the table and put the kettle on to boil. Aunt Bessie and Aunt Rose, I just bet the pair of you are dying for a good cup of tea."

CHAPTER 28

Surprise!

S now blanketed Mark's Point on Saturday morning, yet it was a beautiful sunny day. Even the harbour and the calm sea around it twinkled from the sun's reflection.

Rose was in the sunroom, looking out a window admiring the wintery scene and turned to speak to Bessie as she came into the room.

"After that terrible weather yesterday, we are left with all this snow, and yet it's one of the nicest days we've seen in weeks. And look, it's not even ten o'clock, and Bobby and Michael are already clearing our snow, and if my eyes don't deceive me, there are two more little helpers on their way up here."

Bessie answered the door to Daisy and Marigold a minute later, who shook their heads when invited indoors, saying they had come to work.

"Bobby said he and Michael was clearing the snow from your driveway, and Daisy and me wants to help. We've got our shovels, and Bobby said maybe we could dig the snow from around your door and out to your store. Mom said it was fine with her, but we had to ask you first. Can we do it, Mrs. Bessie?"

When Bessie said it was an excellent idea, the girls' faces lit up. Their smiles increased at Bessie's next suggestion.

"Maybe later, you could take your sleds over here and slide down the garden. It's a fine sunny day, with lots of snow, and everyone tells us we have a great slope for sliding down."

"Marigold, do you hear that. We needs to get our sleds out of the store when we goes home."

"I can hear Daisy, but right now, we have to clear this snow. You know what Mom always says, 'Work before play,' so get your shovel and start digging." Marigold ordered her younger sister.

Bessie asked Rose if they had anything sweet to give the youngsters when they finished clearing away the snow.

"What about the Cadbury chocolate biscuits we brought out from town? We bought two tins, intending to take a variety from one to Kate's shower and keep the other tin for Christmas. There's a great selection of biscuits in the tin, and for sure, the youngsters will enjoy them."

About half an hour later, four rosy-cheeked youngsters sat around the kitchen table drinking hot chocolate and thoroughly enjoying the biscuits.

"These are some good Mrs. Bessie. Can we make some like them next Saturday when we goes baking with you?" Daisy asked.

"We bought these in St. John's, but I know a recipe for chocolate cookies that we could make. They are so easy; we make them on top of the stove, not the oven. What's more, I'm sure we could make enough to give Bobby and Michael a few."

Hearing this, the boys grinned, and Michael said they wouldn't mind digging snow again in exchange for cookies.

"Pansy and Lily is digging snow too, but it's at the old school," Marigold announced.

"And so is Maggie and Theresa. They've got a meeting there tomorrow with Mrs. Nolan, and it's for mothers too. The twins is some lucky being in high school. They're getting to go to another school far away to play ball, and they'll be staying at other girls' houses. Isn't that right, Bobby?"

When Bobby appeared lost for words, Bessie said she had heard about the volleyball team. She agreed that the older girls were lucky to go on a school sports trip but reminded Daisy and Marigold that they were just as fortunate, having just spent a weekend with their friend Beverly.

Completely distracted, the young girls then monopolized the conversation with stories about their adventures with Beverly until Bobby finally told them it was time to return home if they intended to slide later.

Shortly after lunch, it was Maggie and the twins' turn to visit when they came to see the shower gifts bought by Bessie and Rose. Their expressions and sounds of delight when they saw the crib mobile and teddy bear were enough to let the women know they made good choices.

"We have the school path cleared of snow. And tomorrow when we're in mass, Pop will light the stoves in the school, so it's warm for the shower at three o'clock. Mrs. Kate will be some surprised when she sees everyone and finds out it's a shower for her," Maggie said.

"It's awful hard trying not to say anything in front of Mom, Marigold and Daisy. We couldn't tell the little girls about the shower because they wouldn't be able to keep it a secret. But we're not leaving them out of things. Dad will bring them to the shower after Mom gets there so they can see what's happening. Is it okay to leave our gift with you to bring once we wrap it because we don't want Mom seeing it?" Lily asked.

That wasn't a problem, Rose replied, producing wrapping paper, cards, and a pen for the girls saying they needed to sign the card before putting it with the gift. Maggie asked if she, too, could leave her gift.

"I can't take it now as I'm going back with Lily and Pansy. Mrs. Kate wants them with Marigold and Daisy when they come here with their sleds. I remember the great fun I had years ago sliding down your garden. The other night when I was on the phone with Mom, she asked if we had enough snow yet to use her old slide. We didn't then, but we sure have now, so is it alright, Aunt Bessie, if we all use your garden?"

Bessie told the girls she couldn't be happier to see them sledding in the garden, adding she was sure it wouldn't be only her and Rose who would get enjoyment from watching them slide down the slope.

"I'll phone Mrs. Lucy and tell her to look out for you going down the garden on your sleds. She's still not allowed to do too much, which makes time long for her. She will enjoy seeing you having fun."

When the girls left to go back to the Browns, Bessie decided to walk over to Lucy's house instead of phoning her. She wanted to return Lucy's soup boiler and give her a few pork sausages to try.

When she knocked and walked into the Pearce kitchen, it was evident Lucy had watched her coming. She not only had the kettle on to boil, but she had set the table 'fit for royalty,' as Bessie later described it to Rose.

"Come in, come in, my dear. I'm some glad to see you after that terrible day you had yesterday. I said to my Jim, 'Bessie's a strong, sensible woman, and if anyone can drive through a storm like this, it's Bessie.' I prayed to St. Christopher all afternoon and promised him I'd be the best neighbour anyone could have if he only kept you and Rose safe. And he answered my prayers like I knew he would. Every time my boys travel to and from Newfoundland, I prays to St. Christopher, and he always listens because he looks after travellers. He and St. Anthony are my two favourite saints. I keeps losing things, but I never worries because St Anthony is the patron saint for finding lost things. Bessie, all you need is faith, and although you're not a Catholic, I tells my Jim that I believe you've got more faith than an awful lot of folks around here."

Back in Martin House, Bessie was telling Rose about her visit with Lucy. The women had waited until evening to have their main meal of the day. After enjoying sausages, liver, and onions, they relaxed at the table with a cup of tea.

"Having Lucy treat me like an honoured guest made me feel like a hypocrite when I thought how often I've complained about her. However, she did appreciate the sausages and would love to have some suet to use in her Christmas pudding. You should see the baby's set Lucy knit for Kate's shower. She did a lovely job on it. Jim wasn't too keen on her going to the shower, but Lucy put her foot down, saying not only was she going to the shower, but she would also be at mass tomorrow morning. She told him although she wouldn't go lifting anything heavy, it was time she returned to a normal life, and it seems Jim has accepted that."

The following day there was little doubt Lucy was back to normal when she brought a plate of freshly baked raisin buns to the shower.

Sitting down next to Agnes Dawson, she said she only took the buns out of the oven half an hour earlier and left some for Jim,"

"I didn't know what I was going to bring because I haven't baked since I came out of the hospital. But like I told Jim, 'enough is enough,' I've been home for two weeks, and it's time to get back to normal. And honestly, I think he's happy to turn the housekeeping back to me. As a matter of fact, it was my Jim that suggested I make raisin buns, and I'm sure it's because he's been missing them."

Even while carrying on a conversation, Lucy missed none of the activities in the school. Her eyes never stopped surveying the room, taking in the decorations, the food table, and the gift basket while noting that those attending came from several communities. Agnes said the twins and their friends spent hours getting the school ready when Lucy mentioned the decorations.

"Didn't they do a grand job? They stayed with Sharon in school one day to make the decorations. They were here last night to decorate while supposedly helping Sharon prepare the school for a meeting. Then they came early today, just making sure everything was in place. I never saw a busier, more excited group of girls, and it's not just the girls from Mark's Point; there must be at least another six of their friends who are only too happy to be part of this."

"It's good to see them learning charity at a young age. It's just too bad that Robert had a poor season at the fishery this year, 'though it's a good thing Kate has her pay from the post office to help them make ends meet. I think the women doing this to help with clothes and stuff for the new baby is the right Christian thing to do." Lucy said.

"What are you talking about, Lucy?" asked Rose as she joined the women.

"Where did you get the idea that Robert didn't do well fishing this year. From what I hear, he and his brother-in-law, Tim, had one of their best seasons ever."

"Then how come all the women got together to do this? Not that I mind, of course, and I'm enjoying being out of the house. For sure, I'd have got the new baby a gift anyway, and I liked knitting with the lovely soft wool Bessie gave me. Me and my Jim talked about this party today, and we figured that money-wise, Robert and Kate might be having a hard time. We wondered how we could help them as we don't want their youngsters doing without things."

"Not at all, Lucy. Although it's the first time we had a baby shower in Mark's Point, they are popular in most places in Newfoundland. I went to quite a few baby and bridal showers in St. John's. Baby showers are a time to celebrate and a way for a mother-to-be like Kate to prepare for her baby. They

WELCOME TO MARTIN HOUSE

are also a social activity for women and girls, and showers are usually great fun. We'll be playing games, so stop worrying about the Brown's finances and sit back and get ready to enjoy yourself," Rose said.

Kate would be out of here like a shot if she thought people believed she and Robert needed help, Rose thought. She knew how independent the Browns were and that they didn't need financial assistance from anyone.

Just then, one of the twins, standing on a chair to look out a window, called out that Patsy had arrived and had just parked her car. She and Kate would be in the school in a minute.

"All right, everyone, not a word until Kate is in the door, and then we'll all shout surprise," Sharon said in a loud voice.

Apart from a few muffled giggles, there was complete silence for the next few minutes, only broken when Kate and Patsy came through the porch into the school.

When the loud 'SURPRISE' broke out, there was no doubt Kate was surprised. She looked almost in shock when she saw so many women in the hall.

"What's going on? What kind of meeting is this?" she asked in bewilderment.

"Come in and sit, Kate," Patsy told her. "This, my dear, is a baby shower, and it's your baby shower. Mrs. Nolan and the girls came up with the idea, and everyone has worked hard to keep it a secret from you. By your face, I'm guessing the surprise was successful."

"Sit down here, Mom. We have this specially decorated chair for you because you're the guest of honour," an excited Lily told Kate.

"Are you really surprised, Mom?" Pansy asked.

"Like Mrs. Patsy said, it's been some hard keeping this a secret, and there were times we almost put our foot in it. Dad and Bobby knew about the shower, but we couldn't tell Marigold or Daisy, but Dad is bringing them here in a few minutes to let them take part and see everything."

Kate was settled down in her chair and gradually accepting what was happening when the two youngest Brown girls ran into the school. Daisy was the first to see Kate, and approaching her, announced they were here for the baby's party.

"How come you never told me and Marigold about it?" she indignantly asked the twins.

"Yes, how come?" Marigold added her voice.

"We would have got our new baby a present. You shouldn't come to a party without a present."

"We have a present, and it's from all of us, Dad, Bobby, the two of you, and us. Mrs. Bessie and Miss Rose got it in St. John's, and you're going to love it. We didn't forget you. This shower is just supposed to be for women and high school girls, but you are here because you'll be the baby's big sisters, just like Pansy and me are your big sisters. There's no other girls of your age here," Lily informed them.

The youngest girls' indignation turned to pleasure as they looked around when they realized Lily was right. When Sharon began talking, welcoming Kate to Mark's Point's first baby shower and telling her to relax and enjoy herself because the twins and their friends had worked hard to make the event special, they joined everyone clapping in appreciation.

"We'll be playing some games, including a few games of bingo, and to get us in a party mood, we want everyone, except you, Kate, to stand up and look at the bottom of your chair. Two chairs have a paper taped to the bottom of the seat, and if one of them is yours, you win a prize."

There was much laughter and movement at Sharon's words, and seats were soon turned bottom up. Maggie and Theresa invited the lucky winners Nora Ryan and Flo Kavanagh to pick their award from a box filled with prizes. Flo was first to tear open the paper from her package to reveal a pack of clothespins, which she declared would come in handy. Nora discovered a pair of face cloths was her prize and raised laughter when she said they were almost too pretty to use on her face.

After more than an hour of games, Sharon, seeing only a few prizes left, said they were keeping them until later, but now it was time for Kate to open her gifts. Calling on the twins to sit one on each side of their mother, she passed Lily a notebook and pen to record who gave each present and what it was, then asking Pansy to display the gifts once Kate opened them.

The Brown family gift, placed conveniently on top of the large decorated basket, was first to be opened, and Kate's pleasure in it was second only to that of Marigold and Daisy. As Kate opened it, and Pansy started the crib mobile rotating to the sound of Brahms' Lullaby, the little girls' faces were pictures of wonder and delight.

"Didn't we tell you we had a nice gift for the baby from us all? Isn't it lovely?" Lily asked her younger sisters.

The girls' faces and quick nods answered the question. By then, Kate had unwrapped her second gift, which turned out to be the sweater, cap and bootee set knit by Lucy.

"Oh Daisy, look how tiny and beautiful the clothes are. I can't wait for our baby to come and wear them."

Daisy, enthralled by everything, hardly heard Marigold speak. As the gifts continued, it was evident that the Brown family's expected addition would want for nothing. Pansy displayed nightgowns, diapers, vests, T-shirts, and bedding before placing them in a large plastic baby bath that held baby powder, soap, oil, and shampoo gifts.

Daisy's most enthusiastic reaction came after Maggie's gift was revealed.

"Look, Marigold, our baby even has its own teddy bear, and it's beautiful. I bet our baby will be some glad to see it and look at the quilt Mrs. Bessie made. It has Humpty Dumpty on it and Jack and Jill. We can learn our new baby all the nursery rhymes on the quilt, Marigold."

It took almost half an hour to open everything, and as the last gifts went around the circle of women, Bessie, Rose, and Agnes put the kettles on and started preparing the lunch. Removing cloths, they uncovered two tables filled with a variety of sandwiches, cookies, and cakes.

"We have tea, coffee and soft drinks available, although we only have Styrofoam cups. I'm sure you'll agree the delicious lunch will make up for any shortcomings in the cup department. You will notice the girls have tables set up with forks, spoons, and serviettes, so bring your chairs over, and once you get something to drink and filled your plate with goodies, have a seat. Kate will cut her cake in a few minutes and will sit at the top of the table."

"It's no problem hearing our Sharon when she uses what I call her teacher's voice. It's loud enough to get attention," Agnes said.

"I don't know about that, but she certainly knows how to get things going. It was a great idea of hers to have this shower. You can see by everyone's faces, especially the twins and their friends, just how much they enjoy it. And thanks to you too for organizing it with Sharon and getting the decorations, the quilt material and baby wool. Did you see the expressions on Daisy and

Marigold's faces when they saw the nursery rhyme characters on the quilt?" Bessie asked Sharon's mother.

"Yes, I'd say this shower will be the talk of their classrooms tomorrow. They certainly enjoyed themselves. It seems all the Brown girls are looking forward to the arrival of the baby."

Both women had successfully collected a plate of food and managed to carry them and their cups to the table when Sharon announced there were still prizes to be won. She then told everyone to look for an X on the bottom of their plates and cups.

Mina was one of the four winners when she discovered an X mark under her plate. Opening her prize, she found a box of stationery, which delighted her two daughters, who said it would come in useful when writing Chrissie.

It was more than an hour later before the activities came to an end. Robert and David, who had watched for the women to start leaving, arrived to help clear the hall.

"You must be some pleased with yourself managing to keep this baby shower a secret from me. I'm still wondering how you and the twins managed it," Kate said to her husband.

"Bobby and every woman in Mark's Point knew and so did most of the men, but nobody told you," Lily added.

"They never told us either, did they, Marigold?" Daisy said.

"I wonder why that was," their father said, trying not to smile.

"I think Lily and Pansy wanted it to be a happy surprise for you too. Don't forget; they asked me to get you here before the shower started. Did you enjoy yourselves?"

The two little girls agreed they had a wonderful time, then remembering all the shower gifts, insisted Robert come and inspect them.

While the men made light work of stacking the tables and chairs, the older girls swept up and put the former school back to rights. By then, the women had not only packed the gifts and cards for Kate to take home, but they also had, much to Marigold and Daisy's delight, a variety of cookies and some shower cake ready to send back to the Brown house.

"Mrs. Bessie, will we be baking these the kind of cookies at your house on Saturday?" Marigold asked.

"There's a couple of different kinds here we might try. I know you love snowballs; what if we try making shortbread, which I know your father likes and maybe peanut butter cookies?"

Marigold and Daisy were only too happy to agree and spoke about Penny arriving and how they knew she would just love learning to bake cookies with them.

"You know what, Mrs. Bessie? When I'm big, I'm going to be a cook and work in a big hotel, and I might even cook dinner for film stars," Marigold said.

Daisy, not to be outdone, spoke up.

"I'm going to be a baker and open my own shop and sell cherry cakes and all kinds of cookies. That would be good, wouldn't it, Mrs. Bessie?"

"It certainly would. A smart pair of girls like you and Marigold can do anything you want. Whatever you end up doing, I know you will do well."

"According to their prate, I think the girls would make better politicians. I'm sure they'd give Joey Smallwood or Frank Moores a good run for their money in a few years. What do you think, girls, about one of you being the first female premier of Newfoundland?" Robert asked.

The disgusted looks on Marigold and Daisy's faces showed their father precisely what they thought of his joke, and Marigold quickly retorted.

"If you don't want us baking, Dad, you won't want us making shortbread with Mrs. Bessie on Saturday."

The women burst out laughing, not only at Marigold's quick response but by the look on Robert's face.

"Marigold has you there, Robert. You keep tormenting your children, but you should know by now they can give as good as they get," Kate said.

"Marigold, as Mrs. Bessie says, whatever you want to do when you grow up, your father and I know you'll do well. As for making shortbread, that's for Mrs. Bessie to decide, but I hope you remember that I love cookies made with peanut butter."

Bessie remembered the Browns' banter the following Thursday night when she and Penny discussed what they would bake. Penny, who arrived by taxi that afternoon, was delighted to be back in Mark's Point.

"Tomorrow, we'll make the fruit cakes. You said Bishop and Mrs. Harris love dark fruit cake, and I need to make one for Gabe. It's just as easy to make two as one." Bessie said.

"I brought out a box of dried fruit and other supplies for baking. I asked a lady in the store for advice on what to buy. Apart from Beatrice, I didn't know who else I could ask."

When Bessie said there was no need for her to bring anything, she already had fruit and baking supplies; Penny said it was the least she could do since Bessie was giving her baking lessons.

"I'm so looking forward to this and also to Saturday when Marigold and Daisy come here, and we make cookies."

"You'll see them tomorrow. Kate decided not to tell them you were arriving today, or they would have tormented the life out of her to come this evening. She says they have homework, and Marigold needs to study for her weekly spelling test. I am sure that before the school bus pulls out of Mark's Point tomorrow afternoon, the two of them will be on our doorstep," Bessie told Penny.

Bessie's words were proven correct the following afternoon when Penny, who watched the school bus pass by, called out that Marigold and Daisy were on their way.

"They must have stopped long enough to drop their book bags and come on. They're almost at your gate already," Penny called out to the women.

"They will be hungry after a full day at school. I'll get out cookies and glasses for milk. I might as well put on the kettle for us to have a cup of tea because I'm sure we're in for an hour or more of entertainment from the girls. David, their school principal, says they told their teachers all about their 'missing Harry' from Africa and how you should come to their classrooms," Rose said.

"Is Penny here?" was the first question asked by the girls.

Then, smelling baking from the oven, Marigold wanted to know if they'd been making cookies without her and Daisy?

"Yes, I'm here," Penny said, coming forward and hugging the girls.

"It's so good to see my two smallest friends, and of course, we wouldn't make cookies without you. Mrs. Bessie showed me how to make a dark fruit cake to surprise my brother, Bishop Clarence and my sister-in-law, Beatrice. We're making cookies tomorrow, and Mrs. Bessie says, we're going to decide what kind of cookies we will make while you are here. Isn't that exciting?"

During the next half-hour, the girls and Penny shared stories of what had happened in their lives since they last saw each other. Penny spoke about volunteering with children in the after-school program and as a Sunday School teacher in her church. Meanwhile, Marigold and Daisy had plenty to share, telling Penny about their school, their 'bestest' friend Beverly, and Kate's baby shower. Seeing how quickly the time passed, Bessie reminded them they should decide what they wanted to bake because no doubt Kate would soon phone to say it was time they came home. That way, the women could get the ingredients ready for the next day.

"I spoke to your mother, and she's agreed you can stay for lunch tomorrow, which means we have all morning and afternoon to make cookies. Why don't you plan to be here by 10 o'clock and we will begin by making snowballs? We start them on top of the stove and then put them into the fridge to cool. Once cooled, we roll them into balls and coconut. What else do you fancy making?"

Once the girls got over their excitement at being allowed to stay the entire day, Daisy asked could they make peanut butter cookies for their mother.

"And what about shortbread for your Dad. Isn't shortbread his favourite?" Rose asked the girls.

"Yes, he loves them. I suppose we should make some for him, even though we said we wouldn't 'cos he tormented us. But if we make shortbread, that's three different kinds, and Penny, you never said what kind you wants to make." Marigold said.

Penny said she was only too happy to participate in the activity and didn't care what they made. When Daisy asked Bessie if three different kinds were too many to make, Bessie assured her they had all the ingredients and plenty of time to make that amount. It was two happy little girls who left Martin House a short time later.

"Aren't they precious?" a beaming Penny asked.

"They're such lovely girls, and although I didn't tell them yet, I have something for each of them. I had aprons made by a lady in our parish, and she even embroidered their names on them. I'm looking forward to seeing their faces when they get them."

It was just before ten on Saturday when Marigold and Daisy arrived. Robert, who dropped them off, said the girls had been sent back to bed by

Kate at six o'clock and again at seven before being instructed not to leave their bedroom for at least another hour.

"I got up with them at eight o'clock, and if I had given them the slightest encouragement, they would have left to come here then. I reminded Marigold and Daisy that you said 10 o'clock, but it wasn't until Kate threatened if they didn't stop tormenting, they wouldn't be allowed to stay for lunch that we got any sense from them. I'd say good luck to the lot of you. I hope you have earplugs handy."

When Penny produced five aprons, the women were as surprised as Marigold and Daisy. Each apron had one of their names embroidered on the bib, resulting in squeals of delight from the girls.

"Bessie and Rose, I know you never expected them, but these aprons are my way of trying to say thank you to each of you. My life took on a purpose once again when I met the four of you, and now, I think it's time we begin baking. I can't wait to get started," Penny said.

"Thank you, Penny. These aprons are perfect gifts, aren't they girls? But in addition to an apron, every cook follows a recipe and Rose, and I thought each of you should have your own recipe book. You probably saw me use this old hand-written book when I made the cherry cake from a recipe passed down by Mrs. Martin. Rose and I each have books in which we write recipes we like and want to use again. Some of mine came from my mother, grandmother, mother-in-law, and friends. Now it's time you begin your recipe books."

With this, Rose opened a kitchen drawer and passed out hard-covered notebooks to Penny, Marigold, and Daisy.

"You will notice we printed RECIPE BOOK on the cover, and inside, Mrs. Bessie and I wrote out four recipes. One is for cherry cake, which we put in a section of your book under CAKES, and the other three are the cookies you will make today, and they are in the COOKIE section. We bought these books when we were in town, and now, whenever you want to bake cookies, you'll have these recipes. The books look clean and pretty empty right now. Over the years, we are sure you will add many more recipes. And don't worry if you get flour and grease on them. Like ours, it will show that you use your recipe books."

When Kate came at four that afternoon to bring the girls home, Marigold and Daisy were so happy and proud; they didn't know what to begin showing their mother.

"Look, Mom: we have aprons and recipe books of our own, and look at all the cookies. We made your kind with peanut butter and even Dad's shortbread ones and wait until Bobby and Michael sees the snowballs we made. We promised them we would give them some when we were shovelling snow, that's right, isn't it, Mrs. Bessie?"

Daisy interrupted her sister to say Kate would never guess what they had for lunch.

"We had stew, Mom, and it was some good. And guess what, Miss Rose had a lemon meringue pie made for our dessert, and when she saw you coming, she put the kettle on."

Laughing, Rose said Daisy was right, the kettle was on, and before Kate left, she should have a cup of tea and a piece of lemon pie.

"But first, I know you've heard all about Penny, and Penny, I know the girls speak about Kate all the time, but I don't think the pair of you have actually met."

Rose began pouring the tea, asking if Kate would prefer some of the girl's cookies.

"Don't forget you and Penny and Mrs. Bessie; all baked the cookies with us. And Mom, if you wants to make any of our cookies, you can use the recipes from our books. I'm bringing my apron and recipe book to our next Show and Tell in school. Wait until Beverly and the rest of my class sees them," Daisy said.

After Kate and the girls left, Penny asked the women if they knew when Kate's baby was due? On hearing Kate had at least two more weeks to go, Penny said she thought it might have been sooner.

"After I completed nurse's training, I spent another year training as a midwife before I went to the missions where I delivered hundreds of babies. Kate appears to be carrying this baby low down, and I wouldn't be surprised if she had it quite soon."

Bessie said she hoped that wasn't the case because the cottage hospital recently closed its maternity ward. It meant Kate had to travel to a hospital in St. John's, and her booking date for the hospital was December 9, just two days before her due date.

Penny appeared uncomfortable that she had raised the subject and began speaking about the taxi instead.

"With the taxi not going into town on Sundays, it's good of you providing all these meals for me. I'm afraid I never thought about the taxi schedule when I asked to come and stay, but because it is Sunday and you have a church service, do you think your priest would mind if I attended?"

"Of course not. Father Kiely would welcome you, and you could come with me," Rose said.

You'll get an opportunity to meet Father Kiely tomorrow because he comes here for dinner after Sunday mass. I think you already met Gabe and his granddaughter, Maggie; they'll also be here," Bessie told Penny.

"And speaking about meals, it's almost five now. What if we wait until later before having supper. I feel like I've been eating all day, and all I'll want is something light for my evening meal."

"Me too. That last cup of tea with Kate finished me. I'd say we wait even later and maybe have a sandwich around seven o'clock. Is that okay with you, Penny?" Rose asked.

"I think that would finish off a perfect day. Bessie and Rose, thank you so much for this. I've enjoyed myself. Beatrice and Clarence knew I would be making cookies, and they will love them, but I can't wait to see their faces when I produce the cake and tell them I helped make it."

CHAPTER 29

Another Surprise

Sunday morning saw Bessie preparing dinner in Martin House while Rose and Penny were in Mass. She was using a family recipe not tried for many years, one requiring puff pastry. Using two enamel deep pie dishes she brought from Scotland as a young bride, Bessie poured the partially cooked steak, kidneys and onions in well-seasoned gravy, into the dishes, before covering them with the pastry.

I hope they are as good as I remember them. Steak and kidney pie was one of my favourite meals growing up in Scotland, and I'll be so disappointed if these are a failure. It's many years since I tried making one.

But Bessie wasn't disappointed with her efforts when she saw how much her dinner companions enjoyed the meal.

"That was a delicious meal, Bessie. I think that's the first time I've ever tasted steak and kidney pie, and was it ever tasty. I'd describe it as out of this world. Don't you agree, Gabe?" Father Kiely asked.

"I suppose you being a priest, would have heaven in your mind when you say it's out of this world. Being a more down-to-earth man myself, I'd say it's good. Bessie don't need to hear fancy words to know I enjoyed my meal," Gabe replied.

Before the two men could start tormenting each other as they usually did, Bessie interrupted by asking Penny what she thought of mass in Mark's Point.

"It was a beautiful service. Thank you, Father Kiely, for allowing me to attend. Rose, you and the choir did an excellent job. I was surprised at the similarities between your service and our Anglican one. And thank you too, Bessie, for this lovely Sunday dinner. I had never tasted steak and kidney pie, and it was delicious".

When Maggie added her compliments to Penny's, Bessie said it had been years since she last tried making it.

"I could never get any kidney, or for that matter, any good steak, since coming to Mark's Point. And the last time I tasted steak and kidney pie was when we were on holiday in Scotland; do you remember Rose? Now I know we can get meat from a proper butcher. I'll be making it more often."

"Maggie, did you tell Bessie and Rose the news from your mother?" Gabe asked his granddaughter.

"Guess what! Mom will be home for almost a month. Her classes finish on December 10. She's working all that weekend but hopes to fly to Newfoundland on the 13th. She doesn't start classes again until January 10th. Isn't that good? I can't wait to see her."

"It is excellent news. Don't forget that you wanted to make a light fruit-cake for your mother. Why don't we plan that for next Saturday? Bessie asked Maggie.

"Aunt Bessie, I know it's a lot to ask, but do you think the twins could come with me and also make a cake. Mrs. Kate usually makes one, but the twins don't think she'll have time this year with her going into hospital soon. But if it's too much to ask, don't worry. I'm sure Mom wouldn't mind me giving them half of her cake."

"It's not a problem at all. Maggie. As a matter of fact, I thought about Kate and intended to make her a fruit cake, but if the twins want to try baking, they can come here. You're a good friend thinking about them," Bessie said.

"If the twins are half as enjoyable as their younger sisters, I'm sure you'll have a good day," Penny added.

The ring of the telephone broke into the conversation, and Rose went to answer it. On her return, she said taxi driver, Ted Brown, wanted to speak to

Penny. After talking to him, Penny asked Bessie and Rose would it be alright if she stayed an additional day.

"Mr. Brown says the forecast calls for snow tomorrow and quite a lot of it. He wanted me to know if that happens, he won't be making the trip to St. John's."

After Bessie and Rose assured Penny that they would be glad to have her stay longer, Maggie wondered if the weather would be bad enough for the schools to close.

"I'm sure it will. I was looking at the sky this morning and thinking we're in for a good batch of snow. By the signs, I'd say we're going to have a major storm. Miss Harris, you might be stuck here for a few days yet," Gabe prophesized.

It was barely dark that evening when the first snowflakes began falling and continued that way for almost an hour. Looking outside, Rose said Gabe must have been wrong in his weather forecast as nothing much seemed to be happening.

"I wouldn't be so sure of that. Alex always said Gabe was the best one in Mark's Point for predicting the weather," Bessie said.

Just then, they heard the sound of a shovel scraping near the back door. When it opened, Gabe appeared from the porch, saying he had come to check the generator and make sure there was enough gas in it.

"I don't doubt we might lose power because the wind is shifting around. I'd say we're in for a dandy of a storm. Now Bessie, do you remember how I showed you to turn on the generator? If we lose the lights, you're going to need it."

To make sure she knew how to start it, Bessie put on her coat and boots and went with Gabe to the generator shed. Once Gabe was satisfied she knew how to turn it on, he said he would bring in a few armfuls of logs and stack them in the porch.

"The generator is good for the lights and some appliances, but if the power goes off, it's hardly strong enough to work the furnace and everything else. You still have your oil stove in the kitchen, and you could use the oil heater in the front room, but with wood, you can also use the fireplace. Now, what about flashlights? Have you got them handy?"

Assuring Gabe that she had several flashlights and batteries in convenient places in the house, Bessie told him he should get home before the weather turned too bad.

"Yes, I should get back to Maggie, but don't none of you women go out in this weather. If you needs anything, phone me, and if such a thing the phones goes out, I'll be checking on you," Gabe said.

Around nine that night, the storm began with a vengeance as snow and wind began battering Martin House.

"Rose and I are used to the wind hitting against the house, and hopefully, with your bedroom at the back of the house, you shouldn't find much of it once you go to bed, Penny," Bessie informed their guest.

But used to it or not, Rose and Bessie agreed the following morning that the wind, which was still blowing hard, had kept them awake most of the night.

"Gabe was right, this is a major storm, and it doesn't seem to be giving up. It's a wonder we haven't lost power. After breakfast, I'm going out to dig a path to the generator shed. I want to make sure there's access to it."

Penny wanted to know if Bessie had an extra shovel, saying she would help clear the path. It had been years since she shovelled snow, but she would like to help. Telling her she would need warm clothes to go outside, Bessie said her clothes would probably go around Penny twice before suggesting Rose's things would be a better fit.

Rose agreed and took Penny upstairs to give her a selection of slacks and sweaters to try on, saying once Penny found something to fit her to come downstairs to see what outdoor clothing and boots would do.

Although fully dressed for the outdoors, the two women were shocked when they opened the back door. Not only were they facing snow past their waists, but it was blowing so hard, they couldn't see where to start shovelling.

"I can't see the sense of the two of you going out in this weather. You might clear some away from the door, but before long, it will be just as bad," Rose said as she struggled to hold the door open to allow them out.

Rose wasn't far wrong, Bessie thought to herself a few minutes later. She and Penny were making little progress in their efforts to get to the generator, and as she tried looking back, it seemed the path was filling in as quickly as they moved the snow. Grabbing Penny's arm, she motioned her to turn around and go back to the house where a thankful Rose was anxiously watching for them from the porch window.

"This is a day for staying indoors, and that's just what we'll all be doing until this storm stops. Didn't I tell you it was a waste of time trying to clear away snow, especially in this wind?"

Interrupted by the sound of the phone, Rose left to answer it. By the time she returned, Bessie and Penny had their outer garments off and were warming themselves by the kitchen oil stove.

It's times like this that make me glad Alex convinced me to keep the oil stove when we installed the electric one, Bessie thought, before telling Penny to move her chair closer to the stove and enjoy the heat.

"That was Gabe, wanting to know if we were alright. He'll be over to clear a path to the road as soon as the wind dies down, which he says might not be until tomorrow. He says almost three feet of snow is forecast to fall before the storm calms down in this part of the province. According to the radio, this wind could result in six-foot drifts and even higher. Gabe's last words were not to attempt to go outside in this, so I thought it best not to mention your expedition."

Their next phone call came from Lucy, who wanted to know how they were managing during the snowstorm.

"You might think I'm foolish, but I love a day like this, being all warm and cozy inside while the weather goes crazy outdoors," Lucy said.

She was looking forward to baking and planned to make at least two fruit cakes. Lucy added her sons looked forward to home baking whenever they came home, whether bread, cakes or cookies.

Phone calls also came from David and Robert, wanting to know if the women needed anything. David and Sharon were enjoying their day off, but it was far from a holiday for Robert.

"The five youngsters are home and driving me crazy with both the radio and record player on high. If I hear the song, *Everything is Beautiful* one more time; the record player might mysteriously disappear. I told them they'd all have to shovel snow when this wind and snow die down. That's when they'll see how beautiful everything is outdoors."

When Bessie said at least Kate wouldn't be working due to the weather, Robert reminded her that Friday had been Kate's last day in the post office for several months.

He and Jack Martin had moved everything from the post office on Friday afternoon, including the big old safe, over to Martin's shed that Patsy would use as her office. According to Robert, Jack built a counter and shelves in the shed, and it was now ready for business.

"I'm happy Kate will have a break for a few weeks before the baby comes. I made her go back to bed this morning because she was awake most of the night. Kate says the wind kept her awake, but I've seen her sleep through far worse storms than this. When I asked her was she having any pain, she told me not to be so foolish. She said the baby wasn't due for weeks yet, but I'm worried. What if something happened? I can't get her to hospital in this weather, and Nurse Holland wouldn't get out of Murphy's Cove until the storm's over and the roads plowed."

When Bessie told Rose and Penny about Kate having a restless night and how Robert was worried because of the storm, Penny said Robert was right to worry, adding Kate might be in the early stages of labour. She suggested Bessie call Robert and let him know she was a midwife, and if Kate needed her, she would get there somehow. Penny spoke about seeing Kate on Saturday and thinking she wouldn't be surprised if she had the baby soon.

"If Kate needs you, there isn't a man in Mark's Point who wouldn't get out and dig a path to get you there. I remember Nora Ryan had one of her boys during a February storm over 20 years ago. Poor old Mrs. Jose Martin, God rest her soul, had been the local midwife years earlier, and when word spread about Nora, men and boys got out shovelling. Before long, they had Mrs. Jose on a sled pulled by a horse, with the men digging a path ahead, all the way to Ryan's house. Mrs. Jose delivered the baby successfully a few hours later. I believe it was Sean who was born at that time. I'll phone Robert letting him know you are here and that you're willing to come if needed. I'm sure that will relieve his mind."

"Thank God," was Robert's response.

"I know Kate is feeling poorly, but when I asked her again a few minutes ago, she denied it. I've never known her to stay in bed until this time of day. What's got me even more worried is her not being up and around when she knows all the youngsters are home. That's not like Kate at all. We're going to have lunch now, and then I'm going to try Kate again and see if she fancies something to eat. I'll let you know what happens, but I feel easier in my mind knowing we have a trained midwife handy."

It was still snowing a few hours later, but the wind had turned, making it less blustery. Bessie noticed the weather change when she rose to answer the phone to an exceedingly worried Robert.

"Kate's definitely not well and is spending her time between the bedroom and the bathroom. She says it's a stomach bug, and truthfully, she looks sick. But what if it's the baby? I'm worried, and I know the twins are also worrying. If I get ready and come over on my snowmobile, do you think Penny would come back with me and see what she thinks?"

"I know she will. How long do you think it will take you to get here?"

When Robert said it would take him at least half an hour to dig a path to his store and get his machine out and started, Bessie told him to hold on until she spoke to Penny. But Penny had been listening and said she would be ready whenever Robert arrived.

"First of all, I'm going to find Alex's old parka because you'll need something warm to wear and you can choose from the boots, mitts, and caps in the parch. Now Penny, when you get there and think Kate is in labour, the best thing we can do is get the children out of the house. They can come here for the night. Ask Robert to call me, and we'll see how to arrange this."

As Bessie spoke, the phone rang again. It was Gabe asking if she had heard from Robert and if she knew if Kate was alright.

"Maggie's been talking to the twins, and they're really upset and worried about their mother. They think the baby might be coming early. Kate's mother is on the mainland, and her sister Jean can't get here from Mark's Landing in this storm. That's why I wondered if I got Nell and the slide out of the stable if you might want to go over there. You're as close as any relative to Kate. What about it, Bessie? From what I hear from Maggie, those youngsters need someone to calm them down."

Bessie told Gabe what she'd heard from Robert and agreed to go to the Brown's house with him when he arrived. Hanging up the phone, she told Rose what was happening. Rose agreed with Gabe, saying not only would

Kate prefer Bessie to anyone else, she thought it would be good for Penny to have her there.

The women were dressed and waiting for almost 15 minutes when the phone rang again. On answering, Rose was surprised to hear Nora Ryan.

"Rose, there's been a change of plan. Instead of Robert and Gabe, my boys are on their way to your place. They will pick up Bessie and the midwife. Sean was out on his snowmobile when he saw Gabe digging a path to the stable and stopped to help. When Gabe explained what was happening, Sean told him to stay with Maggie, and he would get you. He came back to tell me, and I sent him to stop Robert before he left. Robert needs to stay with Kate and the youngsters. Nick is home for the weekend, and he's coming with Sean and driving his father's snow machine."

As Nora was speaking, Bessie had risen to the window at the sound of the snowmobiles, announcing the arrival of Nora's sons. She met Sean at the back door looking for shovels, so he and Nick could clear away the snow from around the door. In a couple of minutes, he was back and ready to start the journey.

"Now, Mrs. Bessie, are you and your friend well dressed for this weather? I don't know if any of you were on a snowmobile before, but you'll sit behind Nick or me, put your arms around our waist and hold on tight. It won't take us long to get over to Robert's house, and I know he's waiting for you. He's right worried about Kate."

Once outside, Bessie had only time to notice the wind had died a lot, and the snow wasn't falling quite so fast before getting behind Nick on his machine. When the Ryan boys were satisfied that the women were safely seated, the powerful vehicles took off.

Despite navigating through large drifts of snow, the trip between the two houses only took a few minutes. Robert opened the door and couldn't hide his anxiety while waiting for Bessie and Penny to remove their clothing layers.

"Bessie, I think the baby is coming because as much as she denies it, I can see Kate is poorly. When I told her the pair of you were on your way over, she finally admitted she'd been having pains almost all day. The youngsters are worried because they know she's sick and can't get to a hospital. Dad's in town for a couple of days, or I would have sent them all next door to his house to stop them fretting."

"First things first, Robert. Take us to Kate, and then we'll see about the youngsters," Bessie told him.

When Robert brought them upstairs, it was evident Kate was relieved to see them.

"Bessie, Penny, am I ever glad to see you. I don't think this baby is going to wait for the storm to finish. He or she seems pretty determined to see this world."

Shooing Robert out of the room, Penny proceeded to examine and question Kate. After a few minutes, she nodded, saying Kate was right; she was definitely in labour, but it would be a few hours yet before Miss or Master Brown appeared. Penny reassured Kate by saying she and Bessie would be staying with her and not to worry. Then drawing Bessie aside, Penny suggested that she go downstairs with the children.

"I thought the children were too quiet and worried-looking when we came in. Is it possible for them to stay with a relative or a friend? I don't think they should stay here tonight. I believe Kate will be more relaxed knowing they're not in the house when she's in labour."

Kate, hearing this, was in complete agreement, saying she had been worrying about the children and how scared they might be if they heard her moaning or crying while in labour.

As Bessie went downstairs ready to suggest the youngsters could go to Martin House, she heard Robert arguing with the twins.

"Any other time, you'd be delighted to go to Maggie's house and stay overnight. And you too, Bobby, Mrs. Nora says you should stay with Michael. Look, here's Mrs. Bessie, see what she thinks. Maggie wants the twins to go over there for the night, and the Ryan boys would bring them by snowmobile, but they want to stay here. Isn't it better for them to go, Bessie?"

"Girls, it's what your mother wants, and it's the best thing for all of you. Lily and Pansy, why don't you have a quick visit with your Mom and then pack your nightclothes and go to Gabe's house. Bobby, you know Michael and his family enjoy having you there, so Robert, why don't you bring him to Nora's house on your snow machine. Once you talk to Sean and Nick about taking the girls, come back because we are going to need you," Bessie said.

"What about us, Mrs. Bessie. Nobody wants me and Daisy," a tearful Marigold cried.

"That's because everyone knows you'll be going to Martin House, that Miss Rose and I wouldn't let anyone else take you. When your Dad gets back from Ryan's, and Nick or Sean drops off the twins, they'll bring you over to Miss Rose, who is waiting for you. Why don't you get your pyjamas and toothbrushes and be ready to go? What do you think?"

With that, Marigold and Daisy threw themselves at Bessie and hugged her, while a much happier looking, Robert nodded thankfully. Within minutes Bobby was ready, and he and his father left for Ryan's.

Bessie then called Rose to alert her to the younger girls' arrival, adding that she would stay with Penny and Kate for now. Discussing where the girls would sleep, they decided it was best to put them in an upstairs bedroom near Rose. After asking about Kate, Rose said to tell the little girls how much she was looking forward to having them.

"Ask them whether they'd like to help me make macaroni and cheese for supper. It will be late, but I'll make a double lot, and Robert can come and get some for the rest of you."

A more relaxed Daisy and Marigold were happy when Bessie relayed Rose's message about making macaroni and cheese. When Bessie added they should bring their recipe books to enter the new dish, they became even more enthused about their upcoming visit to Martin House.

Within a half-hour, the five Brown children were gone to their temporary homes, but only after Bessie promised the twins their mother would be well looked after, and she would phone and let them know as soon as the baby arrived.

Daisy and Marigold were the last of her children to leave, Bessie told Kate. She recalled how good Sean and Nick were, each carefully placing a small girl at the front of their snow machines.

"The boys told them to hold on to the handles, then hopped on, snugly protecting the girls from behind. By then, Marigold and Daisy were so excited it took their minds off you, Kate. And now, what can I get the pair of you to eat and drink? Robert tells me you hardly ate a bite today Kate."

A more relaxed-looking Kate, thanks to Penny, who had helped her sponge bath and change into a clean nightgown, said she wasn't hungry.

However, Penny insisted that Kate eat something light to keep her strength up because she intended to have the mother-to-be up and walking around the bedroom and hall.

"Before going to Africa, I would have kept you in bed, but over the years, I watched African women stay active until almost the last minute before birth. Now I believe it speeds up labour, and the mother is also much more relaxed and comfortable. But before you start walking, you should at least have a cup of tea and maybe some toast. Why don't we have the same, Bessie? If you don't mind getting it ready, I'll help you carry it up here," Penny said.

When Robert returned home to an empty kitchen, he rushed upstairs to find the three women laughing and talking while enjoying their tea and toast.

"Oh, thank God, Kate, you're not in labour after all. I'm so glad you're feeling better and enjoying a cup of tea."

"I'm sorry to disappoint you, but I am in labour. However, being in labour doesn't mean I can't enjoy a cup of tea and good company. What's more, I'm getting out of bed when I finish this and walking around to get some exercise," Kate cheerfully replied.

"Bessie, what does Kate mean? Miss Harris, you're not going to let her out of bed, are you? She needs to be taking care of herself," a distressed-looking Robert said.

"Don't worry, Robert. It's Penny who wants Kate to start walking, and Penny knows what she's doing. She's delivered hundreds of babies and if she says walking is good for Kate, then I'm sure she's right. Now, I'm just about to take this tray downstairs; come with me, and I'll get you a cup of tea and a snack. That should do you until Rose has the macaroni and cheese ready."

Once back in the kitchen, Robert asked Bessie how confident she was in Penny? He said having Kate walk around upstairs didn't seem right to him.

"Robert, what do we know about delivering a baby? Nothing, and that's why I think we need to let Penny handle this her way. Think about Kate; doesn't she seem much more relaxed since Penny arrived?"

When Robert reluctantly agreed, Bessie said once he got something to eat, he should be thinking of getting the baby's cot ready. She wondered where Kate put the new diapers and clothing from the baby shower, knowing they needed washing before the baby used them. When she went upstairs and asked Kate, the mother-to-be got upset.

"Oh my, Bessie, I never washed them yet. I thought I had lots of time before going to the hospital. What am I going to do?" a distressed Kate asked.

"You can tell me where they are, and I'll get them washed and dried in no time at all. It's at a time like this that I bless the invention of washers and dryers. Don't stop walking, just tell me where the clothes are. Robert is out in the store bringing in the small cot. He tells me it's ready to use, that he gave it a new coat of paint a few weeks ago. He also showed me the cot mattress you ordered from the catalogue and, once the baby clothes and bedding are washed and dried, I'll make up the cot."

The baby items were washed, dried, folded, and the cot made up with fresh bedding in just over an hour. Bessie, trying to keep Robert's mind off what was happening upstairs, kept him busy by getting him to fold the clothes and engaging him in conversation.

"When the new arrival makes their appearance, we can bring the cot upstairs, but for now, it's better to leave it here in the warm kitchen. Tell me, Robert, have you and Kate picked out any names for the baby?

"Kate wasn't due until December, and because we thought it might be a Christmas baby, we spoke about names like Noel or Christopher for a boy and Holly or Carol for a girl. But this is November 29, not December, I don't know what Kate will want now, but for sure, she'll include a saint's name, just like the rest of our youngsters. Do you know if this is a saint's feast day?" Robert asked.

"No, but like every good Scot, I do know whose feast day it is tomorrow. It's November 30 and St. Andrew's Day. He's the patron saint of Scotland and the patron saint of fishermen."

"I'm a fisherman, but I never knew fishermen had a patron saint. And the only country I knew had a patron saint was Ireland," Robert replied.

"With you being a Catholic, you'd know St. Patrick was the patron saint of Ireland. Wasn't he supposed to have converted Ireland to Catholicism? But I'd have thought, being a fisherman, that you would have known about St Andrew. I wasn't a Catholic, but as a child, I had to learn all the patron saints of Britain, including St. George of England and St. David of Wales."

The telephone rang then, and when Robert answered it, Bessie heard him talking to one of his children, saying Kate was good. After saying he would leave to come over, he asked was there anything else they needed.

"That was a three-way conversation with Marigold and Daisy, who say they've made the macaroni and cheese as well as the 'bestest' ever raisin buns. Of course, they wanted to know about Kate. I don't think they realize she's having the baby, but because they've never seen her in bed during the day, they were worried. Now I need to look for their tea set because they're having a tea party. Poor Rose, I wonder if she knows what she's in for?" Robert said.

It was after seven before Robert returned with the food. His first thought was for Kate, asking how she was and was there any sign of the baby arriving?

Bessie, who had come downstairs a few minutes earlier after spending time with Kate and Penny, said there was no change.

"Penny believes this little one is in no hurry to get here, and Kate agrees, although she has some labour pains now and then. Your wife also gave me a message for you. She said the best thing you can do is to sit down and enjoy your supper. Kate has agreed to have some tea with one of the raisin buns the girls helped to make.

A short time later, Bessie carried a tray with two cups of tea and raisin buns up to the bedroom, where she was thanked by Penny, saying she was looking forward to a raisin bun and tea. She was surprised when Bessie replied the second tray setting was not for her.

"I'm staying up here with Kate, and you're going downstairs with Robert to have a good meal and to relax for at least an hour. Robert and I agree that looking at this storm, it will be Wednesday at the earliest before you get back to St. John's. It's gradually decreasing, but it may be tomorrow afternoon or even later before the main road is open. When Robert was at Martin House, your sister-in-law Beatrice phoned, wondering how you were coping. Rose told her what was happening and that you were all right, but Robert wants you to call and reassure your family."

Kate was also in favour of Penny phoning her family, saying no doubt they were worried. She asked her to tell Bishop and Mrs. Harris how grateful and fortunate she and Robert were to have Penny in Mark's Point at this time. Her final words to Penny were not to come back upstairs for at least an hour.

Penny reluctantly went downstairs, telling Kate to call her if anything changed. Meanwhile, a relaxed Kate sat on the side of her bed, enjoying her tea and a raisin bun, and chatting to Bessie.

"I hope when this baby arrives, it will be as undemanding as it is now. He or she is certainly not looking for attention as there's been little movement in the past hour or more. Maybe it's just enjoying all the walking." Kate said.

Apart from a few grimaces of pain, the next hour passed uneventfully for Kate as she walked around and talked to Bessie. When she heard steps on the stairs and saw Penny appear, she shook her head, saying there was no change.

"It's almost nine now. I don't think this child has any intention of making an appearance tonight. I think it must be a boy, slow and steady just like Bobby; not taking after the girls who are far more impatient and always have to be doing something."

"I think maybe it's you who are impatient. This baby may be taking its time, but look out when it's ready. We will see who is slow and steady then. Bessie, you need to have a break and eat something. I spoke to Beatrice and Clarence, who wish you both well, and Kate, they said they are praying for you and the baby."

On the way downstairs, the phone began to ring, and Bessie heard Robert answer. As she passed the living room, he called out to her, saying Nurse Holland was on the phone and would Bessie talk to her about Kate.

"Bessie, I just heard Kate is in labour and that a trained midwife who is staying with you is looking after her. Is this right? How is Kate doing, and am I needed?"

Bessie answered Nurse Holland's questions for the next few minutes while assuring her that Kate was in good hands by relating Penny's training and experience. Once satisfied that Kate was doing well and in capable hands, the Public Health nurse wanted to know more about Penny's nursing background.

Bessie told her how Penny was a missionary nurse in Africa for many years and visiting Martin House for the weekend. When asked where Penny was working, she replied she wasn't working, nor did she know her plans.

"I might have known it was Lucy who told Nurse Holland," Bessie said to Robert after she concluded the phone call.

Nurse Holland not only heard from Lucy but also Millicent Murphy. Hearing Kate was in labour, Millicent said her husband Dave was ready to organize a group of men to take the nurse to Mark's Point by snowmobile.

"That's why Nurse Holland wanted to hear for herself that Kate had a trained nurse with her. She was ready to travel by snowmobile, saying it wouldn't be her first emergency. Two years ago, she was called out to Mossy Brook during a storm and went by snowmobile. She says when the roads get cleared tomorrow, she'll come regardless if the baby has arrived or not. In the meantime, she said to tell Penny not to hesitate to call her.

"Lucy will never change. She just loves relaying news. However, Nurse Holland did say Lucy insisted Kate was in good hands, saying Penny had to be good if Rose and I trusted her because we wouldn't let anything happen to Kate."

Noticing how jumpy Robert was, Bessie suggested he nap on the day bed while he had the chance. But it was the last thing on Robert's mind as he paced between the kitchen and the bottom of the stairs. When Kate, who was walking around the hall upstairs, saw him, she asked was he keeping time with her.

"Are you alright, Kate? Is there anything I can get you?" a worried-looking Robert asked.

Taking pity on him, Kate asked if he could bring her a glass of cold water. The words were scarcely out of her mouth when Robert had ice cubes from the fridge freezer placed in a tall glass and had the tap running until the water was icy cold. Taking the stairs two at a time, he passed over the glass of water to his wife, asking what else he could get her.

"Why don't you do the same as me and relax? Didn't I hear Bessie telling you to take a nap? I think that's a great idea because once this baby is born, neither one of us will get a lot of sleep."

But Robert had no intention of lying down, and to keep him occupied, Bessie, who had opened the back door to check on the weather, came up with another suggestion.

"I know it's after 10 o'clock, but for sure, the Ryans or Gabe have not gone to bed yet, knowing Kate is in labour. The wind has died down, and it's not snowing nearly as bad as it was earlier. Why don't you take a run over on your snow machine to check on Bobby, then swing by Gabe's house and see the twins? I imagine the three of them could use some reassurance that their mother is okay."

Robert's objection that he couldn't leave Kate was quickly squashed by Kate, who had been listening at the top of the stairs. She agreed with Bessie, saying it was a great idea.

"I'm not worried about the little ones because they don't realize I am having this baby, and I know they are having a great time with Rose. It's different with Bobby and the twins, who know I'm in labour. They could be imagining all kinds of things. It would take a load off my mind if you saw them and told them that I'm doing well. Say that I know they're looking forward to meeting their new brother or sister, but that won't be happening very soon, that they should go to bed and get a good night's sleep."

Kate's prediction that nothing would happen was quickly proven wrong when shortly after 11, Penny called out to Bessie, asking her to come upstairs. When she went into the bedroom, a flushed-looking Kate was lying on the bed.

"We're thinking this baby is starting to get serious about seeing the outside world. Bessie, perhaps you'll help me make up the bed with this rubber mattress protector and these sheets while Kate sits on the chair," Penny said.

"I've older sheets to put under me. I don't want to use my good ones, and Penny is right; I'm sure this baby is ready to see the world. Is Robert still gone?" Kate asked.

When Bessie said he was, Kate replied that was a good thing as he would probably get upset when the baby started to come in earnest.

"Poor Robert, I don't think he has any idea about what a woman goes through at this time. With the others, he just had to drop me off at the hospital and wasn't allowed to see me again until after the baby was born."

Once the bed was re-made, Bessie got a basin of warm water from the bathroom to sponge down the expectant mother. Meanwhile, Penny checked items Bessie and Robert had picked up for her earlier, including scissors, string, clean towels, face cloth, a receiving blanket, and baby clothes.

"Good, and I see there's an electric outlet by the bed. Bessie, do you think you could bring up another bowl? And I will need a kettle of water that I can boil here to sterilize the scissors."

Bessie was following Penny's instructions when Robert returned. Seeing her with the kettle on her way back upstairs, he wanted to know what was happening.

"Kate's doing fine. Penny just wants this kettle handy upstairs, but the other kettle is still on your wood stove. When I come back down, I'll get you a cup of tea. Meanwhile, Kate is sure to ask about Bobby and the twins. How were they?"

Bobby was the best kind, but according to Robert, the twins were 'skittish.'

"It's easy to see they're worried about Kate, but I told them nothing was happening right now, that it looked as if the baby would wait until tomorrow. They're glad Kate's fine, but they also want this baby to arrive soon. I did get them to promise to go to bed, saying I'd be over to pick them up first thing in the morning."

Looking at the clock, which now read 11.15, he added that it looked as if the baby wasn't in a hurry, and it could be well into the following morning before it made its entrance.

Robert was correct in one respect. It was the following morning, although just an hour later before anything happened. At 16 minutes past midnight, Kate delivered a healthy baby boy. When Penny cut the umbilical cord, and the newest Brown family member gave a small cry announcing his arrival, she passed him over to Bessie, who wrapped him warmly in a blanket before putting him in Kate's arms. Then going to the top of the stairs, she called out to Robert, telling him to come up.

"Kate, Kate, are you alright?" a frightened Robert asked, rushing in the door. Then looking at her, he noticed the baby.

"Oh my God, Kate. The baby is here, and I didn't even know. I never heard a sound from you. Why didn't you call me?"

"And pray tell me, what could you have done?" Kate asked, laughing.

"Now, do you want to see your baby son or not?"

"A boy? You had a boy? Oh my, Bobby will be some happy to have a brother, and so will all the girls. Oh, Kate, what a beauty he is."

"We'll be cleaning him up soon, and I also have to attend to Kate. While I'm doing that, do you have a measuring tape you can get so we can see how long he is? Kate tells me you have bedroom scales that we will also need. If you go and get them, I'll let you know when you should return," Penny told Robert.

Bessie, who now had another pan of warm water, gently washed the tiny baby while Penny tended to Kate. Patting him dry, she diapered and dressed him and snugly wrapped him in another clean blanket.

"I wonder how heavy he is? As I dressed him, I was trying to guess his weight, I don't think he's as heavy as a seven-pound bag of flour, but he weighs a good bit more than a five-pound bag of sugar." Bessie said to Kate.

Once Penny finished with the new mother, she called Robert, who not only had the tape and scales ready, he had brought the cot from the kitchen and had it by the bedroom door.

When Kate asked Robert to step on the scales and tell them his weight, her mystified husband asked why? The baby needed weighing, not him.

"As smart as I know he is, I can't see our baby hopping onto the scales, can you?" Kate asked.

"Once Penny sees how much you weigh, she'll hand you the baby and see what the pair of you weigh, then deduct your weight. That's how we'll know how heavy our son is. Bessie thinks he might be over six pounds."

The weighing over, Penny said Bessie's guess was close as the baby was 6 pounds, 3 ounces. Then using the tape measure, she announced he was 21 inches in length.

"Robert, if you go downstairs and put the kettle on, Bessie and I will help Kate to the chair then make up the bed with clean sheets. When Kate gets washed and changed, we will leave the pair of you in peace with your new son.

"After all this, I'm sure we could all use what Bessie calls a 'good cup of tea' and Kate, how do you fancy one of Marigold and Daisy's 'bestest' raisin buns?"

CHAPTER 30

Decisions – Decisions

T he Brown's kitchen was never quiet at the best of times. The morning of November 30th was no exception as the younger family members began to gather.

"Where's our new baby? Is it a sister or a brother? Where's Mom? Why do we have to sit here? Bobby, did you see the baby? Where's the twins?"

The questions came pouring out from Marigold and Daisy, who were unhappy that their father had restricted them to the kitchen after the Ryan brothers dropped them off at their home.

"We're waiting for Lily and Pansy. As for Bobby, he knows no more than you. Everyone will see the newest member of our family together. Nurse Harris and Mrs. Bessie, who were here all night, are waiting to find out the baby's name when you do. As soon as Lily and Pansy arrive, your mother will bring the baby to meet you," Robert said on his way upstairs.

A few minutes later, the twins came rushing into the kitchen and were not at all pleased to see their sisters and Bobby already there.

"Did you see our baby?" Pansy demanded to know.

"You are all going to see the baby together, and now you're here. I would say that is about to happen because I hear someone coming downstairs," Bessie said.

It was Penny carrying the baby and behind her was Robert holding Kate's arm. Guiding Kate to the rocking chair, he stepped back to let Penny gently lay the baby in her arms. As the children rushed forward to see him, Robert said, "Meet your brother, Andrew Harris Martin Brown.

"He was born early this morning, November 30, and is named after St. Andrew, whose feast day this is. His second name is Harris, called after Nurse Penny, who brought your new brother into this world. I don't know what we would have done without her. And of course, Martin is for our good friend Mrs. Bessie, who stayed here since yesterday making sure everything went well. Now, what do you think of your new brother?" Robert asked, looking around at his children.

While the four girls started to argue who would hold the baby first, Bobby was content to stand behind Kate, gazing down at his brother.

"Sit down, Bobby, and I'll let you hold the baby. You've finally got a brother, and one of these days, he'll be sharing your bedroom," Kate said.

"I don't care. Wait 'till Michael sees him. He's some small now, but we'll show him how to play hockey and ride a bike when he is big," replied Bobby.

"We like his name, don't we, Daisy?" asked Marigold.

"When is it our turn to hold him? Wait till we tell Beverly and our teachers and friends. Aren't we lucky to have the most beautiful baby brother?"

"Yes, Marigold, he's beautiful, but how come he was born here? I thought babies was born in hospitals. Isn't that right, Penny? What does Dad mean you brought him? Nobody could get any place to get anything in the storm."

With that, Kate interrupted, "Daisy and Marigold, you said your new brother was beautiful. Your father and I thought for sure you would say he was the 'bestest' baby ever."

"You tells us it's not a word. We're big sisters now, and we're not going to say it anymore; are we, Daisy?"

Daisy was too busy watching the baby to speak, although she nodded her head in agreement. At Lily's insistence, Bobby had reluctantly passed Andrew over to her, and Daisy was watching for an opportunity to hold her baby brother.

The phone, which had been ringing nonstop since the early hours, rang again. Nora Ryan, who called, said the plow had arrived in Mark's Point, and the main road would soon open to traffic.

It was almost noon before Bessie and Penny arrived back at Martin House. Once the main road was clear, Gabe, David, Dan Ryan, and his sons got together and shovelled the driveway to the Bed and Breakfast, while Robert and Bobby cleared their own much smaller driveway allowing Robert to get his car out to drive the women home.

Before leaving the Brown house, Penny had insisted Kate go back to bed once the baby successfully fed again. Giving the twins a quick lesson on changing their brother's diaper, she promised to return and check on Kate and the baby that night. At Martin House, Rose was eager to hear the news of Kate, the newest Brown family member, and the children's reactions to their baby brother.

"You both must be tired, but before you lie down for a few hours' rest, have a light lunch. I'm making stew for our main meal this evening. I hope, Bessie, you didn't plan to use those two packs of stewing meat for anything special because I took them out of the freezer last night. There's over four pounds of meat, more than enough to feed us, and the Browns. I told Robert to come back at five, and I'll have a pot of stew for their supper.

"Meanwhile, Lucy has also been thinking about the Browns. She's mixing bread, and when Robert picks up the stew, Jim is bringing over several loaves. Lucy says having six children now, the family will need lots of bread."

Bessie and Penny were resting later that afternoon, and Rose was preparing the evening meal when a knock came at the back door. Opening it to find Nurse Holland, Rose ushered her into the warmth of the kitchen.

"I was here in Mark's Point, visiting Kate and her baby, and I wanted to speak to Nurse Harris before she left for St. John's. Is she here, Rose?"

Saying Penny and Bessie were still resting but had planned to get up about this time, Rose went and knocked on Penny's door, then returned to her visitor in the kitchen.

"I'll put the kettle on, so we can have a spot of tea. What did you think of the baby? I haven't seen him yet, but Penny and I are dropping over after supper. From what I hear, he's a little beauty."

"He certainly is. Kate's so lucky that Nurse Harris was visiting here. She did an excellent job. According to Kate, it was her easiest delivery; much better than any of her hospital births."

When Penny came into the kitchen and met Nurse Holland, Rose suggested the nurses go into the sitting room, where she would bring them tea and biscuits. It was almost half an hour later before they came back, with Nurse Holland saying she had to get home before it got too late. However, her parting words to Penny left the sisters-in-law puzzled.

"Kate having her baby at home now might be the best thing to happen in this area for a long time. I'll expect your phone call by Friday at the latest, and I'm hoping it will be good news. You should tell Bessie and Rose about our talk. I'm sure they will agree with me."

When Nurse Holland left, Penny looked slightly bemused.

"That was an unexpected conversation. Perhaps when we finish dinner and are having a cup of tea, we could discuss it. Is that alright with you? I'd like to do so before speaking to Clarence and Beatrice, who are calling at six."

As they relaxed after their meal, Penny spoke about her surprise when she realized what Nurse Holland had in her mind. Thinking she wanted to talk about Kate or the baby, it came as a shock to Penny when Nurse Holland asked about her future nursing plans. She then said her job was available and suggested Penny should apply for it. Nurse Holland had hoped to retire earlier, but there was no response when the government advertised her position. With no one to take her place, she felt she couldn't leave the area without a nurse.

But Penny said she had given up on the idea of nursing since learning she couldn't return to her life as a missionary. Knowing the need for nurses in Africa, she felt she had let her patients down.

"Nurse Holland told me I didn't have to go to Africa to be needed, asking if I felt needed when I helped Kate. You know, I hadn't thought of it that way, but she's right. Kate did need me, and it was such a good feeling being there, reassuring her and helping bring Andrew into the world."

As Nurse Holland spoke about her work, Penny realized it wasn't much different from her African nursing duties. They both ran pre-natal classes and well-baby clinics. They also treated minor illnesses for people of all ages and changed dressings for patients recovering from surgery.

"Nurse Holland tells me there is a three-bedroom bungalow provided in Murphy's Cove next to the clinic. I would need a car, but the strangest thing about this is that I took a driver refresher course after my first visit to Martin

House, thinking it was time I stopped relying on my family for transportation. I've also considered buying a small car since receiving a lump sum payment from my insurance because of my hospitalization with the tropical disease."

Bessie and Rose agreed Penny should seriously consider taking the position. They pointed out the benefits, not only for the area but also for Penny.

"I know you would like to speak to your brother and Beatrice first, but you say you feel as if everything is falling in place, and that's exactly what I am thinking. Deciding to come here with Bishop Harris and Beatrice was fate taking a hand in your future. Without that visit, you wouldn't have returned or been here to help Kate during the storm. It makes me even more certain that this is the place and job for you. What do you think, Rose?"

Rose agreed and wasn't the only one. When the Bishop and Beatrice rang, they were quick to give the idea their blessing. Although they would miss having Penny if she accepted the position, they said they would enjoy visiting her in such a beautiful part of the island.

"We talk about this job as if it were mine for the taking, but what if I'm not suitable. I'll need a medical and may not pass it, and it's almost 20 years since I trained in Newfoundland. Perhaps my skills are out of date."

Beatrice, on the other end of the phone line, reprimanded Penny.

"Where are you getting all those doubts? I thought you were back to your old, enthusiastic, and positive self. I'm not saying you should make a final decision tonight. Take time and seriously consider it. Why don't you spend a few more days in Mark's Point, and perhaps you can hire someone to go to Murphy's Cove. Look at the set-up of the clinic and maybe visit some of the communities where you would work if you did accept the position."

Penny was still thinking about Beatrice's advice when she visited Kate to check on the new mother and baby. She found herself telling Kate about the job opportunity.

"Now, Penny, you don't need to ask me what I think. Robert and I are your biggest fans. Neither one of us want to imagine what might have happened without you. Take the job. It's the new start you need, and I know two little girls who will be over the moon if you stay. Then too, there's been plenty of worried people in these communities knowing Nurse Holland wanted to retire, and no one seemed interested in taking her place."

A knock on the bedroom door ended the conversation, and Penny quickly asked Kate not to mention her news to anyone apart from Bessie or Rose. Nodding her agreement as Penny opened the door to a young woman, Kate introduced her sister Jean to the nurse.

"Jean couldn't get here yesterday because of the storm. She insists she's making up for it by staying until Friday evening when the twins finish school for the weekend."

"Someone in the family should be here. Mom was so upset when she heard the baby was born in the middle of a storm. Thank you, Nurse Harris, from both of us. Mom imagined all the things that might have happened if you weren't here to look after Kate."

As the women chatted, Penny asked Jean if she had any children.

"We have three boys, and our only girl turned 11 last week. My husband Tim is looking after them. He and Robert are fishing partners, and with the season over, he spends most of his time in the store mending nets and gear. Kevin, our four-year-old and the only one not in school, loves to be with his father in the store. Tim figures he's the next fisherman in our family."

Jean said she brought over the second small cot that once belonged to the twins before Kate passed it on to her. Jean thought the extra crib should be kept in the kitchen. The baby could use it during the day while the other cot would stay upstairs for his use at night. It had a mattress, but Jean wanted sheets and a light blanket to make it up.

Kate agreed that having the second cot downstairs made good sense. Laughing, she also promised to return it if Jean needed it in the future.

"Don't you go worrying about that possibility. I've no intention of trying to catch up with you, considering the size of your family. Although looking at this little beauty sleeping so peacefully, I do miss having a baby around the house," Jean said almost wistfully as she left the room.

"I really don't need Jean to help, but I will enjoy having her here. I could be downstairs now, but with the youngsters all fussing over the baby, I told them he and I both needed a nap. Tomorrow I'll get up and dress when the school buses leave and bring the baby downstairs for most of the day."

Rising to leave and promising to return the following day, Penny told Kate to take advantage of Jean's help, as she needed to regain her strength.

Thursday was a sunny, crisp day when Penny, Rose and Bessie drove to Murphy's Cove to visit the clinic and the nurse's house. It had been a quiet morning at the clinic, according to Nurse Holland. She didn't travel on Thursdays but had a drop-in clinic in the morning and pre-natal classes at two. Apart from dressing a cut hand, filling out medical forms and calming down a young mother, who mistakenly thought her toddler had measles, her morning had been uneventful.

"A doctor, usually Doctor Hann from the cottage hospital, has clinics here two days a week. I check the patient's temperature, pulse and blood pressure before the doctor sees the patient, and sometimes I'm asked to stay during examinations. There's plenty of variety with this job, and I've enjoyed working here since the clinic opened in 1960. My youngest daughter was in university at the time. Now both my girls are married, and I'm looking forward to retiring back to the city and spending more time with them and my grandchildren."

After viewing the nurse's house, Penny met some of Bessie and Rose's friends on the return journey home. Millicent was in her shop when the women picked up a few groceries, and Penny was introduced to Mina when they stopped in Murphy's Cove East long enough for Bessie to give her friend some suet and minced meat. After travelling through Basket Cove and Fisherman's Creek to Mossy Brook, she met Maureen when Rose and Bessie made appointments to have their hair styled before Christmas. Having visited Freeman Beach during her earlier visit, there was no need to head in that direction. Instead, they returned to Mark's Point before continuing to Muddy Brook Cove and Mark's Landing to allow Penny to see that part of the district.

"When you go back to St. John's tomorrow, you'll pass through Northfield and two communities with names you're sure to like: Penny's Cove and Lower Penny's Cove. They are at the farthest end of the nursing district. The roads we travelled today usually have quite a bit of traffic, and of course, school buses go to and from Murphy's Cove each weekday," Rose told Penny.

When taxi driver Ted Brown stopped at Martin House the following day, Bessie asked if he would point out Penny's Cove to the nurse when he approached the community.

"Not too many people can boast of communities bearing their name. Don't you think it's a sign you are supposed to return here permanently?" a smiling Bessie asked, giving Penny a goodbye hug.

The house seemed quiet after Penny left, but it wouldn't stay that way much longer, Rose pointed out. Not only was Maggie scheduled for a piano lesson after school, but David and his four guitar students were also coming to practice a Christmas carol with her.

"They'll be here directly off the school bus. That way, the boys from Muddy Brook Cove don't have to turn around and come back. David will drive them home after practice. Four growing boys will most likely be hungry and would probably appreciate sandwiches and cookies. The bus usually arrives at quarter to four, and if we give them 15 minutes to relax and eat, they will have about an hour to practice. We should be finished by five," Rose said.

"With lots of time before our first weekly bingo game in Mark's Point," Bessie remarked.

"How can I forget, considering that's about all Millicent spoke about yesterday when we were in Murphy's Cove. I never saw anyone so excited about a game. She couldn't believe it when I told her I wouldn't be there. I don't mind going when it's my turn to work and, according to the schedule Sean made up, that's in two weeks. Who else is on your group tonight?"

"Sean, Kelly, Nora, and Patsy. Robert is also in our group, but David is taking his place tonight. Now, if we're going to make cookies, we should get started. It's a good thing I stocked up on extra baking supplies at Millicent's, knowing Maggie and the twins were planning to make cakes tomorrow. Did I tell you only Lily is coming now? Pansy is staying home to help Kate."

"For a house with only two middle-aged women, we seem to have a fair share of young folks around here lately, and I must say I enjoy their company," Rose said.

"If you're making cookies, I'll strip Penny's bed, then clean the room after I put the bedclothes in the washer. I don't say we'll have many guests this month."

Rose was on her way upstairs as the phone rang, and Bessie answered. It was Jack looking to stay at Martin House on the 13th and 14th of the month.

"Angela flies home on the 13th. I'm picking her up at the airport and driving her home. She's phoning Gabe and Maggie tonight to tell them. That way, they will know we are friends, and I'll be able to visit her while I am in Mark's Point. What do you think, Bessie? I hope Maggie and Gabe will be alright with Angela and me seeing each other."

But Bessie was sure both Maggie and Gabe would welcome Jack. She told Jack how much she and Rose enjoyed using his apartment when they were in town, and by way of returning the favour, would not be charging Jack to stay in Martin House during his upcoming visit.

The following morning, Maggie and Lily had plenty to talk about as they prepared their cakes for the oven. Maggie's practice with the boys was the first topic raised by Lily.

"Are Bobby and Michael as good on guitar as they think they are? Me and Pansy want to learn to play guitar when Mr. Nolan starts classes again, but not if Michael and Bobby teach us. They say when the new lessons start, they will be helping Mr. Nolan teach. Did you ever hear the like?" an indignant Lily asked.

When Rose and Maggie agreed the boys were doing well on guitar, Lily shook her head. Changing the subject, she said Pansy had been close to winning the $50 bingo jackpot.

"She was," Maggie confirmed.

"Pansy waited for ages for B14, and it never came out. A woman from Freeman's Cove won the consolation prize, and next week the jackpot is going up to $60. Mrs. Millicent was some lucky. She won twice, $10 each time. There was a big crowd at bingo, wasn't there, Aunt Bessie?"

Bessie agreed, adding it looked as if the weekly bingo game might be a good fundraiser. Noting Lily wasn't at bingo, she asked her if she didn't like the game.

"I do, but for now, I'm taking turns with Pansy at doing things. It's my turn today, and that's why I'm making the cake, and Pansy is at home. We don't want to be leaving Mom on her own with the little girls and the baby. He's some good baby. He hardly cries at all even 'though Marigold and Daisy are always poking at him, wanting to be holding him."

"Your mother is a lucky woman having you girls to help, and speaking about mothers, you must be excited Maggie with your Mom coming home," Rose said.

When Maggie said Angela was flying into St. John's on the 13th, Lily asked if she would be home for the elementary school concert.

The school's first-ever concert was taking place on the 14th, she said, and when Marigold and Daisy were not talking about the baby, they were practicing their parts or singing carols. Daisy had the innkeeper's wife's role in the Nativity play and was singing with her classmates. Marigold was also singing and reciting a verse of a Christmas poem.

Once the cakes were in the oven and the dishes washed up, the girls prepared to leave, knowing it would be a couple of hours, at least before the cakes were ready to come out of the oven. Lily wanted to get home to check up on the baby while Maggie and Gabe went to Murphy's Cove to buy Christmas tree lights and decorations.

"Did you know Pop didn't put up a Christmas tree for years? He didn't have any lights, but we found a few decorations in a box in the attic. Next Saturday me and Pop are taking Nell and going in the woods to get a tree. Pop says he's going to cut one for you at the same time. We'll decorate our tree next Sunday; that's the day before Mom arrives, and when we come home from Murphy's Cove today, I'm going to start cleaning to make sure the house is ready for Mom and Christmas."

"Is your Pop going in for your Mom, or is she coming by taxi?" Lily asked

When Maggie said Mr. Jack Matthews was driving Angela home, Lily asked why. Looking at the women as if for confirmation, Maggie said he and Angela were friends, and he would be staying at Martin House for a couple of days.

Later, Bessie was telling Rose that listening to the girls made her smile.

"You wouldn't know, but they were housewives. What with Lily talking about looking after the baby and Maggie about house cleaning. It's serious business to them, but I know for sure Angela couldn't care less about how clean the house is; it's Maggie and Gabe she wants to see. As for Kate, although she appreciates the twins helping, she might let them take turns staying home this week, but knowing her, she'll make sure neither Lily and Pansy miss out on anything after this."

Later that night, while most Mark's Point residents were attending Saturday night mass in the local church, Bessie wrote Christmas cards to her relatives in Scotland. She had just finished a long newsy letter to enclose in her brother Duncan's card when she thought she heard voices coming from the porch. She had a pleasant surprise when Nora and Dan Ryan appeared.

"I hope you're not busy, Bessie, because we hoped to talk to you and Rose. I mentioned it to Rose after mass. She's practicing some Christmas music with the choir but told us to come over, and by the time the kettle boils, she'll be home," said Nora.

"That sounds like Rose," Bessie said, laughing.

"Come and sit down. You know you don't have to ask or wait until you have something to talk about before visiting us."

"Gosh, Bessie, it's ages since we were here because we were away the time of Rose's birthday. I was just saying to Nora that we hadn't played any cards since Alex died. I think that's why Pat was so eager to see weekly cards games begin. He also misses coming here. With Gabe making up six, we had some wonderful grand games of 120s in your kitchen," Dan reminisced.

Bessie admitted she was glad when the weekly card games started. She had previously considered having cards again in her house, but Rose wasn't much of a card player. But when she reluctantly tried playing cards at the school, Rose enjoyed herself. It had Bessie thinking about getting her friends together again for a game in the new year. Alex always liked playing cards, she told Nora and Dan, and he'd be the first to say the weekly games should continue.

True to her word, Rose pulled into the driveway as Bessie began to pour the tea.

"Just what I needed, a good cup of tea. Honestly, the Brown girls, who are usually so good, were in a right snit with Bobby and Michael all through practice. It's all about guitar lessons, and of course, David wasn't at practice tonight to sort it out. He left right after mass to go to the school to help get the stage ready for the Christmas concert."

Rose related how the boys took great delight in tormenting the twins by saying Mr. Nolan asked them to help with guitar classes.

"Telling the girls if they wanted to learn how to play the guitar, they would be their teachers, did not sit well with the twins," Rose recalled.

Bessie said she knew Lily was far from happy about the possibility of the boys teaching guitar because she spoke about it earlier that day when she and Maggie were mixing their cakes.

"But enough about guitar lessons, we'll leave David to fix that situation. What is it that you want to talk about, Nora and Dan?" Bessie asked.

"That Michael. I'll speak to him about tormenting the girls. Meanwhile, it's two other sons of ours that we want to discuss. Tell me, Bessie, did Alex ever sell his land by the crossroads?"

"I know the land you mean, Nora. Alex would say it would make an ideal spot for a garage, with it being on the main road. When Sean took the mechanics course and later worked at his trade in St. John's, Alex always said the land was his if he came back to build a garage. Instead, Sean came home and starting fishing with you, Dan. Is he thinking about starting up a garage? I hope he knows the land is his if he wants it."

"Yes, he wants to open a garage, but this is about more than Sean. It's also about Sam and his wife, Denise. You know Sam has been in the Army for ten years. Well, he's decided not to re-enlist but to come home and become Dan's fishing partner. They are going to invest in a long-liner. Meanwhile, Denise is a head cook in a hotel, but she has always wanted to open a restaurant. Sean and Denise hope to join forces and open a garage with an attached restaurant. That's why we're asking if the land was still available."

Nora continued talking about her sons and daughter-in-law's plans, saying the new school's opening was a factor in Sam and Denise's decision. They had one boy who would be starting school next year and a younger daughter. Although eager to return to Sam's home, the idea of their children attending a one-roomed school had not appealed to them.

"There's something else. Because this a big investment, Sean has accepted a six-month position as a mechanic in Frobisher Bay and begins work next month. We'll miss him, and so will Kelly, but going up North is his opportunity to make good money. Between his earnings and savings, and Denise's investment, they will have enough to start construction in Spring. They hope the business will be ready to open next year. That young fellow in Mossy Brook, Jerome Maloney, will be in charge of the construction and is hiring two other workers to help. Sean's heart was never in the fishery, but at the time, there was no one else to fish with his father, and he didn't want him alone in the boat." Nora said.

Later that night, Rose and Bessie were still discussing Nora and Dan's visit. The Ryan family had not planned in haste. It was evident that a great deal of thought and research had gone into the decision. Sean moving away for six months would be a loss to their committee, but a future garage and restaurant was encouraging news for the entire area.

"I thought we were going to have a battle on our hands after Sean arrived, and he started talking about the price of the land," Rose said.

"Sean, Nora and Dan were so insistent about paying the full land value, saying their family had budgeted the cost into their plans. When you said it was Alex's wish for Sean to have the land to use for a garage, then put the bill of sale in his name, asking him for one dollar to make it legal, did you notice his face? It was a mixture of emotions, but there was no mistaking his feelings when he held that piece of paper. I almost cried when he thanked us, saying he would never forget what the Martin family did for him, nor would he ever give us cause to regret the decision. It's a good thing you did here tonight, Bessie. Alex would be proud."

"You are right, Rose. Alex often said we needed a good garage in this area, and we had a prime piece of land to put it on. When Sean began his mechanic's course, Alex told him if the day ever came when he wanted to build a garage, the land by the crossroads was his. There's also more land if he or Sam wanted to build a home near the business. Yes, the more I think about it, I feel sure Sean made a good decision and speaking about decisions, I wonder when we'll hear from Penny?"

On Monday evening, Rose answered the telephone to an excited Penny, saying the job was hers. She had visited the Department of Health offices that morning to fill out an application and returned for an interview in the afternoon.

"I was shocked they wanted me back that soon. After being interviewed by a government official and a nurse, they said Nurse Holland told them if I applied, to make sure I didn't leave without agreeing to accept the job. They knew I delivered Kate's baby. After asking lots of questions, they wanted to know when I could start work. They've set up a medical for me tomorrow, and if all goes well, I'll train in town for two weeks, then spend January with Nurse Holland. After that, I'm on my own as your Public Health nurse."

After telling a delighted Bessie about Penny accepting the position, Rose called Kate and shared the good news.

"Isn't that wonderful? Just wait until Marigold and Daisy realize Penny will be living and working in this area. I can hear them now announcing the news to their teachers about their friend Penny. And while I have you on the phone, Robert talked to Father Kiely about baptizing Andrew. It's next Sunday afternoon, and David and Sharon have agreed to be his godparents. Of course, we want you and Bessie to be there. Lily wants to use the cake she baked for the christening, and Agnes, who is arriving on Thursday, has offered to decorate it."

The days flew past as Rose and Bessie caught up with house cleaning and baking as they prepared for Christmas. Saturday morning found them trying to decide what to bring to the reception following the christening.

"We have cookies, and there's that half-pound of cheese we picked up at the shop the other day that would go well with crackers. I think I'll run over to the shop and see what kind of crackers I can get to do up a cheese platter," Bessie said.

As she went out to go to the shop, she was met by a rosy-faced Maggie, asking her to come down to the road and choose her Christmas tree.

"Mr. and Mrs. Nolan came in the woods with us. We cut three trees, and we had a boil-up over a fire Pop made. We had a great time Aunt Bessie. The three trees are lovely, and Pop and Mrs. Nolan say you should pick the tree you want first."

As they walked down the garden path, Maggie was all talk about Christmas trees and how she had convinced Gabe to put lights on his big rose bush. She had just told Bessie that Gabe was making another trip to Murphy's Shop to pick up outdoor lights on Monday when Sharon, who was perched happily on Gabe's slide, called out.

"Bessie, what a wonderful time we've had. Gabe made a fire, and we fried baloney and heated beans. It was a great feed, and we made tea over the fire. It's the best time I've ever had outdoors, and look at Nell; isn't she a grand horse? Remember Gabe telling us about going in the woods and looking for a buddy; well, if I didn't have to teach, I'd be going with him all the time. I had such a great time, and now I feel guilty having so much fun while Mom stayed at home decorating the christening cake and making cookies."

By now, Gabe had a large fir tree hauled from the slide and held it up for Bessie's inspection. When she declared it perfect for Martin House, Gabe brought it up to her store, saying it would need at least a day to dry before bringing it into the house. The teachers and Maggie then joined him on the old wood slide and made their way home.

Christenings in Mark's Point were generally small affairs, but quite a few people came the following day to witness Andrew Harris Martin Brown's welcome into the church.

Bessie, Rose, and Agnes had volunteered to get everything ready for the reception at the Brown's home and left the church as soon as the ceremony finished. While the others stayed to have photographs taken, the women were busy preparing food and refreshments in Kate's kitchen.

"It's just like a party, isn't it, Daisy?" Marigold said, eyeing up all the food when the family returned.

"But how come the twins and Bobby's friends are here, and lots of grown-ups and none of our friends was asked to Andrew's christening?"

"Marigold! These are all our friends. I'm sure Mrs. Bessie and Miss Rose would be hurt to hear you say you had no friends here, especially after them doing so much for the pair of you," Kate said reprovingly.

"Your school friends don't live in Mark's Point like Maggie, Theresa, and Michael, but you do have your cousins here from Mark's Landing, so don't let me hear you talk that way again."

After the christening party, Bessie stayed behind with Kate when Rose, Robert and the children went back to church. Taking advantage of the church being warm because of the christening, Father Kiely had decided to schedule Benediction.

"Lily and Pansy are happy since they heard Bobby and Michael would only help David with guitar lessons for younger beginners. David will continue to teach the older ones. It's a good thing, considering I had two guitars come from the catalogue weeks ago for the twins' Christmas. I thought I might have to send them back, knowing there was no way they would take lessons from Bobby and Michael.

"And speaking about lessons and music, are you going to the school concert, Bessie? There are two concerts, one in the afternoon to allow parents with small children to attend."

When Bessie said she and Rose planned to go at night, Kate asked if she'd consider looking after Andrew to allow her to go to the afternoon performance.

"Robert will have to go at night to take the youngsters back and forth, but he wants to drive me that afternoon in case of weather. Marigold and Daisy would never forgive me if I didn't see their first school concert. I could take the baby, but the girls would be inviting their classmates to meet their new brother. Just think of the coughs, sneezes, and grimy hands he'd be exposed to if I did bring him."

Bessie was happy to be asked, saying she would gladly babysit at any time. As Kate began to get the baby's bottle ready to feed him, Bessie asked to do it, saying if she was going to babysit Andrew, Kate needed to see she could do it properly.

Later, when Robert and the younger girls arrived home from Benediction, Daisy was all talk about the upcoming concert.

"Mrs. Bessie, is you and Miss Rose coming to our concert? I'm the inn-keeper's wife, and our play is all about Baby Jesus. I told Miss that our baby would be a good Baby Jesus because he's called after a saint, and that's pretty holy, isn't it, Mrs. Bessie?"

"And what did your teacher have to say about that?" Bessie asked.

"She said she didn't think Mom would want a bunch of children carrying our new baby, and you know what else she said? She said she could always count on me to come up with ideas. That's good, isn't it?"

Bessie assured Daisy that it was good, adding she and Rose wouldn't miss the concert for the world. When the girls left the room to start their home-work, Kate shook her head, saying she sometimes wondered what went on in their heads or what they would say.

But even Kate was surprised at what Daisy had to say on Tuesday after-noon during the Christmas concert matinee. She and Robert thoroughly enjoyed the performance, breathing a sigh of relief when Marigold recited her verse without missing a word and joined in the laughter when her class sang 'All I want for Christmas is My Two Front Teeth.' Daisy also sang a Christmas carol with her classmates, and finally, it was time for the Grade One Nativity play.

Kate and Robert watched the rendition of the age-old story as a very tired Mary and Joseph tried to find a place to stay, with Joseph going from door to door, only to hear over and over that there was no room available.

"Some of them could talk a bit louder. I bet there's no trouble hearing our Daisy when it's her turn," Robert whispered to Kate.

At last, Mary and Joseph arrived at the inn, where Daisy was waiting with her innkeeper husband. When the innkeeper said 'No' to a request for a room, the small Joseph pitifully said his wife was going to have a baby, and he needed to find a place for her. Keeping to the script, the innkeeper informed Joseph that he and Mary could sleep in the stable and the baby would be born in a manger.

At that, Joseph's words of thanks were interrupted by Daisy, who, fully caught up in the drama, and living up to Robert's prediction, spoke clearly and loud enough for all to hear as she declared.

"And that's what they won't. Mary, you can't have your baby in a stable. You and Baby Jesus can have my bed."

While the rest of the cast looked stunned, and the surprised audience wondered whether this was a new version of the nativity, there was total silence. Then, in a loud stage whisper, the Grade one teacher addressed her students.

"It's time to sing, *Away in a Manger*," and began singing the first verse. As the class gradually followed her example, the curtain came slowly down.

Kate was relating this to Bessie when she returned home, resulting in Bessie laughing so hard the tears ran down her face.

"Trust Daisy, I can hear her now. Well, the teacher did tell her she had good ideas. Maybe that's why Daisy thought it was time to change a story that is 1971 years old. I can't wait to see this Nativity Play. Did the play stop then, before Mary and Joseph ever got to the stable?" Bessie asked, still laughing at the thought of Daisy.

"No, when the curtain rose again, they were in the stable, and Baby Jesus had arrived. I wouldn't mind if Daisy had a soft voice like some of her classmates, but oh no. If the audience heard nothing else in that gym, they certainly heard Daisy. Now, Bessie, the girls will be home soon; don't you go encouraging her. It was bad enough having Robert laughing. I pitied the poor teacher; she must have been embarrassed."

Bessie was still at the Browns when the two excited girls arrived, asking if Kate could see and hear them and whether she thought they did well.

"Yes, you both very well, and I loved the concert, but Daisy, why did you change the words in your part when you practiced the correct ones at home?" Kate asked.

"But Mom, I thought of our baby. We wouldn't want Andrew in an old smelly stable, would we? Miss says she knows I'm kindhearted, but I've got to use the words she gave me tonight because it's a true story. I promised Miss I would, although it's not nice putting baby Jesus in a stable with animals. I'm some glad Miss used a doll and not our baby," Daisy earnestly declared.

That night, although Bessie and Rose half hoped Daisy might give another impromptu performance, they watched as both girls performed flawlessly. Sitting with the women were Sharon and Agnes. They had heard about Daisy's afternoon performance from David, who thought it was hilarious.

"David says it's things like Daisy's performance that make school concerts memorable, and from what I hear, this afternoon's show was certainly that," Sharon said as the women were putting on their coats following the concert.

"Now correct me if I'm wrong, but Angela and Jack are a couple, aren't they? David told me I was foolish back in September, that I was seeing things that weren't there when I said there was a spark between them. Now, I hear Jack brought her out of St. John's, and although Maggie and the twins are with them, it's evident Angela and Jack are very much at ease in each other's company."

Bessie, taken by surprise, said she expected Sharon felt that way because she and David were happy and wanted to see others sharing that feeling. Sharon, however, laughed.

"Bessie Martin, I can see by your face, and you too, Rose, that you know something, but you're not prepared to talk about it. Never mind; call it my instinct or whatever, but I'd say those two are more than casual friends.

"It's still early, so when we get back to Mark's Point, why don't the two of you come to our place? And it's not an excuse to ask more questions. Mom made a new cookie recipe, and she wants you to try it. Anyway, you haven't seen our Christmas tree. David and I decorated it last night and, if I say so myself, it's lovely. Come on; you know you're always ready for a cup of tea. This way, you won't have to make it yourself, and you can try Mom's baking."

CHAPTER 31

Where Did The Year Go?

*I*t feels strange to be alone. During the pre-Christmas rush, there is always *someone coming or going here in Martin House. Although I enjoy being busy and having company, I have to admit that it's nice at times just to sit, relax, and gather my thoughts.*

It was Christmas Eve, and Bessie was in the sitting room. Mass would begin in Holy Family Church in just over an hour, and Rose had already left with Maggie to practice the hymns she would play that night. A second rehearsal with David and the four boys playing guitar would also take place before the service.

The church had been a hive of activity all week as women from Mark's Point, Mark's Landing and Muddy Brook Cove took turns thoroughly cleaning its floors, walls, pews, kneelers, and sacristy in preparation for tonight's service. Once the women were satisfied with their efforts, it was the men's turn. They began by cleaning all the windows, requiring ladders for some of the higher ones. It was then time to bring the traditionally handcrafted stable from storage. After placing the stable inside the altar rails, they covered its floor with sawdust and boughs in readiness for the nativity figures. The men's last task was to erect a tree with lights outside the church. That afternoon, Rose helped Nora complete the preparations by changing the altar cloth and setting out colourful house plants gathered from several homes for the occasion.

It had been a busy week for Rose. With the furnace on all week, she and David had taken advantage of the heated church to hold either choir, organ or guitar practices most nights. Playing for the first time in public during Christmas Eve mass, the four boys on guitar were every bit as nervous as Maggie and, like her, practiced as often as possible.

Although not a Catholic, Bessie had always attended Christmas Eve mass with Alex. This year she would have company in the Martin family pew. With Sharon and David in the choir, Agnes would sit with Bessie, Angela and her father. Gabe was keeping his promise to Maggie to attend mass and hear her play the organ.

What a difference Maggie has made in all our lives, Bessie thought.

Gabe is a different man, much more relaxed and willing to get involved in things. Rose is giving Maggie music lessons, and I not only enjoy baking with her, but I also love how Maggie is so at home here, dropping in and bringing her friends. Although the twins and Theresa have always lived in Mark's Point, I've got to know them so much better since Maggie came home. And if I hadn't been baking with Maggie, Marigold and Daisy would never have asked me to help them make a cake for Kate.

She smiled, thinking about the two youngest Brown girls.

The Brown family has become such a big part of our lives. Alex always had a soft spot for Robert, and I know he would be pleased to see the Browns spending time in his home.

Yes, it's certainly been a year of new friends and experiences, and a large part of that is the result of opening Martin House to guests.

Bessie's chain of thought was interrupted when the telephone rang, and on answering, an excited Agnes began talking.

"Bessie, you're going to think I've got some nerve, but can you manage one more person for dinner tomorrow? Jerry just called from Toronto, and he's getting on a plane to come home in the next half hour. His boat tied up early, and it's such a wonderful surprise. Sharon doesn't know; she's already left for church, but she's going to be so happy. It's been years since Jerry got home for Christmas. He'll stay in town tonight and leave early tomorrow morning to drive here."

Agnes abruptly stopped and apologized, saying she was asking too much when Bessie stopped her.

"Nonsense! We've loads of food Agnes. Of course, Jerry must come for Christmas dinner. I'm delighted for you and Sharon that he will be here. Don't forget you insisted on bringing dessert, so he'll also be eating your food. And Agnes, remember Rose said we should get to church early as there's always a crowd on Christmas Eve, so I'll pick you up just after six-thirty."

Sitting down again after her call with Agnes, Bessie's thoughts went back to the summer when Sharon and David arrived at Martin House after being offered positions in the schools.

They were among our first guests, and now it's as if we've always known them and Agnes. Yes, Rose and I have made some good friends through our business.

Several Christmas cards lining the bookshelves came from guests who stayed with them during this first year of business. The cards brought back good memories of their visitors from New York, Boston, Ontario, Nova Scotia, and St. John's.

Here I am, daydreaming when I should be getting ready for mass. It's a good thing I have my clothes laid out, ready to wear.

As she rose to go upstairs and get dressed for church, a card near the end of one shelf caught her attention. Unlike the others, it hadn't arrived by mail but was hand-delivered by Lucy the previous night.

This time last year, I wouldn't have appreciated Lucy's company. I always tried to avoid her because of her nosiness. Since seeing her reaction to being asked to help at the fair and her hard work making the baked goods stall a success, I've got to know a side of Lucy I never considered. She wants to be friendly, and now she realizes her way of doing so, passing on gossip she thought people wanted to hear, is not the way to make friends.

Her neighbour had dropped over with the card and a package shortly after Rose returned from choir practice. When she asked them to open the gift, they discovered two sets of white fluffy towels and facecloths. On examining them, they saw the words *Martin House* was beautifully hand-embroidered on each item.

Lucy emphasized it was not a Christmas present; it was a thank-you for all the two women did for her, not only when she was sick but also for getting her involved in the community and especially for being her friends. She had wanted to give them something to use in their business and thought guests using the towels would remember their stay in Martin House.

Her gift left the women lost for words, but Lucy didn't notice; she went on to speak about her sons Leonard and Lawrence, who arrived home two days earlier.

It's a good thing we ordered and wrapped an extra bottle of wine. While I poured tea for Lucy, Rose went to the spare room and got the wine. Writing Lucy and Jim's name on a gift tag, she attached it to the bottle.

Bessie remembered Lucy's surprise and pleasure when she received the wine.

It made me feel guilty yet glad that we made Lucy happy, and Rose confessed she felt the same way.

Shaking her head at her foolishness, Bessie went upstairs to get ready for mass.

Half an hour later, she and Agnes walked into the church to the sound of Christmas carols playing on the organ.

"The church looks lovely. And everything is shining. Just look at the stable and altar, and what a lovely smell of pine boughs. Doesn't the organ sound great? There's a true feeling of Christmas sitting here waiting for mass to start." Agnes whispered as they joined Angela and Gabe in the pew.

Just then, Bessie, sitting at the end of the pew, felt a tug on her arm and heard a voice, trying hard to whisper.

"Mrs. Bessie, Daisy is carrying baby Jesus in the procession to the stable. I did it last year, but I had to share Jesus with Jerry Fleming from Mark's Landing. Bessie gets to do it by herself because she's the only grade one student going to our church."

Kate, who turned back when she discovered Marigold was not following her, shook her head at her daughter before catching hold of her hand. Robert had continued walking and joined his father, Rob, in their family pew. He held the carrycot where Andrew lay asleep when Rob spoke loudly to the amusement of those around him.

"Lost your wimen folk, Robert? I guess it's just us three Brown boys here in our family pew tonight."

At this, Kate appeared, still holding Marigold by the hand and gave both men dirty looks, much to her father-in-law's amusement. When he invited

Marigold to sit by him, Kate emphatically said 'No,' adding Marigold was bad enough without her grandfather encouraging her.

Ten minutes later, the organ thundered out *Come All Ye Faithful,* and the congregation rose as Father Kiely, altar servers and Daisy processed from the back of the church down the middle aisle.

"Look at Daisy. Doesn't she look angelic carrying Baby Jesus? See how serious she is."

The whispered words were no sooner out of Bessie's mouth when Daisy spotted her and gave her a huge smile as she held on tightly to the small clay figure of the Infant Jesus. As she passed by their pew, Angela spoke.

"I bet Kate's holding her breath, wondering what Daisy might say or do. But doesn't Daisy look proud? She's doing a great job."

They watched Daisy walk up to the altar and, with Father Kiely following her, cross over to the stable. She then gently laid the statue in the manger, but not before adding her personal touch to the ceremony by kissing Baby Jesus on the forehead.

Bessie could see Kate shaking her head at her youngest daughter's action, but when Daisy skipped her way back to her parents, Kate quickly gave her a smile and a hug.

Before starting mass, Father Kiely welcomed everyone and praised the choir members and organist Rose for the beautiful musical introduction to Christmas Eve mass.

"And not only do we have organ music, we also have guitars. It's wonderful to see the enthusiasm of the choir. It's especially good to see so many young people taking part in our music ministry."

Father Kiely's words appeared to have inspired the choir and musicians. When it came time for the Offertory, Maggie confidently played *Angels We Have Heard on High,* and the choir responded with enthusiasm. Looking over at Angela and Gabe, both focusing on Maggie, Bessie wondered which one was the most nervous. As Maggie played the final notes, Angela's pride was evident, while Gabe appeared almost awestruck.

"When it comes to music, Rose is never wrong. She said Maggie would do well, and she certainly did. Why don't you both relax and enjoy the rest of Christmas Eve mass."

Bessie's words made Angela smile, and she whispered back that she believed her father was speechless.

"Maggie knew he was nervous for her, and she let him think that's the only Christmas carol she would play, but she's also playing *Silent Night* after communion. The boys on guitar will accompany her, and only the high school choir members are singing. It's going to be a surprise for their parents. I only know because I picked up Maggie from practice and heard them singing. It sounded beautiful, but I promised Rose and Maggie that I wouldn`t tell Dad or the other parents."

As mass continued, Bessie recalling Agnes's reaction on entering the church could see why she felt that way. It wasn't easy to describe the feeling or atmosphere, but she felt at peace with the world. Alex was very much in her thoughts, and she believed it was because he, like Rose, had always felt so at home in the church.

Before the final blessing, Father Kiely thanked everyone who helped prepare the church by cleaning and decorating, then praised the music again.

"There isn't a church congregation in Newfoundland that wouldn't be proud to have the music ministry we heard tonight. When I asked Rose earlier this year if she would consider playing the organ with the hope of getting a choir started, little did I imagine how much she would accomplish. Thank you, Rose, and thank you, David, to the choir and our young people. Everyone did an excellent job. You should be proud. I think you deserve a round of applause."

Once the applause was over, the choir began their final carol, *Joy to the World*. Turning to Bessie, Agnes said it was the most beautiful Christmas Eve service she had ever attended.

"When you told Angela and Gabe to enjoy the rest of mass, I thought it was the strangest thing to say because honestly, although I always attend mass, I can't say I ever thought of it as enjoyment. But tonight, it was sheer pleasure, starting with the entrance procession and Daisy carrying Baby Jesus. Then there was the music and Father's lovely sermon, which was so meaningful. The entire atmosphere was beautiful, and yes, it was enjoyable.

"The choir did an excellent job, and Rose must be proud. I don't think I will ever forget Maggie and the boys playing as they and their friends sang *Silent Night*. It was so touching; I was almost in tears," Agnes recalled.

'I agree; it was a beautiful mass. Well, Gabe, what do you think of your granddaughter's playing? Didn't she do well?" Bessie asked.

Gabe appeared overcome as he nodded his head in agreement. He had come to church to support Maggie, hoping for her sake that she would do well. Knowing she had spent many hours practicing, he had wondered if she found it difficult. After listening to Maggie play the organ alone and then with the boys accompanying their friends singing, he was lost for words.

Once mass was over, the women were surprised when Maggie didn't come to hear their reaction to her playing. She and other choir members remained to talk around the organ at the front of the church.

"Something seems to be going on. There's a lot of excitement among the choir, and the only ones moving are the boys."

Bessie, who had been looking around, could see something was also happening at the back of the church. The group, consisting of Nora, Dan, Lucy, Kelly's parents, and Lucy's sons, talked, laughed, and shook hands.

As the boys left the choir, Daisy and Marigold ran down to tell Bobby and Michael how good they were on guitar. When Bobby stopped to talk to his parents, Michael and the two other guitar players continued up the aisle until Bessie spoke to them.

"Congratulations, boys, you all did a great job on guitar. Your parents must be proud of you. But tell me, what's going on in the choir? Why are the other members still hanging about?"

"That's females for you, Mrs. Bessie. And Mr. Nolan and Mr. Jim Pearce are every bit as bad. They're all going foolish over Kelly because Sean gave her an engagement ring for Christmas. Who wants to see a ring anyhow? Huh, she and Sean only got engaged before mass, and that crowd is already asking them when they're getting married. I don't know what Sean is thinking about getting engaged. He's got enough on his plate with him going up North next week," Michael said, shaking his head at the idea.

"Engaged!" said the women in unison.

Realizing the engagement was the cause for all the excitement, the women went and joined the choir members, offering congratulations and hoping to see Kelly's ring. It seemed no one was in a hurry to leave, and it wasn't until Father Kiely said he needed to go and prepare for Midnight Mass in Murphy's Cove that people gradually left for home.

It was a night for good news Bessie discovered when Angela, Gabe, Agnes, Sharon, and David dropped into Martin House after mass. The women had declined a glass of wine in favour of tea with a slice of fruit cake, while the men agreed the occasion called for a drink of Bessie's special Scotch brand. As they relaxed in the sitting room, Agnes was still talking about the service.

"What a lovely mass that was. Who would have thought last Christmas that we would take part in such a beautiful service or be relaxing in Martin House tonight? I'd never heard of Mark's Point, and if anyone had asked me about a Bed and Breakfast, I wouldn't have had a clue what it was. Now, Sharon and David, you live and work here while feeling right at home and part of the community. You've made good friends, and since my first visit, I've felt the same way."

"You're right, Mom. David and I realize how lucky we are. I don't mind saying that we both had doubts at first, even after accepting positions in the schools. It was such a change from city life, and we didn't know how we would get on or how people would react to us either at work or in the community. We never imagined how happy or contented we'd be or how much this community would come to mean to us. It seems fitting that Dad arrives tomorrow and will share in our first ever Christmas in Mark's Point," Sharon replied.

With that, David, who had been nodding in agreement with both his mother-in-law and wife, looked over at Sharon and said, "I'd say this is the right time, Sharon. What do you think?"

Sharon smiled in agreement, saying, "Mom knows what we are about to tell you, and so does Dad and David's parents because it was our early Christmas gift to them. David and I are expecting a baby, and we couldn't be happier. We wanted to share our news with you as we consider the four of you our good friends.

The baby was due in June, Sharon said, and she hoped to continue teaching until then. She and David preferred to keep the news within their family and close friends for now.

"You can see why I've been so excited recently," Agnes said when the congratulations finally died down.

"Fancy Jerry and me going to be grandparents. I can hardly take it in. I was hoping, Bessie, that you would help me with baby knitting patterns. I can knit, but I'm hopeless with patterns, and isn't it a grandmother's job to knit for her grandchild?"

When a smiling Bessie said she would be happy to do so, the friends went on to talk about their plans during the Christmas holidays. Angela said Jack would arrive on Monday but might have to return on Wednesday because of his work.

"His whole family always gets together on Boxing Day, but he hopes to leave early the next morning to come here. He'd like to stay, or at least get back, here for New Year, but he won't know until next week."

"Who knew when Albert decided to run in this district that his brother would be making so many visits back to Mark's Point and not because of politics," David said, laughing.

"I had an idea, but according to you, I imagined it. Didn't I say there was a definite attraction between Jack and Angela?" Sharon asked her husband.

"Jack's a fine man, and I'm happy knowing he and Angela are such good friends," Gabe said, looking around as if defying anyone to contradict him.

"And speaking of elections, Jack was telling me that we might soon be seeing him and Albert campaigning out this way again. He says the government can't carry on the way it is, with neither the Liberals nor Tories having a proper majority. Albert thinks there could be another election held by the Spring, and this time, he believes the Conservatives might well get a majority. I hope he's right, and we see the last of Joey Smallwood."

Bessie and Rose looked at Gabe in astonishment. It was rare for him to mention personal matters, and now he was telling them he approved of Angela's relationship with Jack. And for someone who never had time for politics, it was a complete turnaround for him to discuss an election.

"Well, well, Gabe O'Brien. When did you start having opinions on politics?" Rose asked him.

"Jumping Joseph, Rose Martin! Is there a law that says it's just retired principals that's allowed to voice an opinion?" an indignant Gabe asked.

"Okay, Dad," Angela broke in.

"It's Christmas and time to call a truce, but knowing you and Rose, I guess that's a lot to expect. Instead, let's change the subject. David, do you have enough chaperones for the Christmas dances on Tuesday night? I wouldn't mind helping, and I'm sure Jack would also help."

Bessie, used to Gabe and Rose picking at each other, wished they didn't choose tonight to start and hoped David, Sharon and Agnes wouldn't make too much of the exchange. Following Angela's lead, she joined the conversation, saying she was looking forward to chaperoning the younger age group's dance.

The dances were proving to be a success as well as a money-making venture, David said. The schools were alternating dances with the committee, and by arranging for buses to transport students, all had a chance to attend,

"It's hard to believe, but Maggie has much more of a social life now than she had when we lived in Toronto. She loves staying with Dad, especially with all the benefits offered by your committee and the high school. When I mentioned this to her, she agreed and said not to forget her music and baking lessons in Martin House that she would never have in Ontario," Angela said.

She then asked why the adult dance was planned for Old Christmas Day and not New Year's Eve?

"Our committee did speak about having a dance on New Year's Eve, but Turner's Club is planning a New Year Ball, and we didn't think it right to compete with the Turners when the club is their livelihood," David answered.

An hour later, their friends left Martin House. Angela and Gabe planned to pick up Maggie at the Browns' house, while Agnes wanted to get back and check to see if Jerry had arrived in St John's As the two women relaxed in the sitting room, Bessie spoke about the upcoming dance in Mark's Point.

"January 6th is a suitable date because some people prefer to stay home on New Year's Eve. I'm one of them, but that's because I got homesick for Scotland on that date for years.

"New Year's Eve, or Hogmanay as it's called in Scotland, was a big holiday when I was growing up, and memories of celebrating it with my family and neighbours always returned. That's when Alex came up with the idea of inviting people here on that night. He was determined to make it just like home for me and had Dan Ryan go outside before midnight and return on the stroke of 12 to 'first foot' us."

Bessie's words had Rose smiling as she recalled her first New Year's party in Martin House.

"The year I came home for Christmas after leaving the convent, I didn't have a clue what was going on when Dan left the house only to come back after midnight with a lump of coal in his hand. It seemed I was the only one who didn't know what was happening. Nora, who sat beside me, told me about the Scottish tradition of 'first footing' and how bringing coal was a symbol that the house would be warm all year round. She said Dan did it every year.

"I remember asking Alex later why it was Dan who always brought in the coal, and he told me it was because Dan had the blackest hair in Mark's Point. When I asked what the colour of Dan's hair had to do with anything, he told me a black-haired man had to be the first person to put his foot across the threshold on New Year's Eve."

Bessie laughed, saying Alex was right because a black-haired man meant good luck. A woman or a fair-haired man would never be the first visitor to enter the house after midnight. She also recalled how the Ryans, Rob Brown, Pat Martin, and Gabe were regular New Year's Eve visitors to Martin House, and in the last couple of years, Robert and Kate would leave the twins in charge and come over for at least an hour.

"Earlier tonight, when Agnes said she had never heard of Mark's Point a year ago, I got thinking again how this is our first Christmas and New Year without Alex. He'll be gone a year on January 21. It doesn't seem right to be celebrating, but he always enjoyed having people visit or for a meal, so I'm sure he'd be happy knowing that both old and new friends will join us for Christmas Day dinner. But I've told Dan and Nora that I don't feel like celebrating New Year's Eve this year, and they understand."

"Nonsense Bessie; Alex may have started the 'Hogmanay' tradition for you, but he loved doing it and having your friends share the fun. You'd be keeping his memory alive by continuing the tradition. Anyway, it's still a week away and lots of time to change your mind. Meanwhile, I will give you your Christmas present now because I want to get your mind off the past and begin making new memories instead. I'll get it from my bedroom."

Rose soon returned with an envelope and, passing it over to her sister-in-law, said she hoped Bessie would like it, although it didn't look much like a Christmas gift.

A puzzled Bessie removed an invoice for a room at the Newfoundland Hotel for four nights in January. Her second surprise was a pair of tickets to a traditional Burns' Supper on the 25th of January.

"It's the anniversary of Alex's passing on the 21st, and I know it will be a sad time for you. But I'm also sure if Alex had known the Burns' Supper took place in St. John's, he would have been the first to buy tickets for both of you. That's why I got them. I booked a room at the Newfoundland Hotel for two days before and after the supper, mainly to make sure we get a good day to travel, but also to give us time to shop and relax."

Bessie was surprised and delighted, saying Rose had put a lot of thought into choosing the perfect gift. She was still gushing over it when a smiling Rose cut off her thanks.

"Bessie, I'm starting to feel a real hypocrite. I'm glad you like your present, but I must admit to being selfish when choosing it. I'm looking forward to the Burns' Supper every bit as much as I hope you will."

"If that's the case, I hope you'll also enjoy the present I have for you. I don't have to go upstairs because it's here in the sitting room."

Standing up, Bessie took an envelope from the top bookshelf, where she put it before going to mass. Laughing, she said it looked as if envelopes were the latest fashion in wrapping presents this year.

"As Lucy said last night, this is not only a Christmas present; it's a thank you for your support this past year. Before I say anymore, why don't you open the envelope?" Bessie asked.

To Rose's absolute astonishment, she discovered a ticket in her name and another in Bessie's for a return airline flight from Gander to Prestwick, Scotland, departing on April 5 and returning on the 25th.

Almost stuttering in shock, Rose's first words were, "How did you manage to get these?"

Before Bessie could reply, Rose continued speaking.

"This is the best Christmas present I ever had. I wondered if we could take another trip to Scotland sometime, but I thought you might not want to go with Martin House open to guests. It's the most wonderful idea ever, and although I hate winter, it will fly past when I know we're going to Scotland in April."

"That's the reaction I hoped to see. When I wondered what to get you, I remembered how much we enjoyed our holiday in Scotland, which led us to discover what a Bed and Breakfast was," Bessie said.

"We have our own Martin House Bed and Breakfast now, and I thought it was time we returned to Scotland because there's no way I'd let you go without me. Of course, we would visit Duncan and his family, but we could also tour Scotland, staying in various Bed and Breakfasts to see how they operate. In a way, it would be a workman's holiday. What do you think? Bessie asked.

"I think it's wonderful, and as Marigold and Daisy would say, it's the 'bestest' present. Saying thank you doesn't seem enough to say. I thought after Mass that this day couldn't get any better, but it just did," Rose replied.

Bessie said they had to thank Jack for getting the tickets. He contacted the travel agent who usually arranged his business flights and hotels to book the plane tickets to Scotland.

"All I had to do was give Jack a cheque. I knew you'd want to be home for Holy Week and Easter services and asked him to book a flight after Easter Sunday, and that's what he did. The weather should be good because Spring is one of the nicest times of the year in Scotland."

When Rose said it would mean closing Martin House for three weeks, Bessie had a suggestion.

"You know how we were saying what a great thing it would be if Mina could attend Chrissie's graduation in Halifax but knew if we offered to help with the cost, she'd never accept. What if we paid Mina to look after our business when we are on holiday? She's more than capable of looking after Martin House. Mina and the girls would stay here, and the girls could catch the school bus with Maggie. It would help us, but don't you think it would be good for all three of them to have a break?"

Bessie reminded Rose that Sue and Bob planned to fly to Newfoundland around the middle of April to hire a contractor and buy materials for their house. She knew they wouldn't mind staying in Martin House on their own, but it would be a good reason to ask Mina to look after the Bed and Breakfast.

"Knowing Mina, she might refuse to accept payment from us, but even if she did, we could buy her a plane ticket and tell her it's non-returnable. If she knew Katy and Isabelle could stay here with us when she's gone, I believe she would go to Chrissie's graduation."

Rose said it was a great idea. Not only would it allow them to go on holiday knowing Martin House was in good hands, but Mina deserved to go to Chrissie's graduation. She sat silent for a minute before speaking again.

"I'm looking at you, and do you know what I'm thinking? We started talking about our holiday, and right away, you saw it as a way to help Mina. That's you all over. After losing their husband, some women are ready to give up, taking no interest in anyone or anything. Others become entirely self-centred, expecting help from people, but not you. You never changed. You're still thinking of ways to help others," Rose said.

"Rose, Rose! What foolishness you come up with at times. Here I am, priding myself on being a hard-headed businesswoman, and you are making me out to be soft. That's enough of that nonsense. It's like hearing your mother talk when you come out with comments like that," Bessie said, laughing.

Rose shook her head at this, but knowing Bessie had never been comfortable receiving compliments, she changed the topic by saying she would put the Burns' Supper and plane tickets in the small safe where they kept their important papers.

"Yes, thanks, Rose. And about Mina, I'm glad you think it's a good idea. We'll talk to her on Tuesday when she and the girls spend the day with us. I'm looking forward to meeting Chrissie, and maybe if we tell her about our idea, she'll try and convince her mother to attend her graduation."

Rose agreed, saying if Chrissie let her mother know she wanted her at the graduation, it might be the best way to convince Mina to attend.

"Let's try and get Chrissie alone and speak about it when they come here on Tuesday. And while we are talking about next week, Bessie, I think you should reconsider your decision not to celebrate New Year's Eve.

"I know it was a terrible start to the year when Alex died. It was hard, and we will never forget him, but we had to continue our lives. We not only did that, but we also changed our future by opening Martin House to guests. No one would be prouder than Alex. That's why I believe continuing the New Year tradition he began so many years ago would be a positive thing," Rose said

Bessie realized she hadn't considered Rose or her opinion when she cancelled the annual event. Instead, she had thought only of her own feelings and how she would miss Alex at the party. Yet Rose, whose loss was as great as hers, favoured continuing the New Year party.

"You are right, Rose, and we will go ahead with it. It's traditional to anticipate the future on the last day of the year, and we should start 1972 as we mean to carry on. After all, we've already started making plans for next year with tickets for the Burns' Supper and our trip to Scotland. So yes, we will continue Alex's tradition.

"And we do have a lot to celebrate. I look around at times and thank God for Alex's vision when he built Martin House. It is the ideal home for our business, and it gave us a reason to work together. We will always miss Alex, but I think we can truthfully say the year that began so badly turned around and opened a new world for us," Bessie said.

"I feel the same way," Rose replied.

"There's one other thing we should do tonight. New Year's Eve is usually the time for toasts, but while there's only the two of us here and because Christmas Eve is also a special night, I'd like to open a bottle of wine and make a toast."

Without waiting for Bessie to agree, Rose left the sitting room before returning with two glasses and an opened bottle of wine. Carefully pouring wine into the glasses, she passed one to Bessie.

"Merry Christmas, Bessie. Here's to Martin House and us. May we continue to be successful in our business and make many new friends in the future," she said, raising her glass.

"To us and our friends and neighbours in Mark's Point," Bessie replied.

"Here's hoping 1972 will be a good year for us, our neighbours, and our guests who became our friends. Merry Christmas, Rose."